"An engaging and inventive picaresque novel that illuminates the life of Isabel, a beguiling Renaissance woman who was the only daughter of one of the world's most recognized writers, Miguel de Cervantes. Historical fiction readers: get ready to swoon, not over the famous author of *Don Quixote*, but over the feisty woman who fought for legitimacy and her place in a man's world."

—Nita Prose, #1 New York Times bestselling author of *The Maid* and *The Mystery Guest*

"*A Daughter's Place* is a pure pleasure to read from beginning to end. Isabel and the Cervantes women are powerful, disparate female characters revolving around a man who led a life of such adventure. Through Bátiz's impressive research and engaging storytelling, the Golden Age of Spain, a fascinating period of social and political upheaval, comes to life."

—Roberta Rich, #1 bestselling author of *The Midwife of Venice* and *The Jazz Club Spy*

"A *Daughter's Place* is a joy to read, immersive, erudite, and compelling. In seventeenth-century Spain, the Cervantes women—wife, lover, sister, illegitimate daughter, and niece—lived stories of wit and strong-will, recklessness and determination, to have any small measure of freedom in that convention-bound society. Bátiz reinvents the untold stories of the women around Miguel de Cervantes, and they are as ingenious as the sad knight himself. Read this wonderful book."

—Kim Echlin, bestselling author of *The Disappeared* and *Speak, Silence*

Praise for *No Stars in the Sky*

"*No Stars in the Sky* offers wonderful, haunting writing that burrows deep into the reader's heart. In these stories, Latin American women scramble with courage and stamina to persevere in the face of violence, illegal incarceration, abandonment, migration, solitude, and ruptured relationships. Bátiz's prose is raw, honest, and immediate. To appreciate its beauty, one has only to take in the opening sentence to the story 'Uncle Ko's One Thousand Lives': 'When no one expected his return anymore, when almost everyone believed he must be dead, he appeared out of nowhere at our door.'"

—Lawrence Hill, author of *The Book of Negroes*, *The Illegal*, and *Beatrice and Croc Harry*

"Profoundly moving and beautifully written, Martha Bátiz's *No Stars in the Sky* spans different countries and timelines but always circles back to keen observances of the human experience. With a writing style so gorgeous and spare, Bátiz has a remarkable capacity to draw out moments both significant and small, to find the deepest meaning in little snippets of time. Each story is its own universe that transports the reader through the characters' joy and pain, turmoil and resilience, from the hills of inland Mexico to the streetcars of Toronto and beyond. A brilliant collection."

—Amy Stuart, author of *Still Mine*, *Still Water*, and *Still Here*

"These are stories for the twenty-first century. Their geography is as vast as their violence. Bátiz has a powerful gift for empathy, entering the mind of a disappeared boy in Argentina, a fourteen-year-old girl exploited at the US/Mexico border, and female asylum seekers sharing their grief. The power of these stories comes from the writer's understanding of the politics of exploitation and her refusal to look away."

—Rosemary Sullivan, author of
Stalin's Daughter and *The Betrayal of Anne Frank*

"*No Stars in the Sky* is a beautifully written, masterfully crafted collection that explores the trauma of loss. Its vivid characters stayed with me long after I finished the book."

—Marina Nemat, author of
Prisoner of Tehran and *After Tehran*

"Brimming with unforgettable characters who find themselves in unimaginable circumstances *No Stars in the Sky* shines with brilliance and will leave you breathless. Bátiz's prose sparkles against the dark background of heartbreaking choices and harsh realities, and lights up the senses. This book is meant to be read slowly and savoured."

—Christina Kilbourne, author of
Safe Harbour and *The Limitless Sky*

"In *No Stars in the Sky*, Martha Bátiz travels across countries and cultures with confidence, humour, and an ear for the musicality of language. Her stories, both beautiful and terrifying, deal with loss, depression, injustice, and the need to love and be loved. A refreshing collection written by an author in full control of her literary style."

—Pura López-Colomé, author of
Speaking in Song and *Borrosa Imago Mundi*

A Daughter's Place

A NOVEL

Martha Bátiz

ANANSI

Published in Canada in 2025 and the USA in 2025 by House of Anansi Press Inc.
houseofanansi.com

House of Anansi Press is committed to protecting our natural environment. This book is
made of material from well-managed FSC®-certified forests, recycled materials, and other
controlled sources.

House of Anansi Press is a Global Certified Accessible™ (GCA by Benetech) publisher.
The ebook version of this book meets stringent accessibility standards and is available to
readers with print disabilities.

29 28 27 26 25   1 2 3 4 5

Library and Archives Canada Cataloguing in Publication

Title: A daughter's place : a novel / Martha Bátiz.
Names: Bátiz Zuk, Martha Beatriz, author.
Identifiers: Canadiana (print) 20240489896 | Canadiana (ebook) 20240518314 |
ISBN 9781487011864 (softcover) | ISBN 9781487011871 (EPUB)
Subjects: LCGFT: Historical fiction. | LCGFT: Romance fiction. | LCGFT: Novels.
Classification: LCC PS8603.A856 D38 2025 | DDC C813/.6—dc23

Cover design: Alysia Shewchuk
Cover artwork: *Two Women at a Window* by Bartolomé Esteban Murillo,
c. 1655/1660, oil on canvas, Widener Collection, 1942.9.46
Book design and typesetting: Lucia Kim

*House of Anansi Press is grateful for the privilege to work on and create from the
Traditional Territory of many Nations, including the Anishinabeg, the Wendat, and the
Haudenosaunee, as well as the Treaty Lands of the Mississaugas of the Credit.*

With the participation of the Government of Canada
Avec la participation du gouvernement du Canada | Canadä

*We acknowledge for their financial support of our publishing program the Canada Council
for the Arts, the Ontario Arts Council, and the Government of Canada.*

Printed and bound in Canada

Children are half of one's soul,
But daughters are the most complete half.
—Miguel de Cervantes

Act One
Madrid
June–November 1599
1

Act Two
Esquivias and Madrid
November 1599–November 1602
79

Act Three
Valladolid
February 1603–January 1606
143

Act Four
Madrid
February 1606–August 1607
233

Act Five
Madrid
October 1607–April 1616
307

ACT ONE

MADRID
JUNE–NOVEMBER 1599

Miguel de Cervantes was born on September 29, 1547, in Alcalá de Henares, a town northeast of Madrid, in the region of Castile. Privileged by the opportunity to receive an education, Cervantes became a poet, but circumstances also made him a soldier. While stationed in Italy, he proved his bravery in the battle of Lepanto in 1571. On his way home he was captured by pirates and held for ransom in Algiers for five years, the time it took his family to gather the money to pay for his liberation. He was released in 1580 and returned to Spain after an eleven-year absence.

Back in Madrid, the Empire's capital, Cervantes became a royal petitioner. He began writing his first book, the pastoral novel La Galatea, *which was published in 1585, a few months after his marriage to Catalina de Salazar. In 1587, he became a tax collector for the Spanish Crown, a job that required extensive travel throughout Andalucía, collecting oil, wheat, and barley in support of the war effort of Catholic Spain against Protestant England.*

In 1588, when Spain's so-called "Invincible Armada" was vanquished by the English navy, King Philip II faced a humiliating defeat. After several bankruptcies, he died in 1598. His son, Philip III, inherited a nation where the price of food and general goods was out of reach of the majority of the population, and the customs checks imposed at the city gates contributed to the scarcity of supplies that afflicted Madrid.

More and more people continued to leave behind the hardships of life in the countryside. By the end of the sixteenth century, the population of Madrid had grown from 20,000 to 65,000. The Spanish people would face drought, famine, and in 1597, a plague that would rage throughout the Iberian Peninsula for five years.

I

ISABEL

MY LITTLE SISTER ANA and I were washing dishes when a knock on the door startled us. We remained still, listening. Grandmother was outside, and we were not expecting visitors. There came a second, more insistent knock.

"Don't answer!" Ana said, her eyes wide. Whoever was outside seemed impatient. But my sister gestured for me to stay put.

When Grandmother failed to appear and the knock came again, I had to see who it was. Laundresses, servants, day labourers, and craftsmen were among our neighbours, and perhaps it was one of them. But just in case, I grabbed the poker that sat by the stove before I opened the door.

A lady greeted me with familiarity as she lifted the impeccable silk mantilla covering her face, though her smile faded when she saw the poker. I laid it on the floor as soon as I recognized her; she was a former client who used to buy wine from us when we ran the tavern. I was so impressed by her hat, which matched her overskirt and bodice, that I forgot to ask what she was doing so far from the tavern. Was that a velvet ribbon around her waist? Mother used to own a velvet waistcoat that she wore to mass on Sundays. It was an item that I should have been allowed to keep, but the doctor said it was contaminated with the foul airs of the sickroom and had to be burned. The only things I had been able to rescue for myself and Ana, and only because no one was looking, were a small mirror and a silver pomander, which I hid so that no one could take them or force me to sell them.

"Are you going to invite me in?" asked the lady.

I moved aside to let her in and closed the door firmly behind her. She frowned in obvious disapproval as she scanned our living quarters, which were nothing more than the room we stood in and the kitchen beyond it: there was the mattress we shared, a straw rug, two worn chairs, and a shelf on the wall that held our few plates, utensils, and rusty pots. There was a bench by the kitchen fire where I, my sister, and our cousins, Jerónima and Marita, sat in the winter to eat our meals and keep warm. Yes, everything was basic and sad looking, but as the lady's frown gave way to a look of pity, I felt a knot of anger in my stomach. What else did she expect to find in this part of town?

Before I could speak, Grandmother appeared in the room. One look at our visitor and her face lost its colour. Her hands grasped tightly onto her skirt. Ana stood close behind her.

"Won't you introduce us?" the lady asked, looking at Grandmother. "I thought you would have mentioned that I was coming." Grandmother looked as if she wanted to say something but had forgotten how to speak, and the visitor shook her head impatiently.

"I'm Magdalena Pimentel de Sotomayor," she said, turning to me with a bow. She seemed to be waiting for a reaction, but I wasn't sure what was expected of me. At the tavern she had simply been another one of our customers. True, not many women came to buy wine on their own, but she always did so in the morning, when the tavern was practically empty. As Mother's *medidora*, I measured the wine and poured it into her leather wineskin.

"Or Magdalena de Cervantes, if you will. Miguel is my older brother. I am here on his behalf." As I continued to stand there, she examined me from top to bottom. The expression in her eyes revealed that she was satisfied with what she saw.

"You are his spitting image, no question about that. You always have been." I could feel the hair on my arms stand up.

"What do you mean?" Four simple words, but I had to push them out. They were tangled in the knot my throat was knitting. Ana was biting her lower lip the way she did when she was nervous, a habit she had acquired after Mother's death. I had to remind her constantly to stop—she was making her skin bleed.

"You look just like him." Magdalena was smiling. "Your father."

I was only seven years old when Papa passed away. But as a frequent customer, she must have met him. He was a silent, serious man. My sister never knew how big his hands were or how angry he could get when I didn't follow the rules. Once I almost choked on a piece of orange I tried to hide in my mouth. I wasn't supposed to eat between meals, and when he saw me doing so, he hit me. Mother didn't speak to him for two full days after that. Yet despite those memories, I was proud of Alonso Rodríguez, *tabernero de la corte*, an innkeeper for the Crown and the one we had to thank for our Tudescos tavern and former home.

"Isabel, my child, there's something you need to know." Grandmother's voice was heavy and dark, like Papa's eyes before he hit me. "You are not Alonso Rodríguez's daughter."

Ana let out a cry and ran over to hug me. The knot in my throat unravelled, releasing a sudden sob.

"I don't understand."

Grandmother spoke slowly, aware of the pain every word was causing me. "Alonso Rodríguez wasn't your father."

None of them dared to break the silence while I absorbed the news.

Not my father.

The man who had raised me and made sure that Mother, Ana, and I had a roof over our heads and food on our plates— the man whose soul I prayed for every night—was *not my father*.

"Then who is?" I cried. My question was directed at Grandmother, but our visitor answered instead.

"My brother, Miguel. I'm your aunt."

My aunt! How could she have come to the tavern so many times and never said a word? I hardly remembered her saying hello or goodbye. All sorts of questions were brewing in my head, yet the only thing I managed to blurt out was, "Have you always known about this, Grandmother?"

"Yes." Her eyes were fixed on the floor. It seemed as if she wanted to swallow the words rather than speak them. "I knew this would happen one day, especially with your dear mother gone."

"And what about Aunt Luisa? And Uncle Juan? Did *they* know?"

Luisa was my mother's sister and Ana's godmother. She couldn't have agreed to such a lie. My mother's brother, Juan, was a priest. Priests always told the truth, didn't they? I needed Grandmother to look me in the eyes, but she was gazing at a point beyond the wall behind me.

"Juan, no. But he'll find out now," she said. I gave a sigh of relief. At least I could still trust my uncle Juan.

"Luisa did," she added. "That's why she's not home right now. She didn't have the courage to face you." I shook my head in disbelief. She could not face *me*? How could I face *her* after this?

"Is Papa *my* father?" Ana blurted out, trembling.

Grandmother nodded. "He is."

Her sigh of relief was the final blow. Ana Rodríguez y Villafranca, my sister, was Alonso Rodríguez's daughter. Like me, she was an orphan. But Alonso was her legitimate father. No one had shown up to take that certainty, the privilege that such status afforded, away from her. No matter how poor she was, how destitute, she would always be respected in a way that I would never again be. I knew this, because I remembered the contempt with which men and women at the tavern pronounced the word that now defined me: *bastarda*. How many times had I heard them spit out this word like it was a fly they had found floating in their wine?

"So I'm illegitimate?" I asked quietly. I was a daughter of sin. And my mother, I suddenly realized, the woman who had always emphasized honesty and purity of body and soul, was a sinner. A sinner whose soul was now probably burning in hell. The thought horrified me.

Magdalena was speaking. "Now that your mother is no longer with us, your father has decided to do what is right."

"How?" My words came out loud and shrill.

"To begin with, we will provide you with an education. Do you know how to read?"

I shook my head. None of the women I knew could read. Papa didn't know how to read either.

"Do you know how to sew?"

I shook my head again.

"That needs to change if you're going to have any kind of future in this world."

But I already had a future! I had the tavern on Tudescos Street. It was mine and Ana's. We were entitled to equal shares once we turned twenty-five.

"Fetch your belongings, my child. You are coming to live with us, and we need to get going."

Letting out a cry, I turned to Grandmother. Wasn't she going to stop this?

"Señora Magdalena's right. You must go to your father's house. They'll provide for you better than I can."

Ana had embraced me, her face was buried in my bosom. We were both crying.

"Don't cry, Isabel." Grandmother's wrinkled hands cupped my face and wiped away my tears. "And promise me you'll always do as Señora Magdalena says." Stepping into the kitchen, she reached behind the stove, where she kept a bottle of liqueur, and poured me a glass. I drank it in one gulp. "This is a man's world. You'll benefit from your father's protection."

Magdalena nodded in approval. I stared at her while appealing to Grandmother. "But her brother never cared about me before. Please let me stay here!"

"Yes, let her stay!" Ana cried, her face red and damp.

"Your father did care about you." Magdalena said, staring back. "When I bought wine at your tavern, I gave your mother money to help support you, money your father sent especially for your upkeep."

I turned to Grandmother. Was this woman telling the truth? She nodded. Magdalena went on. "Your father's name is Miguel de Cervantes. He has spent years travelling all over. He is in Andalucía right now, working as a tax collector for the Crown. But as soon as he found out about your mother's death, he asked me to bring you home. He is a writer, you know. One of the best in all of Spain."

"Really?" I said, unsure of whether I could believe that. Writers came to the tavern all the time. "I've never heard of him." Mother had served wine to the great Lope de Vega. Who was this Cervantes in comparison? A nobody.

"You have never heard of him because you're too young. He is also a war hero."

"A war hero?" Despite myself, I had to admit this sounded exciting.

"My sister doesn't want to go with you, no matter what he is!" Ana said, positioning herself between Magdalena and me, stretching out her arms like a fence. How could I be expected to leave my little sister behind?

"Please tell your brother that I appreciate his offer, but—"

"That's enough. You will come home with me now." Magdalena was taller than me, especially with her hat and the thick cork platform of her *chopines*, and she spoke like she was used to being obeyed. "And hurry. It's a long walk to Calle Leganitos."

Calle Leganitos! Steps away from our tavern, just on the other side of Plaza Santo Domingo. My father and his family had been living so close to me, yet we had never met. And now I'd be back in the neighbourhood I loved, but away from the place where I grew up and yearned to return to. It all seemed like a big, cruel joke. I did not move.

"Isabel, do you want to end up at in a *casa de recogidas*?"

Casa de recogidas? Why would Grandmother even

mention that? Those were horrible places where they locked up women who had no family. But I did have a family. I had her and Ana. I had Luisa and Juan, and Luisa's daughters, my cousins Jerónima and Marita.

"Don't you see, Isabel? We can't afford to keep you!" Grandmother cried out. *So this was the reason.* "Luisa can look after Ana when the Lord calls me home, but she can't care for the two of you on her own. She has more than enough with her own daughters!" She was so agitated that I thought for a moment she was going to faint. We all remained quiet until she managed to catch her breath. Then she dealt me the final blow. "You must go home with your aunt. Now."

Home? What did the word even mean? Who was I now?

Magdalena cleared her throat. "You are going to live under my roof. I will feed you, clothe you, and teach you how to sew and how to manage a house. You will receive a yearly allowance of twenty ducats." When she saw that I had stopped crying, she continued. "May I assume this sounds fair to you?"

Ana's eyes were pleading as I stood still, my arm around her shoulder.

"Yes," I said. Ana let go of me and ran to the kitchen, sobbing. Grandmother followed. I wanted to go to them, but Magdalena took me by the arm.

"I can tell you are clever, Isabel," she said. "This is the only opportunity you will have to improve your lot. I'm glad you understand this."

I nodded and went to the cupboard. I placed my few belongings—my best dress; my brush, shawl, mantilla, and ornamental combs—in a cloth sack. My hand reached for my mother's mirror but stopped. No, I would leave that with Ana. The silver pomander was still hidden at the bottom of my bag. My fingers found it and rubbed it gently, and I asked for Mother's blessing. I went into the kitchen and bent down over Ana, caressing her long hair one last time. "*Hermanita*, look at me, please," I urged, but she was sobbing and refused to turn her face towards me. "I'm so sorry!" I pleaded.

"We don't have all afternoon, Isabel, let's go." Magdalena was standing by the door, which Grandmother had opened wide.

Ana tore herself away from me. Fighting my own tears, I moved to the doorway.

"May God protect you and guide you, *hija*," Grandmother said, making the sign of the cross over my face. "Do as Señora Magdalena and your father tell you, and take care of yourself." I put my arms around her, hoping she would not let me go, but she gave me a quick, stiff hug and pushed me out into the street.

II

CONSTANZA

"CONSTANZA DE OVANDO!" Andrea's voice fell like a whip-lash against Constanza's back. Her mother always called out her full name when she reprimanded her. "Siesta is over! Get back to your sewing!"

Constanza was lying on her canopy bed, her eyes fixed on the exposed beam ceiling above it, pondering the space she had taken for granted. *No es justo*, she thought. It wasn't fair! After today, she would have to share her bedroom, and her bed, with a stray she was being forced to welcome as her cousin.

"Dear God!" She turned around and buried her face in her pillow, muffling a cry. Had Pedro de Lanuza not broken their engagement, she would be preparing for her wedding and sewing her own trousseau. "Why must everything bad happen to me?"

"Constanza, *hija mía*! Time to get back to work, I said."

Would her mother ever stop treating her like a child? Taking her time, Constanza stood up and opened the wooden shutters that protected her from the light and the heat. The afternoon sun bled through the window. While she fixed her hair with her fingers, she could hear the lazy clip-clop of horses' hooves and the gentle cooing of pigeons in the distance.

"Coming!" Constanza dried the sweat off her forehead and the back of her neck with a freshly starched handkerchief—thank God for Teresa, who always kept such important garments clean!—then turned around and looked at her room. These were to be her last moments of privacy. The wool rug that kept the tile floor warm in the winter was rolled up in the corner next to the dormant brazier. A simple wooden chest meant for Isabel's belongings had been placed next to Constanza's. Hers had been a present to her mother from Signore Francisco Locadelo, an Italian gentleman Andrea had helped care for when her father, Rodrigo de Cervantes, worked as a surgeon. Brought all the way from Germany, made of oak with dovetailed boards and carved geometric designs that made it unique, the chest was one of Constanza's most precious belongings. At least she would not have to share *that*. As the only child of Andrea de Cervantes and Nicolás de Ovando, *que El Señor lo tenga en su Santa Gloria*—God rest his soul—she had grown up enjoying the undivided care and attention of not only her mother, but the entire family. Until now.

"Mother?" She found Andrea spinning yarn in *el estrado de las damas*, the name they sometimes used to refer to their sewing room. This was Constanza's self-contained world. Located by the front entrance next to the foyer, and one of the biggest rooms of the house, it was both spacious and cozy at the same time, and featured carved lattice doors in two parts, the lower half of which remained closed when customers visited. In the centre of the room, on a large podium covered with a hand-woven rug, stood a wooden distaff, spindle, and winder for spinning wool, as well as several large soft cushions where the women could sit while working or chatting. On one wall was a chest even larger than Constanza's, although not as elegant. Next to it, a tall, finely carved cabinet, which they affectionately called *nuestro bargueño*, was fitted with small drawers and pigeonholes that stored their supplies. Against another wall was a table that held their dressmaking guide, *Geometría y traça para el oficio de los sastres*, by Diego de Freyle. By now, they knew most of the patterns almost by heart, but they showed them to the customers for inspiration and to prove that their work was as good as that of the male tailors they competed against. Constanza missed the days when they were required to sew padded hose, pinked doublets and bodices, and finely embroidered scarves instead of the simple everyday shirts, chemises, and mourning garments that made up most of their orders lately.

"I've been wondering, Mother." Constanza sat down in her special sewing chair and cleared her throat. "With my cousin moving in, perhaps you and I could consider living on our own again?"

Andrea continued to spin without looking up. Her fingers moved with agility and speed, as if they had a life of their own, independent from her hands and arms "You know the answer to that, *hija*. Let's not talk about it."

Constanza gazed at the garment on her lap, a half-finished shirt. How many had she personally tailored for Pedro, even embroidering his initials on them, all for nothing? She let out a sigh.

"Stop thinking about him," Andrea said. Her hair was up in a bun, drops of sweat condensing on her forehead. "It's no use. Luisa de Silva y Portocarrero will be Pedro de Lanuza's wife."

"I wasn't thinking about him, Mother," Constanza retorted.

"Yes, you were. You can't fool me." Constanza braced herself to hear about the money she had received in reparation for the broken marriage promise. She regretted accepting those 1,400 ducats because now she felt she had no right to complain. After a four-year engagement, and at age twenty-four, she would have much preferred to be Señora de Lanuza than to receive all the riches in the world.

"As your Aunt Magdalena said—"

"I know," Constanza said, cutting her off. "I got the best possible deal: the money without the man."

Andrea smiled. "Exactly. Remember that when Magdalena was in your situation, and Juan Pérez de Alzaga broke his wedding promise, she received—"

"I know, I know," Constanza emphasized. "She received merely three hundred pitiful and humiliating ducats." If they weren't in the middle of a plague, if they were allowed to go out and meet with people like they used to before, Constanza wondered, would they still be talking about the same subjects and saying the exact same things in endless circles? "Why must we always do what Aunt Magdalena says?"

This time Andrea stopped spinning and looked at her daughter. "We are not doing what Magdalena says. We are doing what your uncle Miguel has asked us to do. We owe it to him to take care of his daughter."

"Now that you mention it," Constanza said as she continued sewing, "are there two dowries in our future? I assume my cousin will need one, too."

"She's only fifteen years old. We don't have to worry about that just yet."

"Are you expecting her to be ugly like me and still a *solterona* when she's almost twenty-five?" Constanza asked, turning her face towards the window to avoid her mother's gaze.

"*Hija.*" Andrea's voice softened. "You're not ugly. You have the same chestnut eyes and hair as your father, and I assure you that you are as pretty as he was handsome." Constanza's expression didn't change. "And you're not a spinster. You'll find someone else. Someone better than Pedro de Lanuza."

Constanza held back a tear. Where would she find someone else, at her age and in the midst of a plague? Theatres were closed, and the only public gatherings that were still taking place were at the Plaza de la Cruz Verde, where heretics were burned. The Cervantes family stayed away from those. The smell of burnt hair and skin, the cries for mercy, the cheers of the crowds were too much for them to bear.

"How can Pedro and Luisa be consumed with wedding arrangements at a time like this?" Constanza asked, breaking into tears. "People are hungry, they're dying every day. How can they be so insensitive?"

Andrea put down the yarn and rose to her feet. She went to her daughter, leaned over her in her chair, and embraced her. "You need to stop thinking about those two, *hija,*" she said, handing her a handkerchief. "It's not good for you."

"You want to know what else is not good for me? Having a stranger sleeping next to me in my own bed."

"She's not a stranger, Constanza."

"To me she is! I never knew she existed until Uncle Miguel's letter arrived last week!" Constanza blew her nose. "She may be his daughter, but she's a stranger, and to make matters worse, she grew up in a tavern!"

Andrea sighed and returned to her seat at the spindle. "Believe me, it will be fine."

"Fine?" Constanza was stabbing at the shirt in her hands with her needle. "Once Uncle Miguel recognizes Isabel as his legitimate child, she'll always come first."

Andrea shook her head as she spoke, her voice gentle and reassuring. "No one will ever take your place in this house."

Feeling encouraged, Constanza pressed on. "And what about Teresa?" she asked, referring to their longtime servant. "There is enough to do around the house to keep poor Teresa occupied day and night, without having to wait on another person."

"We will have to make do with what the Lord has given us and be grateful."

"If we're taking Isabel into our service as a maid, can't she be in charge of some chores, at least until Uncle Miguel comes back? *That* would be useful."

"You know very well that Isabel will not be our real maid. She's family, and regardless of how we manage to keep appearances, we'll treat her as such."

"Good luck making people believe she's a maid if she shares our last name," Constanza snapped.

Andrea shook her head. "If I were you, I wouldn't worry too much about that."

Constanza stopped sewing and stared at her mother. "Why?" She frowned. "Why do you say that?"

Taking her time, Andrea cut the yarn with a pair of scissors and rolled it into a ball. When she was done, she turned to look at Constanza, lowering her voice. "Don't tell your aunt I told you this, but your uncle is not giving Isabel his name."

"He's not?" Constanza said loudly.

Andrea frowned and put her finger to her lips. "What did I just say?"

"Sorry!" Constanza whispered. "He's not giving her his name?"

"At least for now he isn't, no."

"How do you know?" she asked. Andrea signaled for her to resume her sewing as she placed the ball of yarn in a basket. Constanza obeyed but she found it impossible to concentrate.

"All I can tell you is that tomorrow she and Magdalena are going to see a lawyer. Your aunt is requesting legal guardianship of Isabel."

"And?"

Andrea lowered her voice even more. "Miguel requested that she be officially registered as Isabel de Saavedra."

Constanza pricked her finger and let out a cry. As she sucked on the wound, she tried to digest the news. Saavedra was the nom de plume Miguel had started to use after returning from Algiers. At first, he told them he had taken the name of their cousin Gonzalo Cervantes Saavedra, a poet Miguel had praised in his first book, *La Galatea*. But later he confessed the truth. While he was held captive in Algiers, because of the wounds he received in the Battle of Lepanto, he was given the nickname *Shaibedraa*, meaning defective arm. Constanza never truly understood why, but Miguel had grown fond of the word—fond of its sound rather than its meaning, he said. After five years in those faraway lands, it became part of his identity, and upon his return he felt that a new name would be fitting of a new beginning. He dropped his mother's last name, de Cortinas, and became Miguel de Cervantes y Saavedra, a name that he believed held the promise of a better future.

"Isabel de Saavedra?" Constanza asked. "Why not de Cervantes?"

"Perhaps he wants to protect Catalina."

"My aunt still doesn't know about her?" Constanza's eyes grew wide.

"I don't think so, no."

"She'll be devastated when she finds out," Constanza said. Then, after drying the sweat from her forehead with her hand-kerchief, she resumed her sewing.

III

ISABEL

AS WE ENTERED Calle Leganitos, the only sound was the singing of sparrows getting ready for the evening. How could they and everyone else go about their business as if nothing had happened, when my existence would never be the same? There were so many questions I wanted to ask but, afraid of upsetting Magdalena, I remained silent. I could feel the sweat running down my back.

We stopped in front of a heavy wooden door. Magdalena unlocked it discreetly, pulled it open and entered, but I hesitated to follow her inside. This was it. I was standing at the threshold of my new life. My life as a *bastarda*.

"What are you waiting for? Hurry up before a thief notices our door is wide open!"

The exterior of the house was plain, but the moment I stepped inside I understood why Magdalena had shown such contempt when she entered Grandmother's apartment. I stood still and allowed my eyes to take in my new surroundings. We were standing in an elegant foyer with a fireplace and three leather chairs. On either side of the foyer was a spacious room. The one on the left held a distaff; the one on the right had a desk and many books. The fourth side of the foyer led to a hallway and, beyond that, a staircase.

"There are two floors?" I said, unable to hide my surprise.

"We're home!" Magdalena called out. She signalled for me to help remove her overskirt. Once that was done, she collapsed on a chair.

"I can't stand on my feet anymore!" she declared as her *chopines* fell noiselessly to the tiled floor. I had never seen shoes like these before. They had a thick platform and were lined with velvet. The shoes that Mother, Ana, and I wore were flat, simple leather ones.

Two women came down the stairs and through the hall to greet us. One of them seemed close in age to Magdalena. But whereas Magdalena had light-brown hair and hazel eyes, this woman's blond hair and blue eyes reminded me of a painting of the Virgin I saw at church every week. The other woman was still young, but older than I was. There were dark shadows under her eyes and her chestnut mane fell like a veil framing her face. I gazed at the two as they approached. Magdalena remained seated.

The older woman opened her arms and embraced me. "You're his spitting image!" she exclaimed. "I'm your aunt Andrea, Miguel's sister."

"*Aunt?*" Even though the young one had spoken in a whisper, I could hear her clearly.

There was an uncomfortable moment of silence. My hands were sweaty and my stomach was uneasy. I had felt like this the day when Ana, Grandmother, and I left the tavern after Mother's executors took it over, the day that—until now—I had considered the worst of my life.

"Let's go into the sewing room." Magdalena stood up and took my arm. "Isabel, I told you we are going to pay you, right?" she asked. I nodded. "That is because, for the time being, to the outside world you will be our new maid." Before I could say anything in response, the other two followed us into the next room, and Magdalena turned around to face the younger woman, signalling for her to come closer. "Now, let's try this again, shall we? Constanza, this is your cousin, Isabel."

Constanza made a slight bow, and I bowed in return, noticing with embarrassment the difference between the clothes the three women were wearing and my own. Their blouses and skirts were made of fine fabric, and not a single garment had patches on it. I would not even need to masquerade as their maid: I was already dressed the part. My throat felt as dry as leather.

"You must be very thirsty after that walk!" As if she had read my mind, a short, plump woman emerged from the hallway holding a tray with glasses. When she looked at my face, she let out a little shriek. "My Lord! This girl is Mistress Leonor come back to life!"

"Leonor?" My voice was raspy.

"Isabel, this is Teresa. She has been working for us for years helping to run the house as smoothly as possible," Magdalena said. Teresa smiled and made a slight bow, which I tried to mimic.

"Leonor de Cortinas was your grandmother. And yes, you do resemble her quite a bit." There was a spark in Magdalena's eyes as she said this.

I felt myself blush. Constanza picked up a glass from the tray and the rest of us followed suit. I noticed her fingers were slender, her nails rosy and clean. I brought the glass to my nose. Fresh water with cinnamon! I drank it almost in one gulp, admiring the beautiful crystal, then dried my mouth with the back of my hand. Then I realized that the others were sipping their water; their glasses were still half full. Nobody spoke, and I felt very uncouth.

Magdalena broke the silence. "Follow Teresa into the kitchen, Isabel. She has everything set up to help you get ready for the night. I left some clothes for you—an underskirt, an overskirt, a petticoat with laces at the side so you can dress yourself, and a couple of chemises. You can wear those while we get your new wardrobe ready. Nothing too fancy because there are rules to be followed, but it should suffice."

While my aunt was speaking, Teresa had taken my sack and Magdalena's overskirt from the foyer. She came back to where we stood, and with a gentle hand on my back, guided me down the hall.

Together, we entered the most delightful kitchen. The blue and yellow tiles on the wall were the first thing I noticed. There had been no such decorative frills at the tavern, much less in Grandmother's apartment. On the far side of the spacious room, French doors opened onto a small patio, where the evening's exhausted rays of sunshine still shone. In the middle of the room was a big wooden table surrounded by half a dozen chairs. Cauldrons of different sizes hung on a rack by the stove, and there were wooden shelves along the walls with plates and jars and skimmers and baskets. Best of all, there were ropes of dried meat hanging from a hook! I looked at it in delight. I hadn't seen a rope of *chorizo* since I moved in with Grandmother. My mouth began to water.

"Would you like some?" Teresa asked. I wasn't sure if she meant the meat or something else, but I was ready to accept anything she had to offer.

"*Chorizo*," she said.

Such a delicious word! The sound of it made me smile.

Teresa pulled out a chair for me to sit. Then she cut a piece of meat and placed it on a heavy dish. She brought out cheese from the pantry and poured more water from an earthenware pitcher. If only Ana were here! Knowing she would go to bed with an empty stomach while I enjoyed this feast made me feel guilty.

As I ate, I noticed a mattress rolled up against the wall in the far corner of the room. "Is that where I'll sleep?"

"No, no!" she said with a laugh. "That's where *I* sleep! You'll be upstairs, in your cousin's bed!"

A piece of meat got caught in my throat and I began to cough. Teresa patted my back and gave me more water to drink until I caught my breath again. My eyes had teared up, not only because I was choking, but because the thought of sharing a bed with an elegant woman who was clearly unhappy to see me was frightening.

"Señorita Constanza is not a bad person," Teresa explained, as if she had read my mind, her smile sweet and sincere. "She's simply getting over a broken heart. She was engaged for four years to an idiot who is going to marry a woman with more money." I took in this information, intending to ponder it later.

As my eyes continued to roam around the kitchen, I saw a large basin of water on the floor by the fireplace. Next to it was a stool with a folded towel.

"What's that for?"

"Señora Magdalena asked me to bathe you before you go to bed," Teresa said. "And she wants me to take a look at the belongings you brought with you."

"You mean the clothes I packed in my sack?"

Teresa nodded. She picked up the sack and handed it to me.

"Why? All I have is my best dress and a shawl."

"Yes, give them to me." She held out her hand. Not wanting her to see my silver pomander, I opened the sack and brought out my dress and my shawl. She took them and laid them over her arm.

"I'll take the sack, too." She held out her hand again. "It needs a good scrub."

"But where will I keep my clothes?"

"There's a trunk for you upstairs, in Señorita Constanza's room."

"A trunk?" I smiled with pleasure. Deciding to trust Teresa, and I took the silver pomander out of the sack and held it out for her to see.

"This belonged to my mother," I said. She took it from my hand with a smile.

"It's very beautiful. You will want to keep that in your trunk," she said, putting it on the table and taking the sack. With a feeling of relief, I went over to touch the water in the basin. What a pleasant surprise to feel that it was lukewarm, not cold!

"What about the clothes I just gave you?" I asked.

Teresa shrugged. "Your aunt will probably give them to the poor," she said.

"But my Sunday dress is as good as new!" I replied, distressed. Teresa shook her head. "Well, almost new." I conceded. "And this skirt is special," I protested, smoothing it out against my leg. "Very special."

"You'll have to talk to Señora Magdalena about that. Now, take off your clothes." I hesitated, taken aback, and my excitement faded. I had never exposed myself in front of a stranger. "I will wash your hair, too. Your aunt said so."

Crossing my arms in front of my chest, I looked around as if trying to find a way out.

"Come on, *mi niña*. It's getting dark fast. I still have to brush your aunt's overskirt, and God knows I didn't warm up all that water for nothing."

With my face on fire, I opened my shirt. Teresa offered to help me undo my skirt, but I asked to do it on my own. I wanted to say goodbye to it, to touch it silently for the very last time. I remembered the day Mother had brought it back to our apartment above the tavern. Ana and I were getting ready to go downstairs and help serve our customers. My task was to measure the wine, and she helped Mother at the *bodegón de puntapié*, the stall we had set up outside the tavern door when the new rules prohibiting the sale of food inside came into effect.

Mother burst into the room, proudly holding up the skirt as if it were a flag.

"Isabel, look what I have for you!" She was beaming. "Luisa Benzón gave it to me, and I think it will fit you perfectly." Luisa Benzón was a famous actress, one of the first women to work on stage. She had given the skirt to Mother in exchange for wine. With the theatres closed because of the plague, actors were having a hard time covering their basic needs.

"You will look all grown up and fancy wearing it, *cariño*. Try it on!" I put on the skirt and Mother and Ana clapped in excitement. "It's perfect!" Mother exclaimed as she hugged me. "Look at you, so tall and beautiful! I'm proud of you!"

I felt a pang in my stomach. Would she be proud of me now?

"Do you think we could save the skirt for my sister? For when she's older?" My voice broke as I spoke. "It used to belong to Luisa Benzón."

"The actress?" Teresa's asked with wide eyes.

"Yes," I said proudly.

"Well, aren't you full of surprises!" Smiling, she examined the skirt more closely. I held my breath, but after a few seconds of silence she shook her head. "I don't think it can be saved. It's too worn. Too thin. And too stained. It has certainly seen better days."

"Haven't we all?" I said mournfully.

"Look at you, talking like an old lady!" Teresa said with a laugh. "How old are you, anyway?"

"I turned fifteen in April."

"Not November, on Saint Isabel's Day?"

"No. Mother named me after her baby sister, who died shortly before I was born. She said it was her hope that I would live for us both." My name had always made me feel accompanied, protected. Why did I feel so alone now?

"April!" Teresa sighed. "*Las mañanicas de abril son dulces de dormir ...*" But instead of completing the happy saying, she handed me a cloth to dry my tears. Then, without another word, she helped me remove the rest of my clothes, and I stepped in the basin. I crouched down so she could lather my head with an olive-scented soap that reminded me of my childhood and made me yearn for Mother even more. Teresa scrubbed my scalp and my back while I washed my arms and legs. Then she helped me rinse off the soap and dry myself with the linen towel. Her hands were strong but gentle, and by the time I had put on the clean chemise I would wear to sleep, I was feeling much better. As a last step, Teresa applied orange blossom oil to my hair before combing it.

"Your father will be amazed when he sees you," she said when she was done. "You look exactly like ..."

Like him, whatever that meant. Or like Leonor—as if I cared. As if resembling a couple of strangers had any meaning for me. All I could focus on was my old skirt, which lay abandoned, like a dead animal, on the floor. It had not only seen better days, it had seen my *best* days; yet here I was, turning my back on it. Feeling like a traitor, I followed Teresa out of the kitchen and up the stairs to the room I was to share with my new cousin. This time, the pain in my stomach was not hunger but the realization that I had exchanged everyone and everything I loved for twenty ducats.

IV

CONSTANZA

"BEING A SEAMSTRESS is an art." Magdalena walked into the sewing room, the *estrado de las damas*, followed by Andrea and Isabel. "Clothing is a form of language, a code. There are so many things to understand and consider."

It was early in the morning and the sun seeping through the window shutters promised another scorching day. Constanza had eaten breakfast at dawn, and she was already working on the shirt she had started the previous afternoon.

The white blouse, brown overskirt, and dark-brown vest they had selected for Isabel fit her well, and with her clean hair, now in a braid that fell over her shoulder, she looked even more like her grandmother Leonor and uncle Miguel. Constanza knew her chestnut mane and dark gaze were a trait from her father's side, yet she could not help resenting Isabel's hazel eyes and sunny hair—hers was the complexion poets wrote sonnets about. Why did her cousin have to be the one who looked like a true Cervantes?

"As you know, moral laws call for austerity," Magdalena explained. It was evident she was enjoying sharing her knowledge with someone new. "The colour black—referred to in clothing as *gala negra*—is in fashion, but only the very rich can afford it. Why? Because there are different kinds of black dye, and the best one comes from New Spain. Fabric that has been dyed with it is called 'raven's wing.' Would you like to see it?"

Isabel nodded. Andrea opened one of the small drawers in the *bargueño* cabinet and withdrew a small bottle.

"The carvings on that piece of furniture are beautiful!" The tone of Isabel's voice irritated Constanza.

"I'm glad you like our *bargueño,* Isabel!" Andrea said.

"What?"

"That's what the cabinet is called." Constanza did not need to look at her mother to know that she was smiling. "And, *mi niña,* when you need someone to repeat their words to you, you must say 'pardon' instead of 'what.'" She handed the bottle to Isabel, who held it in her palm reverentially.

Magdalena opened the large trunk, which held their finest, most expensive fabrics. Constanza stopped sewing to watch her take out a roll of their most exquisite gabardine, wondering how much longer they would interrupt her peace. Magdalena continued talking.

"Black garments, once ready, are accessorized with gold chains, buttons, and jewellery."

Isabel came over and gazed at the beautiful material. She was too afraid to touch it. Magdalena smiled as she carefully placed the roll back in the trunk. Next she extracted a roll of silk and a basket of ruff collars.

"I've seen those before!" Isabel exclaimed. "Some of our customers at the tavern wear them at times, but I never had the opportunity to take a close look at them." She reached for the basket and stared at the ruffs in admiration.

"These are made with the finest lace imported from Flanders. We also make cuffs to match. The measurements for each piece have to be very precise so they fit elegantly around the neck and wrists." She picked a ruff from the basket and offered it to Isabel to touch. The girl opened her mouth in awe.

"I always thought they looked stiff, but these feel so soft!" she said. Andrea and Magdalena both laughed.

"That's because they still need to be starched!" Andrea explained. "But don't forget the golden rule." She took the ruff from Isabel, put it back in the basket, and placed the basket in the trunk again. "Great care must be taken to limit the excess of luxury. We can be punished if we craft an ostentatious piece of clothing for someone who doesn't have the right to wear it."

"You can get punished?"

"Exiled for two years, or worse." Andrea's voice was serious, but not as serious as Constanza thought it should be.

"Fortunately," Magdalena continued, "most of what we sew now is men's shirts. They only require a few days' work, compared to an elaborate dress, a skirt, or even a petticoat, which can take weeks to complete."

"Speaking of which," Constanza interrupted, finally losing her patience, "perhaps we should stop talking so much and start working." Aware that her cousin was watching her, she nonchalantly opened the little drawer underneath her chair and extracted a pair of scissors.

"That's Constanza's sewing chair," Andrea pointed out. She frowned at her daughter for being so rude, but Constanza ignored her. "She won't do her work anywhere else."

"I can see why. It's so smart to have a drawer in a chair!" Isabel's happy voice made Constanza cringe. "Everything here is so beautiful! In our apartment above the tavern we had some sturdy pieces of furniture, but nothing like this. And the tavern, as you know," she said, looking at Magdalena, "has a cobblestone floor instead of tile and is furnished with very plain wooden tables and benches. But here in your house ... look at this rug! It's so thick and soft. And look how big that mirror is! Is the frame made of gold?"

Andrea and Magdalena shook their heads and laughed, but Constanza remained silent.

"Come look at yourself, Isabel." Magdalena extended her hand, and she and her niece stood side by side facing the mirror, contemplating their images. "I don't think you've ever looked better, and this is just your first day with us." She sounded very pleased. But her words were like darts hitting Constanza's back. She didn't need to turn towards her cousin to appreciate the beauty of her complexion. Next to Isabel, a rose preparing to blossom in a new garden bed, she felt like a weed.

"Aunt Magdalena," Constanza said, trying to hide her irritation. "What time is your appointment with the judge? It would be unfortunate if you and Isabel arrived late."

Magdalena looked at her sister. "You told her?"

"The appointment isn't a secret, is it?" Andrea replied, taking her spot at the distaff nonchalantly.

"What appointment?" Isabel asked.

"We have an appointment with a judge today," Magdalena replied. Andrea began to weave and Constanza returned to her sewing.

"I don't like judges. They ruin our lives."

Men ruin our lives, Constanza wanted to say, but she held back. Her cousin would learn that lesson soon enough.

V

ISABEL

MAGDALENA AND I left the sewing room and crossed the foyer to the room on the other side. I tried to remember all the new things I was seeing so that I could share the details with Ana the next time we were together.

"This is your father's studio. He does his writing in this room when he's at home."

I took in the sturdy wooden desk and the wool rug. Behind the desk was a large bookcase that held more books than I had ever seen in one space. I tried to imagine my father—that mysterious man who I was said to resemble—inhabiting this space. As I gazed at the shelves I wondered why anyone would need so many books; they all looked the same to me.

"When was he here last?"

"It's been five years since he left for Granada and Seville," Magdalena said. Five years! I felt a knot in my stomach. "But he promised he would come back soon; he can't wait to meet you!" she assured me. And before I could pose any more questions, she clapped twice. "Time for your first lesson!"

"My first lesson?"

"I will teach you how to walk like a lady," she said in a cheerful voice.

I didn't know there was a problem with the way I walked. Magdalena was scanning the books on the shelves, sliding her index finger over them. She picked out a thick, compact volume. Then she stepped over to the foyer and placed the book on her head. Maintaining the book in perfect balance, she walked across the foyer, into the sewing room, back into the study, and sat down on one of the leather chairs without letting the book fall off. I wanted to clap but I held back, unsure if it would be appropriate.

"Your turn now," she said, offering me the book. I let out a startled laugh.

"I'm serious, Isabel. You need to master this. Come on, give it a try."

She handed the book to me. I placed it on my head—it felt so heavy!—and took a step. Immediately, the book fell to the floor with a thump. Since it landed on the rug it wasn't damaged, but I was mortified. Would I be expected to pay for it if it did get damaged?

"Could I maybe practice with something else? This looks very expensive. I couldn't possibly pay for it."

"Don't worry about that. Try it again! It's not an important book anyway."

Carefully repositioning the volume on my head, I began to walk. This time, I was able to take two steps before the book slid off. I was embarrassed, but my aunt's smile made it clear she was amused, not angry.

"Why spend money on a book you don't care about?" I asked. I bent to pick it up and tried to get it back into its original shape. The pages were wrinkled and folded in a way that made it hard to close. At the tavern, my parents never bought anything unless it was considered essential. Mother would not have paid a single *maravedí* for an item she considered poor quality or simply ornamental, like a book.

"Your father didn't purchase that book, don't worry. He received it as a present." What strange people. Shouldn't that make it more valuable? Mother had always taught me to appreciate a gift more than any other object, which was why parting with the skirt she had given me still hurt, even though I loved my new clothes. They were not as elegant as my aunts' and cousin's but, for a maid, they were beautiful.

"Come on," Magdalena said. "Put it back on your head and try again."

I did as she asked and focused on keeping the book still as I moved. I took several steps before it slid off, but this time I caught it before it hit the floor.

"Aunt Magdalena," Constanza called out from the other room, "is that the Pasamonte book?"

"Of course it is!" she said. The three of them laughed.

"Perhaps Isabel would feel better if she knew that Uncle Miguel always thought the author of that book had no talent," Constanza suggested.

"Constanza!" Andrea chided her. With the lattice doors open, it felt as if we were all in the same room. "Gerónimo de Pasamonte is not a bad writer, he's just boring. He has connections, and that's what matters."

"Don't let anyone hear you repeat that outside these walls, Isabel." Constanza's voice was firm but friendly, or so it seemed. I nodded, smiling, even though she couldn't see me.

"One thing you must know since you are going to be part of this family is that Madrid's literary world is very small, so you don't want to make anyone angry at you—if you're a writer, that is."

Taverners have a similar code of conduct, I wanted to say, at least those who were honourable. I was not completely ignorant. But instead, I put the book on my head and managed to take four steps before it slipped, making a loud sound as it fell on the stone floor.

"If the author comes to visit and sees that his book has fallen apart, won't he be upset?" Not only were the pages wrinkled from the falls; some of them had come loose, and the corner of the cover was damaged.

"We can always tell him it came undone because we all read it and enjoyed it so much!" Magdalena exclaimed, which made us burst into laughter.

I tried balancing the book once more, this time concentrating on every motion of my body. I kept one hand close to my head until I felt steady; the weight of the volume forced me to stretch and stiffen my neck. While my aunts and my cousin remained silent, I took a deep breath and proceeded slowly, keeping my back straight. Across the foyer: one, two, three, four, five steps. Into the sewing room: one, two, three, four steps. I avoided looking at Andrea and Constanza so as not to get distracted, but I could feel their eyes on me as sweat broke out on my face. I turned around ever so gently and headed back towards the study: one, two, three, four, five, six, seven, eight, nine steps. The silence around me was full of expectation; I could almost savour my triumph! Now I only had to sit down without letting the book fall on the floor. Facing the bookshelf, I stood still for a moment staring at its contents, barely breathing.

"Did my father write any of those books?"

"Yes!" Aunt Magdalena replied. "That one." She pointed towards the first book on the left side on the lower shelf. "It's called *La Galatea*."

"*La Galatea*? What does that mean?"

"It's a pastoral novel," Constanza replied. I stared at Magdalena blankly, trying to prevent the book from falling off.

"Don't worry, my child. You're doing very well. It's a story about shepherds and life in the countryside."

"Oh!" I said, nodding instinctively in thanks. Of course, down slid the book. Fortunately I caught it, and after placing it on the desk I reached for my father's book. Funny that a war hero would write about life in the countryside, I thought, leafing through the pages, wondering what they said. All shepherds ever did was watch their sheep eat grass. How could that fill up so many pages? It was a thick book, almost as thick as the one I had been balancing on my head. Besides, as far as I knew, everyone had left the countryside and moved to Madrid. The city was overcrowded, or so Mother used to say—never as a complaint, though, since it was good for business. Why would city people want to read stories about shepherds? No wonder I had never heard a word about my father's books.

VI

July 1599

My dearest Miguel,

I hope that God continues to protect you and that this letter finds you in good health.

Andrea, Constanza, and I are faring well. The three of us have been busy sewing all manner of clothing; mourning garments, however, tend to be very much in demand now. Every night and every morning I entrust ourselves to God that we might continue to be spared.

I write with news about your daughter, Isabel. We have already met with a judge, and I have officially petitioned to be appointed her legal guardian. How time-consuming and frustrating this procedure will eventually be remains to be seen, especially since you have insisted that we pay no bribes. In any case, I have no hopes for this to be resolved soon, which gives us time to deal with another concern: how long we will be able sustain the pretence that she is but a servant. Not only does Isabel look too much like you, but it is clear that the years she spent at the tavern gave her a maturity beyond her years. Every time I visited that god-forsaken place I was impressed by her mother's beauty and the self-confidence with which she carried herself and which you found so unique and appealing. Although she does not realize it yet, Isabel has inherited those traits from her mother, which might be a cause of suffering for us in the future. For now, however, I have created a detailed, busy schedule that shall keep her occupied and out of trouble until the fall.

Aware as I am of how much I owe you and all the sacrifices you have made for us, there still are some things I refuse to do on your behalf. You are the one who must tell your wife about Isabel. Think how painful it will be for Catalina given she has not herself provided you with a child. And you must also be forthright about Isabel's birth at a time when you were already engaged to Catalina. What were you thinking, my dear brother, when you got yourself entangled in this web?

I must confess to you that while I worry about the consequences that your choices might bring you—and, by extension, all of us—I feel very proud of the generous man that you are. Instead of abandoning your illegitimate child, as most men do, you have acted nobly and chosen to provide for her, and bring her into this, your home, our family's home. She is very fortunate, as I am, and as Andrea and Constanza are, to have you. If there is an ongoing source of hope in my life, it is the strength of our ties. Of our family.

Have you received any news from our dear Rodrigo? I try not to talk about him these days because the lack of information as to his whereabouts weighs too heavily on my heart, but I pray for his safety every day, as I pray for yours. Are these drought days for you, or have you been able to write some more? I know that those six months in prison in Seville were painful and most unjust, but at least they afforded you the opportunity to pick up your pen again. We miss you every day and pray for your safe return, *hermano mío*.

May God bless you and protect your every step.

Your loving sister,
Magdalena

VII

CONSTANZA

"ISABEL, WAKE UP!" It was a hot August night. Constanza reached over, placed a hand on Isabel's shoulder, and shook her firmly. "Stop moving so much, you're kicking me!"

They had switched sides and now it was Isabel who slept next to the wall. But that had not yielded the desired results. Isabel still tossed constantly in her sleep, and Constanza feared she'd be pushed to the floor. Now, to make matters worse, they were sweaty and the sheets stuck to their skin.

It was a moonless night and all Constanza could see was her cousin's silhouette. "Please forgive me, Constanza," Isabel said with a yawn. "It must be the heat."

"*Aire castellano, malo en invierno y peor en verano*, Teresa says." Constanza nodded in agreement; it was true that the air in Castile was bad in the winter and even worse in the summer.

"Isabel, the mattress is barely wide enough for us both, and you're making it impossible for me to sleep. And if I don't sleep well, I cannot sew well."

"I'm sorry." Isabel's dismissive tone irritated Constanza. This was a serious matter.

"Sewing is not just *any* business. You've seen the attention it requires. How long did it take you before you stopped pricking your fingers?"

"I still do! I'm not good at sewing."

"But you see, I *must* be good at it," Constanza stressed, "and for that I need my sleep."

"Sorry, I'll try not to bother you again."

"*Gracias*." Constanza lay down and closed her eyes. The next morning, she would be embroidering a *gilecuelo*. The fitted vest was one of her specialties, and the filigree embroidery around the edges required her full attention and energy. With the end of summer approaching, people were ordering new wardrobes, and *gilecuelos* always paid well.

"It's just that ..." Isabel wiped her face with her hand, then grew silent.

"What's wrong?" In the three months since Isabel's arrival, Constanza had been watching her. How eager she was to please. How hard she tried to learn what she was taught. How readily she offered to help Teresa with chores and accompany her to the market. Constanza had tried to remain indifferent at the beginning, but as the weeks went by, she couldn't help warming slightly to her cousin.

Constanza sat up again and it prompted Isabel to do the same. They both stared into the darkness with their backs against the headboard. They were swaddled in hot air and silence.

"What were you saying?" Constanza asked.

Isabel let out a sigh. "I'm afraid of crying if I talk about it."

Constanza wanted to say, *You already cry in your sleep*, but instead she said, "Don't worry, just speak."

"I miss my little sister and my grandmother. I haven't seen them at all since I arrived here."

Constanza nodded. She knew this.

"Every time I ask Magdalena if I can visit them, she finds a reason to say no. No, because I have to study letters and words and read out loud. No, because I have to learn how to add and subtract on paper, even though I am perfectly able to do it in my head. No, because I have to accompany Teresa to the market or go with your mother to buy more fabric. No, because I need to practice my sewing, or practice how to walk, sit down, and get back up wearing that wretched farthingale that only rich ladies can afford, so why should I learn to move in it?"

Constanza noticed the effort her cousin was making not to break into tears. "Every day I do as I am told, I try my best, and when I ask again for permission to visit them, Magdalena again says no, because it's too late, too early, too hot, or too risky. She always says no."

"Magdalena is doing what she thinks is best for you." Constanza tried to sound convincing, but she sensed she was doing a poor job. On the one hand, she agreed that keeping Isabel away from her family was beneficial while she was being educated. On the other, her aunt was not the one being kept up at night by Isabel's restlessness and constant nightmares. Constanza had tried to convince her mother to intervene, but to no avail.

"I know," Isabel acknowledged. "She says I need to prove my worth to my father. That once he comes back, he'll want to see how much progress I've made. But why can't I go one day, just one day, to visit my sister to see how she is?"

"I'm sure she's doing well."

Isabel's voice was harsh. "You don't understand."

"I do. You're not the only person who has problems, you know."

"You think I don't know that?" Isabel's voice trembled. Constanza regretted her words. Her cousin was crying now.

"I wasn't even going to say anything. You're the one who asked!" Isabel turned her back to her cousin and lay down again, crying into her pillow. Constanza remained in her seated position. She wondered what to do. Light a candle and find a handkerchief for her? No. That would make it even harder for her to go back to sleep. Something simpler, quicker, was in order.

"I'm sorry, I didn't mean to upset you," she said.

Isabel took a few seconds to respond. "Apology accepted. I'm sorry, too. I guess I'm nervous because of tomorrow."

"Tomorrow?"

"Because of the appointment we have with the judge."

"Right!" Constanza hit her head with the palm of her hand. How could she forget? "Why are you nervous?"

"He's ugly."

"I'm sure he is," Constanza said, laughing. "Magdalena says that men with power have a tendency to be ugly even when they're handsome."

"She's right," Isabel agreed. "But that's not all."

"What else is bothering you?"

"It will be our third time there."

Constanza nodded. Everyone knew that the Spanish Empire was as powerful as its clerks were slow.

"What if the papers aren't ready yet?" Isabel asked.

"Then you'll have to wait and go again."

"But the longer it takes, the longer I remain a *bastarda*!"

Constanza tried to imagine what it felt like to be illegitimate. She shivered at the mere thought. She felt guilty for not sharing the information she had, but she knew she had to remain quiet. Although she was aware that keeping a secret was not the same as lying, she still crossed herself.

"Try not to think about it."

"It's all I can think of—that, my sister, and the tavern."

"Didn't Magdalena tell you she'd help you claim the tavern once you're old enough?"

"Yes."

"Stop worrying about it, then."

"I'll try," Isabel said uncertainly. "*Buenas noches*."

"Wait!" Constanza said. She still felt uneasy. No matter how big a menace Isabel was for her future, she had to do something to help her.

"What if you send a message to your sister so she knows that you're thinking of her?" she asked.

Isabel laughed. "Ana can't read. And I still can't write that well."

"No, not a letter. A parcel. Some marzipan, perhaps? Does she like marzipan?"

Isabel sat up again. "Yes! She loves it." She paused to think. "She loves *chorizo*, too. But she needs shoes, and a new chemise. A dress. She was already outgrowing her clothing when I left, and without me there, she won't have any hand-me-downs."

Constanza shuddered as she imagined someone inheriting the skirt Isabel had been wearing when she arrived.

"I think we have some old dresses and shoes that we could send her with Teresa, but first you'd have to see if they would fit her."

"Really?"

"I'm sure it's possible. But we have to ask my mother and Magdalena."

Feeling a burst of hope, Isabel tried to hug her cousin, but instead she hit her elbow against the wall and let out a faint cry.

"Are you all right?"

"I'm so clumsy!" Isabel said, giggling. "That's why I'll never be a great seamstress like you!"

"Don't say that. You'll learn. It just takes time."

"Everything takes time. Who has time for that?"

Constanza laughed. How ironic, she thought, this hunger for life that guided Isabel's every step. She was only fifteen, whereas Constanza herself, at almost twenty-five, had wasted four precious, irrecuperable years engaged to Pedro de Lanuza. If only God gave her another chance, she would do everything differently. She would have never moved into the family home to begin with. That rare, precious independence she and her mother used to enjoy seemed so far away, so unattainable. Freedom and honour, Uncle Miguel said, were the only things worth risking your life for. If only she were brave enough!

"*Buenas noches*," Constanza said, hoping her cousin would not hear the sadness in her voice.

VIII

ISABEL

ISABEL DE SAAVEDRA, the ink said.

For the second time, a judge had ruined my life. The first time, the judge had ruled that the tavern was to be left in the care of Miguel Hernández and Pedro de Herrera until I turned twenty-five. This time, another judge had given me a name that would hang over my head forever, announcing my shame like a stench: Isabel de Saavedra, *la bastarda*. I felt branded, like an animal.

"I am sorry for the loss of your mother, Isabel," the judge said. He was missing most of his teeth and the few he still had were dark yellow, almost brown—it was impossible to tear my eyes away from them as he spoke. "But you are certainly blessed to have Señora Magdalena de Sotomayor as your tutor for the next two years. You will receive a salary and have a roof over your head, food on the table, and clothes on your back, and will learn how to serve a household in the proper manner. I would say you're more fortunate than half of the people in our country right now."

He frowned and shook his head in annoyance when he saw a tear roll down my cheek. Everything in his office smelled old and stale and dusty, and there were so many people around us waiting for their turn that I had to make a huge effort to remain composed. But it was impossible not to cry. Never would I have imagined that knowing how to read could make me so unhappy.

Isabel de Saavedra, the ink said. It felt like a slap in the face.

It was almost eleven o'clock and the city was bustling with *madrileños* coming and going as we made our way back to the Cervantes house. I stood in silence next to Magdalena. All the excitement I felt that morning, when I was preparing a parcel with clothes, food, and even a pair of shoes for Ana, was gone. Everything looked different to me. Nastier. Fouler. All I could focus on was the garbage on the streets, the stench of horse and donkey dung littering the roads, the flies buzzing incessantly just like my thoughts.

A gentleman carried by two *silleros* arrived at the court-house as we were leaving. When I was little it was my dream to some day be carried about town this way, clean and comfortable above the dusty streets. Now that I had been openly declared an illegitimate child, I would never be able to afford to pay even one *sillero*. The realization that even such a foolish desire was beyond my grasp made me even sadder. All the sacrifices I had made, all my efforts to please my new family over the past two months, had been useless.

I had become used to the relief I felt every time I walked through the front door, relieved by the coolness of the thick walls that protected us from the heat, but also by the fact that I was secure and had hope for the future. This time however, when Magdalena opened the door, my chest felt tight. It was as if I had swallowed all of Madrid's dust and it had formed a rock beneath my ribs. What was the point of anything, really? No one knew when my father would return. He had been away for five years! And now that Magdalena was my legal guardian, and my only prospect was to continue acting and dressing like my family's maid, there was nothing for me to look forward to. All I wanted was to hide in a corner and cry. But as soon as we stepped inside, Andrea and Constanza emerged from the sewing room and I felt ambushed.

"Welcome home!" Andrea said. "What did the judge say?"

"Will you have to go to the courthouse again, or are you finished?" Constanza sounded anxious.

"Success!" Magdalena announced, waving the guardianship document in the air. "Isabel is ours!"

Before I even had time to remove my mantilla, Andrea took me in her arms. This was all I needed to start sobbing.

"Magdalena, look at her! She's crying with joy! Isn't she the sweetest thing?" Andrea said. She hugged me tighter and started crying, too. "See what you've done?" She rocked me in her arms and kissed my forehead. "You're safe now, my dear. You have nothing to worry about anymore."

Isabel de Saavedra. Not even after Mother's death had I felt so destitute, so helpless.

Constanza wasn't smiling. If she understood that my tears were not tears of joy, she didn't show it.

"You'll also be happy to know Teresa has returned from delivering the parcel to your sister. And she's doing fine," she said. Hearing these words only made me cry harder. I had been separated from my sister only to be declared illegitimate!

"Isabel, dry your tears! It's time to celebrate." Magdalena removed her mantilla, went into Father's studio, and locked the guardianship document in a drawer. Then she made her way to the kitchen. "Is everything ready?" I heard her say.

I was wiping my eyes and my nose with Andrea's

handkerchief when Teresa appeared in the hallway to let us know that food was served. The aroma of a tasty stew enticed me, and I let Andrea guide me to the table.

"What is all this?" I said in surprise. On the table were the finest, most exquisitely decorated plates I had ever seen.

"It's Grandmother Leonor's *talavera*, which we only use on very special occasions," Constanza said solemnly.

"Surprise!" Teresa, her round face as bright as fire, led me over to the stove. "Niña Isabel," she said, "I prepared my very own *olla podrida* for you!"

Rotten pot! It was one of Mother's favourite dishes, but I could already tell there was something different about this one.

"What kind of meat is in it?" I asked. At the tavern we used to cook it with bacon, chickpeas, and various types of *zarandajas* such as celery, sprouts, and carrots. On special occasions, Mother prepared it with beef. The butcher we bought it from had access to cows and oxen that were used for work in the field. The meat was tough, but simmering it for a long time rendered it soft enough that even Grandmother could enjoy it despite missing so many teeth.

"It's mutton!" Andrea replied proudly. "Have you had mutton before?"

I shook my head. I was certain I had not. The spices and vegetables Teresa had cooked it with gave it a mouth-watering scent, and despite feeling so dejected, I was also hungry.

"It's our family tradition whenever possible to celebrate momentous occasions with mutton," Magdalena explained, gazing at me warmly. "I am very happy to be your legal guardian, Isabel, and to welcome you into our family. You will be part of it forever." Her smile was broad and sincere, but I was confused.

"I don't understand. The judge said you would be my guardian for two years. The contract has to be renewed every two years."

"That's a formality we can ignore, Isabel. We're family! You're ours to keep. Nothing will ever change that."

Theirs to keep, like the branded animal that I was.

"And what is a delicious *olla podrida* without wine? We must toast!" Andrea gestured for Constanza to begin filling the glasses.

We washed our hands in the basin and took our usual seats: Magdalena at the head of the table, Andrea on her right, Constanza on her left, and Teresa and me closest to the stove and the pots so we could serve the food easily. I watched my aunts and my cousin place their napkins on their laps and followed suit. Teresa looked very proud as she served the stew on the colourful *talavera* plates.

Magdalena raised her glass and we all took a sip.

"Is this *vino de retorno*?" I asked.

Andrea and Constanza looked surprised. "How can you tell?"

I explained to them that at the tavern we didn't serve *vino precioso*—which was very expensive and reserved for the court—but *vino barato*, which almost any customer could afford. And occasionally we served *vino de retorno*—wine that had been on a round trip from Spain to our colonies and back. I had heard Alonso say that the movement of the ocean gave this wine a distinct, richer taste. It was my favourite.

Constanza refilled my glass. I watched as they used what looked like a ridiculously small fork to pick up their food. I wanted to follow their example, but I wasn't sure how to hold my fork properly. When Magdalena noticed I was struggling, she demonstrated how to position my fingers on the strange implement. She watched as I pinched a sliced carrot, which broke into four tiny pieces and fell off the fork. She showed me again, more slowly, how to pick up a piece of food and lift it to my mouth—as if I could ever do anything as elegantly as she did!

"You'll get better as you go, don't worry," she said, her voice firm yet reassuring.

"These are called *bracas*," Constanza said, waving hers in the air. "They are originally Italian, but they were brought to us from France, right, Mother?" she asked. Andrea nodded; it was clear she was proud of them.

"Yes. Sante Ambrosio gave them to me as a wedding present."

"Sante Ambrosio?" The name surprised me. My cousin's last name was de Ovando, so Andrea was not talking about Constanza's father.

"My second husband," Andrea explained. "He was Italian, from Florence. A most wonderful man who was taken from us too soon, just like Constanza's father, Nicolás de Ovando." She crossed herself and Constanza followed suit. I shouldn't have been surprised to learn that my aunt had been married twice; she was so gentle and beautiful. Now I wondered why she hadn't found a third husband yet.

"Let's not talk about sad things, shall we?" Constanza asked. "Sante was a very cultivated man. Since he imported French and Italian books for the court booksellers, he travelled a lot. He brought these forks especially for my mother. They are very popular among refined people in France and Italy," she said, and she took another bite.

"Since we're celebrating and this is a special meal, we thought it would be a splendid occasion to teach you more sophisticated table manners," Magdalena said, smiling.

I had to contain my annoyance. Why did everything have to be a lesson or a test? Surely a *bastarda* would never have occasion to use sophisticated table manners. I would have enjoyed Teresa's dish more without this reminder of my status. I rejoiced when the meal was finished and I could stay in the kitchen to help Teresa clean up.

As soon as we were alone, I burst out eagerly with the question that I had been dying to ask since I got home. It was the only subject that gave me any hope or pleasure: my sister, Ana. "Tell me, did you see my sister?"

"No. She wasn't home," Teresa said, rinsing the plates carefully one by one, so as not to break them. "Your grandmother said she was with your aunt."

This was good news. Ana loved spending time with Luisa and her daughters, Jerónima and Marita.

"And how's Grandmother?"

Teresa shrugged. "She didn't say anything. She took the parcel and closed the door."

"That's it?"

She nodded, and a pang of anguish hit me. "Did she ask about me?" Teresa shook her head. Disappointment washed over me. "Did you give her the money?"

"Of course! I had it very well hidden in case anything happened on the way there, but no one paid attention to me. There are advantages to being an old and homely servant."

I gave Teresa a hug. I could only hope Grandmother would spend my earnings wisely and give Ana the entire contents of the parcel, instead of selecting a few items my sister could keep and then selling the rest, as she had done with Mother's belongings. And for what? We were always hungry anyway.

"Tomorrow is market day, don't forget," Teresa said. I could tell she wanted to change the subject.

"I know. But I think Andrea wants to bore me to death by making me spin some yarn with her."

Teresa shook her head. "I told her how well you bargained when we went shopping the other day. A charming girl who knows her way around numbers can do wonders."

"I guess there are advantages to being a young servant," I said with a laugh.

"A young and *attractive* servant," she corrected me. "Your aunts are not as *duras de pelar* as they sometimes seem." She winked. "I have a feeling that the next time you go out to purchase fabric and sewing supplies, your aunts will let you do the talking."

My sweet Teresa, the one who made this house a home.

IX

November 1599
My dearest Miguel,

I hope these words reach your eyes in time for me to warn you that, despite all the progress I have made with Isabel, she continues to be restless about her condition as an illegitimate child. Catalina has not sent us any letters so far, but have you made up your mind yet as to when you will reveal Isabel's existence to her? The girl also misses her maternal grandmother and her little half-sister. As you requested, I have continued to find ways of preventing her from visiting those people so that she can fully integrate as a family member here. But it is getting increasingly difficult to offer good excuses.

One positive item of news is that Isabel is innately talented with numbers and has exhibited an exceptional flair for bargaining. Teresa first discovered this on their outings to the market for foodstuffs. And just yesterday, you would have been so proud of the way she helped me bargain for a bolt of silk. You have no idea how hard it has become to source fabrics and notions that were readily available even last summer. In fact, I am so grateful for her skill that I have presented her with our dear mother's turtle-shell hair combs.

Andrea and I are doing well, considering the circumstances. Constanza has been working hard and has grown
quieter than usual, but I believe that she and Isabel are
getting along better than before. The braziers are back on
and Andrea's tapestries are hanging on our walls, keeping
the rooms warm and beautiful, just the way you like them.
Sometimes I feel guilty because I have so much when so
many others have so little, but we thank God every day for
all His blessings and make sure we never waste anything.

I know that people in Seville are facing even worse conditions than we are. But still, please do be careful and avoid
arriving here in Madrid at night. It is not safe outdoors once
the sun goes down. Forgive me for treating you as if you were
my child instead of my older brother. But you know I do it
out of affection. I cannot wait to have you back with us in
Castile, where you belong.

We are praying to the Virgin every day for Her to shelter
you under the mantle of her protection, so that you may be
spared of danger and illness on your journey home.

Your loving sister,
Magdalena

X

ISABEL

AWARE THAT MY father would arrive soon and looking for ways to impress him, Magdalena suggested I memorize one of his poems. She selected one of his most recent, written just before he left for Seville. It had won a national poetry competition organized by the Dominican friars of Zaragoza to celebrate the canonization of San Jacinto. As a prize, my father was awarded three silver spoons. So it was that, in between errands, I sat down with my aunt to read over the poem and memorize its lines. I did not understand very well what it meant, but if it had earned a prize of silver it had to be good. One particular stanza captured my attention because, even though I knew it was about San Jacinto, it made me think of Mother. To my mind, she was the finest jewel in heaven.

El cielo a la Iglesia ofrece
hoy una piedra tan fina,
que en la corona divina
del mismo Dios resplandece.

As I walked to the market with Teresa or helped her in the kitchen, and while I shopped for fabric for the winter orders with Andrea, I would repeat the stanzas to myself. And then one morning, I was warming my hands against the stove and going over the poem in my head as usual when I was interrupted by a cry from Constanza.

"He's here! He's here! I heard his voice!"

My palms grew damp and a chill travelled down my spine. I swallowed hard. Could it be? More shrieks and cries of joy left no doubt.

"Miguel! My dear Miguel! You're home!" Magdalena's voice was jubilant.

"My dearest brother, welcome home!" Andrea was ecstatic.

"Uncle Miguel! I missed you so much!" Constanza couldn't contain herself.

My knees felt as if they were made of wax and the fire had started to melt them.

"Niña Isabel, your father is home!" Teresa cried out.

I had been anticipating this moment and played it in my mind so many times! How he would come into the house. What I would say. How we would embrace. And now I was unable to move.

"Isabel!" Magdalena called out. "Come and see who's here!" I could hear the words and the questions my aunts and my cousin rained down on him, but I had yet to hear his voice.

Teresa gave me an encouraging pat on the shoulder and fixed my hair with her fingers. "You look wonderful, Niña Isabel." Then she pushed me out of the kitchen. "Go meet your father."

I took a deep breath and stepped forward, wiping my

palms against my skirt. The whirlwind of voices became silent
as I entered the foyer. The pungent smell of horses and manure
assailed my nostrils. My aunts moved to the side, Constanza
holding her mother's arm.

In the middle of the room stood a man that in no way
resembled the Miguel de Cervantes I had nurtured in my
imagination. His boots were caked with dried mud, his jacket
covered in dust. I could tell that his salt-and-pepper hair had
once been the same colour as mine, but he was old, surely
much older than Mother. I had not expected him to be so old.
I examined his face. He had a thick beard.

"Here, dear brother, is Isabel," Magdalena said, beaming
with joy. My heart was beating so fast I couldn't pronounce
a single word.

"Aren't you going to say anything, Isabel?" Still unable to
speak, I bowed instead.

"Forgive her, Miguel. She's normally very outgoing," my
aunt explained.

"Come closer, my child. I won't hurt you," my father said.

His voice was strong and deep. He was smiling, but I could
not smile back. He lifted his right arm and, bending his fingers,
beckoned me towards him. Slowly, I moved closer. The foyer
smelled like a stable. And he must have eaten in some cheap
tavern on the way home because garlic and onions tainted his
breath. Reaching out, he cupped my chin and inspected my
face. After a moment, he spoke.

"Magdalena, my dear, when you told me she looked just
like our mother I could not picture exactly what you meant.
But you were right. This is a miracle. Let me hold you, my
child." He wrapped his right arm around me briefly. His left
arm didn't move, it hung limply at his side.

"What happened to your arm?" I asked, taking two steps back to see him better.

"I was a *harquebusier* during the war. Did nobody tell you?"

I shook my head, not sure I understood what he meant.

"A *harquebusier* is a cavalry soldier, armed with a carbine called 'harquebus.' It's very heavy, right, Uncle Miguel?" Constanza explained to me, her words lilting in excitement.

"Magdalena only told me you were a war hero," I said, ashamed of my ignorance.

"I don't know if I would go as far as calling myself that. But I received three shots during the battle of Lepanto. One of the bullets entered my chest and now my left arm is useless."

His handicap distracted me and made me feel ashamed.

"He spent six months in the hospital after that," Andrea said. "We were so scared."

They all nodded and fell silent again. How would I ever face my sister to tell her I had been claimed as a bastard daughter by such a man? He was still gazing at me. "You take after your grandmother Leonor, certainly. But I can see a lot of your mother in you. A lot." He was silent for a moment. "You are a very beautiful young woman."

I felt the tension in my shoulders ease a little, and my chin trembled. No one in this house had ever acknowledged my mother's existence. I was happy to hear that I looked like her. It seemed like a wonderful compliment.

"Isabel has a surprise for you," Magdalena said. "We've been working hard preparing for it. But perhaps you should clean up and rest first, Miguel."

"Yes, Teresa can help you with whatever you need," Andrea added.

Teresa, who had been standing behind me, took the signal

and picked up the leather bags my father had brought with him. One of them was so full of loose sheets of paper it did not close properly.

"Place that one," he said, pointing at the bag, "next to my desk, please."

Teresa bowed and did as she was told. I excused myself, saying I would help warm up some water so my father could wash. But as soon as I was back in the kitchen, I had to open the door to the courtyard to get some fresh, cool air while I tried to comprehend what I had just discovered. My father was a cripple. I wished Mother were alive to tell me what on earth she had seen in this man, because I certainly did not see it.

XI

TERESA HAD PLACED sliced oranges and wine on the table, and they all sat down with Miguel while his favourite rabbit stew simmered on the fire.

Her uncle's presence, the warmth of the stove, and the smell of the food made Constanza feel truly happy for the first time in months.

"Magdalena, have you received any news from Rodrigo?" Miguel asked. This was not the first question Constanza had expected to hear.

"Who is Rodrigo?" said Isabel. Miguel looked at his sisters with concern.

"Rodrigo is your uncle," Magdalena answered, then lowered her head as she turned to her brother. "We pray for him every day, don't we?" Constanza and Andrea nodded. "We don't talk about him very often. It makes it easier to deal with his absence and the fact that there is nothing we can do about it."

"It is one thing to be affected by his absence," Miguel said, speaking in a slow and deliberate manner, "but not mentioning him at all, as if his existence were a secret ..."

Magdalena shot him a sharp glance that Constanza

immediately understood. How could he complain about keeping someone's existence a secret after hiding Isabel for fifteen years?

"He's a soldier." Constanza lowered her voice as she explained the facts to Isabel. "He's currently serving in Flanders, and we haven't heard of him or from him in a long time."

"A *very* long time," Andrea emphasized.

"I'm sorry," Isabel said. "I had no idea." She looked upset, and Constanza wondered why. She should be thrilled to finally meet her father.

"That is not your fault," Magdalena reassured her. She offered Miguel some of the orange slices that were on the table, but he brushed them away and drank some wine instead. Maybe he was thirsty, but Constanza sensed that something else was going on because he drank the contents of his glass in one swallow and helped himself to more.

"Luisa is a prioress now. I don't know if her letters reached you," Magdalena said. Constanza noticed that she wasn't touching the orange slices either. Miguel nodded.

"Luisa? My mother's sister is also called Luisa," Isabel said, making an effort to smile.

"*Our* Luisa lives in a convent in Alcalá de Henares, a few steps from the house where your father was born," Andrea explained, her voice uneasy. This was not the way things were supposed to be, Constanza thought. Every other time that her uncle returned to the family home, they had engaged in lively talk, catching up on details, eating and drinking gleefully together. What was going on?

A silence fell and they all watched intently as Teresa stirred the pot. It felt as if that rabbit was taking forever to cook.

Constanza's mouth watered. Was she the only one who was hungry?

"Your father, my child, is not the only war hero in this family. Rodrigo, our brother, fought with him in Lepanto and was captured in Algiers, too. While Miguel decided to work as a tax collector for the Crown, Rodrigo continued with his military career in the Azores and, later, in Flanders." Magdalena tried to sound cheerful, but a heaviness cloaked her voice.

"Isn't there a war in Flanders?" Isabel asked. There was another uncomfortable silence, but she carried on. "How do you even know he's still alive?"

"We don't. We haven't heard from him in over a year. I have sent him letters, but we have yet to hear back." Magdalena voice rose, and her chin trembled.

"Magdalena," Andrea said, placing a hand on her sister's. Then she looked at her brother pleadingly. "This is why we don't talk about him. Now do you see?"

"It is inexcusable," said Miguel, his voice suddenly bitter, "that after fighting for the empire in Italy and Portugal Rodrigo has not received the promotion his loyalty and courage deserve. Did he not complain in his last letter that he was still a second lieutenant?"

"*Sí*, Miguel," Magdalena spoke softly now.

"And did he not mention as well that his salary had not been paid yet? Some soldiers who returned as war heroes now enjoy wealth, prestige, and good jobs with the government, but not Rodrigo. And certainly not me."

Why didn't anyone change the subject? Life as a soldier was hard. Administrative incompetence often meant soldiers were left to starve. Many returned home sick, injured, or as invalids, yet they received no help. These men were easy to spot on the street, often maimed, begging for food. They were in plain view at church on Sunday; out of pity and shame, Constanza forced herself to look elsewhere. This was one of the reasons they should all be rejoicing now. At least Miguel had made it back, and if they had heard nothing of Uncle Rodrigo, surely it meant that he was doing all right. Otherwise, wouldn't the authorities have notified them?

It took Teresa to break the tension. "*Cada ollero alaba su puchero*, Señor Miguel," she said. "But believe me when I say you'll lick your fingers when you taste this stew!"

"*Gracias*, Teresa," Miguel replied, the flicker of a smile brightening his face. Constanza's eyes were on her plate. She couldn't believe none of them had touched the fruit yet, and oranges were so precious at that time of the year!

Rodrigo had wanted to quit the services and return to Madrid, following in his brother's footsteps as usual. But he was unable to buy his way out. Magdalena had been putting money aside to help him, but Andrea had recently shared with Constanza, confidentially, that the higher prices of food and fabric, as well as the extra costs of Isabel's needs, had forced her sister to put those savings towards their everyday necessities.

"I'll ask about him now that I'm back in Madrid," said Miguel, putting an end to the discussion. He finished off his glass and poured himself another. Constanza was taken aback. Did he think he was at a tavern? She had never seen him drink like this. Was it really because of Rodrigo? Or was he uncomfortable with Isabel's presence, or her gloomy expression?

"Are we forgetting that this is a celebration?" Constanza reminded them. "Uncle Miguel, tell us about Seville. I am sure you have a host of fascinating stories to share with us."

"I have no fascinating stories to tell you this time, my dear niece. Life in Andalucía today is very hard, harder than it has ever been. The only good news is that while I was there, I was inspired by an idea for a story. And I think it can make a good book, one that might do well. I've already written a few pages."

"A new book!" Andrea and Magdalena exclaimed, almost in unison. Finally, there were smiles all around the table.

"What is your new book about?" Constanza asked.

"Just a crazy idea that I came up with one night when I couldn't sleep."

"Miguel, tell us! Come on!"

"Yes, tell us!"

His eyes shone, and he even looked stronger at that moment. This was the Miguel Constanza had sorely missed! Finally, here he was, back among them in all his glory.

"Do you really want to know?" he said teasingly.

"*Sí, sí, sí!*" the three chanted. Teresa stopped stirring the pot and looked at Miguel, waiting to hear what he said. The only one who had not spoken was Isabel.

"Promise you aren't going to tell anyone?"

"*Prometido!*" Magdalena put her right hand on her chest and raised her left arm. "You have our word." Andrea and Constanza imitated her, and they all laughed.

"This is serious, you know!" Miguel warned them.

"Uncle Miguel, stop it! Just tell us!" Constanza loved it when he teased them, but she was so curious about this new book she didn't want the game to go on any longer. He had not written in such a long time! This was wonderful.

"All right. Only because my favourite niece requests it, and because Isabel is here, I will share my secret with you."

His favourite niece. Constanza had been so afraid when Isabel arrived that the way her uncle behaved towards her would change. Now she wanted to get up from her seat and hug him. But the dark expression on Isabel's face held her back.

"It's a chivalry novel."

Magdalena burst into laughter and Andrea followed suit.

"But you hate chivalry novels!"

"I do not hate chivalry novels, *hermana mía*. Who said that?"

"You! So many times, I have lost count!"

Miguel put his hand on Magdalena's forehead. "I think you have a fever! Or perhaps it's aging that's making you imagine things?"

"Aging!" She slapped him playfully. "I'm your baby sister. If there's anyone here who is old, it's you!" Constanza had forgotten about Isabel and was enjoying the interaction between her aunt and uncle. But she couldn't help feeling bad for her mother. In the affectionate play between Miguel and Magdalena, there appeared to be no room for anyone else. Andrea was smiling, but she must have felt left out. A wave of tenderness rose in Constanza's chest.

"There are times I wish you didn't know me so well, Magdalena," Miguel admitted, laughing. "You are right in what you say."

"I knew it!" she cheered. "I always am."

"Not always," Andrea complained. She wagged her finger at Magdalena, who caught it in her hand and pretended to bite it. Andrea let out a playful little cry. Now that the three siblings were laughing together, Constanza realized how much she missed these moments. This was the reason family always came first.

"If you really must know," Miguel went on, assuming a

solemn tone, "I am writing a chivalry book that mocks chivalry books. It's time someone showed the public how dangerous those fantasies can be. Real life is hard, and people need to be taught how to behave more honourably if we are ever going to improve this world. There are so many problems, so many injustices that need to be confronted and resolved ... "

"That sounds like a good theme." Andrea said.

"How long do you think it will it take you to write the book?" Magdalena asked.

"I'm not sure. I will have a better idea once I arrive in Esquivias and can get down to work."

Suddenly Isabel spoke up. "Esquivias?" Constanza had almost forgotten she was there. "Where is that? Aren't you staying here?" The displeasure in her voice startled Constanza. During the time that her cousin had been living with them, she had never spoken like this. And no one spoke like this to Miguel.

"Isabel, your father is a very busy man," Magdalena explained. "He has businesses to attend to in Esquivias." This was an evasive answer if Constanza had ever heard one. It was not like her aunt at all.

"What businesses? I thought you were coming home so that you could write. Why can't you write here? You have shelves of books and a desk waiting for you."

"Isabel, he cannot stay and write here because we don't have enough room for him to work in silence, and—"

"Magdalena, if you'll allow me, I think I can answer my daughter's questions without your help."

Magdalena lowered her eyes. So did Constanza and Andrea. The playfulness and joy that had been in the air moments earlier dissipated. Teresa, who was waiting to serve the stew, stood quietly next to the stove, pretending—or maybe wishing—she were invisible.

Addressing his daughter, Miguel spoke softly. "Isabel, I am married. Catalina, my wife, lives in Esquivias. She has a house there, and that's where I must live. Not here."

"A wife? No one told me anything about a wife."

"Isabel, I'm sure—" Andrea tried to intervene, but Isabel interrupted her.

"Forgive me, Aunt Andrea, but I have been living in this house since June. Now it's December. And this is the first time I'm hearing that I have an uncle who is a soldier and an aunt who is in a convent, and that my father has a wife. I asked questions before that none of you bothered to answer. Why didn't it occur to you, or to Aunt Magdalena, or even to Constanza, to share these details with me?" Isabel's face was flushed. Constanza didn't know if she was about to scream or burst into tears.

"I think it's better if Isabel and I talk about this. We'll go to my studio, if you don't mind, so that we can have some privacy," Miguel said as he rose to his feet.

"But the stew is ready, and you haven't even tried the oranges. They are such a rare treat! Can't it wait? You can talk all you want after we eat." Constanza's eyes welled up. This was exactly what she had been afraid of, that Isabel would ruin everything.

"Yes, first we should eat and then you can talk all you want." Andrea seconded her daughter.

But Isabel stood up as well. "I have lost my appetite. Excuse me," she said, and left the kitchen. Miguel called out to her as he followed her from the room.

"They'll be back soon," Magdalena said. "Let us say

grace and ask God for forgiveness for not saying Rodrigo's and Luisa's names out loud in such a long time." Constanza wanted to remind her aunt that it had been she herself who established the rule of silence. Magdalena had thought that perhaps, if they did not speak the names, the words, the fears that lurked inside their hearts, it would keep the terrors at bay. Tears rolled down Constanza's cheeks as the four of them proceeded to eat in silence.

XII

❧❧❧❧❧❧❧

ISABEL

FATHER CAUGHT UP with me and asked that I hear him out. I nodded, and he led me to his study.

"I don't know where to begin." He closed the door, signalled for me to sit in the chair facing his desk, and took his seat behind it.

"Does your arm hurt you?" I asked.

"Only when the weather turns cold," he said with a sad smile.

I couldn't wait any longer to learn the truth. "How did you meet my mother?"

He waved his hand from left to right and laughed. "Did I miss the part when they hired you to work for the Inquisition?"

"I'm not joking, I want to know. And I don't think the Inquisition is a laughing matter."

He became serious and sat up in his chair. "You're right."

"They burn people alive."

"I know."

"How did you meet my mother?"

"At the tavern."

I knew it.

"Were you a regular?"

"Once I fell in love with her, yes. I was."

"Did you know she was married?"

"Isabel, there are things that children—"

"I'm not a child. I'm almost sixteen and can handle this family's finances better than your two sisters and your niece combined. I need to know." I had not planned to talk to him like this; I was surprised at myself. All the emotions I had been holding back were brewing together in my stomach, waiting to come out. Grandmother had asked me to do what Magdalena wanted, and I had dutifully obeyed. But she never mentioned anything about this family—the one that I was supposed to devote myself to. And Magdalena never answered any questions except to say that I would find out in due time. Well, that time had come.

"All right. Yes, I knew she was married."

"And still you sinned."

He looked me in the eyes. "You have no authority to question my behaviour. But if it helps you to know, I have confessed my sins and atoned for my wrongdoings."

"It does help me to know that, thank you."

"And I'm sure your mother did, too. Her soul is in Heaven, I have no doubt."

With his words, a weight was lifted off my chest. I had been avoiding thinking about Mother's soul, but sometimes at night I dreamed her face was melting in eternal fire and I woke up agitated, incapable of eradicating the fear that had invaded my body.

"Magdalena said you had a surprise for me," he said.

I couldn't let my emotions distract me. "You're the one full of surprises. A wife in—what is the name of that city?"

"Isabel, I owe you no explanations. I don't think we should continue this conversation." He was frowning and the tension in his neck and shoulders was evident.

I couldn't let him end the conversation. Not now. "You let another man raise me as his daughter."

"Because your mother was his lawful wife. And because—"

"Because?"

He shook his head in frustration. "This is wrong."

"No. Talking honestly to me is not wrong. It's what I deserve after years of lies."

He let out a sigh, and I could see his torso relax a little. "You must be mindful of your words and temper. Women are beaten and even killed for speaking their mind like you do."

"Have you ever beaten a woman?"

He shook his head vigorously. "No! But I've seen it happen."

I'd seen it happen, too. At the tavern. And at home, although just once, shortly before Alonso's death. He was upset and he slapped Mother. In response, she hit him with a brass candle-holder and warned him to never raise his hand against her again. As I recalled this incident, I saw the details: the blood oozing down Alonso's face, Mother's dishevelled hair, the blaze in her eyes. By then he was already quite old and frail. When people asked about the bruised cut on his forehead, he said he had taken a fall. No one suspected anything different, and Mother made me promise I would never tell anyone the truth. For a time after this, I was afraid. But as I grew up, I began to understand that if Mother hadn't been such a tough woman, she wouldn't have been able to manage the tavern after Alonso died. She wouldn't have been able to raise us the way she did, without a man by her side. I knew Mother was very different from most women, and I wondered if one day I would be as strong as her.

"And did you think they deserved it?"

"Women are complex creatures. And they can be very difficult sometimes."

"As opposed to men, I suppose."

He smiled. "You sound just like your mother."

"Thank you."

He was silent for a while, and during this pause I watched his chest rise and fall, marvelling at the fact that my father was finally here, in the flesh, talking with me.

"I loved her. She had a zest for life, a vitality that made her irresistible. Your mother was unique."

I nodded. It was true.

"I sent her money whenever I could to help raise you, especially after I heard her husband had died."

"Alonso Rodríguez." It felt strange to speak his name out loud.

"It was an arranged marriage. He could have been her father."

"Why didn't you come back to her when you knew she was a widow?"

"By then I was already married to Catalina."

"And living with her?"

"Yes. Well, not exactly. She was in Esquivias. I was in Andalucía, collecting taxes."

"Does Catalina know about me?"

"Not yet."

I was not surprised. "When will you tell her?"

"As soon as I have the opportunity."

"Will you take me to live with you?"

This seemed to surprise him. "Aren't you happy here?"

"I didn't say that. Will you answer my question?"

"Answer mine first. Aren't you happy here?"

I sighed. "It hasn't been easy, but I can't say I'm unhappy."

I was saving money to help Ana while I waited to reclaim the tavern, but he didn't need to know this. "I miss my sister and my grandmother. But mostly my sister."

"I understand that."

I liked the fact that he treated me with respect. I could tell he was different from other men. Alonso would have never had a conversation like this with me or Ana. He would have slapped us if we said something that displeased him. Any other man would have slapped me for being so blunt. But Miguel, my father, listened to me and gave me honest answers. Maybe that was the reason Mother was drawn to him.

"You're very clever, you know that?" He sounded cheerful now.

"Thank you, so are you," I said.

He let out a guffaw. Then he stood up, came around the desk, and gently took my chin in his hand. As he caressed it with his thumb, a tear rolled down my cheek. He wiped it off. Then he opened the door and called to my aunts and my cousin. But before they joined us, he bent down to whisper in my ear.

"I think we have sorted things out for now, haven't we?"

"Yes, we have." I hadn't asked him about recognizing me as his daughter and giving me his name, but I thought it was wiser to wait until he told his wife about me.

As the women came into the room, my father said cheerfully, "Did someone say something about a surprise?" My aunts were smiling, but Constanza looked annoyed.

"Oh, yes!" Magdalena clapped. "Sit back down, my dear brother. Be ready to feel very proud." He returned to his chair behind the desk. They sat on the leather chairs, while I stood in the middle of the room, facing my father. At Magdalena's signal, I began my recitation.

On this day Heaven presents the Church
With a gem so fine
That on the Lord's divine Crown
It is set to shine.

I could sense my father's admiration as I went on, stanza by stanza, repeating the words he had written years ago. By the time I finished, we were both in tears.

"My child, you're a wonder!" He came over and put his arm around me. Then he said, "Wait a moment! Don't move!" He left the room and Magdalena winked at me. I could see she and Andrea were proud of me. Then Father reappeared holding three silver spoons in his hand.

"That was a wonderful rendition of my poem. I've been saving these for your dowry, but I think you deserve them now." He held the spoons out to me.

My aunts clapped and came to stand close to me, admiring the silver spoons. But Constanza excused herself and left the room. As Andrea went after her, Father and Magdalena exchanged glances. He shook his head.

"I'll speak with my niece later. Right now, I'm hungry. What do you say, *mi querida* Isabel? Shall you and I go to the kitchen and enjoy some of that rabbit stew?"

He offered me his arm and I took it. The spoons made a jingling sound as we made our way to the kitchen. They were the most beautiful objects I had ever held in my hand. I would keep them next to Mother's silver pomander after I finished eating my first meal with my father.

ACT TWO

ESQUIVIAS AND MADRID
NOVEMBER 1599–NOVEMBER 1602

King Philip III was less keen on governing the Spanish Empire than on entertaining himself traveling through Old Castile and the area immediately around Madrid, hunting game at will, regardless of season, and participating wholeheartedly in popular religious festivities. Aware of this weakness, Don Francisco Gómez de Sandoval y Rojas, Duke de Lerma, his trusted advisor or valido, took the reins of power and focused on finding ways to enrich himself. Arguing that Madrid was bankrupt and had become too overpopulated, noisy, and dirty, Lerma convinced Philip III to move the seat of the Court to Valladolid, where Lerma had purchased several properties, including the palace— which the King bought from him.

In the meantime, Spain's economic problems raged on, as the ongoing war efforts to defend the colonies from the English and the Dutch absorbed most of the Crown's supply of riches coming in from the Americas. Poverty and vagrancy increased with the return of unemployed soldiers, whose pensions went unpaid because money was directed to the pleasures of Castilian nobles. Soon, life in Madrid became not only difficult but dangerous for its citizens, and the Cervantes family was no exception.

I

CATALINA
ESQUIVIAS
NOVEMBER 1599

Pater noster qui es in caelis,
Sanctificétur nomen tuum,
Advéniat regnum tuum;
Fiat voluntas tua, sicut in caelo et in terra,
Panem nostrum quotidiánum da nobis hódie,
Et dimítte nobis débita nostra,
Sicut et nos dimittimus detióribus nostris,
Et ne nos indúcas in tentatiónem,
Sed libera nos a malo.
Amen.

PRAISE BE TO YOU, Lord. Yours is the greatness and the power and the glory, for everything in Heaven and Earth is Yours. And after five years of absence—five years when I worried about his wellbeing and feared for his life—Miguel is mine again. His long and loving letters helped alleviate my solitude and eased my longing, but his presence feels like a miracle. Another one of your many gifts to this, your humble servant, my dear God. Praise be to You.

"How are your sisters?" I asked as I scrubbed his back after his long journey. I had arranged for the tub to be placed by the fire and filled with warm water. Clean towels and fresh clothes were neatly folded on a chair close to the brazier so they would be warm to his touch. I had already rinsed the dust of the road from his hair, grey that was once golden. I prolonged this intimate moment as much as I could. Here he was, defenceless in my care—at once my husband and my child.

I was eager to touch his body, to be reacquainted with a territory that felt both personal and foreign. I discovered scars and moles and freckles that were not there before, the result of his many days, weeks, years travelling under the unforgiving rays of the sun, moving from one small town to the next collecting oil and grain for the country's military efforts. If only more people were aware that an empire cannot be run unless everyone is willing to sacrifice!

"My sisters are fine. Despite the circumstances, they have had a lot of work, and they are in good health and spirits, thank God."

"And how about dear Constanza?"

"Slowly feeling better after the disappointment caused by Pedro de Lanuza."

I felt very sorry for our niece, almost twenty-five years old, still unmarried, and without any new suitors in sight, because if there had been anyone else after Pedro, Miguel would have told me. There are no secrets between us, as You well know, Lord.

"Perhaps we should invite all three of them to pay us a visit, do you think? I would enjoy their company. I hope they don't resent me because I didn't see them during your long absence, but I still have to take care of my young brothers, and I thought it safer to stay away from Madrid."

"They know that. You did the right thing. The plague hit

the city hard. There's—" He looked like he was going to say something else and I waited, expectantly, but he shook his head, took my hand in his, and brought it to his lips. The kiss made me shiver.

"I prefer to be alone here with you, my Catalina. I have missed you so much, and I need your company, and the peace and quiet of Esquivias, more than ever before. Let it be you and me only." I smiled and nodded. "And now, let me tell you about my new book."

He could barely contain his enthusiasm as he told me about his novel. It would be a satire of chivalry books, which were so popular and readily available but quite badly written and dangerous to weak minds. He wanted to attempt something no one had ever tried before.

"Just remember to be considerate of those who can't understand your fine use of language," I said with a smile.

He pulled me close and kissed my lips. I kissed him back, letting the water on his face wet mine.

"That's why I married you, Catalina. You're the smartest woman I know."

We had been apart for so long that I wasn't sure how to interpret this comment. Why was he praising my intellect instead of my beauty? Had I aged? Did he not admire me as much as before? I don't wish to commit the sin of pride, my Lord; I just want to be appreciated by the man You joined me with in holy matrimony.

"Just the smartest?" I asked.

Seeing me frown, he caressed the space between my eyebrows with his thumb to smooth it. As if he could read me, he replied, "And the most beautiful, of course!"

What a relief! I playfully pushed him back. With a

mischievous smile, he exited the tub and allowed me to dry his hair and chest and wrap the towel around his waist. Then he went over to our bed and signalled for me to sit next to him. I shook my head no; he nodded his head yes. We both laughed. Then he put his right hand over his heart. What is about this man, I wonder, dear Lord? Ever since I met him, despite our age difference, I crave to have him close to me.

"Take off your chemise and let me look at you."

"Miguel!" I could feel my face blushing.

"Come on, I want to see my beautiful wife. Take your chemise off."

I hesitated, but he asked again. "Please."

Unable to say no, I stood up, turned my back to him, and removed my garment. The room was warm, but my skin was covered in goosebumps as I turned around and stood naked in front of him. Feeling shy, I held my arms and hands in front of me. After all, I was not as young as I was the last time we were together as husband and wife.

"Let your arms fall, Catalina. Let me admire you whole."

I hesitated. My body had changed. Would he still find it attractive?"

"Please."

I obliged, closing my eyes as he gazed at me, memories of past lovemaking flooding my mind. I felt shaken. This must be a sin, I told myself, this fire travelling from my legs to my mouth and over to his eyes, this fire that melted me so that his eyes and lips could slowly drink me in.

"I missed you so much, Catalina." He stretched his good arm towards me, gently inviting me to come close. The brazier was burning; our bed was a perfect womb for the rebirth of our love.

"I missed you, too." I took his hand and moved closer to him. No, my body said. This was no sin. This was my long-gone husband: the man I had been faithful to, the man whose long absences I had patiently endured, the man whose children I longed to bear.

Secure in the knowledge that You, God Almighty, have given us Your blessing, and promising to offer the fruit of our love to You, I opened myself to welcome my Miguel. To welcome his sweat, his seed.

Afterwards, we lay quietly, completely spent.

"Don't think even for a second," I whispered, looking in his eyes while he was still trying to catch his breath, "that this excuses you from attending mass to thank God for your safe return. You need to make yourself presentable." He smiled, reaching for my hand, but I rose from the bed before he could pull me back in.

"Come back!" he pleaded.

I shook my head as I slipped back into my chemise. "Time to get ready!" I brought out a clean shirt for him and held it as if it were a flag; his body, my true homeland.

"Yes, Señora *mía*. Whatever you say." He sat up in bed. "Now let me tell you more about the book."

His excitement was contagious. He had not written for so long! But things would be different now. As I helped him slide his arm into the sleeve of his shirt, he talked about the story that had been living in his head since his imprisonment in Seville. How fortunate he was to have kept the use of his right hand so that he could write to his heart's content! I kissed each one of his fingers as he described his main character, a man who, having read all the chivalry books at his disposal, lost his mind and believed himself a knight.

"A knight?" I lifted my eyes towards his but kept his fingers by my lips.

"Yes, a knight who will have all sorts of adventures all over La Mancha."

I could not hold back my laughter.

"You must be joking! You're writing a book about a man who loses his mind and thinks he is a knight and goes on adventures in La Mancha?"

He nodded, his index finger tracing my lips.

"But didn't you say that nothing ever happens in La Mancha?"

"Many extraordinary things happen in La Mancha."

"Really?" I raised an eyebrow. "And what is the name of this knight of yours, if I may know?"

"That is the thing, Your Majesty. He still needs a name. I've been thinking about that scrawny relative of yours—your great uncle? The one whose last name is Quixada."

I was surprised. "Are you serious?"

"Yes and no. The character resembles him. But he's also based on that landlord I had here in Esquivias, way back when I was courting you. Remember?"

"No. It has been a while."

"He was so pretentious, always thinking he was better than everyone else. So oblivious to what was truly happening around him."

"Really? He sounds annoying. Was he?"

"If you only knew. But I need to go back to the basics. What would you say if I called my knight Sir Quixada?"

"I don't think scrawny Señor Quixada will be amused when he finds out you've named a delusional character after him," I said. "Neither will the rest of my family, I'm afraid. Even if you add the title *Sir*—which sounds ridiculous, by the way."

"Sounding ridiculous is precisely the point. Perhaps I'll call him Quixeda. Or Quixida? I know, Quixoda!" His laughter was so infectious that I couldn't stop, even if none of what he was saying made any sense.

"Quixoda? Come on, that's not even a name! I think a pretentious Esquivias landlord, or a scrawny relative of mine, or whoever you're mocking with that lunatic, deserves a better name."

"You're right, my love, as always. You're right."

"Why don't you name him after a weapon? Or after a piece of armour? I don't know. Sir …" I tried to remember a term, any term, and used the first one that came to my mind. "Sir Gauntlet, or Sir Helmet."

"You're a genius, Catalina!" he exclaimed.

"I know."

"No, I mean it!"

"Me, too!"

"You know the part of the armour that protects the thighs?" I nodded.

"Guess what it's called!"

I shook my head; I had no idea.

"The cuisse! El quixote!"

"Quixote?"

"Yes! Do you see? Quixada—quixote. It's perfect!"

"Sir Cuisse?" My stomach was beginning to hurt from laughing so much.

"Yes. But he's a knight, and a *hidalgo* of course, so he's still a member of the gentry. *Sir* doesn't sound quite right, I agree with you—plus, we don't want to give those treacherous Britons any credit, even if King Arthur was originally theirs.

We have *El Cid*, after all. And mine will be a true Castilian knight as well. He needs a title that conveys respect. How about *Don*? *Don Quixote*. And as your fellow countryman, he must perhaps be named *Don Quixote de La Mancha*. How does that sound?"

"It sounds preposterous!"

"Perfect! It's decided, then!" He kissed me again and got to his feet in order to put on his stockings and breeches. He had regained his energy. Looking into his eyes, I thanked You a thousand times, my dear Lord, as I do now, and will forever, for allowing me to confide in You during Miguel's absence and in my times of sorrow, and most of all for bringing him back to me—this generous husband whose joy is also mine.

II

July 1600
Dearest Miguel,

May God's infinite mercy give you strength as you receive the terrible news I am forced to deliver in this letter. I am crying as I write. I have just received a message informing us that our beloved brother Rodrigo perished in Flanders, at the Battle of the Dunes, early this month. His was an honourable death, but he died without receiving the promotion his bravery deserved. What kind of country do we live in? What kind of empire inflicts such suffering and humiliation upon its loyal subjects?

No wonder all my letters to Rodrigo went unanswered. No one takes any responsibility for anything. They tax us to exhaustion without granting us the slightest bit of respect in return. It troubles me to mention this when sadness and mourning have once again taken hold of our family, but there is also the issue of Rodrigo's backpay, which he never resolved. Andrea said she would look into that, although we have little hope of collecting any of the money he was owed.

Andrea, Constanza, Isabel, and I will be starting a novena for Rodrigo's peaceful rest today. My only consolation is that he is finally in the company of our beloved parents and our brother Juan in Heaven. The ways of God are unfathomable, but now, more than ever, our faith must keep us on our feet. With Luisa in the cloister, only the three of us are left now, and our girls. We must fight to keep our family united and strong despite our suffering. I am painfully aware that Rodrigo's death means that you have not only lost a brother, but the one person with whom you shared the most time and experiences in your life. Rodrigo was your shadow; you, his hero. May San Miguel Arcángel protect you and guide you in this time of overwhelming sorrow.

Love from your heartbroken sister,
Magdalena

III

ISABEL

"THEY ASKED ME to come back tomorrow, can you believe it?" Aunt Magdalena called out from the foyer as soon as she entered the house. "As if I hadn't been there yesterday, and the day before yesterday, and the day before that as well!"

I rushed out of the kitchen, where I had been helping Teresa pluck a chicken, to bring her a glass of cinnamon water. I understood Magdalena's frustration because I had watched Grandmother go through the same problem after Mother's death. And I myself was still experiencing the unfairness, being forced to wait until I turned twenty-five to claim the tavern that was rightfully mine. No one had tried to help me at the time, so I wanted to help my aunt as best as I could. The shadows under her eyes worried me. She had lost weight, and both she and Andrea had become quieter. When they were not at work or reminiscing about the past, I often caught them staring at nothing. How odd, I thought, that they had never mentioned Rodrigo in my presence before, yet now he was all they could talk about.

Magdalena took the glass of cinnamon water I offered and drank it slowly. She shook her head in disbelief. "Come back tomorrow. Unbelievable!"

I offered her a handkerchief to dry the sweat from her face and neck. "Any news from my father?" I inquired. Given my aunts' reaction to Rodrigo's death, and knowing now how close the brothers had been, I was worried about my father's state of mind. Magdalena shook her head. "No. But you don't need to worry. Your father is strong, Isabel."

At that moment, Andrea called me from the sewing room. "Isabel, come here! I need your help for a moment."

The household had eased into a peaceful routine, a steady rhythm. After breakfast, we focused on our chores. Mine still included reading and studying. Once I finished, I might accompany Teresa or my aunts to do their shopping—they could not do without my bargaining skills anymore—or fetch water from the square, or help Teresa in the kitchen. Sewing lulled me to sleep and I often pricked my fingers, so my role in that area was limited to occasionally helping my aunts.

"Let me clean my hands before I help you, Aunt Andrea!" I replied. "I was just plucking a chicken."

"A chicken?" Andrea said. "I don't remember asking you to purchase a chicken today."

"I got it at a great price." I replied cheerfully, leaving out the part where I promised the butcher I'd bring him a hand-kerchief next time. I knew I could make one using a discarded piece of cloth.

"Remember my vow?" Magdalena said, shaking her head. "Besides, I'm not hungry."

I certainly remembered her vow. In exchange for the reso-lution of Rodrigo's back pay, she would be as frugal as possible. Of course, the rest of us would follow her example. So far, her sacrifice to God had not borne any fruit. And since frugality to her meant eating little, she was getting weak.

"You must eat," I insisted. "Otherwise, you won't be strong enough to keep fighting."

"It's too hot. I have a terrible headache, and I'm tired," she replied as she headed towards the stairs.

I knew how she felt. After Mother died, I lost my appetite as well. And I respected her promise. But my plan had been to surprise them by making *manjar blanco*, hoping to lift their spirits. I tried to hide my disappointment, but it seemed to me a sin to refuse good food when so many went hungry. When my own sister was hungry.

"What are we to do with the chicken, then?" I asked.

"Whatever you and Teresa want, as long as it doesn't go to waste." Magdalena was almost at the top of the stairs when she turned to look at me and added, "It's still early. Why don't you visit your sister? Take the chicken to her. Ask Teresa to go with you, but be careful and come right back."

Hearing this, Andrea rushed out to the foyer. "Magdalena, are you sure?"

Magdalena's voice was heavy. "Our brother died. Our loss shouldn't be in vain. Let Isabel visit her sister. It's been long enough."

I shrieked with joy and ran to the kitchen to tell Teresa the news. We packed the chicken inside my old cloth sack so it wouldn't attract attention, and I ran upstairs to my chest to retrieve some of the money I had set aside. Once I had it safely hidden in my bosom, Teresa and I put on our mantillas and went out to the street.

I was so eager to see my sister, I started out walking as fast as I could, but Teresa found it hard to keep up with my pace and I was forced to slow down. As we made our way across town, I remembered the day Magdalena had brought me to live with her. The city had been so quiet then, but not now. Despite the relentless heat of the sun, people filled the streets. Some carried buckets of water from the fountains. Others I identified as soldiers returning from war; they hobbled, or had lost use of a limb, like Father. They were disheveled and dirty, their hair matted and their beards unkempt. The smell of sweat, urine, or dung assailed my nostrils at every corner, along with the more palatable scent of fried bacon. I heard talking, laughing, begging, cursing. Children pleaded for money. My chest tightened just looking at them.

"Shouldn't we give them something?" I whispered to Teresa, who laboured along next to me. I didn't remember so much poverty, so much distress. But the truth was that I had not left Leganitos and its adjacent streets for a full year. With sudden insight, I realized that I had grown accustomed to a level of comfort that was increasingly uncommon.

"No! Ignore them," Teresa chided me. "If they see we have something they want, it will be the end of us—and them."

"What do you mean?" I felt a shiver run down my spine. My eyes fell on a boy no older than five, sitting against the wall, hand extended in the air, white eyes fixed on nothing.

"Their parents do this," Teresa said, trying to pull me closer, but I couldn't stop staring at the child, whose eyes were like grey globes in slimy water. "Some people blind their own children and send them out to beg. They get more money that way."

I gasped in horror. Would Alonso have done such a thing to me, had the tavern not existed? I crossed myself, silently thanking God for keeping me from such a terrible fate. We continued our trek in silence, trying to avoid looking at anyone or drawing any attention.

Finally, we reached the street where Grandmother lived. I looked around me, feeling uneasy. Everything seemed smaller, grimier than I remembered, and the odour was particularly foul. As we approached the door, I let out a deep sigh before knocking.

The door opened almost immediately, and I gazed at my aunt Luisa.

"Isabel!" She opened her arms to embrace me, but I hesitated. The stench that greeted my nose was almost too strong to bear, the odour coming from her and from the interior of the house. My cousins, Jerónima and Marita, and Ana, were standing behind Luisa. Taking a deep breath and holding it, I hugged each of them briefly. I left my Ana for last, as I wanted to hug her longer, but the smell of garlic and onion in her hair was too strong. After a quick hug, I stepped back, grasping her hands in mine, and took a good look at her. I tried to compose myself.

"Ana, *hermana mía*! You have grown so much!" I pressed my lips together, hoping she wouldn't notice I was lying. She was barely any taller than the day I left. But her gaze had hardened. I could see more of Alonso in her face. Could she glimpse my father in mine? Her skin looked darker, too. Was she spending more time than usual outdoors? Fourteen months without seeing her: a lifetime.

"Why didn't you come before?" she asked, frowning.

"They wouldn't let me!" I had to fight my emotion to keep my voice from breaking. "You don't know how hard I tried. Everything has been so hard!" I could see in her eyes that she didn't believe me, so I tried to change the subject. "I can see that the skirt and shoes I sent fit you very well!"

Teresa was standing behind me, and Luisa motioned for

us to come in before offering Teresa one of the two chairs in the room. Nothing had changed.

"Welcome, Isabel." Luisa's hair had started to go grey, and the shadows around her eyes showed her age. I always thought she and Mother looked very much alike, and now I shivered at the thought that she could ever be this dishevelled. Mother was always beautiful, in control, strong, and collected.

I was struggling to find something to say when Grandmother emerged from the back. She approached me as fast as her legs allowed her. She looked like she had shrunk.

"Isabel, *hija*! Look at you, you look so fancy!" I laughed. Fancy? I was dressed as a maid. Ana, Jerónima, and Marita were wearing Constanza's old outfits, but they were stained and dusty. I was disappointed; I had sent those clothes for Ana alone. As much as I loved my cousins, they had a mother to provide for them, whereas my sister only had me. And I had thought the dresses I sent would last Ana for several months, but since they had been distributed among the three of them, I would need to provide new ones sooner than I expected.

"Ana, don't you ever go to the river to wash your clothes, the way Mother taught us?" The look on everyone's face, even Teresa's, made me stop. My words hadn't come out the way I intended. I tried again. "I mean, those dresses look so nice on you, and if you brush the fabric, or at least shake it and wipe the dirt off carefully, they will look nice for much longer." I made a mental note to bring a proper clothes brush on my next visit.

Ana's eyes watered. "Is that all you care about?"

So many times I had dreamed of coming over and telling Ana about my life—how I had learned to walk balancing a book on my head, the rules I had to obey, the cousin I shared a bed with—those dreams meant nothing because now, after fourteen months, I didn't know what to say. I felt completely out of place. Almost as out of place as I felt when I arrived at the Cervantes house. And, as God was my witness, I still didn't feel I belonged there. But now I could see I no longer belonged in my old home, either. I felt dizzy, unhinged, dispossessed.

"Isabel, remember the chicken!" said Teresa, breaking into my thoughts to save the day, as usual.

"Chicken?" Ana and my cousins exclaimed. Teresa opened the sack and extracted the half-plucked capon as well as some carrots. Luisa hurried to help her place everything on the table. The girls stared at the bird in awe.

"What else did you bring?" Luisa's question felt like a punch to my stomach. What else did she expect from me? What did they all expect, and how could I ever fulfill those expectations?

I turned to Teresa for help, and she got up from her chair. "It's late, Niña Isabel. I think we should leave."

"You only just arrived!" Ana protested.

"I know, Ana *querida*. But Teresa is right. It's late, and we have to walk all the way back to Leganitos before it gets dark." I couldn't hold my sister's gaze, but suddenly I remembered the money I was carrying under my dress. I had planned to give the entire amount to Grandmother, but seeing them all together like this, I decided to divide it.

"Here, Aunt Luisa, this is for you and my cousins." Not wanting to approach her, I placed a few coins on the table, next to the chicken. Then I turned to Grandmother and slid some coins inside the pocket of her apron.

"And this is for you and my little sister." Feeling Ana's eyes on me, I turned to her again.

"Here," I said softly as I placed some coins in her clammy hand. When was the last time she had cleaned her fingernails? "Buy yourself something tasty and share it with Jerónima and Marita."

Teresa was waiting for me by the door. I wished I could turn back time and be as close to my sister as before. But I had changed, and she had changed. Everything had changed. Fourteen months ago, I had thought twenty ducats was a fortune, but prices had increased so much that I would need more money if I was to be of real help. And more money required a different life. My head was spinning when we left, so much so that at the corner I suddenly bent down and vomited. Teresa stood behind me, offering an old handkerchief to wipe my mouth. At that moment, I promised myself that I would find my place in the world. The place where I belonged.

IV

CATALINA
Esquivias
September 1600

Ave Maria, gratia plena
Dominus tecum
Benedicta tu in mulieribus,
Et benedictus fructus ventris tui, Jesus.
Sancta Maria, mater Dei
Ora pro nobis peccatoribus,
Nunc et in hora mortis nostrae.
Amen.

THE LORD IS my rock, my fortress, and my refuge. And I need You now, my dear Lord, more than ever. We were sitting together at the dining table. Miguel, shoulders hunched, stared at the food I myself had placed before him.

"You must eat, my love. And my *manjar blanco* is your favourite." He knew I had spent the entire morning in the kitchen with the cook preparing the chicken breast with milk, rice flour, sugar, saffron, salt, rosewater, and cinnamon, the way he liked it, to tempt his appetite. The progress we had made, the harmony we achieved after his return from Seville had been utterly destroyed by the news of Rodrigo's death.

I begged both the Virgen Maria and the Virgen del Prado de Ciudad Real to have mercy upon us. Not even when my mother-in-law, Doña Leonor de Cortinas—may God rest her soul—became ill and passed away did I see Miguel so distraught.

He lifted his face. "Forgive me, my darling Catalina. I know you have worked hard preparing this dish, but I'm not hungry."

He rose to his feet, ready to leave the dining room. Where was he going? To waste the day away in bed? To pace the rooms like a lost soul? We had been doing so well these months. He had gained weight and strength and had been writing every day.

"Why don't you try to write a little?" I suggested gently.

"I don't think I can, Catalina. Not now. Forgive me."

It was as if all those nights we spent talking about his characters and laughing at their adventures did not matter a whit. Lord, have mercy! I can deal with his absence, I can deal with his frenzy and his creativity and his silence, but I do not know if I am strong enough to deal with his sorrow.

V

CONSTANZA

CONSTANZA CAUGHT HIM looking at her. She had been praying for Rodrigo's soul in heaven. She hadn't told anyone, but she was having nightmares about her mother and Miguel and Magdalena dying, leaving her entirely alone in the world. At least during mass, her fears dissolved, like the communion wafer in her mouth.

She sat in the middle of the church at the end of a pew, beside her mother and her aunt. Isabel had a spot at the back, with Teresa. It was an overcast day in October and the church was chilly.

He was sitting across the aisle, also at the end of the pew. Although his head was bowed, he was peering over, looking at Constanza. No, not peering—staring. His eyes seemed to be calling hers. She could feel the intensity of his gaze.

Constanza crossed herself and prayed harder, but even though she was saying the right words, her mind was elsewhere, and her head, as if it had developed a will of its own, kept turning towards him. She could feel herself blush, and hoped her mantilla concealed it. He was the first man who had paid her any attention since Pedro de Lanuza had broken their engagement.

She had seen him before, of course. They both attended

church every Sunday. When her family prayed the novena for the eternal rest of Rodrigo's soul, she noticed that he was present at every service. Constanza thought it was odd, but she was so overwhelmed that she didn't give it much thought. After all, everyone went to church, and the most pious of Catholics make a point of attending mass every day. She assumed he was one such Christian. But then she observed that every week he sat one pew closer to her, until that Sunday morning when he was directly beside her and she felt as if he could touch her with his eyes.

Her head bowed in prayer, she also glanced sideways. His hair was dark and curly. He was tall, his shoulders broad and strong. The wool coat and leather gloves he wore made it clear that he belonged to a well-to-do family. After the humiliation of Pedro de Lanuza, Constanza had promised herself she would be more careful with men. But then their eyes locked briefly, and she felt that delicious but frightening flutter in her stomach. Who was this man and what did he want?

When mass was over and he followed her down the aisle towards the exit, she didn't know how to react. Should she say something to him? Tell her mother? No, she couldn't trust her in a matter such as this. She would have to resort to Teresa. As the group gathered in front of the church and prepared to return home, he stood by like a lost lamb, directing a pleading look towards her.

"Mother, would it be all right if we stroll down the square for a few minutes?"

Andrea, Magdalena, and Isabel looked at Constanza with surprise. It was a cool, windy day. They had to hold on to their mantillas or tuck them under their capes to stop them from flying off.

"You want to stroll in this weather?" Magdalena asked, blowing warm air into her gloved hands. It was hard to pretend it was not a nippy morning.

"Yes, why not?" Constanza said, gesturing with her arm, "People will leave, and we can have a bit of fresh air just for ourselves. It will be good for me. I seldom have a chance to be outside. Please?" She turned towards Teresa, hoping she would agree.

"I can walk with her, Señora Andrea. We won't be long, and the way back is short and safe." Constanza smiled; she knew Teresa wouldn't let her down. So the others headed home, leaving Constanza and Teresa to walk around the square. Constanza was excruciatingly aware of the young man following closely behind, but she did not look back. Teresa was obviously equally aware of his presence.

"You have a very nice reason not to feel cold today, Señorita," Teresa said with a smile, rubbing her hands.

Constanza laughed. "You won't tell, will you?"

"Of course not."

"Not even Isabel?"

"*Gallina ponedora y mujer silenciosa ...*" Teresa said, crossing herself as she spoke. Constanza laughed out loud at the expression. Nothing was more valuable than a laying hen and a discreet woman.

"What do you think?" she asked Teresa.

"I think he's quite handsome. What do *you* think?"

"Shhh! He'll hear you!" There were people in the square, but they all seemed to be heading somewhere. They were the only ones strolling around, taking slow steps around the trees and the fountain.

"Would you like to know his name?" Teresa inquired.

"You know his name?" Constanza's eyes opened wide. She had forgotten how full of surprises Teresa could be.

"The maid who works at his house washes the laundry at the same creek. We're friends."

"Really?" Constanza indicated with her head that she was waiting to hear the name.

"Francisco Leal."

Leal. Loyal. She liked that.

"I wonder how old he is," she said softly.

"Old enough to marry."

"Teresa!" Constanza raised her voice inadvertently and was mortified when she saw Francisco Leal smile in response. "Oh, my God. What do I do now? What do I do?"

"We could walk home along the creek. I'm sure you can find some privacy there."

"Are you crazy? That's dangerous! And we're alone!"

"It's not dangerous on a Sunday morning. And I'm sure the gentleman will happily protect you if we run into trouble."

"Teresa!" Constanza cried again, then erupted in laughter when she saw Francisco smiling at her maid's words.

The women turned and walked along the creek. Once they were surrounded by trees, Teresa started heading towards the water.

"Where are you going?" Constanza asked.

"Stay there, Constanza. I want to look at something," Teresa replied.

"Look at what?"

"I'll be back soon." Constanza stood still as Teresa continued in the direction of the brook. There was nobody nearby and for a minute it was very quiet. Then she heard footsteps coming in her direction.

"It's a lovely day, isn't it?" asked Francisco Leal as he came to a stop in front of her.

In fact, the sky had turned grey and dark. Was he being ironic?

"If you say so," Constanza responded. *Why did I just give such a stupid answer?* she reproached herself.

"It's lovely because I finally have a chance to talk to you," he declared, giving a little bow. The warmth in his eyes beguiled her. "I've been dreaming of this moment for weeks."

"You have?" The air was cool, but her entire body felt like it was on fire. Sweat beaded at her temples.

"And let me assure you that my intentions, beautiful Constanza de Ovando, are serious."

"How do you know my name?" she asked in shock.

"*Se dice el pecado, mas no el pecador.*" Name the sin, but not the sinner. Constanza suspected Teresa was behind this. No wonder she had disappeared.

"I want to marry you," Francisco declared calmly.

Constanza was stunned. She said the first thing that came into her head. "Marry me? You haven't even courted me yet!"

"What good is it to court a woman for a long time if his real intentions are not honest?"

Those words hurt. Teresa must have told him about Pedro de Lanuza. And if it hadn't been Teresa, it meant that news of her humiliation had travelled far and wide, which was worse.

"I need to go," she said, moving away from him, flustered.

"Please, wait!" He took a step towards her. Before she could push him back, he pressed him lips against her mantilla as if kissing her face. She felt the moisture of his lips through the texture of the lace. Now she was unable to move.

"Allow me to rephrase those words: I want to court you,

and if you accept me, it would be my honour to have you be my wife."

Seeing that she did not protest, Francisco lifted the edge of her mantilla and kissed her cheek. Constanza's heart was a wild bird flapping against her chest. She didn't have the strength or the will to stop him.

She heard Teresa speaking to her from the path. "I think we should go home, Señorita Constanza." Her voice was happy and light. "I'm sure there will be an opportunity to take a stroll again tomorrow."

"Tomorrow?" Constanza asked, looking at Francisco.

"Tomorrow," he said, placing her mantilla gently over her face.

VI

CATALINA

Credo in Deum Patrem omnipotentem, Creatorem caeli et terrae
Et in Iesum Christum, Filim eius unicum, Dominum nostrum:
Qui conceptus est de Spiritu Sancto, natus ex Maria Virgine,
Passus sub Pontio Pilato, crucifixus, mortuus, et sepultus,
Descendit ad inferos,
Tertia die resurrectit a mortius,
Ascendit ad caelos, sedet ad dexteram Dei Patris omnipotentis,
Inde venturus est iudicare vivos et mortuos.
Credo in Spiritum Sanctum,
Sanctam Ecclesiam catholicam,
Sanctorum communionem, remissionem peccatorum,
Carnis resurrectionem,
Vitam aeternam.
Amen.

My Lord, Your mercy knows no limits. My dear Miguel has
recovered his zest to write and live and love. He is eating well
and is making good progress with his book, which I pray will
fare well despite the bizarre events depicted in its pages. His
deranged knight attacks windmills, believing they are giants.
Then he frees prisoners on their way to the galleys because
he thinks their punishment is too cruel.

"Too cruel?" I said to him the other night, shaking my head after he read that scene out loud to me. "It's a punishment, it's not supposed to be pleasant."

"May God always spare your beautiful eyes from what I have seen during my travels, my beloved Catalina. Being confined to the galleys is a punishment no one deserves."

Perhaps he is right. What do I know about ships and prisoners and galleys? But I know about women. I decided it was time to address the matter that had been bothering me.

"Who is Dulcinea based on, Miguel?" I finally asked.

"Whenever I think of Dulcinea," he said, "I see your angelic face."

He certainly knew how to bring colour to my cheeks. But something told me to dig deeper.

"And Aldonza Lorenzo, the real Dulcinea?" I was aware that chivalric convention demanded that Don Quixote dedicate his quest to a lady. But because the knight is delusional, the person he renames Dulcinea is actually Aldonza Lorenzo, a boisterous, muscular peasant. I knew there was a girl named Aldonza Lorenzo in the nearby town of El Toboso. Miguel had chosen the name because he liked the alliteration. And he was determined to make the book as realistic as possible by infusing the characters with traits of people he had met in his travels. For this reason, I was afraid that Dulcinea, or Aldonza, could be a woman he was acquainted with during his time in Andalucía.

I pressed further. "*A falta de moza, ve con la Aldonza.* That's what they say, right? In the absence of a lady, go search for a ... you know what I mean."

I lowered my gaze. Men were allowed so many liberties, but I had married Miguel because I knew he was not like the others.

And we were bound together by a sacred promise. The mere thought of him seeking refuge in the arms of a woman who sold her body, one of those sinful creatures who "work" in taverns and other lowly places, made me shiver. But I had to find out if Aldonza was a character based not only on the musical name of a girl from El Toboso, but also on a real woman, the opposite of me, who was available to him in my absence. I had to find out if she was a woman he had known and was unable to forget.

"When I think of Aldonza Lorenzo," he replied, "I *don't* think about your angelic face." I slapped his cheek playfully.

"I'm serious here, Miguel. I need to know."

"Are you jealous?"

"Jealous? Of a character in your book? Of course not!" I bit my lip.

"Aldonza can be any peasant, or any taverner in Spain, my love. Any woman who is nothing like you." He took my face in his hands and looked into my eyes. "And no one matters to me except you, my Catalina. You have nothing to worry about."

Of course I have nothing to worry about! Silly me! I went to sleep with the certainty that his book told a captivating, entertaining tale. Then last night he stayed up writing a few chapters about a wealthy orphan called Marcela, who chooses to become a shepherdess so that she can live freely in the mountains. When I woke up, he called me over to his study and asked me to read through the chapters he had just finished and tell him what I thought. First I had to open the windows and clear the air because the smell of wax and candle smoke was so strong. This time, he wanted me to read the pages myself, instead of reading them aloud to me as we had done before. I agreed, on the condition that he allow me to sit on his lap while I did so. I had missed his body next to mine all night long. With his right arm around my waist and his chin resting on my shoulder, I took the sheets of paper in my hand and began deciphering his scribbling.

"You really should do something about your handwriting, you know?"

"What are you talking about? I was the student with the best handwriting in the entire class!" he protested.

I shook my head, smiling. "I can think about many things that you excel at, but penmanship isn't one of them." He tickled my stomach. I wiggled happily, then placed my left hand on his right, locking our fingers together, and began to read.

After a few lines, I felt compelled to stop. I wanted to make sure I understood his words correctly.

"My love, are you sure about all this? First, you are describing an old man who has lost his mind, comparing him to famous knights. As if that were not audacious enough, you have placed your story not in the past, where chivalry novels are set, but in our present day. And to make matters worse, instead of traveling through our enemies' lands or an imaginary kingdom, the man is right here, in Castile!"

With his chin still resting on my shoulder, Miguel assented, inviting me to continue reading. I carried on. Next, a shepherd named Chrysostom dies of unrequited love for a young woman named Marcela. The other shepherds blame her for his death and accuse her of being cruel. But on the day of Chrysostom's burial, Marcela appears, and tells the shepherds (and Don Quixote), her side of the story.

I come to vindicate myself, and to let the world know how unreasonable those are who blame me for their own suffering, or for the death of Chrysostom. Therefore, I beg of all here present that they hear me with attention, for I need not spend much time, nor many words, to convince persons of the sense of the truth. Heaven, as you say, made me handsome, and to such a degree, that my beauty incites you to love me, whether you will or no. And in return for the love you bear me, you pretend and insist that I am bound to love you. I know, by the natural sense God has given me, that whatever is beautiful is amiable, but I do not comprehend that, merely for being loved, the person that is loved for being handsome is obliged to return love for love. Besides, it may chance that the lover of the beautiful may be ugly, and what is ugly deserves to be loathed. It would sound odd to say, "I love you for being handsome; you must love me, though I am ugly."

I burst out laughing. "She has a point, you know, my love? Lucky for us, you fell in love with me because of my wit and I love you back because of your looks." Miguel let out a guffaw. What a blessing it was to feel his joy! He was enjoying writing this new book, and his joy was contagious.

But, supposing the beauty on both sides to be equal, it does not therefore follow that the inclination should be so, too: for all beauty does not inspire love, and there is a kind of it which only pleases the sight but does not captivate the affections. If all beauties were to enamour and captivate, the wills of men would be eternally confounded and perplexed, without knowing where to fix, for the beautiful objects being infinite, the desires must be infinite, too. And, as I have heard say, true love must be voluntary and unforced.

I stopped to ponder my husband's words. I marvelled at his wisdom, his sensitivity, and the eloquence with which he placed his thoughts on paper. We had spoken about this subject many times before. Our marriage had not been forced upon me. He courted me and I fell in love with him precisely because of his gentleness, his honesty. Aware of how fortunate I was, I thanked God again, but a certain uneasiness brewed in my chest as I continued reading.

I was born free, and that I might live free, I chose the solitude of these fields: the trees on these mountains are my companions, the transparent waters of these brooks my looking glass; to the trees and the waters I communicate my thoughts and my beauty. Those whom the fight of me has enamoured, my words have undeceived. And if desires are kept alive by hopes, as I gave none to Chrysostom, nor to anyone else, all hope being at an end, sure it may be said that his obstinacy, rather than my cruelty, killed him. If it be objected to me that his intentions were honourable, and that therefore I ought to have complied with them, I answer that, when in this very place, where they are now digging his grave, he discovered to me the goodness of his intention, I told him that mine was to live alone in perpetual solitude, and that the earth alone should enjoy the fruit of my reservedness, and the spoils of my beauty.

"Miguel, this is beautiful! Beautiful—and yet so dangerous." I couldn't help but frown and shake my head. It was one thing for Don Quixote to commit irrational acts. But for a female character to speak this way! This would incite men's anger. And there was nothing more dangerous, I knew, than angry men.

Let him who is deceived complain; let him to whom I have broken my promise despair; let him whom I shall encourage presume; and let him pride himself, whom I shall admit: but let not him call me cruel, or murderess, whom I neither promise, deceive, encourage, nor admit. Heaven has not yet ordained that I should love by destiny, and from loving by choice I desire to be excused.

"And after this speech, she goes away to live alone in the mountains, without a husband or a father or any man by her side?"

"Yes."

I put the pages down on the desk and was quiet for a moment as I chose the words I would say next. There was no way I could hide my alarm, and I wasn't about to.

My voice was soft but serious. "Do you want to be hanged?"

"Hanged?" He opened his eyes wide and his expression conveyed such innocence that I couldn't help smiling. Once again, I slapped him gently on the cheek.

"Yes, Miguel. I'm serious. Hanged. How many husbands and fathers do you think will thank you for creating a character like Marcela?"

"She's just a character, not a real woman! Besides, I don't care about the husbands and fathers. I care about the sisters, the daughters, the nieces, and all the young girls who are forced to follow men's wishes against their will."

"And if we had a daughter, would you feel the same way?"

He opened his mouth as if he was going to answer. He gave a long sigh before finally speaking. "I have two sisters and a niece, and that is exactly how I feel."

I shook my head. We both remained silent for a moment,

the air tense between us. Miguel had spoken the truth, and I had to trust what he was doing. Trust is a wife's most treasured gem.

"I will remind you of this conversation if Constanza one day decides to become a shepherdess and leaves everything behind to go to the mountains."

Miguel laughed. When he tried to kiss me I had to turn my body around. I held him in my arms, his face against my chest and slowly descending as his hand lifted my skirt. I feel terribly sorry for any woman—shepherdess or princess—who does not know what it is like to have a man like my Miguel in her life. Yes, my Lord, Your mercy knows no limits. And I am, and forever will be, blessed.

VII

Royal Edict
January 11, 1601

King Philip III, by the grace of God, King of Castile, Leon,
Aragon and the two Sicilies, Jerusalem, Portugal, Navarre,
Granada, Toledo, Valencia, Galicia, The Majorcas, Seville,
Cordoba, Corsica, Murcia, Guinea, Algarve, Gibraltar, the
Canary Islands, also of the Eastern and Western Indies and the
islands and terra firma of the Ocean Sea, archduke of Austria,
duke of Burgundy and Milan, count of Habsburg, Barcelona,
and Biscay, and lord of Molina, to the royal children, prelates,
dukes, marquees, counts, masters of military orders, priors,
grandees, knight commanders, governors of castles and forti-
fied places of our kingdoms and lordships, and to councils,
magistrates, mayors, constables, district judges, knights, offi-
cial squires, and all good men of the noble and loyal cities of
Madrid and Valladolid, and to barons and women of whatever
age they may be, and to all other persons of whatever law,
estate, dignity, pre-eminence, and condition they may be, and
to all to whom the matter contained in this charter pertains
or may pertain: salutations and grace.

You know well or ought to know, that whereas I have
been made aware by the loyal Duke of Lerma that in this,

our Capital city of Madrid, the plague and many undeserved
hardships have befallen us, offering God-fearing residents little
opportunity to enjoy the blessings and mercy of Our Lord, and
posing risks and challenges for the respected members of this
Royal Court. Therefore I, with the counsel and advice of said
Duke of Lerma, prelates, great noblemen of our kingdoms, and
other persons of learning and wisdom of our Council, having
deliberated about this matter, resolve to order the transfer of
the Royal Court and all of its members and powers, to the
city of Valladolid, situated about 220 kilometres northwest of
Madrid, where the Pisuerga and Esgueva rivers meet, and from
whence the heart of our kingdom shall shine in new splendour.

VIII

ISABEL

TERESA AND I set down the sacks of grain and vegetables in order to remove our mantillas and winter capes. I went into the sewing room, expecting to find Constanza and my aunts at work, but although the brazier was still lit, the room was empty.

"Aunt Andrea?" I called out. "Constanza? We're back from the market!" Father's studio was empty as well. Assuming they were in the kitchen, we picked up our purchases and made our way to the back of the house. But the fire burned untended in the kitchen, too.

"Did they say they were going out?" I asked as I put away the beans and potatoes in their baskets and Teresa stowed away the rest.

"No, they should be home," she said, warming her hands at the stove. "Something must have happened."

"Do you think they all went for a walk together?" Since the autumn, Constanza had been complaining about shortness of breath. Saying the fresh air made her feel better, she had started going for daily walks with Teresa.

"I don't think so. She only goes out with me," she replied. When I looked puzzled, she smiled in a knowing way. "It's not only fresh air she needs at her age. She's been *pelando la pava.*"

"She's been meeting a sweetheart?" I exclaimed. Teresa slapped my hand, shushing me.

"Who is it?" I was hardly able to contain myself. "How did they meet? Tell me everything!"

Teresa didn't have to be asked twice. She was clearly eager to share information.

"His name is Francisco Leal. You should see the way they look at each other, Niña Isabel!" she said, beaming.

"So *that's* why she's been in such a good mood lately!"

"*Amor, fuego, y tos, descubren a su poseedor.*" This was true: coughing, fire, and love could never be hidden.

"Do my aunts know, Teresa?"

"No, Niña Isabel. If they knew they might send me away. But Señorita Constanza has experienced a lot of sorrow through no fault of her own. Señora Andrea and Señora Magdalena have lived their lives as they have seen fit. I think it's time for you young girls to do the same."

I was moved at Teresa's selflessness. She was taking a big risk to help my cousin, and I hoped wholeheartedly for both of them that it would be worth it. I gave her a quick hug.

"Let's find out what they're doing," Teresa said, pushing me away gently.

We left the kitchen and quietly went up the stairs to the bedrooms. The doors were closed and neither of us dared to open them or knock. Instead, we put our ears against the wood, trying to make out any movements on the other side. Of course, I could have walked into the room that I shared with Constanza, but I hesitated. Perhaps Magdalena and Andrea had made a last-minute decision to go out—they were still not finished all the paperwork regarding Rodrigo's death—and Constanza, taking advantage of their absence, was having a rest.

I put my ear against the door again and struggled to make out any sound coming from our bedroom. Now that Teresa had shared my cousin's secret with me, I wondered if Constanza had left the house to meet this Francisco Leal by herself. Perhaps she was tired of her life and her routine. If she didn't find a husband soon, she would become a spinster. Despite my aunts' assertion that it was better to be alone than to be with a bad husband, I was not convinced that the life of a spinster was desirable. And I knew Constanza would do anything to avoid it.

Hearing nothing from the room, I gently opened the door and looked around. My cousin was nowhere to be seen. We repeated the process in the next bedroom. Something was not right, I could tell. I had a feeling in the pit of my stomach. Teresa and I approached the last door. Just as I was placing my ear against it, the door opened, revealing my aunt Andrea. Startled, all three of us cried out, then burst into laughter. What a relief!

"What are you two doing here?" Andrea asked, her hand on her chest as she caught her breath. Magdalena and Constanza were sitting on the bed. Magdalena was laughing, too.

"I'm sorry, Aunt Andrea." I wiped a few tears from my eyes; it had been a while since I had laughed that hard. "We expected you to be downstairs as usual. We were worried when you weren't there."

"Why didn't you call out for us first?" Constanza asked, annoyed. "Wouldn't that be better than prying?"

"Prying? I wasn't prying!" I said indignantly.

Magdalena signalled for me to come inside. Teresa stood in the doorway, expectant.

"Come here, dear child. I have wonderful news for you—for us all." Magdalena made room for me to sit next to her on the bed. Constanza rose to her feet and moved towards her mother.

"What is it?" I asked, feeling as if a thousand ants were crawling inside my stomach.

"We're moving to Valladolid!" Magdalena exclaimed joyfully.

At this, Constanza ran into our room and slammed the door. Andrea went after her. Teresa sighed and made her way towards the stairs.

"But what about my sister?" I cried out. Although I hadn't seen Ana again since our last sad, uncomfortable visit, I still sent her money and bits of food every month. If we moved to Valladolid, how would I be able to help her? She would be even worse off than she already was!

"Madrid's wealthiest people—our clients—are all moving to Valladolid. We'll be left with very little work. We might not be able to afford the rent for this house. We don't really have a choice."

"But Ana—"

"Isabel, listen to me. Your father got an advance payment for the book he's currently writing."

"He did?" I said, my emotions a jumble. On the one hand, I was happy for him, and for us. This money would help our living situation. On the other, I was angry. I had been hoping he would come to visit us, but he hadn't because he was *too busy writing*. For this long? Esquivias wasn't that far from Madrid, only two days' journey. Wasn't he interested in getting to know me better? Now I was supposed to leave the only place I had known, as well as my sister? My chin trembled and Magdalena took my hand in hers.

"Apparently, the publisher really likes what Miguel has submitted so far, and your father wants us to use that money to live in Valladolid together."

"*Together?*" My heart skipped a beat. Father wanted us to live together? Like a real family?

"Yes, together. We must decide what to bring along and what to sell. Once the Royal Court leaves Madrid, the city will be dead for a man like your father." She sounded proud, hopeful, but her clammy hand suggested a different story. She was nervous. "He must be in the company of other intellectuals, other writers, and meet people in positions of power. His talent needs to be recognized, and perhaps this book will make that miracle happen."

It was hard not to feel a little bit excited at the prospect of living under the same roof as my father. But I couldn't stop worrying about what would happen to Ana when I was gone. I felt torn.

"How did you find out? Did Father write you a letter?" I asked.

Magdalena nodded and gave me a long hug. But I couldn't hug her back.

"What will happen to my sister and my grandmother?" I said quietly.

She looked puzzled. "Nothing. The move will not have any impact on their lives whatsoever. They will stay here and go on as they always have."

"I'll never see them again."

"Of course you will, my dear!" she replied. Her face was

all smiles, but her pleasure was no comfort to me. I could feel it in my gut: if Ana and I were separated, each in a different city, we would lose each other forever.

"Can we bring my sister along?" I asked in desperation.

Magdalena looked surprised. She shook her head.

"When your father has received the recognition he deserves and full payment for the new book, things might change."

"But—"

"Life will be better for us there. Anyone who matters has to be close to the King's Court. And we're the ones who sew their clothes, remember?"

I remembered. But this didn't change the fact that I would be losing my sister.

IX

CONSTANZA

"CONSTANZA DE OVANDO, stop crying!" Andrea was sitting at the edge of the bed next to Constanza, who had buried her face in her pillow. How could she be expected to stop crying? She had finally met a man who made her forget all her troubles, and now she had to leave him behind in Madrid.

For weeks, with Teresa's help, Constanza had been meeting Francisco Leal. In the beginning they took strolls by the creek, where he held and kissed her hands in an effort to warm them up. When the weather got colder, he invited her to meet him at an inn that belonged to a friend of his. At first Constanza refused this invitation, aware of the danger it posed to her honour and the good name of her family. But Francisco insisted that there was nothing to fear. He gave her his word that he would ask for her hand in matrimony as soon as his business investment came to fruition.

Constanza didn't need much coaxing. The fire burning between her legs proved stronger than the fear of being dishonoured, and she began visiting the inn twice a week, telling her aunts she was going to church. Had it not been for Teresa, who walked with her and cautioned her to be discreet, she would never have been able to contain herself.

Every minute she spent in Francisco's arms felt like God's response to her prayers.

"What do you mean, 'Stop crying,' Mother?" Constanza wailed, afraid that Andrea would deduce the real reason behind her tears. "Why must we always do what Uncle Miguel wants?" Before she met Francisco, Constanza would have never dared to voice such a complaint. But the turmoil in her heart made it impossible to remain quiet.

"I explained that the Court is moving to Valladolid," Andrea repeated. "And anyway, Miguel knows what's best for us."

Constanza sat up and faced her mother. "Really? Like he did when he fled Spain like a coward and was captured by pirates on the way back?"

At these words, Andrea slapped her. Constanza immediately stopped crying. Her mother had never hit her before. With a hand on her throbbing cheek, she collected herself as best as she could.

"Please just tell me this. Why do you and Aunt Magdalena feel that you owe him eternal obedience?"

"Miguel is the man of the family," Andrea said quietly.

"No, that's not it. I want the truth. I want to know what happened," Constanza insisted.

"What are you referring to?"

"Why do you and Aunt Magdalena never question his decisions and always do what he tells you?"

"I told you already. Because he's—"

"No. I want to know. I'm entitled to know."

"You're not entitled to anything," her mother said coldly.

"Then I'm not going to Valladolid with you. I'm the best seamstress here. I can earn my own living."

"Alone? In an empty city?"

"Even people in an empty city need clothes."

"You wouldn't do that. You can't stay alone here."

"Why not? I'm an adult."

"But what would people say?"

Constanza shrugged. Andrea clenched her teeth and made a fist. Constanza thought she was going to hit her. But instead, her mother lowered her voice and locked eyes with her.

"No one can ever know this story, Constanza. No one. Do you understand?"

Constanza nodded vigorously and managed to hide a triumphant smile. She was going to get what she wanted. Her mother put her finger to her lips, then began talking.

"Miguel was a successful, promising poet. He had just published his first work to great acclaim. Everybody was impressed by his talent. He was just twenty-two, younger than you are now." The reference to her age was like another slap in the face, but Constanza forced herself not to react. She had to pay attention because Andrea's voice was barely above a whisper.

"Around that same time, he met a gentleman named Antonio di Sigura." Constanza nodded. She had heard the name, but all she knew about the man was that he was the reason her uncle had left Spain all those years ago.

Andrea paused in her story and took a few deep breaths. She looked uncomfortable.

"Antonio di Sigura seduced me."

Constanza's mouth opened wide in disbelief. It was the last thing she had expected to hear. She stared at her mother in alarm.

"He seduced *you*?"

Andrea nodded. "He was an Italian painter and sculptor. King Philip II had brought him to work in El Escorial. I was young. He made so many promises ..." her voice faded away.

"King Philip II? You had access to the court?" Constanza said in disbelief.

"Your uncle did. Because of his writing."

"Did di Sigura pay you a compensation?"

Andrea nodded. "Two hundred ducats." *So little?* But Constanza held her tongue, and both women were silent for a minute.

"Did my father know this happened to you?" Constanza asked quietly.

Andrea nodded again. "But that's not all di Sigura did." She paused again and seemed unwilling to go on. Constanza sat still, staring at her mother, waiting for her to gather the courage to continue.

"He took advantage of Magdalena—not like Pedro de Lanuza did with you," she hastened to explain. "It was worse." Andrea's voice quivered. She had to pause again, and Constanza thought she would faint with suspense. What could be worse than being tricked by your fiancé?

"She was abducted."

"Abducted?" Constanza's heart was pounding. "*How?*"

"With the help of a group of his friends."

Constanza's voice was a whisper. "Are you saying Di Sigura dishonoured Aunt Magdalena, too?"

Andrea nodded slowly. "He held her captive for three days." Constanza's hand flew to her mouth in horror.

"But Magdalena refused financial reparation. She couldn't stand the thought that years later, someone would find out what had happened to her." At this, she looked at her daughter entreatingly. "Remember what I told you: no one must ever find out about this. Do you hear me?"

Constanza nodded vigorously. She realized Andrea was not finished with her story.

"But your uncle couldn't stand by while di Sigura went unpunished. He challenged him to a duel."

As the mystery surrounding the powerful loyalty her mother and her aunt displayed to their brother finally became clear, Constanza started to cry again. And these tears were more bitter than any she had shed before.

"Antonio di Sigura was badly wounded, and his family sought revenge. Miguel was condemned to ten years in exile. But his right hand would be cut off first."

Constanza had to suppress a cry. "But if they knew what di Sigura had done to Aunt Magdalena, wouldn't they forgive Uncle Miguel?"

Andrea shook her head. "We agreed to tell no one what Magdalena had gone through. She was the youngest, and we had to protect her. Miguel went to Italy and joined the army to clear his name and restore his honour. You know the rest of the story. He would have never been on the ship that was captured by pirates if he hadn't wounded di Sigura. He would have remained here in Spain and by now he'd be as famous as Lope de Vega. He wasted his best years trying to rebuild his reputation and lost the use of his arm—for us. Now do you understand?"

Constanza nodded slowly. It was almost too much to take in.

"Not a word to anyone about this, Constanza!" Andrea's voice was the quietest her daughter had ever heard, but her warning was the strictest. "I have trusted you with our gravest family secret. I expect you to prove you are worthy of keeping it."

X

CATALINA

Sálve Regína, Máter misericórdiæ!
Víta, dulcédo, et spes nóstra, sálve.
Ad te clamámus, éxsules filii Hévæ.
Ad te suspirámus,
geméntes et fléntes in hac lacrimárum válle.

I pray to You, Holy Mother, Virgin Mary, to give me strength
to hide my pain from my beloved Miguel. Today once more,
our bedsheets were stained by my monthly blood, a curse that
reminds me time and again of my barren body and my empty
arms. How many nights I have prayed for the miracle of life
growing inside me, life created by the power of our love, of
our days and nights together in our home, in this home where
my husband has finally found some solace.

His book is now several hundred pages long, and it seems
to me that the longer it gets, the smaller my chances of seeing
my dream come true. If only I could give life to a baby the
way he gives life to characters and dialogue. I offer my heart
to my husband and, with it, my entire body and soul, without
shame or secrets, for there cannot be any secrets between two
people who love each other as much as we do. But still my
womb is empty. And soon my bed will be empty, too. Miguel

must depart for Valladolid. Even though he has been happy here, writing to his heart's content, never lacking paper, ink, or inspiration, he is not a man who can live in a small town.

I have yearned for a baby because I thought perhaps if he became a father, he would never leave again. Alas, I have failed. My body has betrayed me. Perhaps there is a lesson to be learned in this. Perhaps the secret to our union is the perfect way our bodies fit within each other, like they were meant to be together. Perhaps another body, the body of a baby growing inside me, nourishing itself from me, would ruin that perfect fit. I would then stop being my husband's main sustenance. Something in our bond would be broken. I tell myself this and try to find consolation in that thought. There cannot be any children between us. We are meant to be alone, just him and me. And we have been joyful since his return. Thank God for that.

I must focus on this as he prepares to leave once again Even though he has promised I will join him in Valladolid, even though he has promised he will come back to visit me often, I know that the city and its theatres and salons can better satiate his thirst. I know that there are certain promises he cannot keep, like remaining in a single place for too long. On our wedding day, he promised he would never leave me. And then, after only twenty-eight months together, he turned back into the traveller he was before we met. I have finally come to understand that my Miguel is very much like his errant knight.

Here I shall remain, Holy Mother of God, alone and barren, dry yet hopeful, until he returns and his mouth breathes joy into my days again.

XI

ISABEL

I WAS STRUGGLING in vain to fall asleep when I heard banging on the front door. It sounded desperate, urgent. Someone needed help; someone wanted to come in. I sat bolt upright in the bed and listened closely in case I had dreamed it. But it was real. Banging on the door, a faint cry for help. I shook Constanza's shoulder, trying to wake her.

"Constanza!"

She pushed my hand away and turned her back against me. I insisted. "Constanza, wake up, can't you hear that?"

She opened her eyes, and there it was again. The banging on the door, louder, more desperate than before. Constanza got out of bed, calling out for Magdalena and Andrea, and we ran downstairs. At the same time Teresa emerged from the kitchen. It was still dark outside—it was a moonless, late-November night—and it took us a few moments to light our candles. My aunts appeared, wearing woolen shawls. A cold shiver ran down my spine.

"We have to open the door!" I said. If someone needed help, the Christian thing to do was to give it.

"Are you out of your mind? We can't open the door!" Constanza's voice was agitated.

"Please, help me!" It was a woman banging on the door. Her voice sounded weaker than before. I approached the door, intending to unlock it, but Andrea blocked my way.

"Don't open that door, Isabel!"

"It's too dangerous!" Magdalena pulled me back.

"But a woman needs help, can't you hear her?" I protested, distressed.

"Yes, but we can't let her in! Whoever she's running from will come after us, and we're alone."

"We're not alone," I said. "There are five of us here."

"Isabel," Magdalena stood in front of me, blocking my access to the door. "We are wearing nothing but our night-gowns and shawls. It's the middle of the night. They can do whatever they want to us. Don't you understand?"

I had never seen Magdalena so scared. She was shaking. I could see the veins throbbing in her neck. But I pushed past her and proceeded to unlock the door. Magdalena grabbed the dagger that she kept by the table every night. I pulled the door open and a woman stumbled in. Her face was bruised and bleeding, her clothes were torn.

"*Gracias, Dios mío, gracias!*" I could barely understand what she was saying, her lips were so swollen. Before I could touch her, a man appeared at the threshold and prevented Andrea from closing the door.

"Give me back my wife!" he screamed. In the darkness I couldn't see what he looked like. My one clear thought was this: If the devil could speak, that would be his voice. Holding her shawl with one hand and her dagger in the other, Magdalena stood before the man, Andrea close behind her. Teresa had grabbed the poker from the fire and Constanza the iron pot, ready to attack.

"Get out of here!" Aunt Magdalena screamed. She trembled as the icy wind blew into the room, raising goosebumps on my skin.

The man laughed and made a gesture as if to draw his sword. We all took a step back.

"Mencía! If you don't want these ladies to pay for your sins, come out now!"

The poor woman had fled into the sewing room. Now the five of us watched helplessly as she came out whimpering, her head bowed, and limped towards her tormentor.

"I know who you are, Sir," Magdalena said, "And where you live. And as soon as there's daylight, I shall inform the authorities of what you've done to your wife."

"And I know you, Señora," he said with a hiss. "And believe me, you don't want me to inform the authorities about your household in return."

In a second, he and his wife had disappeared into the darkness. Magdalena lowered her arm and dropped the dagger. Constanza and Teresa also put down their makeshift weapons. Shivering, her teeth chattering, Andrea pulled the door closed and locked it. As I started to ask what the man's words meant, Constanza hushed me.

"Tonight did not happen, do you hear? Don't ever talk about it with anyone, is that clear?" I nodded helplessly, trying to quell the sense of dread that filled me.

It was only in the morning that Teresa discovered the handprint, a bloody mark on our wooden door. Together, we stared at it in silence. Then Teresa got a pail of water and soap and scrubbed it clean.

XII

November 1601
My dearest Miguel,

I trust that God is keeping you safe. This letter will be short, but you mustn't worry, nothing bad has happened. We are healthy and continue to work as usual. It is important for me to stress, however, that Madrid is becoming harder and harder to live in, and my nightmares have returned. It is therefore of utmost importance for us to leave here. As soon as possible, please. It doesn't matter if the new house doesn't resemble the one we live in now. Any dwelling—big or small, within or outside the city walls—will do. Being together again and away from here is all that counts now.

May God help you find suitable accommodation for all of us in crowded Valladolid, and may He bless you until we are together again.

Your loving sister,
Magdalena

XIII

CONSTANZA

"MOTHER, AUNT MAGDALENA. There's something I need to tell you."

The four women were in the sewing room. Andrea and Magdalena put their work down and lifted their eyes towards Constanza, ready to listen. Isabel was sitting on a cushion in the corner, reading. She had been so quiet lately that sometimes Constanza forgot she was there, but now she saw her cousin put down the volume of poetry she had been skimming through and turn to look at her, too.

"I'm in love," Constanza said simply.

Andrea stared at her daughter, perplexed. "What are you saying?"

"His name is Francisco Leal, and he wants to ask for my hand in marriage. He's requesting that you receive him tomorrow."

Magdalena was unable to conceal her distress. "And where did you meet this man, if I may know?"

"At the square, outside the church."

"So is that what you were doing every day," she said, her voice full of reproach, "when you went out for 'fresh air' with Teresa? Meeting with this man?"

"We're in love. We want to get married. What's wrong with that?"

"Everything is wrong with that! You don't go out and exhibit yourself on the street with a man, to begin with. And you don't surprise us with news of an engagement before we've even had a chance to find out who he is, what his family does, and where they come from."

"I know who his family is," Andrea said quietly, deliberately. "*Conversos*."

"That's not true!" Constanza protested.

"Yes, it is, *hija*. Your grandmother Leonor knew them well. She mentioned their name when we moved to this neighbourhood. She didn't want us to have any dealings with them."

"You're lying!"

Her mother shook her head. "I would never lie about something as grave as this, Constanza. We can't afford to establish ties with a *converso* family. You know the consequences it could have. People would shun us. We'd lose customers. How would we earn a living then? Besides," she added, "we're about to move to Valladolid."

"I don't want to go to Valladolid, I want to stay here! I want to marry him. The rest of you can go to Valladolid without me," Constanza protested, making a huge effort to hold herself together.

"And who gave you permission to do that?" Magdalena's voice was deep and composed. "It has been decided we are all going to Valladolid."

"Not me. I'm marrying Francisco and staying in Madrid," Constanza replied petulantly.

"Who will you sew clothes for if you stay in Madrid? The poor?"

"Magdalena, allow me to explain this to her, please." Andrea fixed her eyes on Constanza's. "This will be a ghost town soon. The fact that he wants to stay here should warn you!"

"His family has business abroad, in the colonies. They are already asking for the necessary permits for him to travel there."

"To the colonies?" Andrea left her sewing on the rug and stood up. "Do you want to live among savages?"

"His family has a property in—"

"Silence!" Magdalena's voice echoed against the walls. "You're not going anywhere except Valladolid. Period."

Constanza let out a wail. "But *why*?"

"Because he comes from a family of *conversos* and you cannot marry into that," her aunt insisted.

"So I cannot marry into that?" Constanza's jaw was so tense her temples hurt. "Have you forgotten that we come from *conversos* ourselves?"

"You are *conversas*?" Isabel exclaimed, her voice raspy and weak. It was the first time she had spoken in days.

"No, Isabel, we're not *conversas*. But this subject is none of your business. Please leave the room."

"No, Isabel, don't leave!" Constanza protested, turning to look at Magdalena fiercely. "Don't lie to her. Tell her how the family of Grandmother Leonor, whom she so deeply resembles—as you and Mother have pointed out many times—comes from a line of *conversos*."

"I'm not a liar! And we're not *conversos*. We're Old Christians, do you hear? And you're not marrying into that family."

"I'm not asking for your permission, I'm letting you know what is going to happen. If you don't want Francisco to ask for my hand in marriage, that's fine. I'll run away with him. I'll be his *amancebada*."

Andrea had been standing by the door, her hand on her mouth. When she heard these words, she cried out. "*Amancebada*? The Inquisition will parade you through the city for living in sin, then throw you in jail or execute you!"

"If that were true, they'd have to jail or execute hundreds of women my age all over Madrid! Don't pretend you didn't know that, Mother," Constanza replied.

"Have you thought about what that would do to our family's honour? And to your Uncle Miguel's reputation?" Andrea demanded.

"How dare you—any of you—talk about reputation!" Constanza said. There was an audible gasp.

"What do you mean?" Magdalena asked, her face suddenly pale. Andrea looked at her daughter with fury. Constanza knew her mother regretted confiding in her. But right now, she cared about no one except Francisco Leal.

"I know everything!" Constanza practically spat out her words. "I know about you and that Italian."

"What Italian?" asked Isabel, getting to her feet.

"You told her, Andrea?" Magdalena spoke quietly, which made the question sound ominous. Andrea stood by silently, her expression pleading.

"Besides," Constanza continued, "Francisco and I have no choice but to marry."

"Why?" Andrea cried out. "Did he abuse you?"

"No. He loved me. And I loved him back." Constanza paused before delivering the final blow. "I am expecting a child."

There was another gasp. Andrea approached her daughter, a mix of pity and anger on her face.

"You foolish girl," she said, reaching an arm out as if to comfort her. "Do you understand what you've gotten yourself into?" Constanza stepped back, out of her reach.

"Teresa will pay for this." Magdalena said, her voice sharp as a blade.

"Teresa?" Isabel was trembling with confusion and fear.

"Yes. She clearly helped Constanza conduct this sordid affair." Magdalena turned to Isabel. "I asked you to leave the room."

"And I asked her to stay," Constanza retaliated. "And Teresa has nothing to do with this."

Magdalena let out a mirthless laugh. "Look at her, Andrea. She turned out exactly like you."

Andrea looked wounded. "Calm down, don't say anything you might regret later."

"You told her my deepest secret, why shouldn't I tell her yours?"

"I beg you, please. Don't!"

"What are you talking about, Aunt Magdalena? What secret?" Constanza asked. She felt dizzy, she was afraid she was going to vomit.

"Your mother can explain that to you. I think we've had enough for one day." Magdalena, arm held out as if to warn the others not to follow her, left the sewing room.

Constanza looked into Andrea's eyes. "What secret?"

"Don't pay attention to your aunt." Her mother sat down. "She's angry, she only said that to get back at you."

Suddenly they heard the sound of crying coming from the kitchen. Worried, Constanza and Isabel immediately rushed back there. Teresa stood by the stove, her eyes on the floor as tears rolled down her face.

"Why are you crying?" asked Isabel, putting an arm around the maid.

"Teresa is leaving right away," Magdalena announced.

"But why?" Isabel repeated. Constanza knew she should be the one protecting Teresa, but at that very moment a cramp pierced her abdomen, preventing her from speaking. She rubbed her belly and took a deep breath, hoping the pangs would subside.

"Isabel, no one owes you an explanation," said Magdalena. "Go to your room and let me deal with this."

"No, I won't."

"Niña Isabel," Teresa urged, trying to pacify everyone, "please do as your aunt says."

"No! It's unfair and—" She couldn't finish because Magdalena slapped her on the cheek. Sweat ran down Constanza's back and she felt weak. She had never seen her aunt lose control this way before.

"Silence! This is my house, and you will do as I say. Teresa, get out! You have betrayed this family's trust. I never want to see you again. And as for the two of you—" Magdalena glared at her nieces, her eyes full of rage, "go to your room right now."

Teresa began to collect her belongings. Constanza could barely walk but, afraid of making things worse, she headed towards the stairs.

"How can you just let this happen, Constanza? We need to defend Teresa! Help me!" Isabel insisted. Constanza could barely hear her. Holding on to the railing, she was climbing the steps slowly, breathing heavily. She was almost on the second floor when a bolt of pain hit her, making her feel as if her body was being cut in two. Losing her grip on the railing, she tumbled down the stairs like a marionette whose strings had been cut. Her upper body slammed against the stone floor. Magdalena and Andrea came running to find Constanza lying in a heap at the bottom of the stairs.

"Constanza, *hija!*" Andrea yelled, running to her side. Magdalena was already kneeling beside her, holding her head in her hands. Her eyes and mouth were open, but she couldn't speak. She tasted metal in her mouth and felt warm liquid between her legs. Two Teresas, cloth sacks on their shoulders, stared at her from the foyer. Constanza wanted to scream—for help, for forgiveness, for mercy. Then there was nothing but darkness.

"Andrea, lock the door after Teresa," Magdalena said.

Constanza remained unconscious while the three women struggled to carry her up the stairs. During the time they cared for her—applying compresses and poultices, changing her clothes, wiping her skin clean—she never heard them praying.

ACT THREE

VALLADOLID
FEBRUARY 1603–JANUARY 1606

Wanting to prevent the newly arrived madrileños from building "casas a la malicia" in Valladolid, the Duke of Lerma decreed that all houses must be three storeys and their facades painted in blue and gold. Only wealthy citizens could afford these houses. Others were forced to establish themselves in suburbs outside the city walls. In the early months of 1601, fifteen thousand people moved from Madrid to Valladolid, a city whose infrastructure was insufficient to accommodate so many.

With the death of Queen Elizabeth I in 1603, King James I ascended to the English throne. In 1604, the Treaty of London between England and Spain was negotiated. It was signed in Valladolid in 1605, the same year that Don Quixote: The Ingenious Gentleman of La Mancha *came to light. Spain was taking steps towards peace with France and the Netherlands.*

All these events proved auspicious for the Spanish people in general and for Miguel de Cervantes and his family in particular—at least in the beginning.

I

ISABEL

AS WE APPROACHED our new home on Calle Rastro de los Carneros—Slaughterhouse Street—and the ox-wagon carrying us and our belongings advanced down the dirt road, we had to cover our mouths and noses against the stench of blood and rotten meat.

Magdalena and Andrea had informed their most loyal clients we were moving to the new capital and, after selecting the few belongings we would bring with us, they sold the rest. My aunts insisted we would leave Madrid soon, but we had to wait for our new quarters to be ready. New houses had to be built to accommodate all the *madrileños* who, like us, were uprooting themselves to follow the King. Finally, in February 1603, we departed. Andrea had just delivered the embroidered shirts the Marquis of Villafranca had commissioned and collected 788 reales in payment.

Father came to pick us up and accompany us on the journey so we would be safe. He travelled with us in the carriage until we approached the city walls, when he chose to stretch his legs and walk next to the oxen. He looked strong and moved with ease. I had to agree with my aunts: his time in

Esquivias and his enthusiasm about what Valladolid had to offer had improved his health and his spirits.

"We left our house in Madrid for *this*? We're not even within the city walls!" Constanza said, bending down. I was afraid she would vomit—the stench had made me nauseous as well—but instead she scratched her legs until they were bleeding. The fleas in the last *venta* where we stayed on our way to Valladolid had feasted on all of us, but they were the most merciless with her. She had not stopped complaining. Complaining had become her favourite activity since my aunts had prohibited her from contacting Francisco Leal and kept a grim watch over our every move.

"*Hija*, access to the city through la Puerta del Campo is close enough. Do you have any idea how fortunate we are that your uncle was able to secure suitable accommodation for us?" Andrea responded. She looked haggard. Two days travelling down dry and dusty roads on a wooden cart pulled by oxen, purchasing whatever food was available along the way, and sleeping in flea-infested quarters had exhausted us all, but especially Andrea. Despite this, she still tried to comfort my cousin.

"This is *not* a good neighbourhood," Constanza insisted, staring at the river. "How can we expect to serve respectable clients from a place like this?"

She was right. The wooden bridge over the river was crowded with servants and labourers. There was a line of men, women, and children who looked like vagrants—perhaps they were beggars, or destitute soldiers—outside of a building that stood next to the slaughterhouse. The water was so dirty we would not be able to wash anything in its stream. Would there be a fountain or a well we could rely on? I wondered. There was no square in sight.

"That river is La Esgueva. It converges with the city's main river, El Pisuerga, which runs through the city itself." Eager to share his knowledge with me, Father walked next to the cart and raised his voice over the din of the crowd so I could hear him.

"Remember that Valladolid used to be the Empire's capital, but King Philip II moved the court out of the city a year before the Big Fire of 1561. That's why everything here is new. After we unpack and organize ourselves, we will take a stroll within the city walls so you can see that the city is prettier than Madrid."

Constanza continued to look displeased, but Magdalena opened her arms with enthusiasm and exclaimed, "Valladolid, at last!" Father smiled.

"I do not have good memories of the last time we were here," Andrea declared. I had heard the story already. Unable to repay a loan, Grandfather Rodrigo had been sent to jail and his belongings confiscated. "But I want to believe that this time around things will be better."

Magdalena nodded, behaving as if the smell of rotten meat and the noise of people yelling all around us didn't bother her. I knew that my aunts didn't want to upset Father after all the efforts he had made to bring us together under the same roof. Constanza, however, was too unhappy to hide her disappointment and frustration. Oblivious to her, Father went back to walking ahead of the cart, asking people to move aside so we could pass. Eventually we came to a stop in front of a newly built brick house close to the end of the street. Father waved his hand to let us know we had arrived. To my delight, I saw that there was a tavern on the main floor.

"A tavern!" Constanza and Andrea sounded distraught. Magdalena remained silent, but her grimace said it all.

"The apartment is on the second floor," Father said with a big smile. "Everyone who is anyone is in Valladolid. We will not regret moving here!"

He led the way upstairs, telling the porters where to place our belongings—the desks and the chairs, along with the rugs, the tapestries, and the rest of the basics. Magdalena had kept the *bargueño* desk and Grandmother Leonor's *talavera*, hoping to use it to entertain Father's important guests, but sold the large mirror that adorned the wall of the sewing room.

In the midst of the confusion, since no one was paying attention to me, I took the opportunity to go into the tavern. I was greeted by the owner, Anastasio, a burly man from Toledo, and his wife, Prudencia, who appeared to be a Moor. I admired the red floor tiles and the tall ceilings. The smell of wine and pigskin filled the air, reminding me of home.

Here and there, groups of older men occupied the tables and I could sense them leering, their eyes fixed on me. For a moment I felt intimidated, but then I recalled the way Mother used to walk around our tavern, clearly in control with her firm voice and no-nonsense attitude. Standing tall, chin raised, I cooly returned their stares until they dropped their eyes. If this was to be a clean start for the Cervantes family, it would be a clean start for me, too. I would soon be eighteen, and if I had learned anything it was that my life would be nothing like Constanza's. No one could stop me from lending a hand at the tavern in my free time. A bit of extra income would be welcome, especially since I had given most of my savings to Grandmother to provide for my sister and my cousins. "I worked as a *medidora* at my family's tavern back home in Madrid," I said loudly enough that the men closest to the bar could hear me. "If you need help around here, I'm available. My name is Isabel de Saavedra."

Anastasio smiled and raised his arms. "You're the answer to our prayers, child!" he said. "Welcome to the neighbourhood, and to our tavern. You will have noticed the slaughterhouse already, and up the street you'll find the Hospital de la Resurrección, where some of our most illustrious neighbours compete for a place to sleep and a meal to eat," he said with a wink. I nodded; this explained the line-up of people in rags. I liked Anastasio's sense of humour. He continued.

"Having said that, if you do not have an animal to slaughter and don't need charity, but would like to know where the market is, my wife, Prudencia, can help you." Prudencia gave me the warmest of smiles. Perhaps living in Valladolid wouldn't be so bad after all.

"Isabel!" Father's voice was loud enough for me to hear him from the tavern. It was early and there were not many customers. I thanked the taverners and went upstairs. Father stood on the landing outside our new home.

"Sorry, I was introducing myself to our neighbours."

He shook his head. "We need you to help bring some order to the chaos upstairs."

Constanza and my aunts were already inside. They looked troubled.

"Isabel, where were you?" Magdalena called out to me. She was trying to decide where the carriers should place the heavy pieces. She directed them to take Father's desk and bookcase to the room on the left of the foyer. The *bargueño* desk, the chests, the rugs, and all the sewing material were being placed in the room on the right. The *Talavera* was taken past the hallway to the kitchen, which was at the back.

"We left Madrid for this?" Constanza repeated.

I looked around. As far as I could see, besides the foyer, those were the only two rooms: one to the right, with a divided door and a wooden platform framed with tiles, which would be the sewing room, and another to the left, which would be Father's bedroom. All three rooms faced the street and had large windows and thick wooden shutters. As I went in search of the kitchen I passed by our mattresses—three of them in total, piled one on top of the other, the straw and down held inside their fabric sagging already—and arrived at what I guessed was the dining room, our table and chairs having already found their new place. There was a small hatch to allow food to be passed from the kitchen, an opening through which I could see the stove and the bench placed at its side for sitting on a cold winter's day. I looked out the kitchen window and rejoiced when I saw a courtyard with a well and a fountain. At least fetching water would be easy. When Father entered the kitchen and found me at work sorting the pots and pans, he smiled and offered me a hug, which I received like a flower welcomes the sun.

II

CONSTANZA

"PEOPLE OR FLIES," Constanza hissed, shutting the window. "I don't know which is worse! It will be impossible to work in peace here!"

They had arranged the sewing room to resemble the one in Madrid, although this room was smaller and didn't have a mirror. Constanza did not miss it. She could do without confronting her imperfections, and Isabel did not need a reflection of her beauty. Madrid had been a familiar beast in whose chaotic embrace Constanza had learned to find solace. Valladolid was an entirely different animal—and as far as she was concerned, they were trapped in its mangy tail, where the filth accumulated. The clamour from the street started at dawn and grew louder by the hour until darkness lulled insects as well as beggars to sleep. Constanza's back ached, and she was still having trouble getting used to the smells that emanated from everything she saw and touched.

"I think Valladolid is wonderful," said Isabel, as if determined to contradict Constanza's inner thoughts. She sat spinning yarn next to Andrea. Magdalena and Miguel had gone out.

"I think it's amazing that four carts can drive side by side along Calle de la Platería. And there are so many fresh hares, partridges, and quails at the market!"

Constanza took her seat again and shook her head. If only she were as simpleminded as Isabel, everything would be easier.

"There must be thousands of windows and porches at the Plaza Mayor, and they gleam as if they're made of pure gold!" Isabel sounded as gleeful as a little girl. Miguel had taken the family out the day before to explore the city. The streets in the area where they lived were narrow and unpaved, strewn with debris. But when they entered the walled section of the city it was like another world. The roads were clean and wide. Elegantly dressed citizens, many of them transported by *silleros*, circulated in a leisurely fashion as if they were on display. The atmosphere was that of a Sunday or a holiday.

The Cervantes women stood in awe, admiring the luxurious merchandise offered in the shops. How was it possible, Constanza wondered, for these people to be oblivious to the misery that prevailed just outside the city walls? Had everyone already forgotten about the plague? Were they no longer afraid of God? She wanted to ask these questions out loud. But because Miguel was so obviously excited to be here, among fellow poets and playwrights and painters, she kept her concerns to herself. Surely such amnesia, such indifference would inevitably attract divine punishment. She had learned that joy always preceded misfortune.

Constanza tried to focus on her work, but her head was buzzing like the flies with these kinds of thoughts. Once again, she examined her situation. Her hopes of creating a family with Francisco Leal had dissolved in a stream of blood and tears. She had yearned to bear a child who would resemble him. A boy, Francisco Leal de Ovando. Or a girl—would he have wanted to call her Francisca? Or Constanza?

"Constanza de Ovando!" Her mother's voice startled her. "Stop it!"

"Stop what?" Constanza snapped.

"Stop thinking about whatever it is you're thinking. I know that face."

Constanza clenched her teeth. Sometimes she wished she could hide in a room that was shut off from everyone and everything, where she could escape the constant demands of her own head and heart. The sound of the front door relieved her from these ruminations and she rested her needle gratefully.

"I'm home!" Magdalena announced as she made her way towards the sewing room. She was followed by a scraggy looking young woman who had to be their new maid. She must be desperate, Constanza thought, if she accepted the job in exchange for food and board only, especially in this part of town.

"Hello," Andrea said. Constanza bowed her head but barely gave the woman a glance. She had yet to forgive her aunt for the way she had dismissed Teresa.

"Nice to meet you!" cried Isabel, getting up, eager to abandon the task of spinning.

"This is Maria. Isabel, help me to explain to Maria what her duties will be," Magdalena said, heading to the kitchen.

Constanza thought about her uncle. Miguel was still working on his knight's story but he spent his days outside talking to other writers and trying to find a patron. Constanza knew that, as the man of the house, this was what he needed to do, but she resented his freedom and comforts. She now understood why they had been unable to bring their beds—there was simply nowhere to put them! But why did it have to be *he* who slept in the only bedroom in a canopied bed while she continued to share her mattress with Isabel and, this time, it was on the floor, as if they were paupers? How could it be that, no matter how hard they all worked, they never seemed to be able to pay off the family's debts?

The front door opened again and Miguel came in. Constanza was surprised; it was too early for him to be back. Something must be wrong. Her uncle closed the door and came into the sewing room.

"Did you find a patron?" Isabel asked with excitement, rushing in from the kitchen.

"Not exactly," Miguel said. "I need to tell everybody something."

Constanza could read the rhythm of her uncle's voice. She could tell his heart was galloping.

"Isabel, could you please ask the maid to put together some provisions for me? Bread, cheese, and grapes will do. And some wine," he said. Isabel went back to the kitchen to attend to this. She returned shortly.

Miguel closed the doors to the sewing room. Constanza and her mother had remained seated, while Isabel stood near the door and Magdalena stood next to Miguel. This was most unusual. Constanza shivered.

"I need to go back to Esquivias," he said.

"What?" Isabel's voice cracked. "But we just moved here so we could be with you!"

"I know, but I need to tend to some unexpected business."

"What about us?" Constanza asked. For once, she agreed with Isabel. How could he be leaving them already?

"You will remain here, of course. Magdalena, you and Andrea can have my bedroom until I come back."

"And when will you be back?" demanded Andrea, her eyes travelling from Miguel to Isabel to Constanza. She avoided looking at Magdalena, who remained silent.

"I'm not sure," Miguel said wearily.

Isabel's chin trembled and she started to cry. Miguel's expression was hard to read, but he seemed distressed by her tears. He appeared not to notice Constanza, who was making an effort to contain her own sadness.

"Isabel, *hija*, please. Don't cry," Miguel begged her.

"We came here to be together, didn't we? Family first? Or was that another lie?" she flung at him.

"Isabel!" Magdalena exclaimed, but Miguel gestured for her to be quiet.

"I thought you said your wife was coming to live with us," Isabel continued.

"She is. I'll bring her with me when I return."

"And when will that be?"

"It's hard to say. When the book is finished."

Isabel ran to her father and buried her face in his neck, letting out a sob. Miguel held her and caressed her hair, rocking her gently as if soothing a baby.

"I promise I will make it up to you," he said softly.

Make it up to her? *What about me?* Constanza wanted to ask. But she kept silent and looked at them. Isabel seemed inconsolable. Constanza had never seen her cry like this, not even the day she arrived to live with them.

"Isabel, *mi niña*. What can I do to make you stop crying?" Miguel asked. She lifted her head away from his neck so she could look in his eyes.

"Take me with you," she said softly. The meekness in her voice made Constanza's stomach turn. They were behaving as if there was nobody else in the room. Miguel shook his head. Isabel hadn't expected him to deny her, and her cousin could see she was searching for a way to sway him. Could no one else see this? There was a pause, then Isabel's tone of voice changed. It was firm.

"Then let me work at the tavern," she said. It sounded more like a demand than a request. The women let out a joint cry of disapproval.

"That's out of the question!" he said.

"Why? It's just downstairs. I worked in our own tavern for years. What could go wrong?" Isabel wiped her eyes with the back of her hand. Miguel looked torn.

"A lot could go wrong."

"A lot can go wrong even if you only go out to church."

"What do you mean?"

Andrea stretched out her arm and took her daughter's hand. Constanza held her breath.

"I mean I will be careful. May I please help out at the tavern?"

"Absolutely not!" Magdalena had finally had enough. Her eyes were on fire. "Miguel, someone must be reasonable here. As Isabel's legal guardian, I refuse to let her work at any tavern. And I will take no responsibility over whatever happens to her if you agree to this folly."

Miguel was silent for a moment, perhaps choosing his words carefully. Then he spoke quietly but with conviction.

"Isabel grew up in a tavern, Magdalena. I trust she knows how to handle herself."

Constanza couldn't believe her ears. She had never heard

her uncle contradict his sister this way. Now Magdalena's anger turned to despair.

"All the work I did teaching her to behave like a lady will go to waste if she returns to that world," she said sadly. But Isabel shook her head and faced her aunt, her eyes pleading.

"I promise I will behave just the way you taught me, Aunt Magdalena."

The five family members remained in their places. The sun had found narrow gaps in the window coverings and the temperature seemed to rise. Drops of sweat shone on Constanza's forehead. It was only early afternoon, but the day felt endless.

Miguel finally spoke again. "Isabel, you may help in the tavern—but only during daylight hours, and only after you've completed all your duties here at home. The moment it gets dark, you come back upstairs." Isabel's face broke into a smile.

"And something else," he added. "If I hear any complaints about you from anyone in this house or elsewhere, your privileges will be over."

"Thank you, Father," Isabel said, embracing him once again.

Magdalena and Andrea exited the sewing room in indignation without a backwards glance. Miguel and Isabel stood together silently while Constanza stared at the window, focusing on a single fly that buzzed fruitlessly against the glass, feeling more than ever alive without a purpose, unheard, unseen.

III

ISABEL

NOW THAT I had my father's permission to work at the tavern, in just a few weeks I began a new routine that offered me some respite from the suffocating tedium of the sewing room, which always made me feel like an insect caught in a spider's web. The block of houses where we lived was home to families who dedicated themselves to a wide variety of activities. Some men were *hidalgos* who led a leisurely life. Others worked as clerks in government offices or banks; still others were merchants. The women spent their days taking care of children and cooking, sewing, and knitting—although none were as talented and successful as my aunts and my cousin. While Valladolid seemed to welcome more people every day, I soon learned to identify the faces of our neighbours as I walked past the Puerta del Campo to go to the market or to mass at Nuestra Señora de San Llorente.

Once I had purchased our food for the day, or the taffeta, silk, or linen required to fill our sewing orders, I went downstairs to Anastasio and Prudencia's tavern and helped them measure the wine they sold to the nearby households. I enjoyed the dimly lit space, the sound of people laughing and cups hitting the tables, and the smell of wine and tobacco that helped mask the stench emanating from the slaughterhouse.

"Isabel, help yourself to a glass on the house," Anastasio would urge me.

"*Gracias*, but wine gives me a headache."

Anastasio laughed. He must have known I was simply following my mother's rules. Mother never drank when she worked. Now that I was older I understood how vigilant I had to be to protect myself and focus on my duties.

One afternoon, as I was about to go back upstairs, I noticed that a well-dressed young man was looking at me intently. I looked back at him and we both smiled.

"I would like a glass of wine, Your Majesty, if you please," he said, approaching me. He had an accent that I couldn't place.

"Not until you tell me where you are from, my loyal subject," I said, playing along.

"Your most loyal subject is from Portugal. At thy feet, Majesty."

"I am pleased to meet you, my most loyal Portuguese subject."

He took off his hat. "My name is Simón Méndez."

I gave a small bow, as my aunt had taught me. "My name is Isabel," I said simply.

"A name and manners worthy of a queen!" he exclaimed. Simón had a well-trimmed beard, brown curls, and green eyes. He took my hand in his and planted a wet kiss that would have horrified Magdalena but for some reason did not disgust me. Just as he did this, Alicia de Ayala, the nosy prude who lived in the attic above, passed by the open doors. She stopped and stared. My aunts and I often crossed paths with her on our way to run errands.

"Well, if it isn't one of the Cervantes sisters, out on the

street as usual!" she would say in a nasty, insinuating tone. We tried to avoid her, but it wasn't easy since she spent most of the day sitting by the front door, watching the residents come and go.

Anxious not to give the spinster a reason to gossip about me, I pulled back my hand quickly and slapped Simón on the face before Alicia de Ayala disappeared up the staircase to the upper floors. Simón's hand was on his cheek as I quickly tried to explain myself.

"I didn't mean to do that, but the nosiest woman in the neighbourhood just saw you kiss my hand. I work as a maid for the family upstairs, and I don't want her talking to my employers about me."

"How can anyone as sophisticated as you be a maid?" he asked in surprise. His accent was really quite charming.

"What do you mean, sophisticated?"

"Your manners—the way you stand and walk and speak are not the manners of a maid. Unless you are lying to me, which would break my heart, Your Majesty."

I laughed. Magdalena's lessons had been useful, after all! He took my hand in his again and I felt myself tremble slightly.

"I should go back upstairs now," I said. "Good evening, Simón Méndez, my most loyal Portuguese subject."

He bowed. "Good evening, Isabel ..." he looked at me questioningly.

"Isabel de Saavedra," I said, giving a curtsey.

"What a lovely name! Good evening, Isabel de Saavedra. We shall meet again, you have my word."

IV

December 1603
My dearest Miguel,

May this letter find you and Catalina in good health and surrounded by blessings. I cannot believe it has been almost five months since you went to Esquivias. How far along is your book now? This is going to be the longest piece of writing you have ever produced.

I am writing to you with my worries for Isabel. All the progress we made in three years of hard work in Madrid has been lost during her time at the tavern. I admit that she has been responsible with her duties and never stays out once it's dark; in that regard, she has obeyed your rules. There are rumours, however, that she is seeing a foreigner, a Portuguese merchant. Isabel denied this, and I have no proof. But you know what they say: *cuando el río suena* ... There is a reason for the river to roar.

Anastasio and Prudencia are good people, but Prudencia looks too much like a Moor for her own good. I fear what the Inquisition would do to her if she were to find herself in trouble, and how that might affect Isabel, even if she only works for them as a *medidora*. In short, dear brother, I think it is necessary for you to come back and take matters into your own hands. You are the man of the family, after all.

I have yet no response to my queries about the pay still owed to Rodrigo, and no matter how many times I write to them or go to their office, the answer from those bureaucrats is still the same: the matter is being looked into, come back tomorrow. I have been there almost every tomorrow since you left, and I fear we will not live long enough to reach the tomorrow when they will finally have an answer for us.

Please stay well and consider returning immediately to us in Valladolid. We moved here to be with you, yet we do not have your company. Come back to us safely—and with a finished book.

Your loving sister,
Magdalena

V

CATALINA

Eia ergo, Advocáta nostra,
Illos tuos misericórdes óculos ad nos convérte:
Et Iesum, benedíctum fructum ventris tui,
Nobis post hoc exsílium osténde.
O clemens, o pia, o dulcis Virgo María.

HAIL, HOLY QUEEN, mother of mercy, thank you for answering my prayers. My beloved husband has finished his book, and what a splendid book it is! What does it matter if it is written in the language of everyday people instead of sophisticated verses full of artifice, wordplay, and metaphors? You have watched my Miguel agonize over this! Holy Virgin Mary, Mother of God, please protect my husband and ensure that the people he mocks in the book never read it, and if they do read it, that they do not realize they are the ones depicted, especially my neighbours in Esquivias.

Cover my Miguel with your sacred veil so that people see only the good in him and his words and rejoice in them the way I do. Help him receive the patronage he seeks from the Duke of Bexar so that, when it is ready, his book is granted permission to be printed. You, who sees everything, please make those clerics who inspect the manuscripts understand the good in Miguel's intentions and allow his words to flourish. Grant *Don Quixote* the gift of satisfying the Crown's censors! Please help my Miguel succeed, dear Mother of God. And help me as well as I fight my own fight. A wife should not be left perpetually alone. I want to see what he sees and touch what he touches. I want to share his mornings and his nights every morning and every night. What else is a marriage for if not this tangling of arms and legs and breath in search of the fruit of our love? He argues that the journey from Esquivias to Valladolid is too long and hard for a woman, especially in these early months of the year when it is still cold and the wind shows no mercy. But if his sisters could travel from Madrid to establish themselves in Valladolid, why can I not do the same? How am I different from them? My youth, if anything, makes me stronger.

Forgive me, Holy Mother of God, if I offend You. But I felt I had to make my determination clear, to take matters into my own hands. This dawn, I caressed Miguel as he was waking and asked him to remain in bed a little longer. I placed my head on his chest and closed my eyes to listen to his heartbeat. I swear by Your grace that there is no sweeter sound in the world than the beating heart of Miguel. I caressed him and listened to his heart beating faster and faster until I knew he could not wait anymore, and I guided him so he could become flesh of my flesh, our bodies a single wave. And then, fully aware that He views the ends of the earth and sees everything under the heavens, I pushed Miguel away at the very moment when I knew he was the most vulnerable, betraying my most sacred duty as his wife. Intercede in my favour, Holy Virgin Mary, so I am forgiven for closing my legs and telling Miguel that we would not be husband and wife anymore, not like that, not ever again, unless he took me with him to Valladolid.

VI

ISABEL

"WHAT DID SIMÓN give you yesterday?" Prudencia kept her voice low. She was the only one who knew he was courting me. Aware of the risks to my reputation and wanting to heed Father's warning, I had been careful not to give in to Simón's advances too quickly, but I didn't know what I liked more—the taste of his lips after he had been smoking his pipe or the presents he sometimes surprised me with. Prudencia and I were in the courtyard at the back of the house, just below my kitchen window, so I had to be careful not to speak too loudly.

"A pearl necklace," I said, smiling as I poured water from the well into the bucket I would bring back home. It was never windy in the courtyard, but it was cold. Although I was wearing my wool cape, my fingers felt numb. "It's too bad I have to hide it."

"One day you will wear it in front of everyone, Isabel, you'll see," Prudencia said.

"He's leaving tomorrow morning for Portugal," I confided. "He says he'll miss me."

"And you, will you miss him, too?"

"Of course I will! But I didn't tell him that! A queen has to keep her loyal subjects under control," I said with a laugh.

"That man is besotted with you, Isabel. Don't be too hard on him," she admonished.

I wiped my hands dry on my apron, then brought them to my mouth and blew air on them, warming my fingers. Wanting to return to the coziness of the kitchen and the braziers, I picked up my bucket of water and steadied myself to bring it upstairs.

"I like him, too, Prudencia, but—"

I never had a chance to complete the thought. Suddenly, from the window above, Aunt Magdalena's voice called out to me, "Miguel has arrived. Miguel is here! And he brought Catalina!"

I let go of the bucket, dropping it on my foot. Cold water splashed on my skirt and our feet. Prudencia picked it up, half-full. I cried out in pain, but also with fear. Father was back, and he had brought his wife with him! I had been waiting for this moment for so long, and now here it was. If only I had known they were coming I would at least have tried to tidy myself a little, ensuring that my clothes were clean and dry. I had never thought of it in these terms before, but now that Catalina was here, I knew that I wanted her to like me. I had missed Father. I *needed* her to like me.

"I'm sorry," I said, trying to wring out Prudencia's skirt and my own, ashamed of my clumsiness.

"I can help you carry the water upstairs. You must say hello to your father."

Her words startled me. "How do you know? I never told you."

"You didn't need to."

I closed my mouth tightly, unsure of how to react or what to say. I looked up at the upstairs window. It was closed.

"I can take it myself. It's no trouble," I said, waving good-bye to Prudencia before picking up the bucket and hurrying towards the stairs. At our front door, I stopped to push a few strands of hair back in place and examine my throbbing foot. It was swelling up, and I could feel a bruise announcing itself already. Why did I have to be this clumsy today of all days? My eyes welled up, but I didn't know if it was the physical pain or the anguish brewing in my chest. How would Catalina de Salazar y Palacios react when she saw me? Had Father told her about my existence already, or was I supposed to continue posing as the family's maid? I felt like one of those stray dogs that ran wild in the streets and feared people but also longed to find a master and a place they could call home. Hearing Magdalena and Andrea's voices rising excitedly on the other side of the door, I took a deep breath, exhaled slowly, and let myself in.

When I saw Catalina standing next to my aunts I was transfixed by her beauty. A cascade of golden ringlets adorned her head, and she was still wearing an exquisite *ferreruelo de camino* made of leather and wool, which must have protected her well during her journey. As I took a few steps into the foyer, she looked in my direction. The moment she saw my face, her gaze hardened, her back stiffened. It was as if she was growling silently.

Father kissed Constanza's forehead, and before he even made a move in my direction, I put the bucket on the floor and curtsied to signal my status as a servant. Why would he hug a maid? Father seemed taken aback for a moment but then, as if grateful for the cue, he extended his arm towards Catalina.

"Catalina, this is Isabel."

"We took her in as a second maid, remember?" Constanza

said, not looking at me. I didn't know what hurt me more—my cousin's words or my father's silence. I would have spoken then, but Catalina's eyes pierced me and left me paralyzed.

"It has been wonderful having her," Andrea said. She came over and rubbed my back, the way she used to in Madrid when I was younger. "She's been a great addition to our household." The festive air in the room had completely dissipated, and despite Andrea's efforts, I felt like a dog that has been kicked for pestering people. I found my legs, but it took all my strength to control my urge to run away howling. Instead, I had to muster intelligible words to find my way out.

"I still have chores to complete downstairs. May I please be excused?" I asked.

My father and my aunts exchanged glances, but he avoided my eyes.

"I'm sure that's perfectly fine, Isabel. Right, Uncle Miguel?" Constanza said. Without waiting for an answer, I curtsied again and, hiding my mantilla, ran down the stairs as fast as my swollen foot allowed. By the time I reached the open field on the other side of the river, I was out of breath and my foot was throbbing. I fell on my knees, sobbing, hating Catalina but hating myself even more for harbouring hope that I would ever fully belong to that family, that I could be my father's daughter openly, that I could become a Cervantes.

VII

CONSTANZA

"THAT GIRL WAS no maid!" Catalina's face was flushed and her breath quickened.

"Catalina, allow me to explain—" said Miguel anxiously.

"Explain what?" Catalina looked at each of the women in turn before her eyes settled back on her husband. "How you told your family to lie to me all these years?"

"The girl is ..." Miguel broke off. Suddenly he seemed older and frailer than before. Constanza could barely look at him, and she was too ashamed to look at Catalina.

"The girl is *what*, Miguel? Did you think I wouldn't notice?" Tears rolled down Catalina's cheeks. She resembled a plaster statue of a saint, delicate and doleful.

"I knew this would not end well," Magdalena whispered to Andrea, but her voice was loud enough for the others to hear. Constanza shook her head. This was the last thing they needed.

Catalina turned her head. "And Magdalena, *you* of all people, how could you lie to me? In all the letters you wrote, you concealed this girl's existence!"

"It was not my place to tell you, Catalina, and she only—"

Catalina cut in. "You're right, it was my husband's place to tell me that a daughter *I knew nothing about* was living under his roof! Under *my* roof!" She opened her arms as if to encompass the entire apartment. "How could you do this to me, Miguel?" Covering her face with her hands, she ran into the bedroom, slamming the door behind her.

"Go talk to her," Magdalena whispered to her brother.

Miguel shook his head. "She will never forgive me."

"You must try," she said, gently pushing him towards the bedroom and gesturing for Constanza and Andrea to go into the sewing room. They heard the bedroom door open and close. Constanza was about to pick up the bucket of water Isabel had left by the door when Magdalena took her by the arm.

"Why did you speak that way?" she said in an angry whisper.

"What way?" Constanza whispered back, pulling her arm out of her aunt's grasp.

"Don't play that game with me, young lady," Magdalena shot back, her eyes piercing her niece's face. "Introducing Isabel to Catalina like that."

"Like what? Wasn't it *your* idea to bring Isabel into our family by pretending she was a maid?"

Andrea approached them gently. "Shh! This is not the time to—"

"How can I ever trust you again, Miguel? How?" Catalina's breaking voice could be heard as clearly as if she were standing next to them in the room. The three women stood still, as quiet as possible.

"Remember when you first arrived in Esquivias, Miguel? I was eighteen years old, *eighteen*! I have never known any man but you! And now I discover you have a grown-up daughter you never even mentioned?"

Instead of going into the sewing room, the women approached the bedroom door. Constanza knew that eaves-dropping was wrong, but Catalina was speaking so loudly it was impossible not to listen. She hoped that neither Maria, who was in the kitchen, nor the neighbours could hear the conversation, too.

"I was so naive then, believing you actually cared about me! Talking to you in Latin to impress you, enthralled by your stories about the war and your escape from Algiers, so in awe of the five hundred ducats in gold your family had struggled to scrape together as ransom for your return! I remember thinking: *this* is a family I would be honoured to belong to. A family that knows what loyalty means. Can you imagine?"

Constanza, Magdalena, and Andrea looked at one another, feeling the pain in Catalina's words. Like a wounded animal, she was lashing out at everyone and everything. Ruefully, Constanza reflected that she understood how her aunt was feeling. She knew that no amount of shouting and crying could lighten the weight of betrayal.

"My mother tried to warn me about you. She said I should distrust your constant comings and goings to Madrid, that all you wanted was my money and my land!" Magdalena held her fist to her mouth, and for a moment Constanza was afraid her aunt might burst into the room to defend her brother. But at that moment, Catalina's yelling gave way to sobbing, and Magdalena didn't move. Through her tears, Catalina went on.

"Do you know why I didn't listen to her? Because I fell in love with you! Because you fed me grapes from my vineyard and kissed me on the lips. I felt like a goddess because you christened my skin as your 'New World'! And—"

Then came a pause during which all they could hear was muffled sound. Constanza imagined her uncle hugging Catalina, rocking back and forth with her the way he had done with Isabel. Andrea made a gesture for Constanza and Magdalena to move away from the door. Should Miguel or Catalina suddenly open it, things would be even worse. Constanza knew this, and she was sure her aunt did, too, but they both remained like statues at the door. Andrea stood a few steps back, unsure whether to go to the sewing room or stay with the others.

"A taverner? *A taverner!*" Now Catalina let out another cry. "So you came to Esquivias to tell me you loved me, and then you went back to the taverner to make a child with her?" Constanza bit her lip. She didn't dare to look at her aunt or her mother. Her feet were glued to the floor and her heart was racing.

"How old is she now?" Catalina asked, a little more quietly.

"Eighteen."

"The same age that I was when you and I met. And what was her mother like?"

"She was ..." Miguel paused. How could a man who was so good with words have such difficulty speaking? "Strong."

"Stronger than me?"

"She was nothing like you."

"Dulcinea and Aldonza, right?"

"Catalina, my book has nothing to do with any of this. Yes, Dulcinea's beauty and virtuosity are inspired by you, but that's as far as it goes."

"No. It's not. You know that's a lie. People who we know are in that book. My neighbours in Esquivias. Your niece. Me. You, the eternally errant man. And your lover."

"Catalina, stop. She meant nothing to me," Miguel said bitterly.

"I don't believe you. Stop lying! I want the truth now. I deserve the truth."

Constanza nodded. Catalina was right. Her mother and her aunt were nodding, too.

"I met her before I met you," Miguel explained. "Before I even knew you existed. And she was married."

"Married?"

"Yes. Her husband was old."

"How old? As old as you?"

Constanza could tell the barb had hit home. Her aunt gave a barely audible gasp.

"She didn't love him," Miguel continued to explain.

"But she loved you. She gave birth to your daughter."

"It wasn't like that."

"No? Are you saying that while you were courting me you didn't go back to her?"

"I stopped seeing her once you and I were engaged."

"And the girl was born when?"

"In April."

"And we were married when?"

"The following December. Why are you asking me these questions, Catalina?"

"Because I want to understand. We got engaged in the summer. How many times did you see her before then? And after?"

"I saw her when I met the baby," Miguel said. Constanza almost pitied her uncle, but Catalina was not ready to let go.

"Don't play games with me, you know exactly what I mean," she said, her voice vibrating with anger.

"I saw her a few times."

"A few times! Did her husband find out you were lovers?"

"She never mentioned it. I stopped seeing her and only gave her money to help raise the child."

"And then you rushed our wedding because it offered you the perfect escape from that responsibility."

"I did not escape anything!" Miguel protested.

"Yes, you did. You escaped your lover, your child, your debts, your sisters, and your niece. You hid inside my house, inside my bed, inside my soul, and then you betrayed me."

Constanza's mouth dropped open. She had never imagined that a woman could speak this way to her husband—that a woman could speak like this at all. Any other man would have raised his hand, but not her uncle Miguel. Catalina was taking advantage of him, just like Isabel.

"But I didn't escape. I fell in love with you," he said quietly.

"When your daughter comes back, bring her in, Miguel." There was another pause, a moment of silence during which Constanza silently prayed that the two might be making up. Perhaps he was caressing her hair or giving her a kiss. But then Catalina cried out, shattering her hopes.

"Don't touch me! Don't you dare touch me again!"

As if this were their cue to retreat, the women stepped away from the door and tiptoed into the sewing room. Constanza was working on a special order, a *cartón de pecho*. The garment, when worn together with a farthingale, made a woman's waist look smaller. But she couldn't even think of picking up the piece now. Feeling nauseous, as if she had ingested something that had gone bad, she sat still and avoided looking at her mother and her aunt.

"I'll go fetch Isabel. She should come home now,"

Magdalena whispered, heading to the foyer to grab her mantilla. "Constanza, ask Maria to prepare some chamomile tea. I think we'll all need it tonight. Andrea, you should lie down, you look unwell. I'll be right back."

Constanza picked up the bucket Isabel had left by the front door and made her way to the kitchen. Her mind was racing with thoughts and questions. At least Catalina had enjoyed many years of happiness with Uncle Miguel, she reflected. Those days and nights had to count for something. True, her uncle had fathered an illegitimate child, but so had countless other married men all over the country. There was nothing rare about the situation. But after the altercation they had just heard, the atmosphere in the home seemed menacing, as if a terrible storm were on its way. Constanza understood that she had witnessed the first real fracture in the Cervantes family, and she was afraid that it might be impossible to heal.

VIII

CATALINA

Confíteor Deo omnipoténti,
beátæ Maríæ semper Vírgini,
beáto Michaéli Archángelo,
beáto Joanni Baptístæ,
sanctis Apóstolis Petro et Paulo,
ómnibus Sanctis, et tibi, Pater:
quia peccávi nimis cogitatióne, verbo et ópere:
mea culpa, mea culpa, mea máxima culpa.

HAIL MARY, FULL of grace, the Lord is with You, but He has abandoned me. I am the most wretched of creatures and need your guidance, your strength, your compassion, your help to extinguish the fire of hatred that is consuming my heart. How am I supposed to accept living under the same roof with my husband's bastard daughter, the child he planted in another woman's womb?

I can't stop thinking of the day Miguel and I walked through my vineyard, assessing the firmness of the grapes. When I took one and placed it in his mouth, he kissed my fingers. Then he picked a bunch of grapes and, after wiping them against his shirt, doled them out—one for me, one for him. How his touch made me tremble! Until that day, we had done no more than hold hands. But now, taking my chin in his hand, he kissed me on the lips. So our first kisses tasted like grapes. What did hers taste like? What did she smell like? Not like fresh grapes, no. I was grapes. She was wine.

Holy Virgin, Mother of God, help me, for when I close my eyes all I can see is Miguel with Ana Franca. His mouth exploring her body, her legs around his hips. His child alive under her skin, while my body remains dry and fruitless. If only the child had been brought to me as a baby, perhaps I would have forgiven him. I might have been able to raise her as my own and love her. But how am I to welcome a daughter who is already a woman?—a woman who grew up in a tavern and has none of the innocence that was mine at that age. A stranger who looks exactly like the man I love more than anything, who will remind me of his unfaithfulness every time I look at her? It is too great a trial for this, Your weak, most humble crusader. Hail Mary, full of grace, the Lord is with You. I plead with You to ask Him to be with me, too.

IX

❧❧❧❧❧❧❧❧

ISABEL

PRUDENCIA APPLIED A poultice to my foot, which was swollen and purple and gave me a valid reason to cry so I wouldn't have to explain what was happening. It wasn't my story to tell.

Some time later, Magdalena came down to look for me, and I limped back up behind her without protest. With the memory of Constanza's hurtful words and Catalina's hate-filled eyes so fresh in my mind, I prayed I would be allowed to head straight to bed without talking to anyone. When I entered the kitchen, I realized no one had eaten. The cheese, the ham, even the bread that Maria had served was still untouched. My aunts and my cousin were silent, moving about as if they didn't want to attract any attention, almost as if someone had died.

I couldn't eat either before going to bed, so I was simply sitting by the stove, focusing on the soothing sounds and warmth of the fire, when Father came and beckoned me to come to his room. Seeing as I had no choice, and full of apprehension, I followed him.

The room was in disarray and smelled strongly of melted wax. Had it been dark for so long? Catalina sat on the bed, her face mottled and her eyes puffy. It was hard to believe that this was the same haughty woman I had thought so beautiful only hours earlier.

"I asked your father to call you, Isabel." Her voice was heavy and she sounded exhausted. "We need to talk."

I looked at Father, but he avoided my eyes. I curtsied to Catalina.

"Yes, Madam. At your service," I said.

"You don't have to pretend to be a maid anymore. Call me Catalina."

"Catalina." Her name tasted bitter in my mouth.

"I'm a good Christian, Isabel. An old Christian. And I try as best as I can to follow our Lord's teachings."

I didn't know what to say, so I looked at the floor.

"We will be living under the same roof. You must address Miguel as your father because that is who he is." I felt a slight relief, and raised my head to look at her. Catalina continued.

"You can stop dressing like a maid. You will have a wardrobe like Constanza's. And your father will procure you a dowry. But—" she paused. "There is always a *but* in life, isn't there? Especially for us women. You love someone *but* they betray you. You yearn for something *but* you can't have it." I felt like a band was closing around my throat as Catalina finished speaking. "You will not receive a single ducat from my estate, and you shall never bear your father's last name."

X

CONSTANZA

FOR WEEKS, MIGUEL made every effort to make Catalina happy and regain her trust. He took her to the nicest places in the city and consulted with her regarding every decision. His sisters did all they could to make her feel she was the centre of attention. When Isabel was in the room Miguel was courteous, but he didn't engage her in conversation or sit close to her. Constanza hoped that Catalina would forgive him soon; watching her uncle in the role of repentant, servile husband made her uncomfortable. Pondering how she could make their situation better, Constanza offered to attend midmorning mass with Catalina at the church of Nuestra Señora de San Llorente.

At the ringing of the first bell, the two set off for church. Constanza tried to broach the subject of Isabel several times, but Catalina politely changed the subject. After mass, Catalina would visit her friend Juana Gaitán or other neighbours from Esquivias whose apartments were only a block away. She was homesick, she said, and enjoyed spending a few hours a day with familiar faces. So Constanza went home to continue her sewing.

One afternoon, after leaving her aunt at her friend Juana's, Constanza entered the tavern instead of heading home. She knew that it was too early for Isabel to be there. The smell of tobacco, wine, and sweat almost made her gag. How could her cousin stand it here? Lifting her mantilla, she squinted as her eyes adjusted to the dimness and searched for Prudencia. Some of the customers who sat talking and drinking stared at her in surprise—a lady was out of place there. One of them even dared to offer her a seat beside him. Constanza would have left in a panic if Prudencia hadn't caught sight of her and come to her rescue. Approaching the man who had spoken to Constanza, she reprimanded him.

"Be quiet, Juan! Leave the lady alone. She lives upstairs and is Isabel's cousin."

The young man smiled, got up from the table, and approached Constanza. "All the more reason to want to meet her, then," he said.

Prudencia slapped him playfully on the arm. "That isn't funny, Juanito," she admonished.

"I'm not trying to be funny," he protested. "It isn't every day that a lady walks into this place. I meant no offence," he said, bowing to Constanza.

Prudencia rolled her eyes. "Go back to your seat." Juan ignored her.

"Juan Jiménez at your feet, Señorita," he said, taking Constanza's hand. His skin was soft—it was clear he didn't do any hard labour—and she was ashamed of her own calloused fingertips. He must be a merchant, she decided.

"Constanza de Ovando," she said, then immediately regretted revealing her name. What was she doing talking to a stranger? Hadn't she learned her lesson? And in a tavern, too! Her mother would never allow her to leave the house unchaperoned if she found out.

The man's smile set her cheeks on fire, but there was something impish about his face that made her shiver. He didn't have a foreign accent, so he couldn't be the merchant her mother and Magdalena had been talking about the other day.

"Enough, Juanito!" Prudencia gestured for Constanza to follow her to the back of the tavern. "Please forgive him, Señorita Constanza. Juan's problem is that he always speaks his mind, but he's harmless. How can I help you?"

"I came here to talk about Isabel," Constanza said.

Just as she had expected, Prudencia became defensive. She frowned and crossed her arms over her chest. "What about her?"

"I don't know if she's told you about the situation at home …" she began cautiously. Prudencia shook her head. Constanza suspected the woman was lying, but she played along. "She's not speaking to me. She's not speaking to anyone except about basic, everyday things—food, chores."

"She speaks to everyone here just as usual," Prudencia declared. Constanza's hands were shaking. Coming here had been a mistake. How could she expect the taverner to understand what she was talking about? Since Catalina's arrival, Constanza had been trying to make up with her cousin. Magdalena and Andrea were going to great lengths to make Isabel feel included. Now that there was no need for her to dress like a maid, they chose beautiful fabrics to sew new dresses for her. They prepared her favourite dish, *olla podrida*. But Isabel didn't seem to recognize their efforts. At the dinner table, when Miguel shared anecdotes about other writers he had mingled with that day, she remained detached, there in body but not in soul. Even when he shared the great news—his new book would be printed by the famous Juan de la Cuesta in Madrid—Isabel barely smiled. Constanza wanted things to be as they were before—before Catalina, before Valladolid. Before Francisco Leal. She had made so many sacrifices for her family! Now the conflict between Isabel and Catalina was ruining her days and keeping her up at night.

"Could you please tell her that I miss her? That we *all* miss her?" Constanza asked Prudencia, wringing her hands. As the taverner uncrossed her arms, Constanza caught a glimpse in her eyes of the gentleness that Isabel frequently spoke about. Constanza had always been skeptical—this new Christian was, after all, a Moor.

"I'll see what I can do," she said. "But now, if you'll excuse me ..." Prudencia led Constanza back down the hall.

In order to reach the stairs to the apartments, it was necessary for Constanza to pass through the tavern again. As she came in, she paused. The man called Juan was sitting in the same spot as before, and he caught her eye as soon as she stepped into the room. With a smile, he lifted his glass to her and said some words she was unable to hear. But she could read his lips: *To you, beautiful Constanza*. She rushed to the exit so quickly that she collided with a woman who was coming down the stairs.

"Pardon me, I'm sorry!" Constanza said, and then she realized it was Alicia de Ayala, the gossip from the top floor. The woman smiled maliciously.

"Well, well, if it's not another one of the Cervantes ladies! They seem to be attracted to that place of perdition." Constanza hurried past her without another word.

XI

ISABEL

"LOOK AT YOU, dressed like a queen! Queen Isabel!"

I couldn't believe my eyes when Simón Méndez walked into the tavern. He had been gone so long I had almost forgotten him completely.

"I missed you!" he said with a big smile. As if not a day had gone by, he reached for my hand, but I took a step back. Now that Catalina was living with us and some of her friends from Esquivias had become our neighbours, I was not allowed to do any cleaning or serving at the tavern, but when it was quiet and there were few customers I was allowed to visit Prudencia. The tavern had acquired a mascot, a grey cat that had walked in one day and declared the place was his home. Prudencia had named him Sombra, and I had become very fond of him.

"I'm sorry I disappeared like that, my Queen," Simón Méndez said, looking into my eyes. "I had to prolong my stay in Portugal and I've been travelling since then. Only now was I able to return."

He was carrying a large canvas bag, which he dropped at my feet. When I started to move away from the bag, he grabbed my hand and kissed it. The feeling of his lips immediately took me back to the afternoons we had spent together before. It was hard to pull my hand away, but I did. He had no right to a warm welcome.

"Isabel, allow me to explain. The peace measures enacted by the Duke of Lerma gave rise to opportunities never seen before. I had to go to Portugal and then to Italy to take care of business. But I returned as soon as I possibly could."

"Congratulations," I said cooly. Did he think he was talking to an ignorant girl? I was aware of the latest peace treaty, of course. Father couldn't stop talking about it—how, after almost three decades of war, the treaty between Spain and England would allow our Empire to flourish. He was so optimistic about the future and about his new book, and so busy catering to Catalina's every whim, or eating and drinking with other writers, that he didn't pay attention to anything else. Particularly me.

I turned my back on Simón and tried to walk away from him. But he reached out, gently pulled me closer, and spoke into my ear. I could feel the warmth of his body, and his beard tickled my neck.

"I thought of you every day and every night, my queen. I brought you presents. Please hear me out, give me a chance to prove how much you mean to me. Is there somewhere private where we can talk?"

I turned my face to him and our lips almost touched. A shiver went down my spine.

"Let me ask Prudencia," I said. Simón took my face between his hands and gave me a look that made my legs weak. I broke away to find my friend behind the bar.

"I see your Simón is back, *guapa*," she said with a wink. I knew I was blushing and I couldn't hide my smile.

"Is there a place where we can talk alone?" I whispered. Prudencia discreetly put her hand into the neck of her blouse and withdrew a key.

"Let yourselves into my apartment. I'll make sure Anastasio stays busy and no one bothers you. But don't take too long!" She placed the key in the palm of my hand and closed my fingers over it. "Don't forget that you're the one who holds the key. That applies to the door and to everything else," she said, giving me a serious look. I nodded. I could feel her eyes on me as I approached Simón and quietly gave him the instructions.

Five minutes later we were inside the apartment, and Simón's hands and mouth were making me forget I had ever been angry at him. My body yearned for his, but I wasn't going to give in easily. I still had my honour to think of. When he asked me to remove my corselet so he could touch my breasts, I pushed him back.

"I have to go," I said. It was starting to get dark, and I would need to be home soon.

"No, please. I'll do whatever you want if you stay a little longer."

"Whatever I want?"

"Yes. And I still need to give you your presents."

"All right, let's start with that," I said, adjusting my dress, which was in disarray. Simón let out a deep sigh and reached for his bag. We arranged ourselves on a carpet on the floor, and he took out the gifts from the bag one by one.

"I brought you a present from every single place I stayed," he announced. "Lace from Flanders," he said, placing a beautiful piece of ivory lace in my hand. "Wool from Italy," he said, taking out an exquisite shawl. "Silk from the Chinese merchants in Portugal. I also have a gold bracelet and pearl earrings." The piece of lace was still in my hand as he brought out these items and put them side by side on the carpet.

I had never seen so many beautiful objects on their own, let alone together. I was mesmerized. "All of this is for me?" I said weakly.

"And you deserve more, Isabel. No one in the entire world is as beautiful as you. I can attest to that. I would give you my life if I could."

"Then give it to me. Let's get married!" The words burst out of their own accord, and I regretted saying them the instant they left my mouth. Simón's expression changed from euphoria to disappointment. He looked down at the floor.

"I would love to marry you, Isabel. But—" he paused and remained quiet.

"Forget I said anything!" I cried out, deeply ashamed. What on Earth had possessed me? Now I would have to confess at Sunday mass, and I had no idea how I was going to explain my behaviour to the priest. "I can't accept your gifts. I need to go." He grabbed my arm.

"Isabel, I would marry you right away if I could, but I have a wife already."

My mouth dropped and I sat still, stunned. I should have known, of course. My joy and desire suddenly transformed into rage.

"Get away from me, Simón. Go back to your wife!" I practically spat the words at him.

"No, that's what I wanted to tell you. I won't be going back to her. I returned to Valladolid to be with you. Come and live with me. I will take care of your every need and protect you forever." He gazed at me, distraught.

His proposal took me by surprise. Since I could not have

my father's last name, I dreamed of one day bearing the name of my husband. Living with a man who couldn't give me his name was not at all appealing. Besides, it was illegal. But living under the same roof as Catalina while I waited for my family to arrange a suitable marriage was not tolerable either.

Simón had not taken his eyes off me.

"I will think about it," I said. I put my hand briefly between his legs as if to promise that his patience would be rewarded.

XII

CONSTANZA

IT WAS CONVENIENT for Constanza that Catalina liked to spend time with her friend Juana Gaitán every day after church. Miguel had gone to Madrid to arrange the publication of his book, so his wife had lots of free time. The two women had developed a routine. They walked the few blocks to church together. Then, after mass, Catalina turned down the street that led to Juana's house while Constanza walked the last steps home alone.

One day, as Constanza passed in front of the tavern on the way to her apartment, she saw Juan standing outside. She ignored him and went up the stairs. The next day, he was there again. This time he looked at her with a smile and bowed his head. Constanza thought it would be polite to acknowledge his greeting, so she bowed in return. After a few days of this, Juan came up to her and said hello; Constanza said hello in return. Then she continued up the stairs, chastising herself for feeling slightly lightheaded. She had to be careful, she reminded herself as she entered the foyer and shut the door. She put away her mantilla and went into the kitchen.

Isabel was sitting at the dining room table holding a quill pen and looking over a pile of papers.

"Hello. Where are the others?" Constanza inquired.

"They've gone out to run errands. I need to make the tax calculations," Isabel explained. Constanza let out a sigh as she sat down across from her cousin. She seemed so grown up now, surrounded by receipts and other documents covered with numbers. She looked alert and clever and beautiful. Her hair fell down her back like a waterfall, her cheeks were rosy. *If Isabel were a flower*, Constanza thought, *she would be a lovely rose about to bloom*. She decided to speak her mind.

"I'm sorry about the way I behaved. And I'm sorry Catalina is being so harsh with you. It's not your fault," she said. Isabel put down the pen and looked at her cousin in surprise.

"I'm sorry, too," she said quietly. There was a pause during which Constanza considered whether she should make a physical gesture towards Isabel. Should she give her a hug? But her cousin did not indicate that she expected this. After a moment, Isabel smiled and said something startling. "Juan is nice, isn't he?"

Constanza didn't move. She wasn't sure she had heard right.

"I hear he really likes you," Isabel added. "You don't have to worry. I told you, no one is home."

"Did Prudencia tell you this?" was all Constanza was able to say in response.

Isabel shook her head. "No. Juan told me himself."

Constanza opened her mouth wide. "He did?" *He not only looks like a devil; he is a devil*, she thought. "What else did he say?"

"I promised not to tell!" Isabel said with a smile, stroking her cheek with the quill pen.

"Isabel!" Constanza rolled her eyes. "Don't do this to me!"

Her cousin laughed. "What am I doing? Juan told me he's in love with you. He told Prudencia, too." She sat back and waited for a response.

This was much more than Constanza had expected. She put a hand on her chest.

"You're not lying?" she asked in disbelief. Isabel shook her head, smiling.

Constanza felt giddy, but she was intent on remaining in control this time. After her previous disappointments, she would not allow herself to dream about Juan. She was determined that her heart would remain her own. But she was pleased to be able to confide in her cousin once more. Wanting to demonstrate their renewed friendship, Constanza inquired about her own life.

"How is your merchant?" she asked.

"Who?" Isabel looked confused.

"The Portuguese merchant I heard about."

At these words, Isabel became serious. "People talk too much. Don't pay any attention to their gossip," she said dismissively. And with that, she dipped the quill pen in ink and turned her attention back to the papers in front of her. Disappointed, Constanza got up and went to the sewing room to resume her work.

She had just put some kindling in the brazier and lit the fire when the front door opened and Catalina came in. She bid goodbye to Juana Gaitán, who always walked her back home, even though they lived practically next door to each other. Constanza felt sorry for Catalina and her friends, having moved from idyllic Esquivias to this area of Valladolid, but in a city where rental properties were scarce and over-priced, Miguel always said they were fortunate to have found a place to call home, despite the tavern. Catalina had declared, however, that even the thought of walking past it alone made her feel ill. Constanza considered that it was for the best; this way she wouldn't have to worry that her aunt would see her if she decided to talk to Juan for a few minutes.

"Miguel is about to arrive," Catalina called out from the foyer. "Someone told me they saw him on the road on the way here. Where is everybody?"

"I'm in the sewing room, Aunt," Constanza called out. "My mother and Magdalena should be home soon."

Isabel remained quiet. Catalina went into her bedroom and closed the door. When Miguel wasn't present, the two barely acknowledged each other's existence. Constanza still hoped that the mood in the household would lighten. Perhaps if Uncle Miguel brought good news, the situation would be less tense.

Now the door opened again, and Magdalena's happy voice rang out.

"Hurry up, everyone, we have to get ready!" Constanza understood right away that Miguel had told her to expect him; this was the reason she and Andrea had gone out at that unusual time.

Constanza remained intent on her sewing. She had already wasted enough time that day. Surely her uncle would not be there that quickly.

"Come!" her aunt said.

Isabel was blowing the ink dry and organizing the pieces of paper she had been working on so she could put them away when Constanza joined them. Magdalena took out a few of their special *Talavera* plates. Andrea brought Miguel's favourite cheese, a fresh piece of *chorizo*, and a loaf of bread from the kitchen and placed them on the table. Maria put another log into the kitchen stove to bring the heat up for boiling water.

"Bring the wine! Everything needs to be ready!" Magdalena called out.

"What are we celebrating?" Isabel asked, taking her papers and placing them on a chair in the foyer. The sun made the sky resemble a bouquet of pinks and oranges. The street was still noisy and foul-smelling, but the women had become used to this and didn't seem to notice it anymore.

"It's a surprise!" Magdalena said cheerfully. Andrea smiled, rubbing her hands together.

Constanza looked at the bedroom door, wondering when Catalina would join them. She finally appeared, draped in woolen shawl, when she heard Miguel's steps on the stairs. Isabel hung back, but the others rushed to the door to welcome him and help him with his bags and travelling clothes. He carried a package proudly in his arms.

"Is that what I think it is?" Constanza said with a shriek.

Miguel nodded. It was a copy of his freshly published book. He removed the protective coverings and turned to look at Catalina. "My beloved wife, this is for you," he said, extending the book towards her, but she kept her arms crossed beneath her shawl.

"Let Constanza see it first," she said, "I can wait." Obediently, Miguel handed the book to his niece, but it was obvious that he was hurt. How long was Catalina going to continue to treat him with contempt? What good was all her praying if she couldn't forgive him and celebrate this special moment? Constanza took the book, caressed its modest vellum binding and cover, and brought it to her face to smell the pages. It was so fresh, so new!

"Mother, Aunt Magdalena, look at this!" Leafing through the volume, Constanza was aware that she was holding in her hands a product of incredible effort: 630 pages, 4 parts, 52 chapters—without counting the prologue! The adventures of Don Quixote and his squire throughout La Mancha, from the moment he lost his mind from reading too many books on chivalry, to the time when he was returned to his village restrained in a cage.

Andrea, Magdalena, and Isabel eagerly surrounded Constanza, sharing the book among them. Catalina held back a little, holding on to Miguel's good arm, watching them. As they took turns admiring the book, Constanza felt her chest swell with admiration.

"Listen to this!" Magdalena cleared her throat to read aloud. "'*The Ingenious Hidalgo Don Quixote of La Mancha*, composed by Miguel de Cervantes Saavedra, dedicated to the Duke of Bexar, Marquis of Gibraleon, Count of Benalcazar and Bañares, Vicecount of the Puebla de Alcocer, Master of the Towns of Capilla, Curiel, and Burguillos,'" She stopped, puzzled. "Year 1605? That's still a month and a half away!"

"The book will be available in January. This is one of the very first copies."

"I see!" Magdalena smiled and continued reading. "'Printed in Madrid by Juan de la Cuesta and published by Francisco de Robles, bookseller of the King our Lord.' I am so very proud of you, my dear brother!" Magdalena could not help shedding a tear, and Andrea followed suit.

"I am so glad you managed to keep a good relationship with both Juan de la Cuesta and Francisco Robles after all this time, despite your travels and absences," Andrea said, drying her eyes. "How many years have passed since the publication of *La Galatea*?"

"Let's not count!" Miguel said with a laugh.

"You have always been able to keep your old friends and make new ones everywhere you go, Miguel. That is another one of your talents," Andrea insisted.

"If only our parents and our dear Rodrigo were alive to see this, Miguel!" Magdalena was unable to conceal the melancholy in her voice.

"Let's not think about sad things!" Constanza declared, noticing that Catalina had drawn her husband close to her. "This is a celebration!"

"Let me hold it, let me hold it!" Isabel chimed in, unable to resist the joy of the moment. Now she read out loud from the book.

Notice. I, Juan Gallo de Andrada, scribe of the Chamber of the King our Lord, and of those who reside in the Council of Castile, certify and attest that, the members of said Council having seen a book entitled The Ingenious Hidalgo of La Mancha, composed by Miguel de Cervantes Saavedra, they established the price of each sheet of said book at three and a half maravedís, which, the book having eighty-three sheets, sets its price at two hundred and ninety maravedís and a half.

She looked into Miguel's eyes. "Congratulations, Father! It is the equivalent to about a dozen eggs at 63 *maravedís*, a dozen oranges at 54, and a chicken, worth 127. A full feast for your readers!"

Miguel laughed. "When you put it that way, who knows if it's worth it."

"Of course it is!" Constanza exclaimed. "From what you have shared with us, dear uncle, I'm certain yours is a truly entertaining, fun book!" She hoped her uncle wouldn't take her comment the wrong way. She remembered he once said that it was precisely for this reason that some of his fellow writers, such as the great Lope de Vega, might look down upon it. Ever since Lope de Vega had assumed that three sonnets against him had been penned by Miguel, their friendship had ceased and Lope had become scathing about Miguel's works. She knew how bitterly Miguel felt Lope's contempt.

"For a book this long, it's actually a bargain," Isabel said with a smile.

"Is that so? Perhaps I should have taken you with me to negotiate the price of the book as well as my fee, daughter," Miguel retorted. Constanza looked over quickly to see Catalina's reaction and was relieved that she was smiling, too.

"It's my turn to hold the book now," Andrea said. Isabel placed the book in her hand, and Andrea invited them to follow her into the sewing room.

"I'll go clean up quickly and will be right back," Miguel said, then disappeared into the bedroom, where Maria had placed a bowl of warm water, soap, and a towel. Holding his hand, Catalina followed him and closed the door.

"Don't take too long. There's food and wine waiting for you!" Magdalena said.

Once the Cervantes women were comfortably seated on the carpet in the sewing room, Andrea opened the book again, caressed its first pages and began to read.

"Somewhere in La Mancha, in a village whose name I do not wish to remember ..."

XIII

CATALINA

Credo in Deum Patrem omnipotentem,
Creatorem caeli et terrae;
et in Iesum Christum, Filium eius unicum, Dominum nostrum;
qui conceptus est de Spiritu Sancto, natus ex Maria Virgine;
passus sub Pontio Pilato, crucifixus, mortuus, et sepultus;
descendit ad infernos; tertia die resurrexit a mortuis;
ascendit ad caelos, sedet ad dexteram Dei Patris omnipotentis;
inde venturus est iudicare vivos et mortuos.
Credo in Spiritum Sanctum, sanctam Ecclesiam catholicam, sancto-
rum communionem, remissionem peccatorum, carnis resurrectionem,
vitam aeternam.

WINTER IS BEHIND us, and a glorious spring suggests that 1605 will be the best year of our lives. Thank You, God, for granting us the miracle of resurrection, the resurrection of Miguel's name, now once again valued and respected as a writer, and the resurrection of our love, which for so many months seemed to be dying. I felt so divided, so troubled! You see everything, You know everything, and it was only thanks to Your compassion that I recovered from those dark days when I could not bear Miguel's touch, those dark nights after I arrived in Valladolid when, instead of striving to conceive the fruit of our love, we lay in bed next to each other like strangers. You understood, dear God, that I needed time to heal, time to learn to live with the presence of his daughter. I needed time to overcome the tears, the scars, the resentment that built up inside me in Valladolid, where everything was foreign to me. I missed my brothers, my olive trees, and my vineyard—I even missed having fresh air to breathe!

Thank You, God, for bestowing the gift of patience on my Miguel. You bore witness to the way in which he waited without demanding that I surrender myself to him as is his marital right. He sat next to me at his desk, writing, and finished the most wonderful of books, and Dulcinea has become a beloved figure all over. And now that the new privilege grants permission for the second edition to be distributed to the province of Aragón and even to Portugal, his fame will only grow. *Don Quixote*'s success marks a new beginning for us, and for that I am deeply grateful to You.

Thank You, God, that his book is being read aloud at public squares for those who are illiterate to enjoy. During these past months, as I have strolled the city in the company of my loyal friend, Juana, or my dear niece, Constanza, we have often come across groups of people standing or sitting in a square, or under a tree, listening to someone read the words my Miguel has written, words I was the first to ever read.

Forgive me, dear Lord, if my chest was swollen with pride when, before the bullfight organized by the Duke of Lerma on Corpus Day to celebrate the baptism of the little Prince and the ratification of the peace treaty between Spain and England, a one-act farce featuring Don Quixote and Sancho was presented in front of the crowd, a crowd that included King Philip III himself. The English diplomats will be bringing the book across the sea to their island, where their king might read it, too! Now if only the theatres would welcome Miguel's plays and stage them, making that fervent dream of his come true, this would truly be the most perfect moment of our lives.

And I must thank You, God, especially for this evening. After the royal performance of Lope de Vega's play—when even the great Lope was forced to acknowledge my Miguel's presence and talent—the ardour that I thought dead within me burned bright again. I closed the door of our bedroom behind us and went in search of his body—his hands, his tongue, his soul, which I had so sorely missed. I opened up my heart and my mind and my bosom to claim him again, my husband, to please him again, my husband, to be his wife again and bring You, Lord, down to earth with us. To find You once again in each other's gaze.

XIV

ISABEL

I WAS IN the tavern playing with Sombra and waiting for Simón when Prudencia took me aside. It was a quiet afternoon, there were few customers, and the unexpected June rain shower had freshened the air. Father was busy either crafting what he called his *Exemplary Novels*, or meeting with the important people who wanted to talk to him now that his book had been received with an enthusiasm none of us could have foreseen. Catalina had just left for Esquivias to attend a baptism. Her absence was a relief. Father was more attentive and sweeter to me when we were alone, and I wanted to enjoy those moments in the short time we had left. Once I revealed my plans with Simón, everything would change between us.

Prudencia pulled me close and spoke into my ear, laughing nervously.

"I thought I would be able to keep silent, but I'm burning inside. God forgive me, I need to tell you what's going on, Isabel."

"What is it, Prudencia?" Her breath smelled of cumin and turmeric, like the cushions and the carpet in her apartment, a smell that was now intimately associated in my mind with Simón and his skin against mine. Why was he taking so long?

"I really shouldn't tell you, but I can't keep it to myself. You have to promise not to tell another soul."

"I would never betray your confidence, Prudencia. You know me."

"Yes. I trust you."

"Then tell me!" I said. Feeling giddy, I rubbed my hands together.

"Your cousin came to see me," Prudencia said. It took me a minute to process this information.

"What did she want?"

"She came to ask a favour."

"What kind of favour?"

Prudencia laughed again. She looked to the left and the right to make sure no one could hear us, and lowered her voice.

"She's been meeting Juan in my apartment for a few days now."

I laughed, but dread crept into the pit of my stomach at the same time. If Prudencia was telling me Constanza's secret, how could I be sure she wasn't telling my cousin, or anyone else, about my relationship with Simón?

"That's not all," Prudencia continued. "The other day, Anastasio saw one of your aunts at another tavern. She was coming out of a back room, followed by a man."

I gasped. "One of my aunts? Which one?"

"Not the blond one," Prudencia said.

"Magdalena!" I blurted out. "She was with a man?"

Prudencia nodded. I would have never imagined it. All that talk about honour! But I also understood. How could I not? A man could have any woman he wanted without staining his reputation—on the contrary. Wasn't Lope de Vega celebrated by how many women he had had, how many illegitimate children? At least Father had only me, but now that he was famous he would surely find it easy to be with any woman he fancied. It was the way of the world. I wasn't surprised that Andrea was the only one behaving "honourably." She had had two husbands and was probably done with men. Although how could I be sure? In any case, I would have never expected this from Magdalena!

Hours went by and my head felt like it was about to explode. I had been waiting for Simón, eager to share this new information with him, yearning for him to undress me, to rest his head against my chest and tell me more about his travels. But he failed to appear. It was almost dark when I finally decided to go upstairs.

"Please don't tell Simón that I waited this long for him," I begged Prudencia, trying to conceal my disappointment. As it turned out, my precaution was unnecessary. Days, then weeks went by, and Simón didn't return to the tavern. I pretended not to care, but at night it was impossible to sleep, wondering what I had done wrong, why he had not even said goodbye, seeing his face in the face of every man on the street and every patron at the tavern, and hearing his voice calling me from the midst of every crowd and in the most intimate of silences.

XV

CONSTANZA

"WHAT IS THAT?" Constanza sat up in sudden alarm from the mattress. In the winter, the women slept next to the kitchen fire, but during Valladolid's hot summer nights they placed their mattresses in the sewing room. Everyone else was already soundly sleep, except for Isabel, who was not in bed. She reached over in the darkness to light her candle. The neighbourhood dogs had started up a frenzy of howling. She waited, her entire body tense, and a second later she heard it again, deep, agonized, audible even above the barking.

"Doesn't anybody hear that screaming?" she called out, her hand against her chest.

The other women were awake now.

"It must be men quarreling on the street," Andrea said.

"This sounds more serious than the usual brawling," Magdalena said, when that male voice pierced the night again.

"Where is Isabel?"

"Somebody out there needs help!" Isabel cried out from the other room. Constanza shivered when she remembered the woman who had pounded on their door in Madrid, seeking refuge from her husband.

The three women ran to the foyer, where Miguel and

Isabel were already gathered. Miguel was lighting a torch. Neighbours were awake. The dogs continued their frenzied barking.

"Help me bring that man inside! Hurry!" Isabel cried out as she opened the front door and ran downstairs. Miguel hurriedly put on his boots, took the torch, and exited the apartment behind her. Magdalena grabbed a shawl and followed him. Isabel was already in the middle of the street, crouched down beside a man who lay helpless, screaming intermittently. When Miguel reached them with the torch, Constanza managed to see the man was covered in blood.

"What's your name? Who did this to you?" Isabel was asking. She looked up at her father in distress. "Someone needs to fetch a doctor, call the Holy Brotherhood!"

"Isabel, what are you doing?" Miguel cried. Constanza could hear him over the barking of the dogs.

"We must save this man's life!"

Now another voice could be heard. "Isabel, bring him into my house. I don't think he can be lifted up the stairs, he's bleeding too much." Constanza recognized the voice of Luisa de Montoya, the woman who lived on the main floor across from the tavern.

"Thank God for Luisa de Montoya," Magdalena exclaimed as she came back to the foyer. "Quick, we must help her! Maria, bring hot water. Andrea, tear some linen into strips so we can try to stop the bleeding."

The candles burned brightly in the breezeless night as the women rushed to put clothes on over their nightgowns and do as they were told. Constanza went down the stairs in time to see Anastasio and another neighbour, followed by Miguel, carrying the injured man into Luisa de Montoya's house. By now, other neighbours had gathered outside the entrance to Luisa's house.

"Anastasio, fetch a barber-surgeon, hurry!" Isabel called out. The man nodded and headed out down the street. Isabel knelt at the wounded man's head, wiping his face with a handkerchief. Constanza thought at first that the man was a servant, for he wore a cheap cape, but as her cousin carefully removed the garment, she found that underneath it he wore a fine silk shirt. Was the man disguised as a servant? What was his story?

Magdalena came in and knelt opposite to Isabel. She unbuttoned the man's shirt to look at his wounds. Andrea appeared carrying the linen bandages.

"What's your name?" Magdalena asked. The man was breathing but he lacked the strength to answer.

"Where are Anastasio and the barber-surgeon?" Isabel cried, holding some blood-soaked linen against the man's stomach.

"This man needs a priest. Find a priest!" Magdalena called out. She whispered in the man's ear. "Keep your eyes open a little bit longer, please."

Isabel and Magdalena continued to apply pressure on the man's wounds while they waited for the priest, for the barber-surgeon—for a miracle. Andrea began praying out loud, and the people around her followed suit. Finally, a clergyman arrived.

"I came as quickly as I could. I'm Gonzalo Bravo de Sotomayor," he said to the women. Then, addressing the bleeding man, he said, "Do not be afraid, brother. I have come to take your confession and perform the last rites." His voice was peaceful and melodious. "Your sins will be forgiven, and should Our Lord call you, your soul will rest in Heaven by His side."

The room became quiet, the only sound being Father Gonzalo's words in Latin. Luisa de Montoya lit every candle in the house and arranged them close to the dying man. There was enough light now to see his wounds. They were deep— from his lower abdomen to his groin. Constanza shivered.

Just then, Anastasio burst through the doorway along with a stranger carrying a leather case on his shoulder. It was the barber-surgeon.

"Sebastián Macías," he announced himself, setting down his case. He approached the patient calmly, but when he set eyes on his face he cried out. "Don Gaspar de Ezpeleta!"

There was a gasp. How could they not have recognized him? Don Gaspar de Ezpeleta frequently strolled the streets in the company of his friend, the Marquis de Falces.

"Who would attack such an illustrious gentleman?" Isabel asked. She had blood on her hands, her cheeks, and her dressing gown.

The women and the priest made room for Macías to quickly examine Ezpeleta's wounds. He frowned and shook his head. "There is no time to waste. I need egg whites, all the egg whites you have."

Luisa de Montoya returned with a bowl of egg whites. The surgeon removed some herbs from his leather case—incense, myrtle, and rose powder—mixed them with the egg whites to create a poultice, and applied it to the open wounds, exerting pressure.

At that moment several other men came through the door. Constanza recognized the mayor of Valladolid, Cristóbal de Villaroel, followed by his scribe, Melchor Galván. She remembered them from the peace treaty festivities they had attended just days earlier. The third was the Marquis de Falces himself.

"Don Gaspar de Ezpeleta, Knight of the Order of Saint James was my guest this evening. He must have been attacked after he left my house."

"He is gravely wounded," the surgeon said. "Probably by a sword." He continued to press the poultice against the wound.

"Where is his servant?" demanded the mayor.

The Marquis scanned the room. "There you are!" he said, pointing at a young man who had been cowering behind Miguel. The man came forward.

"Francisco de Camporredondo, at your service," he said with a bow.

Then the mayor called over his scribe. He asked Luisa de Montoya, "Is there a desk where my scribe can make notes?" She indicated a small table against the back wall. The scribe installed himself at the table and took out a sheaf of papers and some ink.

The mayor addressed Camporredondo. "That's your master's cape you're wearing. Did you steal it?"

The manservant looked afraid. "Would I be here if I had done that? My master asked me to switch capes with him before we departed."

Annoyed, the mayor demanded, "Why would your master make such an outrageous request?"

"I don't know, Sir. My role is to obey, not to ask questions."

"Were you there when he was attacked?"

"No, Sir. He was alone."

"And why did you leave your master alone?" asked Isabel. Constanza shook her head. Why couldn't her cousin stay silent? The mayor looked irritated, but he nodded and repeated the question.

"Where were you?" the Marquis demanded.

"My master sent me to deliver a personal message."

"What was the nature of this personal message?"

"I'm not at liberty to say."

"Who was the message for?"

"I'm not at liberty to say that, either. Is he dead?" The servant looked like he was about to cry.

"I think it would be better to ask these questions in private," the Marquis whispered to the mayor, but everyone in the room could hear him.

"One last question," asked the Marquis. "Did your master visit this household often?"

"No. He always—"

"I need water. Bring me more water!" cried the barber-surgeon from the floor.

Luisa de Montoya brought him a pail of water from the kitchen, and he used it to wet Ezpeleta's hair and his forehead, as well as the area between his legs.

"They say that pouring water over a patient's private parts helps stop bleeding," he explained matter-of-factly.

"Please, respect Don Gaspar's privacy!" cried out the mayor. "Anybody who is not essential should leave the room. Leave now!" Most of the onlookers went out the door, and the mayor looked hard at Miguel. "Are you the writer of that book, *Don Quixote*?"

Miguel nodded. "Yes, Sir."

"What are you doing here?"

"I live in this apartment building," Miguel said.

The mayor then noticed Constanza, Isabel, and their aunts. "Who are you, ladies?"

They all introduced themselves. "Why are you two covered in blood?" he asked Isabel and Magdalena.

"We were trying to stop Don Ezpeleta from bleeding to death," Isabel said.

"If he was wounded by a sword at this time of night, it must have been a duel. And duels are often caused by women. Do any of you ladies have a relationship with Don Gaspar?" They shook their heads.

"Was anything of value found in Don Gaspar's clothing?" The mayor asked, turning to the manservant. "Did your master give you anything for safekeeping when you switched capes?"

"No," Camporredondo replied.

"I felt something in a pocket of his cape when I removed it," Isabel admitted.

The mayor turned to her again. "What was it?"

Isabel bent down to pick up the blood-stained cape. She reached into the small pocket and held up her hand. The mayor inspected the objects close to the light.

"Two rings," he said. "Scribe, take note! Both gold. One with diamonds, the other with three emeralds. And a folded note, which I will read later." He put the rings and the note in his own pocket and looked at Isabel. "I was right, then. This was no robbery. What is your relationship with Don Gaspar?"

"I have no relationship with him, Sir. I heard him screaming and ran to the street to help him."

The mayor and the Marquis both looked at Isabel carefully. "Where were you when you heard his cries?"

"I was at home, Sir."

"Is that so?" the mayor said. "Your name again, Señorita …?"

"Isabel de Saavedra."

"Continue, please."

"It was hot, I couldn't sleep and—"

"Silence, please!" The surgeon interrupted. "Don Gaspar is conscious."

His words drew gasps from the people who were still in the room.

Gaspar de Ezpeleta's eyes were open and his lips were moving, but it was impossible to hear what he was saying.

"Has he regained consciousness? We must find out what happened!" the Marquis exclaimed.

"Everyone out! Leave the apartment," ordered the mayor. As the Cervantes women headed to the door, he added, "None of you are to leave Valladolid until we find the person responsible for this crime!"

XVI

Notice: For the Particular and Common Good of the Neighbours of the City of Valladolid

Don Gazpar de Ezpeleta y Río, native of Pamplona, whose family honourably served the Court for three generations, Knight of the Order of Saint James since 1568, valiant soldier who fought in the battle of Ostende, was mortally wounded last night, June 27, 1605, Year of Our Lord. That evening, he dined with the honourable Don Diego de Croy y Peralta, Marquis of Falces, Captain of His Majesty's Royal Guard of the Archers. Returning alone to his temporary place of residence in Valladolid, an inn on Calle de la Mantería, near the Hospital de la Resurrección, he was attacked and mortally wounded using a sharp object, be it a dagger, a sword, or a knife. The parishioners of Nuestra Señora de Llorente, as well as any neighbours living on Calle del Rastro, Calle del Perú, and the adjacent streets near the Esgueva river, are urged to share with the authorities anything they may have seen or heard that may help bring the murderer or murderers to justice. They are expected to fulfill their Christian duty and address themselves directly at the earliest opportunity to the Royal Court Judge and Mayor of Valladolid Cristóbal de Villarroel.

XVII

CATALINA

Agnus Dei, qui tollis peccata mundi: miserere nobis.
Agnus Dei, qui tollis peccata mundi: miserere nobis.
Agnus Dei, quitollis peccata mundi: dona nobis pacem.

LAMB OF GOD, hear my prayer, the most important prayer I
have ever sent You. I have just now received a letter from my
dear Juana de Gaitán, and I cannot stop my tears. You who
can see my eyes, my heart, my soul, hear my prayer. Today,
the sky over Esquivias may be bright and cloudless, but my
heart feels dark and heavy. My beloved Miguel, as well as
his sisters, Constanza, Isabel, and even Maria are among the
people Judge Villarroel, Mayor of Valladolid, ordered arrested.
In her letter Juana said that the mayor interviewed forty-two
people and arrested eleven in his quest to solve the death of
Don Gaspar de Ezpeleta. Eleven! How could this be? Why,
dear Lord, did this have to happen? And just when Miguel's
reputation is at its highest!

Juana heard from Luisa de Montoya herself that Ezpeleta
refused to name his foe or suggest a reason why he was
attacked. If he was wearing his servant's cape, and valuable
pieces of jewellery were found in his possession, yet robbery
was not the motive, on what grounds is my Miguel, together

with his family, being held behind bars? Why, Lamb of God, is human justice this imperfect, when we are created in Your own image and likeness? Please protect him, and make the judge set him free, and clear his good name—which is also mine. And once this nightmare is over, dear Lord, please help my husband realize that, had he travelled with me back to Esquivias, instead of staying in that wretched, filthy city, this would have never happened.

Lamb of God, listen to my prayer. Deliver us from evil, and more than anything, I beg You, deliver us from Valladolid.

XVIII

CONSTANZA

Constanza refused to sit down on the filthy cell floor. The small window let in enough light to see the pile of straw that was to be used as a bed, the wooden pail where they were supposed to relieve themselves—and that had not been emptied since before their arrival—and a bench that an officer brought in out of consideration for Andrea and Magdalena's age. Spiderwebs clung to the ceiling, and the smell of dampness, urine, and feces attached itself to Constanza's hair and clothes, making her nauseous. She stared at Isabel, who was standing with her back against a wall, head down, eyes closed. How could she be so calm? She was the one who had dragged them into this pitiful situation by insisting on helping Gaspar de Ezpeleta three weeks earlier.

Yes, it was because of Isabel that her mother, her aunt, Maria, her uncle—who had been celebrated by the masses mere days before the incident—and even a few of their unfortunate neighbours had been arrested, forced to walk into the street followed by officers of the Holy Brotherhood, and loaded onto an open cart, under the blazing summer sun, and paraded through the streets of Valladolid for everyone to stare at. Eleven of them shared this undeserved ignominy and were thrown together with yellow-hooded prostitutes, drunkards, people who might have committed terrible crimes, who had no morals. Constanza's mantilla was not enough to protect her. Even armour would have felt insufficient; she had never felt so vulnerable, so helpless, as if she were naked for the entire world to see.

Outside it may have been July, but Constanza found it impossible to find solace from the permanent winter trapped within those walls. If only she had thought to grab a shawl! As she watched her mother and her aunt huddle together, praying, it dawned on her how fast and how mercilessly time went by. Both women had silver hair now and looked smaller than she remembered. Constanza would have given anything to spare them the discomfort and humiliation of finding themselves in jail in Valladolid, just like their father decades earlier. She was fully aware this was not the same jail where Rodrigo de Cervantes had been detained. But to Constanza it made no difference. It felt like a curse.

Her stomach growled. Before closing the heavy door behind them, the officer had given them each a piece of bread.

"Your food for the day," the man said, in his voice a warning not to ask for more.

But the bread was stale and hard. Magdalena and Andrea would be unable to bite through it. Constanza knew they would even have difficulty breaking it into small pieces that could be softened inside their mouths.

"Officer, could you please bring us something suitable for my mother and my aunt to eat?" Constanza pleaded. "They have bad teeth."

"Of course! Would you ladies also like some *olla podrida*, perhaps?" The man gave her a nasty grin. He, too, had bad teeth. "This is not a *mesón*, and that," he pointed at the bread, "is what all prisoners eat."

"But they can't chew this!" She held the bread up in her hand, wishing she could throw it at the man's face. It was hard as a rock. Perhaps it would hurt him. She wanted to hurt him.

"Don't worry, *hija*. We shall offer our sacrifice of fasting to our Lord God," Andrea said meekly.

Constanza stared at Isabel once more—her cousin had still not spoken a single word. But just as the officer was about to leave, she approached him and whispered something in his ear. The man smirked, Isabel whispered again, and they exited the cell together.

"What is she doing?" Constanza rushed over, trying to catch a glance of what was happening, but the officer had taken the torch with him, and the light flowing through the small window at the back of the cell did not reach the hallway. The smell of rust filled Constanza's nostrils as she rested her forehead against the metal door.

The women, having no idea where Isabel had gone, were filled with fear and hope. To pass the time, Constanza rubbed her mother's back and shoulders, trying to comfort her, while Magdalena held her sister's hands to warm them up. Maria sat in a corner, praying earnestly and silently.

After a while they heard footsteps in the hall and the door opened. An officer let Isabel in, locked the cell, and went away again. The women stared at Isabel, trembling with expectation. Smiling, Isabel held out her hands to her aunts to offer them each a ripe peach.

"Isabel!" Magdalena exclaimed, "This is extraordinary. How did you manage to get these?" Isabel lowered her gaze.

"I'm good at negotiating, remember?"

AS THE HOURS went by, Constanza had to make a huge effort not to cry. She wanted to remain strong for her aunt and her mother, but she felt weak and afraid. What if they were locked up in this cell forever? It was cold, so cold that her fingers felt stiff. What if she couldn't sew any more after this? What if they got sick? Her mother was already coughing. Did Juan know that she had been arrested? What would he think of her now? As daylight, which offered her a bit of comfort, turned into darkness, she grew more anxious.

That first night, as they huddled together on the straw— Constanza and Magdalena flanking Andrea to keep her warm, Isabel next to Magdalena and Maria at the end—she fought her desire for sleep, afraid of the insects and vermin that might crawl over her if she succumbed to her exhaustion. Curling up into a ball against her mother's back and pressing her skirt tightly between her legs, she hoped to keep spiders and mice at bay. Was the cell where Uncle Miguel and the other men were being held as disgusting as this? Had the jail in Seville looked the same? Constanza marvelled at how he had survived captivity in Algiers.

"I trust that God will make the authorities realize the grave mistake—no, the *huge injustice*—they are perpetrating," Andrea prayed, her voice weak and hoarse.

"We must have faith," Magdalena added.

Constanza would have liked to follow suit with some positive comments, but she could not. "Except that in our experience, forcing the authorities to acknowledge their mistakes and correct them has not been very successful, has it? I'm thinking of Uncle Rodrigo's backpay and the money Uncle Miguel is still owed from his time as a tax collector."

"I know. But we're not talking about money right now.

We're talking about our honour. And honour is a far more serious matter."

Constanza knew her mother was right. Besides, it would soon be Tuesday morning, and they had orders to finish and deliver to customers by the end of the week. What would happen if they were not freed in time to finish their work? They had fought so hard to build a clientele. Would those fine people still want to have their clothes tailored by seamstresses who had been in jail? After this, their name would be forever tainted.

When morning came it was hard for Constanza to believe this was only their second day in captivity; it felt as if they had spent a lifetime in this horrible place. They heard steps approaching their cell. An officer of the Holy Brotherhood opened the door.

"Are you going to set us free now, Sir?" Magdalena inquired politely, but her voice quivered.

"We are still conducting our investigations." The officer handed them each a piece of bread and gave them a jug of water to share. Andrea and Magdalena drank first, then Constanza, Isabel, and Maria. Like the day before, Isabel approached the officer and whispered something into his ear, but this time he shook his head and left. *Maybe that will teach her that she's no better than we are*, Constanza said to herself. She felt that some justice had been served as she watched her cousin return to the corner and make herself small, as if she wanted to hide inside her dress like a turtle in its shell.

Gazing at the blurry piece of sky she could see through the small window, Constanza lost track of time. Her mother and her aunt oscillated between prayers and silence. At some point they began sucking on the bread, as if they were babies. Constanza couldn't stand to watch those two strong, independent women reduced to this. The pail they used as a chamber pot was filling up fast. Constanza was convinced that no amount of washing would be enough to make her feel clean again. She would reek forever.

She could hear yelling in the distance. Crying. Cursing. They dozed off, but none of them managed to sleep properly. *There is no rest in hell*, thought Constanza.

The next morning, the door was opened by a new officer. He was brusque.

"I need the names of the men you ladies are seeing."

"Men?" Andrea asked in disbelief. "There must be a mistake."

The officer smirked.

"Magdalena de Cervantes, Constanza de Ovando, and Isabel de Saavedra, follow me."

They were being separated? Constanza shook her head as if she had not understood the man's words. "And what about my mother?"

"And me?" Maria added.

"What's your name?"

"Maria de Ceballos. I'm the maid."

"No one mentioned you, so you are to stay here." He addressed Constanza. "What's your mother's name?"

"Andrea de Cervantes, widow of Santi Ambrosio."

"No," he shook his head. "She was not reported as living a licentious life."

Andrea stared at Constanza in disbelief. "Officer! I can assure you that my daughter has never conducted a licentious life. You must be mistaken!"

"We have reports of one Constanza de Ovando meeting clandestinely with one Juan Jiménez. Does the name sound familiar?" The man was clearly enjoying their distress. "And one Isabel de Saavedra, who has been described as being *amancebada* with a Portuguese financier named Simón Mendez."

Isabel had emerged from her shell. "I am *not amancebada*," she protested. "I live with my father and my aunts!"

"That will be up to the Royal Court Judge and Mayor of Valladolid, Cristóbal de Villarroel, to decide," the officer replied, lifting his hand to stop her from interrupting him further. "And last but not least, one Magdalena de Cervantes, who has been meeting clandestinely with one Fernando de Lodeña."

"Fernando de Lodeña!" Andrea exclaimed.

"Who is this man?" Constanza cried. Could this nightmare get any worse? First they had all been jailed for the murder of a stranger, and now her aunt, at her mature age, was being accused of meeting with a man whose name Constanza had never even heard of?

Magdalena kept her head down and did not reply. Isabel was the only one with the nerve to look the officer in the eye.

"And what does this have to do with Don Gaspar de Ezpeleta's death?"

"With his murder, you mean to say?"

"What do our private lives have to do with that?"

"This is precisely what the judge is going to assess, Señora," he replied, choosing this title deliberately instead of Señorita to demonstrate his utmost contempt.

XIX

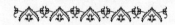

ISABEL

I asked for water to clean myself up before my session with the Royal Court Judge and Mayor of Valladolid. Judges had tried to ruin my life before; I was determined to do my best to prevent this one from succeeding.

When we entered the hall, I identified several of our neighbours among the accused: Father Gonzalo; Camporredondo, the dead man's servant; Juana de Gaitán, who had unfortunately not travelled back to Esquivias with Catalina; Mariana Ramírez, a woman who lived above us and was revealed to be *amancebada* with Diego de Miranda; Luisa de Montoya, in whose home Don Gaspar had taken his last breath; Jerónima de Sotomayor, another neighbour; Alicia de Ayala, the sanctimonious spinster. There were also many others I did not recognize. The room could not hold one more person, but Simón was not there. I had been hoping to see Prudencia and Anastasio among the audience, yet they were absent as well.

The court scribe read out our names, and Judge Villarroel called on Alicia de Ayala to give her statement. The spinster got up, looking prim and self-satisfied, and approached the podium. She stated her name and addressed the court with obvious pleasure.

"Your Honour, the tragedy that resulted in Don Gaspar de Ezpeleta's death could have been avoided if certain women valued their chastity and followed the rules of decency established by the laws that govern our kingdom and our empire."

"Can you explain what you mean, Señorita de Ayala?"

The woman continued, her voice dripping with resentment and envy.

"Of course, Your Honour. You see, I have strived my entire life to live honourably. But recently, I have been forced to tolerate new neighbours who make it very hard for a good Christian like me to live in peace. The women who live downstairs—we call them Las Cervantas—have forsaken all virtue. They receive visits from men day and night."

My mouth fell open in shock. I knew the woman was spiteful, but I didn't realize she hated us enough to try to destroy our reputation with such lies.

Judge Villarroel turned his eyes towards Father, who was standing at the other end of the group of the accused.

"Señorita de Ayala, who are 'Las Cervantas'? Can you point them out among the group of the accused?"

"Yes, Your Honour," the spinster replied, and she pointed at us. "Isabel, Magdalena, and Constanza. They are relatives of the writer Miguel de Cervantes. He allows them to live licentiously while doing business with the men they have illicit carnal relationships with."

I felt my face burn with rage.

"Are you able to name any of these men, Señorita de Ayala?"

"Yes. I made it my sacred mission to gather every detail of their lives so that one day I could bring these women to justice and cleanse our neighbourhood of their filthy ways. And, if

I may add," she said, staring directly at me. "They maintain a close relationship with a Moorish woman who works in the tavern that has invited vice into our midst, and whose true Christian faith I sincerely doubt, as I have seen her leave her post at the tavern to enter her apartment at least five times a day, which coincides with an infidel's prayer habits."

Did this witch understand the consequences of what she was doing? Prudencia's fate would be sealed should the Inquisition decide to take her prisoner.

The judge spoke. "Be it established that since said Moorish woman and her husband have not been located, it is presumed that they fled the city of Valladolid against my explicit orders, a fact that appears to confirm Señorita de Ayala's suspicions. I have personally sent out a warrant for their arrest, and I assume, based on the information currently available, that they are on the way to Andalucía."

I could not believe my ears. Prudencia and Anastasio, gone! I lowered my gaze and bit my lip to stop myself from crying.

"Can you name the men who visit the Cervantes household day and night, and who might be of interest to our murder investigation, Señorita de Ayala?"

"With pleasure, Your Honour. They are one Don Fernando de Toledo, Señor de Hígares; an Italian by the name of Agustín Raggio; and the Portuguese financier Simón Mendez. Also one Juan Jiménez and one Fernando de Lodeña, who arrived recently from Madrid. As soon as I heard about this despicable crime, I took the precaution of noting and sharing these names, as requested in the notice you circulated through the city."

"Thank you, Señorita de Ayala."

My heart ached when she spoke Simón's name. There was much murmuring in the court, but it stopped when the judge called Father's name.

"Miguel de Cervantes Saavedra, please step forward."

Father got up, his head held high.

"You have heard the names in Señorita de Ayala's statement. Do you know these men? If so, what is your association with them, and where were they the night of the murder?"

"Your Honour," Father said, his voice firm, "I do not know where my friends Agustín Raggio and Don Fernando de Toledo, Señor de Hígares, or any of the others, were on the night of the murder. I was at home, as were the members of my family. When my daughter, Isabel, heard Don Gaspar Ezpeleta's desperate cries, she ran out to offer him help."

"Do you admit that the men Alicia de Ayala named visit your house frequently?"

"Yes, Your Honour. All the men whose names were mentioned are acquaintances of mine and have been for some time. Don Fernando de Toledo and Agustín Raggio are contractors for the Crown, as I am sure you are aware. When they visit my apartment, it is to meet with me exclusively. My niece, daughter, and sisters remain in the ladies' room, as the rules mandate."

I was in awe. Father seemed calm and composed as he lied to everyone in the room. He paused briefly to look at us one by one before he continued.

"My sisters, my niece, and my daughter live with my wife and me, and it is regrettable that these visits, which are related to my personal business, are being used as an excuse to tarnish their reputation."

Judge Villarroel nodded at one of the guards. "Bring in the

next witness." I was taken aback as Aunt Andrea entered the court. She looked small, dishevelled, and helpless as her eyes searched for us. The fear on her face was heartbreaking. She had always been the first to console me when I was in distress. Now, seeing her this frail, realizing how much she had aged during the past few weeks, I felt a burst of anger.

"State your name for the court, please."

"Andrea de Cervantes, Your Honour."

"Could you please tell me if you recognize any of the following names, and explain your relationship with those people?" Judge Villarroel consulted his papers and read out the same list of names. Andrea's eyes remained on my father.

"Yes, Your Honour. They are acquaintances of my brother's." Father nodded at her.

"It is a very mixed group of acquaintances, wouldn't you agree? Some of them are almost half his age. How do you explain this?"

"My brother has a very calm and gentle nature, and he makes friends easily. He spent time in Italy and conducted business for the Court in Portugal. He has met countless people during his travels and is well liked by all. Anyone who knows him will confirm that I am telling the truth." Father's shoulders relaxed. I let out a sigh of relief.

"Do you, your sister, your niece, or your daughter have illicit relationships with any of these men?"

Andrea shook her head. "Your Honour, we spend every hour of the day sewing. At this very moment, we are anxious about the orders that we promised to deliver at the end of the week. We should be working on those orders now. We are honourable women who work to earn our living and have no illicit relationships with any men."

Looking at de Ayala to see her reaction to Andrea's words, I saw her frown. How dare she? I promised myself that one day she would pay for her defamation.

"Thank you." Judge Villarroel said. Andrea was dismissed and was led out of the room. Next, he asked Magdalena to step forth.

"Please state your name."

"Yes, Your Honour. My name is Magdalena de Cervantes, but I also answer to Magdalena Pimentel de Sotomayor."

"Can you confirm what your sister has declared?"

"Yes, Your Honour. I confirm that what my sister, Andrea, has declared is the truth."

"Thank you. And I believe there are two more members of your family?"

"There are my nieces, Constanza de Ovando and Isabel de Saavedra."

"Can Constanza de Ovando step forward, please?"

Constanza did as requested. She stated her name, and without even glancing at me, confirmed that the statements of both her mother and her aunt were correct.

The judge consulted his notes, "Could your cousin have been implicated in the attack?"

Constanza shook her head. "Isabel only rushed out to lend support to the victim of this crime." She looked at me but I avoided her eyes. I knew that she blamed me for everything that had happened since that fateful night. The judge turned back to his papers for a moment, then focused his attention back on Father.

"You say your daughter was the first person to offer assistance to Don Gaspar de Ezpeleta, and our reports confirm that information. Please identify your daughter for the court."

"That is Isabel," he said, with a nod in my direction. I stepped forward. Judge Villarroel looked me up and down as he had done the night of the murder.

"State your name for the court."

"Isabel de Saavedra," I replied with as much composure as I could.

"Your father is Miguel de Cervantes?"

"Yes, Sir."

"For the record, could you explain why you do not share his last name?"

The entire city would know I was illegitimate now. I looked at Father, hoping he could see my pain and that he regretted not recognizing me, all to appease a woman who treated him well only when he became famous.

"I am not his wife's daughter. Only his."

"You are his bastard child, then."

I held my head high. "I am his only child."

"Can you describe for us what happened on the night of June twenty-seventh?" I was grateful when the judge moved on immediately, and took a breath. It was a long story.

"It must have been around eleven o'clock when I heard screams coming from the street, screams such as I had never heard before. It was obvious that someone was in terrible distress. I woke up my father and ran outside to help a gentleman lying on the ground, bleeding heavily. As a Christian, I believed it was my duty to help him, and I did not hesitate. With the help of Anastasio, the taverner, my father, and two kind passers-by, we brought the gentleman, whose identity I did not know, to the apartment of our neighbour Luisa de Montoya so that we could tend to his wounds while we waited for the barber-surgeon and the priest."

Villarroel scanned his papers. "This Anastasio is the man who is currently a fugitive?"

"Anastasio is the taverner, and Prudencia is his wife. Prudencia is a devout Christian, loyal to our king and kingdom, and to our church. She attends mass and prays. If she comes and goes between her apartment and the tavern, as was stated here a moment ago, it is because she needs to rest her legs periodically or they become painfully swollen." If Father could lie in court, so could I.

"Is that so?" Villarroel looked from my face to my bosom and back to my face. I should have expected this treatment. A judge is, in the end, nothing more than a man. If he had a weakness, I had to take advantage of it.

"Your Honour, if I may." I pushed my chest forward and tried to appear helpless. He nodded at me to continue. "A hideous crime was committed, but I can assure you that it was not committed by me, by my family, or by anybody we know. That night was tragic, not only because a gentleman died before his time, but also because in the capital of our great kingdom, at the very heart of our empire—an empire built on Christian values, on the teachings of our Lord Jesus Christ and God Almighty—" I looked up and crossed myself to emphasize my point, "there are citizens in general, and neighbours in particular, who are not willing to do unto others as they would have done unto them. We, Your Honour—and by *we* I mean my father, my aunts Andrea and Magdalena, my cousin Constanza, Anastasio and Prudencia, and Luisa de Montoya, of course—we have now discovered that if it were up to neighbours such as those, any one of us could be killed mercilessly on the street and be left to die without anyone to hold our hand or make sure that we receive the last rites. And so it is my turn to ask you, Your Honour," and at this point I had to fight my tears, since I was being completely honest, "should we, the only Christians in the entire neighbourhood who were selfless enough to care for a wounded stranger, who made sure he did not die alone and that his soul was saved, should *we* be judged and punished?" I paused for a moment, waiting to gauge his reaction. He looked completely absorbed by my words, and I knew I had to finish what I had started.

"Every member of my family was wrongfully arrested. We are innocent. My only sin, if you want to call it that, is being a good Christian, one who would never turn her back against a dying brother or sister in God. I beg you, Sir, in your infinite wisdom, punish me if you will for my reckless selflessness, but do not punish my family."

ACT FOUR

MADRID
FEBRUARY 1606–AUGUST 1607

Despite the huge expenses incurred, it proved impossible for the royal family to enjoy in Valladolid the same level of luxury and decorum they had been accustomed to in Madrid. Therefore, King Philip III gave orders to return the Court to its former seat. Most madrileños, among them the Cervantes, left for Madrid en masse, and as many as four thousand Valladolid houses stood empty. Their owners, unable to rent or sell them, faced steep losses as a result.

A few made a handsome fortune, none as grand as that of the king's favourite, the Duke of Lerma. Taking advantage of the royal court's sojourn in Valladolid and the consequent decline in real estate prices in Madrid, the duke acquired a substantial number of properties. These he sold or rented at great profit once Madrid became once more the capital of the Spanish Empire in January 1606.

I

ISABEL

WITH THE FOUR hundred reales Father received as an advance for his *Exemplary Novels*, my family established itself in a house on Calle de la Magdalena, far from our previous home on Leganitos Street but close to my grandmother's. The new house was nowhere near as comfortable and spacious as the old one, but it was a big improvement over the apartment in Valladolid. It had an ample sewing room with windows that allowed enough light for us to see our work, and it was near the fountain on Calle de Atocha. My favourite part was that Constanza and I did not need to share a bed anymore. Before joining Catalina in Esquivias, Father had instructed Magdalena to purchase bedframes and another mattress, so that even though we still shared a room, each of us finally had her own bed.

It was a bright April morning two months after our return to the city when I I walked over to Grandmother's house. I had run out of excuses for delaying my visit. How I wished Teresa were still with us, so she could walk with me like she had done before! Fearing my aunts would once again refuse me their permission, I decided to go alone. I took advantage of everyone's inattention: Aunt Magdalena was in her room with a terrible headache, Maria had gone to the river to do the laundry, and Andrea and Constanza were sequestered in the sewing room.

I quietly let myself out of the house. Since I had money hidden in a secret pouch beneath my doublet, I borrowed my aunt's dagger, the one she took with her on every outing. Even though it was a short walk, I felt safer carrying it in my sleeve. She would not even know it was missing, and I'd be back soon.

Like soldiers who return after a long period at the front, Madrid showed scars of the abandonment it had been subjected to during the time it was replaced as kingdom's capital by Valladolid. Its streets appeared older, dirtier. There seemed to be more beggars, more stray dogs and cats than I remembered. My heart ached for Sombra, who would be alone in the tavern without Prudencia and Anastasio. My Aunts had not allowed me to bring him with us, and he was the only thing I was truly sad to leave behind. He would be on his own in that cursed, half-empty city I wished I could forget.

Simón never returned to Valladolid. He had been convicted of fraud and was serving a jail sentence in Madrid. It appeared that we were all back in the place where everything had started, where we were supposed to be. But we had not returned unscathed. When the court moved back to Madrid, its ways and woes and rumours moved with it. It didn't matter that the judge had set us free and our name was cleared in the Ezpeleta case. People still referred to us with contempt as Las Cervantas, and Father's good name and his success were unfairly tarnished by the entire episode. Word travelled fast, and like fire, it consumed everything and everyone in its way.

Instead of becoming a grand city, Valladolid had revealed its true small-town nature.

Idle men clad in rags stood talking in small groups on every street corner. They stopped to look me up and down, and a shiver ran through me. I was wearing an old overskirt and a very simple shirt and bodice, nothing worthy of attention, and my mantilla fully covered my hair and face. But their eyes felt like hands fondling my body. Coming here alone had been a mistake. I quickened my pace.

When I found myself on the street where Grandmother lived, I suddenly realized that I wasn't even sure my family was still there. What if they had moved? Where would I find Ana? Even if she was still there, would she be happy to see me? I had been imagining how wonderful it would be to treat her to some *buñuelos* or *torreznos* at the *bodegón de puntapié*. I was determined not to share the ugly details about life in Valladolid. I would tell her only the good things—how I had worked at the tavern and made friends with Sombra. Above all, she would never know I had been in jail.

My hands were shaking as I approached the apartment. My aunt Luisa opened the door. It took her a few seconds to recognize me. She looked much older than the last time I had visited. One of her front teeth was missing.

"Look who's here!" she exclaimed. "The princess comes back from the castle!"

Ignoring her barb, I stepped inside and removed my mantilla. After living next to a slaughterhouse and spending two days in jail, I was able to tolerate the smells of the apartment much better than last time. In the dim light of the room, I saw Ana. Instead of running to greet me like a child, she took her time acknowledging my presence. It took me a moment to take in her appearance, but when I did, I was distressed. She was very tall but just as thin as before. Now that she had matured, I saw that she resembled her father, with the same thick eyebrows and angry expression. She wore an old and stained dress that was too big for her, probably a hand-me-down from Luisa. Putting aside my fears, I held my arms open to her, but she wouldn't even smile. She just stood there staring, as if she didn't know me or care who I was.

"Won't you even say hello to me, Ana?" I asked.

"Hello," she said, performing a clumsy curtsey.

I moved towards her. "What's wrong? Why won't you give me a hug?"

Ana shrugged.

"Where's Grandmother?" I said, looking around, expecting to see her coming in from the back. Instead, Jerónima and Marita emerged. When they saw me, they froze on the spot. I smiled at them but, like Ana, they did not smile back. Thinking that they didn't hear my question, I asked again. "Where's Grandmother?"

"She's dead," Luisa said. "While you were having the time of your life in Valladolid, mingling with the royals and your famous father, your grandmother became ill. She couldn't eat, she couldn't sleep, and before we knew it, she couldn't breathe." Her voice became harsher, and she spat the words at me as if they were poisoned. "She died a slow, painful death."

My eyes filled with tears.

"And do you know why she died a slow and painful death? Because we couldn't buy medicine. And we couldn't buy medicine because you didn't send us any money. Did you really think the amount that you gave us when you left would last until now?"

I was in shock. All I could take in was that Grandmother was dead, and this fact was hard to digest. Tears rolled down my cheeks.

"And don't expect us to believe those tears, Your Majesty!" Luisa threw at me.

"When did she—?" I couldn't even finish my question.

"What do you care *when* she died?" Ana's voice pierced me. "She died and you weren't here. That's all that matters."

"I'm sorry, *hermana*. I'm so sorry!" I reached out my arms to her again, but she took a step back. Luisa moved to her side, and Marita and Jerónima joined her. The four of them stood and stared at me, their eyes full of wrath. Four against one. Nothing I could say at that moment would be the right thing.

Taking a deep breath and trying hard to stop crying, I removed the money I had hidden in my clothes and placed it on the table.

"I hope this helps you, at least for now."

"The princess shows her charity at last!" Luisa exclaimed. Why was she treating me this way? She was Mother's sister! I had no obligation to her; my only obligation was to Ana. I wondered if my uncle Juan, a priest, would treat me the same way if I went to see him.

"How is Uncle Juan?" I managed to ask.

"In the parish, as always," Ana replied. Her voice had deepened and was bitter like an old woman's. What had happened to my sister in my absence? She couldn't have changed this much because Grandmother died.

"I'll try to visit him," I said, but I didn't sound convincing.

Ana nodded and remained standing, her eyes radiating resentment. I put on my mantilla and moved towards the door.

"What about the tavern?" Ana asked suddenly.

"What about it?" I replied, not sure what she meant. I couldn't claim ownership of the tavern until I was twenty-five, and she knew this.

"I thought you had been there, that's all," she said quietly. I shook my head and went out the door. I would make sure that my sister received her inheritance—I had made a promise to Mother, after all—but there would be time to discuss this later. I needed to restore my equilibrium before returning home to my aunts and my cousin. The Church of San Sebastián was only a few steps away from there, and if one of them asked where I had been, I would say I had gone out to pray.

Now I found myself alone on the street again, met by the threat of strangers' eyes. As I made my way, I heard footsteps close behind me. I walked a little faster, trying to pretend nothing was amiss, but my entire body was on the alert. I put my hand around the hilt of Aunt Magdalena's dagger and kept walking, taking longer, faster steps. Sweat was running down my forehead and my neck. I was about to take out the dagger and scream when the Church of San Sebastián rose before me. Lifting my skirts so I could move faster, I hurried inside, running all the way to the front pews. My mouth felt like it was filled with sand. My hands and knees were shaking. Taking deep breaths, I looked around for a priest or anyone who could protect me. But I was alone. Whoever had been behind me had not followed me inside.

It was in the silence of the church that the enormity of my losses dawned on me. Grandmother was dead and my sister was lost to me. There was no fighting my tears, and I let them flow. Who knows how long I cried? I had to give myself time, compose myself before heading back to Calle de la Magdalena. I knelt and lifted my mantilla so I could dry my face with my handkerchief. I prayed for Grandmother's soul and for her forgiveness. I prayed for my sister. And I also said a prayer for Prudencia and Anastasio. Desperate for hope, I begged God to have mercy on me and guide my steps. I promised to listen to His signs and follow His lead. After saying a last Amen, I rose to my feet.

As I turned towards the exit, I saw that I was not actually alone. A young man sat noiselessly in the last row. Now he stood up, his eyes on me. He was tall and elegantly dressed in a finely tailored doublet and laced suede boots.

"Excuse me, Señorita," he said with a bow. His blue eyes were so striking that I forgot to lower my mantilla. "I saw what happened."

"Pardon me?" I asked. Who was this man who looked as if he had just stepped out of a divine painting? How long had he been there?

"I saw those vagrants following you and chased them away," he explained. "If you allow me, I would be honoured to see you safely home."

"You saw them following me?" I said, feeling the return of fear. It was terrifying to confirm my fear had been justified.

"If you do not mind my saying so, Señorita, a woman as beautiful and elegant as you should not be walking alone," he declared. I should have known better than to engage him, but I couldn't stop staring at his eyes.

"My name is Diego Sanz del Aguila," he said.

"Mine is Isabel de Saavedra."

"Isabel de Saavedra. What a beautiful name!"

I wanted to say, *I used to be Isabel Rodríguez and could*

have been Isabel de Cervantes. But I was Isabel de Saavedra and in his voice it did have a pleasant ring to it.

I moved towards the door, lowering my mantilla so he wouldn't notice I was blushing. It was late, I had to go. Thankfully, Calle de la Magdalena was not far.

The young man caught up with me. "Señorita de Saavedra—or may I call you Isabel?" he went on. I meant to shake my head no, but instead I nodded yes. I was nervous.

"Forgive my boldness, but may I please have your arm? I believe it would make our journey safer. Where are you headed?"

II

MAGDALENA

May 1606
My dearest Miguel,

May God be keeping you healthy and strong. I received your letter. I had to read it several times to comprehend the gravity of its words; then I forced myself to wait a few days for my anger to subside before writing back. If what you have discovered is true, my faith in our authorities will be shattered. I have decided not to share this information with Andrea or Constanza, and much less with Isabel. For God's sake, *hermano mío*, is there anyone in a position of power in this country who is deserving of trust? I am sure that His Majesty would be devastated if he knew what we, his most loyal subjects, must endure. I agree that your findings must remain yet another secret between us. But are you sure your informant is not mistaken? If Gaspar de Ezpeleta was having an affair with Inés Hernández, the wife of Melchor Galván—the royal scribe who took notes in Luisa de Montoya's foyer on the night of the attack—then he was the one who stood to gain with Ezpeleta's death. Judge Villarroel knew this, and he used us as a distraction, as scapegoats, in order to protect his friend. All this time I was sure we had been the victims of bad luck and Alicia de Ayala's venomous words. No wonder Ezpeleta's servant refused to speak when Melchor Galván was there in the room, staring at him! He would have to be out of his mind to confess what he knew.

I feel such impotence, such rage. The same impotence and rage as you. But almost a year has gone by. Andrea's health and mood are improving every day. Coming back to Madrid has done wonders. We have recovered most of our old clientele. Everyone seems eager to forget Valladolid, the way one forgets a bad dream. Constanza and Isabel have adapted well to our new situation. Knowing that you managed to have the names of Fernando de Lodeña and Juan Jiménez erased from the official records of that terrible night gives me solace. Let us put this bitter experience behind us and never speak of it again.

And on another note ... I did not want to mention this but, since you asked, I will answer: No. With the courts moving back from Valladolid to Madrid, paperwork will be delayed for months. Sometimes I think we will die without recovering what poor Rodrigo was rightfully owed. Sometimes I think about him and imagine his death on the battlefield, alone, full of fear. And for what?

Despite these trials, my dear brother, we must have faith in divine justice, and in the fact that God will, one day, right all these wrongs. Many blessings for you and Catalina.

From your sister who misses you dearly,
Magdalena

III

CONSTANZA

CONSTANZA WOULD HAVE felt at ease in their new home and content with the new routine that they had fallen into had it not been for Isabel and Diego. There was something peculiar, something rather disconcerting in his charming ways that made her uneasy.

"I don't trust him," she finally dared to say one June afternoon after he called to accompany Isabel to purchase fabric. Maria had been assigned to chaperone them; this time, Magdalena was not taking any chances. The Cervantes honour and good name could not sustain another blow.

"His manners are impeccable," Andrea said. "And you must admit that having him help Isabel run errands has made our lives easier. Magdalena and I are not getting any younger."

"Speak for yourself!" Magdalena replied, laughing. They were in the sewing room, embroidering silk shirts. The sun beamed through the window but a light breeze alleviated the heat of its rays. It was hard to believe that just a year ago they had celebrated Miguel's success in Valladolid— and then they had gone to jail. Juan Jiménez had altogether disappeared from Valladolid after his name had been raised in the trial, and Constanza still wondered what would have happened had Ezpeleta not intervened into their lives, only to die. She could not wait for the month of June to be over. She would forever consider it a month of bad luck, and something was telling her that Diego Sanz del Aguila was equally bad.

"We don't know anything about him, really, Mother."

"Your daughter is right," Magdalena was embroidering a sleeve. "His references to his family and his past are vague at best, and our inquiries have not yielded any clear answers about his origin. None of our acquaintances or customers seem to know a family bearing that name."

"What if he is of *converso* origin?" Constanza asked. She was still bitter that her family had prohibited her relationship with Francisco Leal for that very reason.

"How could he be? He looks like an angel with those blue eyes!"

"Are you saying that *conversos* can't have blue eyes?" she demanded. Francisco's eyes were hazel and much more expressive, in her opinion, than Diego's. His were too perfect, like a painting.

"Nonsense! I didn't say that." Andrea replied, laughing. Constanza frowned. She and Magdalena exchanged looks. Was her mother well?

The three continued working in silence until they heard Isabel's laughter outside the door. Ever since meeting Diego, she had turned into a little rattle, making happy sounds wherever she was—humming, singing, laughing. She had finished running errands sooner than Constanza expected, and now she entered the foyer, followed by Maria, her eyes so bright it looked like she had swallowed a ray of sunshine. Maria deposited the basket of assorted threads beside Andrea and

Magdalena, and Isabel laid down the taffeta they needed to fulfill their next order.

"Aunt Andrea, Aunt Magdalena, may Diego come inside, please? He would very much like to speak to you."

Constanza frowned again.

"Of course, let him in, please," Magdalena said, rising to her feet and helping Andrea to do the same. They exited the sewing room. Since Isabel had not mentioned her name, Constanza remained in her chair, all senses on guard. She would hear everything without making a move.

"Señoras," Constanza could visualize Diego taking off his hat, making a bow, kissing their hands. "Thank you for welcoming me into your house."

"Hello, Señor Sanz," Magdalena replied, "please follow us. Would you mind carrying one of these chairs?" They were headed for the studio, where Magdalena would occupy Miguel's chair and Andrea and Isabel would sit across from her. Diego would sit on one of the chairs from the foyer, which they normally used for their clients.

"Maria, please bring us some water with cinnamon," Magdalena instructed. *If Teresa were still with us, she would bring a glass for me, too*, Constanza reflected with a sigh. She wondered what her dear Teresa had been doing the past few years. She hoped she was well.

After some small talk about the weather, and how busy it was on the street and in the market, the real conversation started. Diego wasted no time getting to the point.

"Señoras de Cervantes," Diego addressed them both, "I would like to ask for Isabel's hand in matrimony." Constanza dropped her sewing. Andrea let out a shriek and clapped.

"Isabel is getting married!"

"Not so fast, Andrea," her sister said. *Thank God for Magdalena!*

"Señor Sanz, as you must be aware, we do not have authority to approve such a proposal. I am Isabel's guardian, but she has a father. It is he who needs to grant approval."

"But it would help greatly," Diego replied, his voice soft and sweet, which Constanza distrusted to her core, "if you gave your approval and interceded in favour of our union. Isabel is the most beautiful, most perfect woman I have ever met."

Isabel remained silent, but Constanza was sure she was smiling.

"Señor Sanz, such a petition should be made by the head of your family on your behalf. By your father, to be precise."

"My parents are in the process of moving back to Spain from Italy, where they have been living."

Italy? Isabel hadn't mentioned Italy when she talked about Diego.

"It will be a few months until they arrive and, since they are on the move, I have no way of communicating with them. But I am sure," he paused, "that they will love Isabel as much as I do."

Constanza was now pacing in the sewing room, debating whether she should join the others.

"You are a painter, is that correct?" Magdalena asked, sounding somewhat skeptical.

"*Sí*, señora. I studied in Rome and returned recently. I am in search of a patron, and confident I will find one soon."

A patron? Does he know how hard it is to find a patron in a country with so many artists? Miguel managed to secure a patron only in middle age. What makes Diego think he would fare better?

"Aunt Magdalena, Aunt Andrea," Isabel intervened, "Father said that, when the time came, he would give me his support to marry a worthy man. Diego is everything I could ask for and more. Please give us your blessing and help us to obtain Father's."

"All I can do is send a letter to your father. Keep in mind that he is the only person who can approve this union."

Constanza exhaled. *Good. Miguel will never allow this madness.* The moment he saw Diego, he would feel the same apprehension as she did. It was not jealousy, no—although the thought of sewing Isabel's trousseau made her stomach turn. It was something else, something she hoped to God everybody would see sooner rather than later.

IV

CATALINA

Domine Jesu, dimitte nobis debilita nostra,
Salva nos ab igne inferiori,
Perduc in caelum omnes animas,
Prasertim eas, quae misericordiae tuae maxie indigent.

DEAR JESUS, PLEASE have mercy. Never have I seen Miguel this angry.

"Isabel is getting married?"

"No, she is not!" He threw Magdalena's letter on the desk. "She is not!"

"Calm down, my love. It is dangerous to—"

"How can you even ask me to calm down?"

Since his arrival in Esquivias, Miguel has been writing without interruption, taking strolls with me in the vineyard and through the olive grove. He even joins our neighbours as they discuss current matters, the state of the kingdom in general, and our town in particular, things that men enjoy talking about. With the nightmare of Valladolid behind us, our life has been perfect, and this had been a lovely July morning, dear Jesus, a lovely morning—until Magdalena's letter arrived. Now I stood behind his chair, began to massage his shoulders, and asked him what was going to happen.

"Nothing is going to happen, because Isabel is not marrying a painter without a patron or a family. Period."

He handed me the letter. I shook my head as I read Magdalena's words. This was unacceptable, even for Isabel.

"I agree with you," I said, lowering my hands to his chest and kissing his neck. "She will do as you say, you are her father."

"She'd better," he agreed with a huff. "But she is impetuous."

"I know someone else who is impetuous and has not fared too badly," I teased, covering his mouth with mine.

"Not now, Catalina!" He pushed me away. He had never pushed me away before. "This requires my urgent attention."

I am your wife, I wanted to say, *and I, too, require your urgent attention. I want nothing more than to give you the gift of a child who will obey you, a child born of honour and love, a child from my womb before I am too old.*

But no words came out of my mouth, dear Jesus, I did not have the courage to let my thoughts loose like that. Miguel picked up his quill and began writing back to Magdalena. He didn't even turn to look at me as I left his studio.

I retreated, hoping he would come after me and say he was sorry. He did not. He stayed at his desk, then went to town. He returned late and, instead of lying down in bed next to me, went back to his desk again. He barely touched the food I had set aside. He seems to have forgotten I exist. Never have I seen Miguel this angry. Dear Jesus, please have mercy on him. Have mercy on us all.

V

ISABEL

"YOUR FATHER SAID NO, Isabel. There is nothing to be done." Magdalena was holding Father's letter in her hand. She refused to let me read it, but I could tell she wasn't lying.

"What will I do now?" I protested. I would never escape this house, this life. Waiting until I turned twenty-five to claim the tavern and then facing another judge with my aunts by my side was out of the question.

"Diego must stop courting you. A suitable candidate for your hand in marriage will appear soon enough."

"Like he appeared for Constanza?"

Magdalena shook her head in disapproval. "That comment was unnecessary, Isabel." She made a sign indicating that I should exit the studio. "Now I must reply to your father to inform him that his decision shall be obeyed. He must be worried sick about your future."

Had Father forgotten his promise to me? Here was a gentleman asking for my hand, and he had turned him down. Why did he not even bother to come to meet Diego?

"If he was going to worry so much about my future, he should have made sure I was legitimate," I said angrily.

"Silence!"

But the fire in my aunt's eyes was no match for the blaze burning within me. I was certain that God had taken Simón Méndez out of my path because Diego was the man who was meant for me. He was my liberator. I had to find a solution. But I would have to be smarter than Magdalena and my father.

"Diego will be here at four this afternoon for our stroll," I said. "May I at least say goodbye to him, please?"

"You may say goodbye to him here, in the foyer."

"Aunt Magdalena!" I pleaded. "He has been nothing but a gentleman. Please, let me go out with him as planned. Let this be our last stroll. Maria will come along, as always. Let me be the one who breaks the news to him, I beg you!"

She let out a sigh. "I don't know, Isabel. Your father—"

"My father isn't here, he's in Esquivias. And I'm begging you." I reached out to my aunt and held her hands in mine. They were thick with veins, and her pale skin was covered in dark spots that had not been there when I joined her household. She had changed, and so had I. "Please."

Relenting, she nodded her head. "Don't be out too long! And I want a word with him when you return, just to make sure he knows he's not to come again." I nodded and left the studio. I had a few hours to think about what to do next.

When at four o'clock there was a knock on the door, Maria and I were ready. Diego and I walked arm in arm; Maria followed a few steps behind. It was August and the summer sun had brought a pause to everyday activities, but we liked strolling at that time because there were fewer people in the street. Everyone who could do so stayed indoors to avoid the heat until at least five or six in the afternoon. We relished the peaceful cooing of pigeons, the slow clip-clop of horses in the distance, the lazy barking here and there. And that day, I craved Diego's lips and hands like I had never craved Simón's. How would I tell him that we could never be together?

"*Cariño*, what's wrong?" Diego was always careful to whisper when we were out together so that Maria wouldn't hear us.

I stopped walking. "Father said I cannot marry you." Now that I had uttered the words, they took on a new dimension. I found myself breaking into tears.

He turned to face me, lifted my mantilla, and dried my eyes with his handkerchief. I wanted to kiss his fingers, his mouth, but I controlled myself because he was so calm, so collected. A gentleman. I could not behave as anything less than a lady.

"Fathers say so many things," he replied with a smiled. "If you only knew what mine had said to me once—and look at me now!" He had never spoken about his father, other than to say he was away.

"Tell me!" I said, wondering what he meant. "I want to know."

"Never mind me, *Cariño*. Tell me what *you* want. Do you want to be my wife?"

"I do!" I was crying again. "You know I do!"

"Let's get married, then!" He held my hands, kissed them, and lowered my mantilla again. "I have an idea. It may be an outrageous idea, but oftentimes those are the best." I nodded in agreement. If only I were a man! Life would be so much easier.

We resumed our stroll. "We don't want Maria to suspect anything," he cautioned. "We'll tell her we want to pray together. Let me take care of the rest."

I smiled, enjoying the sense of intrigue, and with Maria

walking behind us, I let him guide me down the streets until we reached the Iglesia de San Luis. This was neither my parish nor his. It made no sense to pray here.

"What are we doing here?"

"You will soon see."

He led me inside and asked me to sit down on a pew while he found the priest. Maria sat down a few pews behind me. I watched as she kneeled in prayer. A few moments later, Diego returned, and both he and the priest sat next to me. Diego spoke to him softly.

"Father, I appreciate your discretion. We have come to join our lives in holy matrimony. Can you marry us now?" My eyes opened wide. Was he joking? Marry him *now*?

As I had expected, the priest said no. He explained that there were rules to be followed. In the first place, we had to be parishioners of San Luis. The publication of the banns had to be considered. We needed witnesses. There was legal paperwork that had to be processed.

Diego smiled. I saw him take a gold coin from his pocket and place it in the priest's hand. "Father, I'm sure exceptions can be made when it's a matter of true love. Am I right?"

I was taken aback. How could Diego dare to bribe a priest? He would be excommunicated! We would be kicked out of there at any moment. Maria would tell Magdalena and she would never trust me again. But instead of protesting, the priest took the coin.

"With all the documentation required, the earliest the marriage can take place is a few months from now— December. I will need your full names and two witnesses. Is this acceptable?"

I felt dizzy. Dizzy, scared, and ecstatic. December?

"Is that acceptable to you, my beautiful bride?" Diego asked, his blue eyes my guiding stars.

"Yes! Yes, it's perfect!" If I managed to keep the secret, I would even have time to sew my trousseau.

"Come with me," the priest said to Diego. "There are papers that need to be signed to begin the process." Diego squeezed my hand and followed the priest while I waited, fidgeting with my skirt, wiping the sweat off the palms of my hands. By December, I would be Diego's bride, and once Father met him, he would understand and forgive me. I had no doubt about it.

When my future groom came back and we left the church, I lifted my mantilla and asked him for a kiss. Our first kiss. He shook his head. Cupping my face in his hands, he kissed my forehead and rubbed the tip of his nose against mine. "What was that?" I asked, laughing. "That was not a kiss!"

"Maria is watching—we must be careful not to raise suspicions. Besides, I respect you too much, *Cariño*. Things taste better when you have ached for them."

VI

✥✥✥✥✥✥✥✥✥✥

CONSTANZA

"IS THAT SILK, COUSIN?" Isabel had never taken any pleasure in sewing, so that crisp fall morning, when she sat down
in the sewing room and began working on what looked like a
bedsheet, Constanza could not hide her surprise.

"It is silk, yes." Isabel was humming, she did not even lift
her eyes towards Constanza.

"I don't remember receiving an order for a set of sheets."

"I am sewing them for myself," Isabel replied, almost
singing. "I've decided to spend my spare time preparing my
hope chest. I want to have my trousseau ready when the time
comes, instead of rushing."

"A wedding is never rushed," Constanza said with a laugh.
"It takes many months to plan."

"Which is why it is even better to have the most basic
elements ready, such as linens," Isabel replied. She was working diligently and with care. No one would have guessed that
in the past she had pricked her finger every time she held a
needle.

Constanza watched her for a few moments. Then she
continued with the alterations of a chemise a customer had
inherited from a relative. It was old and stained, but except

for a pair of holes it was still in good condition. Maria would soak the garment in urine to whiten it, boil it in vinegar, and scrub it with soap, and it would look as good as new. In the past, they wouldn't have accepted this kind of job, but since her mother and her aunt's workload had been reduced, no order could be refused, especially since Maria had introduced them to this method of bleaching. She had set a tub on the back patio to collect the urine from their chamber pots. After the garments had been whitened, boiled, and washed, they were ironed and starched. Repairing damaged garments was proving to be a good business.

"Are you going somewhere?" Constanza asked in a friendly tone.

"No," Isabel replied, still humming. "Why do you ask?"

"You smell good."

"Thank you!" Isabel stopped sewing for a moment to lift her braid to her nose. "I used orange blossom oil. The way Teresa taught me," she added in a softer voice.

"I know. The smell reminds me of her, too." Constanza sighed, thinking it was strange for Isabel to take such care of her appearance when she had nowhere to go, no one to see. After Magdalena had dismissed Diego and asked him not to come to the house again, Isabel continued to act cheerfully. She didn't appear distraught, as Constanza expected. When she mentioned this to her aunt, Magdalena said it showed how much Isabel had matured, to which Constanza replied that maybe she did not love Diego as much as she claimed to. After that, there was a tense silence between the two women.

"Isabel!" Andrea exclaimed as she entered the sewing room. "I don't think I have seen you working here in ages!" She took up her spot behind the distaff and began spinning the wool that Magdalena would use to embroider a shirt.

"Bedsheets?" Magdalena said when she walked in, looking puzzled.

"For the future, Aunt Magdalena," Isabel said. "I may as well do something productive with my time."

"I knew the day would come when you would enjoy sewing, *mi niña*," Andrea said with a smile. "What are you working on?"

"She's working on her hope chest," Constanza replied. "The linens for her trousseau."

"I thought she wasn't getting married," Andrea said. "Are you getting married?"

"Not now, Aunt Andrea," Isabel said calmly. "But one day I will. Aunt Magdalena said I should not give up hope, so I have decided to listen to her."

"It's nice to see you listen to me for a change," Magdalena said, looking pleased. Isabel continued humming. Soon Andrea and Magdalena joined her.

"My mother used to sing a lovely song at the tavern when I was small. I haven't heard it since, but I still remember it."

"Sing it for us, Isabel," Andrea said. "A little music will do us good. I can't remember the last time we sang together."

"Good idea," Magdalena said. "You do have a beautiful voice. Sing!"

Constanza had stopped sewing to observe her cousin, the way she swayed her torso as she sang, the way she closed her eyes.

¿A quién contaré yo mis quejas / mi lindo amor
a quién contaré yo mis quejas / si a vos no?
Esperanza por quien padece / mi corazón

¿a quién contaré yo mis quejas / si a vos no?
Muerto quedo si tú me dejas / mi lindo amor
¿a quién contaré yo mis quejas / si a vos no?

"Oh, I remember that song!" Magdalena said, excited. "Do you remember it, Andrea?"

"I do! It used to be your father's favourite, Constanza!"

"It did?" It had been so long since her mother had mentioned her father that Constanza could not contain her excitement. "Can you teach it to me?"

"Sure! Just follow the melody." Isabel put down her sewing and started clapping the rhythm with her hands and feet, enticing the rest to sing and clap along with her.

¿A quién contaré yo mis quejas / mi lindo amor
a quién contaré yo mis quejas / si a vos no?

Maria came into the room, curious to see what was happening. When Isabel saw her, she rose to her feet and invited her to dance.

"Come, Maria! I'm sure you know this song!"

One by one, Isabel brought them to their feet. When they tired of that song, Isabel sang another, and then another. Where had she learned so many songs? Why hadn't she sung them before? Constanza wondered.

"I haven't felt this exhilarated in years!" Andrea exclaimed, panting, and she sat down to rest. She fanned her face with her hands, laughing. Isabel continued clapping and tapping her feet.

"I think I will sit down, too!" Magdalena said. "This is too much for me!" Constanza felt uncomfortable dancing alone with Maria and Isabel, who were so much younger and more gracious. She returned to her seat and asked Maria to bring them water.

"I never knew you could sing and dance like that," she said to Isabel.

"There are many things about me that you don't know, cousin," Isabel said. When Constanza frowned, she added quickly, "I was fifteen when I came to live with you. I had a life before then."

Maria came back with the water. They each took a glass, and Isabel made a toast as if they were drinking wine.

"What are we celebrating, may I ask?" Constanza could not hide her irritation.

"We are celebrating that we're alive, cousin. And hoping for a better future."

"I will toast to that!" Andrea said, and Constanza resumed her sewing in silence.

VII

November 1606
My dear Miguel,

I do not know how to start this letter or how to explain.
I followed your instructions exactly, yet I failed. I should
have noticed what was going on, but I ignored the signs.
Constanza saw them, but I didn't believe her. Now it is
imperative that you return home. Isabel did not end her
relationship with Diego Sanz del Aguila as we thought.
Wedding banns have already been published and they are
to marry in early December. Isabel says that if you do not
allow her to marry this man, she will leave and cease all
contact with us.

Miguel, I beg you, please come home. The thought of
never seeing her again—my Isabel, whom I have cared for
as a daughter—is intolerable to me. I have lived with her and
taught her everything I could since she was fifteen years old.
She is your daughter, but she is my child, too, and I do not
want to lose her. Please, Miguel, reconsider. Meet Diego.
Now that I have learned the truth, I can assure you that Isabel
is happier than I have ever seen her. If you do just one more
thing for me, let it be this.

May God protect you during your journey to Madrid. Forgive your daughter and lend her your support. She is blood of your blood.

Love from your sister,
Magdalena

VIII

CATALINA

Domine Iesu,
dimitte nobis debita nostra,
salva nos ab igne inferiori,
perduc in caelum omnes animas,
praesertim eas,
quae misericordiae tuae maxime indigent.

IT WAS THE saddest of weddings for the most beautiful of brides, and it pained me that You, who blessed the union between Miguel and me, which was so full of joy and love, were forced to bless this one as well. An empty church, an indifferent priest, an enraged father. Miguel barely said a word on the journey from Esquivias to Madrid. It was December and we travelled by carriage for protection from the fierce grip of winter, which was already squeezing the air, and during all those hours he remained silent. There was nothing I could say or do to calm his anger, to alleviate his pain, his sense of betrayal. I could only wait and pray. Talking to You is my greatest source of strength and solace.

Miguel declared that he would authorize the marriage but withhold any dowry. If Isabel insisted on marrying a man that we knew nothing about, and whose fortune is of questionable origin, so be it, he said. Let her face the consequences. His job as her father was done.

Forgive me, dear Lord, for all the times that I have wished to hear those words. I could see the anguish in his eyes and feel it in his voice. Looking at him, I understood that disowning a child is as unnatural as disowning your own arm or leg. Miguel had already lost an arm. Now he was losing something much more precious, and there was nothing I could do to soothe his pain.

Isabel looked beautiful—so unspeakably beautiful!—but during the entire ceremony she did not smile, the groom's blue eyes were like ice, and once the papers were signed and the priest declared them husband and wife, Miguel took my arm and we left the church without uttering a single word. He did not even look back, but I did, and when I saw Isabel's eyes, I could not hold back my tears. No bride deserves a wedding this sad, my Lord.

During our journey back home, I remembered Miguel's character Marcela, the shepherdess who chose her own destiny and defended her decision to live alone, without a husband. Now I barely recognized Miguel, he was such a different man. He frightened me. Oh, how sweet it would be to exist as a woman on paper alone, instead of in the flesh, a woman who prays for a child but bears none, a woman who yearns for a husband but is forbidden to marry, a woman who loses her father the day she wins a husband. You, my Lord, gave us each a cross to atone for our sins. Give us strength to carry it well. Relieve our load with Your light.

IX

ISABEL

"WELCOME TO YOUR new home, *Cariño*!" Diego opened the door and led me into the foyer. I looked around, trying to smile, but my chin began to tremble and I bit my lip. I was so hurt and shocked at the way Father had behaved at the church. But I didn't want to think about that now.

"I'm sorry, it must be the excitement!" I said. Diego took my chin in his hand, caressing my lips with his thumb. His face was close to mine, his eyes my own piece of sky. He smelled like wine and I wanted to drink him in. I closed my eyes, inviting him to kiss me.

"Your father will regret his behaviour one day," he said.

I opened my eyes, confused. Why hadn't he kissed me? "You don't know him, he's stubborn," I replied.

"But he's a good man, too."

"How do you know that? He didn't even want to meet you," I protested.

"I read his book."

I rolled my eyes. "Everyone in the kingdom has read his book. So what?"

"And I looked into his eyes. He will come around. He loves you."

I shook my head. "Enough about my father," I said. I had to focus on what I had gained—a home of my own, a husband, a new life. Diego led me into the room where he did his work, which was next to the foyer and featured two tall windows that let in a generous amount of light, but right away I noticed an unpleasant odour I couldn't place.

"What is that?" I asked, covering my nose.

"That's my paints," he said. Canvases were stacked against the wall. There was paper everywhere; sketches and drawings were scattered all over the wooden floor. I could see dozens of paintbrushes in various containers. The scene was chaotic, but it was the smell that bothered me.

"It's oppressive!" I complained. My nose was filled with it.

"Is it? I don't even notice it. It must be the linseed oil." He was moving around the room, excited. "This place is freezing. When I light the braziers, *Cariño*, it will be better for you." I had experienced many vile scents throughout my life, so I always made sure I was clean and tried to smell nice for Diego. No wonder he had never appreciated my efforts!

"You'll get used to the scent, and it will be easier in the summer when we can open the window without freezing. I apologize for now," he said, pushing his painting paraphernalia to one side of the room. I rubbed my hands and blew into them. There were no tapestries on any of the walls to help keep out the cold. To take my mind off the discomfort, I began to look through the paintings and drawings. There were some landscapes, but most of the works were naked bodies, both female and male. The bodies had no faces.

"Do you like my work?" Diego called out from the other room.

"I do!" I said cheerfully. In fact, although I had no

experience with art, compared to the paintings I had seen at church, these did not seem very good. I thought they lacked precision, expression. But I told myself not to be so harsh. After all, I knew the altarpieces in church were paid for by wealthy congregants. It wasn't fair to compare Diego's work to paintings done by experienced artists. He was young. He could improve.

I left the room and closed the door, hoping the odour would remain inside. The foyer led to a second room that had a red woven carpet of oriental design. It was the most beautiful rug I had ever seen.

"Where did you buy that?" I asked in surprise.

"That's a Persian rug, *Cariño*."

I stepped out of my chopines and walked on it, then knelt down to feel its texture with my fingers. "Is it made of silk?"

"It might be, but I'm not sure," Diego said. He was still busy with the braziers. I explored the room. It was sparsely furnished, and the few objects in it were elegant but looked somehow out of place. There were two leather armchairs. A dusty cupboard held pieces of fine porcelain, a few silver spoons, and plates that looked as if they had been left behind. I wanted to take in my new home. The bedroom door was half-open. I could see the trunk with my belongings, which Diego had brought here before the ceremony, as well as a canopy bed dressed with the bedsheets I had sewn and embroidered. I had dreamed of entering my marital bedroom holding my husband's hand, but since Diego had still not caught up with me, I followed a narrow hallway to the kitchen instead.

There was a rough table and rickety chairs. A pail held slimy water. To make matters worse, the stove was full of ashes. It looked like no one had cleaned it in weeks.

"Don't you have a servant?" I asked in consternation.

"No, *Cariño*. Servants gossip and can't be trusted. I do have a laundress, though, and she knows how to care for ladies' clothing. I thought we could handle the rest on our own."

I felt a knot in my throat. Handle the rest on our own? By the looks of it, he had not been handling it at all.

"The fire is ready!" he announced as he caught me up and hugged me from behind. "Forgive my untidiness. I'm terrible at living alone," he said apologetically.

Now that I had seen all the rooms, I knew that it would be at least a few days before the place was livable. And I still had to determine which fountain I would fetch our water from—I didn't want to risk an encounter with my family. I brought my hand to my forehead and tried to make sense of the wave of emotions that threatened to break over me. I had finally got what I wanted! So why did I feel such an urge to cry?

"Why are you sad, *Cariño*?" Diego drew me into his arms and kissed the top of my head. "What can I do to make that sadness go away?"

I moved away from him and went to the window. "I find this apartment quite charming," I said as I took in the view of the narrow, graceless street, so close to my family, so far from the prosperous part of Madrid, "and I know I should have mentioned this to you before, but—"

"But what? What's wrong?"

"I was so preoccupied with the wedding and my trousseau ..."

"What? What is it?" He looked at me, eyes open wide. I placed my hand on his cheek.

"As an artist, you have a reputation to uphold. I think that will be hard to do if you live in this area."

I thought he would be angry, but instead he kissed me lightly on the cheek.

"You're absolutely right! Where would you like us to move?"

I had to think for a moment. I hadn't expected him to agree so readily. But perhaps his impetuousness was not a bad thing. I had to seize the opportunity to return to the place I knew best, where I felt more at ease, more like myself, and where I could start my new life as his wife.

"Any artist who wants to be successful must have access to the court. You need to live close to the palace. How else can you find a patron?"

"All right, as long as it's an apartment and not a house, we might be able to afford it. Would that make my bride happy?"

"That would make your bride very happy, yes." I exhaled with relief.

"And now, please do me the honour of coming with me."

He led me back to the main room, where the fire was crackling, and helped me remove my veil and cape. Then he proceeded to take off my wedding dress. His hands were clumsy and he couldn't undo the buttons, so he asked me to do this while he poured us each a glass of wine. The room was warm now, and he smiled when he saw that I almost had the dress off. The wine glasses were made of the finest crystal and they made a lovely musical sound when we toasted.

"To our love!" Diego declared, and he drank the entire glass in one swallow and poured himself another. After the second glass, he resumed his exploration of my body. Once I was completely naked, he asked me to lie down on the rug, and he sat down to contemplate me. I was timid at first, but after a bit more wine I felt more comfortable. Would he kiss me now?

"I knew your body would be as perfect as your face. Perfect!"

"Perfect for what?" I wanted to ask. It was our wedding night. I was expecting him to join me on the rug or take me to the bedroom. I thought he might carry me to bed, but instead he went into the other room and emerged with his easel, brushes, and paint supplies.

"What are you doing?" I asked in shock.

"Don't move! I need to take advantage of the light!" he cried.

"Are you painting *me*?" I protested. "For everyone to see?" I reached for my chemise.

"Don't worry, *Cariño*. These are studies, for my eyes only. None will include your face. But your face will be on my Madonna."

"A Madonna?" I smiled. "But I don't look like Jesus's mother!"

"You, my love, are a goddess. You will be my Venus as well!"

"Venus?"

"I am serious, *Cariño*," he said, demonstrating how to hold my arm, how to bend my leg. His fingers brushing against my skin, the proximity of his mouth, sent shivers all over me. If this was so important for him, I would oblige.

"How long will this take?" I asked.

"As long as necessary."

And that was how the rest of the afternoon and evening were spent—me, fighting the urge to stretch my arms and legs to allow my muscles some rest; and him, painting without speaking a word, his eyes drinking up my body and pouring it onto the canvas. Was this normal? Why did he not want to touch me if he found me beautiful and I was his wife? He drank, praised my beauty, and drank some more.

"I'm cold," I protested, once it was dark enough to light the candles.

"I'm so sorry, *Cariño*!" he replied, flustered, and he helped me put my chemise back on. Then he served some bread, cheese, and *chorizo*, which we ate together, toasting with more wine. At last, he led me to the bedroom. I lay down in bed and closed my eyes, trying to conceal my excitement, waiting for him to touch me. But as soon as he blew out the candles and took his place next to me, Diego fell asleep, snoring loudly.

X

February 1607
Dearest Miguel,

May God be watching over you and Catalina this winter. I
hope that you have been able to write again after your brief
and bitter visit to Madrid. I am not surprised to hear that
you have difficulty sleeping. I have, too, especially since your
daughter's last visit—yes, *your daughter*, whether you like
it or not.

I know you do not want to read this, or hear about it, but
it is important that you do. Isabel came to visit us briefly to
inform us that she and Diego are moving to an apartment by
the Plaza de Santo Domingo, close to her previous home on
Tudescos. She believes it is a better area to live as he continues to search for a patron. Our girl is not looking well, and
I believe this is in part because your attitude has caused her
much sorrow. But I suspect there are other causes as well.
When I asked her how she spends her days, she told me that
she is mostly home alone because Diego goes out to paint, or
to pursue contacts, or to meet with potential customers who
might want to hire him to paint their portrait. I was discreet
when I asked this question, but apparently she knows no
more about Diego than she did before, except that at some

point he received a hit to the head that causes him severe headaches, which he keeps under control by drinking wine.

I worry, Miguel, because I could tell by her hands and her nails that she is doing housework herself. Why, I wonder, if she does not appear to want for anything, does she have no help at home? With so many desperate souls available to perform this kind of work for food and a roof over their heads! Isabel should be a happy, treasured newlywed, and Madrid should be the jewel in our Empire's crown. Instead, your heart would break to behold your daughter, and it would dampen your spirits to see how many people of Moorish and Barbarian origin and looks are populating our streets. Some are even being sold as slaves! I shudder when I walk by them because I think of you, and Rodrigo, and all those Christians who have been held prisoners in Barbary and sold, as you yourself almost were, to faraway lands, never to be seen by their families again. We condemn what happens there and yet we do the same here.

Please think about your daughter, and do not forget the most important lesson taught to us by our Jesus Christ: *Even though we have rebelled against him, our Lord remains forgiving and merciful.*

Love,
Magdalena

XI

ISABEL

THE FIRST FEW days after moving to our new apartment, I had a hard time believing this was my new reality and not a dream. I thanked God every morning for the luxurious and spacious rooms that afforded me a life of comfort and beauty I never imagined would be within my reach. The more I thought about Mother's place above the tavern, Grandmother's house, the family home on Leganitos, the apartment in Valladolid, and the house on Calle de la Magdalena, the more I appreciated our high ceilings and thick walls, a living room where the Persian rug reigned supreme, a bedroom with enough space to move around, and a kitchen and dining room that would have fit my entire family—had Father and my aunts shown an interest in having a relationship with us. When their absence weighed heavy in my heart, I took solace in the fresh air and the view from our balcony, as well as the safety and novelty to be found in my husband's company.

Diego and I soon developed a daily routine that met our needs and allowed us to spend time together. Every morning, we walked to the market to purchase our necessities for the day. Then I joined him on his painting outings beyond the city walls. He carried his canvas and art supplies while I followed behind with a thick blanket.

"Painting is much more than the proper depiction of an object, a landscape, or a person," he explained. "Some men paint in order to become famous or wealthy. My aim, and the purpose of art, is to serve God. When I paint, I strive to achieve bliss, because I see God in every place, person, and thing that inhabits our world."

Wrapped up in my warmest clothes, I sat on the blanket next to him and watched him work. In the beginning, I enjoyed seeing the dedication he put into every brushstroke. But I found that being outside for so long was uncomfortable, especially in cold weather or after it rained, and staring at the countryside for hours on end was tedious.

"Do you mind if I stay home today, Diego?" I asked one morning when the sky seemed to be made of iron instead of air. "I'm afraid I may catch a cold."

"Of course, *Cariño*! Being an artist is hard work. You, as my muse, need to take care of yourself."

But at home, all I did was pace around the apartment, listening to our neighbours chatting outside, watching people coming and going. Now that I was married, I was afraid to go out alone, since I had to protect Diego's honour. But I was also afraid that people could see the void that was growing inside me. Aside from the people at the market, I had no one to talk to. I had nowhere to go, nothing to do. When I suggested to Diego that we get a cat, he shook his head, explaining that "those devilish creatures" made him sneeze without control.

I missed running errands for my aunts. I missed listening to Father talk about his writing. How could I tell them that, rather than a wife, what Diego wanted was a combination of housekeeper and ornament? Was that what wives were supposed to be? Every day, I made a stew and waited for Diego to return so we could eat together. And every day, he came home tired, wanting to eat, drink, and fall asleep.

But one afternoon, he burst into the apartment with a fresh pigskin full of wine and a bouquet of flowers that he had picked especially for me.

"*Cariño*!" he exclaimed. "I have a surprise for you!"

"Thank you for the flowers!" I said, touched by the gesture. I fetched a vase and placed them on the table. I didn't realize that such a humble spark of colour could do wonders for the lifeless room. I smiled at him, pleased.

"That's not the surprise!" Diego said, taking me by the waist and pressing me against his body. I relished his touch, his chin on my shoulder, the salty masculine smell that contrasted with the sweetness of the flowers.

"What is it, then?"

"I accepted a commission!" he said with delight.

"That's wonderful!" I cried. "Who hired you? What will you paint?"

"It's a secret," he said with a smile, letting go of my waist and putting his finger to his lips. "But they gave me this as an advance!"

He produced from his pocket three silver coins and one gold one, which he placed next to the vase. He had never been paid this much. It had to be a large commission for an important customer. I was dying to know who it was, but I knew better than to insist. Instead, I decided to take advantage of the happy mood to talk about something that had been on my mind for weeks.

It was a subject I didn't know how to approach. Diego knew

who my father and mother were. But he didn't know I had a half-sister—he knew nothing about Ana. I was too scared to tell him before we were married because I didn't know how he would react. Then after we married, I was ashamed that I had hidden her. I felt like those knights in Father's library who are fighting a monster and cut off its head only to have two grow in its place. Perhaps I could try to get close to Ana again. But I would need Diego's financial support to make that happen. Hoping that this was a good time to discuss the matter, I decided to tell him the truth.

"Speaking of secrets," I said, lowering my eyes, "there's something I haven't told you."

Diego was pouring wine. "You know you can tell me anything, *Cariño*. Let's celebrate!"

"I have a little sister ..." I began, and I told him the whole sad story. Diego listened without interrupting. When I was done, he drank a full glass of wine before speaking.

"Family can be hard to deal with at times, *Cariño*. I should know."

"Is someone else in your family besides your father hard to deal with, too?" I asked, thinking this question might open the door to his past. But he shook his head and changed the subject to Ana.

"Never mind my family. I agree that you must help your sister. Just be mindful about our money. We have to make it last. Who knows when I will get another commission as good as this one?"

It was hard to say whether I felt grateful or dismissed yet again. But I had this image of Diego: if he were a city, he would be surrounded by the tallest, most impenetrable walls. Could I ever find my way in?

I served him the stew I had prepared. We ate and drank together while he talked about his big plans for the future. This commission would open the door to another, he was sure of it, and who knows? He might even become a court painter. *A court painter!* His blue eyes were so bright that even when I lit the candles they shone like fire.

"Would you like to draw me?" I asked. I had to at least give it a try. I poured him more wine.

"Yes, that's a great idea!" he said. While he fetched his charcoal and paper, I slowly undressed and positioned myself on the rug the way he had taught me. "You are the most beautiful woman in all of Spain, Isabel. Don't move!"

The most beautiful woman in all of Spain? Then why did he never touch me? That yearning I used to feel for Simón, who was always so ready to satisfy me, was now directed towards Diego as never before. His eyes travelled over my skin, and I watched his hand as it glided skilfully over the paper. His fingers were stained with charcoal, and this gave me the perfect excuse. I stood up.

"*Cariño*, where are you going?" he asked. I went towards the kitchen.

"Your fingers are dirty," I said. "If you go to bed like that, it will be impossible to wash the stains off the sheets," I explained, knowing that this was not true. "Let me clean them for you."

"But I'm not finished yet!" he protested. But when I offered him another glass of wine, he put down the paper and closed his eyes. He was tired: here was my chance. Before he knew it, my hand was between his legs, my lips on his, my tongue exploring him the way Simón had taught me to do.

At first he resisted, but when I felt him respond I straddled him and pressed him firmly between my legs. I slid my mouth down to his neck and bit him gently. When I pulled him against me, he closed his eyes and followed my rhythm. Our breath became one, and it was as if the entire room was dancing around us. But I had barely started swaying my hips when I felt his spasm, and his flesh went limp inside me. I stopped and gazed into his eyes, unsure what to do next. He pushed me away and I fell over on the floor, hurting my back and my elbow. Then he looked at me with a mixture of disgust, confusion, and shame that frightened me. Did he realize that I had been with another man? Did he want to avenge his honour? I curled up on the floor and covered my head with my arms, afraid he was going to be beat me. But instead he stood up, went into his workroom, and closed the door.

I didn't know if I should follow him to offer an explanation or an apology. My back ached, my elbow was bruised, and I started to cry. I wanted him to love me the way I loved him.

I washed myself, put on my chemise, and went to bed, but I couldn't sleep. The moment I heard the workroom door open, I leapt out of bed and went to him. Dawn was still hours away, but he was getting dressed.

"Where are you going?" I asked.

"I need to get ready for my commission."

"It's the middle of the night!" I protested.

"A walk at night always clears my mind. It's good for creativity."

"Diego, no one walks alone at night, except those looking for trouble," I replied. The more I tried to make eye contact, the more he avoided looking at me. There had to be something I could say to make him change his mind and stay at home with me. "Tomorrow is *Santiago el Verde*," I said, feeling a knot in my throat that threatened to become a dam. "You promised we would go together."

"I was not on commission when I made that promise. I'm afraid it's impossible." He gathered his art supplies and some of his clothes and placed more money on the table. I tried to fight off a terrible sense of desolation.

"Where are you going? When are you coming back?" I cried, but he didn't bother to give me an answer. He left the apartment and slammed the door behind him. The dam in my throat collapsed, giving way to a flood of tears.

XII

CONSTANZA

WEARING HER BEST dress, a pair of pearl earrings that Andrea had received from her second husband, and a hat especially bought for the occasion, Constanza hurried to meet her aunt, who was waiting by the door.

"You look beautiful!" Magdalena said, her voice high-pitched with excitement.

It was the first of May, a day celebrated in Madrid as *el día de Santiago el Verde*, a day to honour spring and all its renewal. Every year, people from all social backgrounds made the pilgrimage to the church of Felipe y Santiago, travelling by carriage, sedan chair, horse, donkey, or on foot. Over the past few years, the Cervantes women had missed the event—first the plague had made it feel unsafe, and then they had been away in Valladolid. But now that they were back in Madrid, Magdalena insisted they all attend.

At first, Constanza had declined. "I'm too old for that, Aunt Magdalena!" she protested.

"Too old to have a good time? What about your mother and me? We're both going!"

"And what if someone robs our home while we're away?"

"Constanza, no one will be anywhere near the house.

Everyone will be gathered by the river," her aunt said.

After Isabel left to live with Diego, the house felt empty, too quiet. Constanza knew that Magdalena tried to find ways to fill the void left by her cousin's absence. But she chafed at her aunt's clumsy attempts to make her feel better about her situation. Now that Isabel was married, Magdalena was suddenly willing to parade Constanza in front of all Madrid to see if she could pique a man's interest. None of this would be necessary if only they had allowed her to marry Francisco! She would probably have children by now, and on the first of May she would walk alongside them and her husband, like so many other families.

Above all, *Santiago el Verde* was an opportunity for all *madrileños* to show off, to see others and to be seen by them. Women who had the means paraded, sumptuously dressed, in carriages or sedan chairs, their faces plastered white with lead and their lips the colour of vermillion. Constanza knew she couldn't compare to these women, and she didn't expect to receive compliments from strangers like she had in the past. But the music and dancing would lighten her spirits. And perhaps it was not too late, after all, for *her* to be seen. So she told Magdalena she would join them.

The women left early so they could walk at ease, without rushing. They had decided they would go there on foot and hire a mule or a donkey to bring them back. The city was full of life. People sang and horses neighed. Girls and young women wore garlands of roses and carnations on their heads. It would be a pleasant march from Calle de la Magdalena across the city to the river. Maria followed closely behind. Perhaps she was hoping she, too, might find a suitor?

They approached the king's residence in the Alcázar.

Constanza was enjoying herself. It was good to spend a day out in the sun, feeling the breeze as it lifted her hair and played with her dress. It was good to see her mother and her aunt having fun after four months of focusing on their duties. If they were lucky, perhaps the king himself would come out and salute his subjects from his royal carriage.

Constanza recalled the day in Valladolid when the entire city celebrated Miguel and his knight Don Quixote. It had only been a year ago, yet it seemed like several lifetimes. But today, for the first time in many months, she felt a little spark of hope glowing again inside her chest. Perhaps someone would notice and compliment her. Perhaps.

They had just passed the city walls on their way to the Sotillo, the field across the river, between the old bridge to Toledo and the stone bridge where the pilgrimage was headed. Suddenly, Magdalena pulled the other three women to the side. She pointed at a man about twenty feet away from them, standing at an easel, painting a landscape.

"Is that Diego?" she asked.

"I can't tell from here. His hat is covering his face," Andrea replied.

"It looks like him," Magdalena said. "Isabel must be close by." They looked around, but couldn't see any sign of her.

"Perhaps she's already by the river?" Andrea suggested.

"Alone, on a day like this? She's a married woman now," Magdalena protested.

"Where could she be?" Maria asked.

Constanza tried to hide her irritation. She was disappointed that she hadn't received any compliments so far. And now even today had to end up being about Isabel!

"Have you considered that she may be hidden from view

in a sedan chair?" she asked, thinking it was a ridiculous idea, and that it would make the others laugh. Her aunt frowned; her mother smiled.

"That hadn't occurred to me, but you may very well be right," said Andrea. Magdalena hesitated, staring at Diego. Constanza hoped that she didn't dare to approach him to ask where Isabel was. He was busy; he might not welcome an interruption from the family that had rejected him. Isabel had to be around somewhere, perhaps with new friends. Groups of women often travelled together in carts and carriages. One year, a carriage full of women without a male escort got stuck in the mud of the riverbank and it took several mules to pull it free. Witnesses recounted that although the ladies were scared to stay in the carriage, they were unwilling to step down and ruin their best dresses.

The four women continued their stroll, but Constanza's mood had changed. Her aunt's eyes were still searching for Isabel. She seemed to have forgotten why they had come here in the first place.

XIII

ISABEL

I SPENT THE entire *día de Santiago el Verde* crying at home, and in the days that followed I left the apartment only to purchase the very basics I needed to get by. I wanted to be there in case Diego returned to apologize for my behaviour. I sat and waited, paced the rooms and waited, composed letters to him in my head—letters I never had the courage to write. The flowers he gave me finally wilted and I had to throw them away.

That night, the sound of the front door opening woke me up. A wave of relief swept over me. God had heard my prayers and sent my husband back to me! I crossed myself and thanked Him. Waiting for Diego to enter the bedroom, I kept my eyes shut and pretended to be sleeping. I heard footsteps in the foyer and voices whispering. One of them was Diego's, but I didn't recognize the other. I lay in bed, my ears straining to make out any words, but the voices were too soft. The only thing I knew for certain was that Diego was in the company of another man. I remained still, my jaw clenched, my heart beating fast. Something wasn't right. I could sense it.

Minutes went by. Afraid that Diego might be in some kind of trouble, I got up and went very quietly towards the art room. If Diego saw me, I would say I was scared that an intruder was trying to steal his valuables. For a while there was silence. Then I thought I could make out what sounded like moaning. Perhaps I had misheard? I waited, listening intently. The door was very slightly ajar, and I peeked inside. My eyes were used to the darkness and the room was bathed in moonlight. Two silhouettes were in a close embrace. Was Diego lying with another man as he would with a woman? I backed away from the door and returned to bed. Gasping for air, I crossed myself and prayed to God for guidance.

I hated myself for crying again. I hated myself for not seeing the signals, which now seemed so obvious. I hated myself for falling in love with Diego's angelic face, his heavenly lips, his demonic body. Was our marriage still blessed by God? Would he burn in hell alone, or drag me with him to be tormented in its perennial flames? How could I carry on now? I had no one to talk to or go to for advice for simple problems, much less something as grave, as horrifying as what I had just discovered. I tried to imagine what Juan, Mother's brother the priest, would say if I suddenly appeared to request his counsel. He would welcome me with a blessing, then dismiss me with a curse! I closed my eyes and prayed, prayed and waited for morning to arrive. I would be able to think more clearly in the daylight.

I don't know how much time went by, but it was morning when my husband quietly entered the bedroom.

"Diego!" I said, feigning surprise. "You're back!"

He had cleaned himself up in the kitchen, I could tell. He had lost weight during the past few days. His eyes looked bigger, his cheekbones more defined. This is what the Fallen Angel must have looked like, I thought. How could someone be so repellent and attractive at the same time?

"*Cariño!*" As he approached me, I noted how the colour

of his eyes matched the piece of sky I could see through the window.

"I saw you last night." I said without preamble. He stopped in his tracks. "I heard you, and I saw you." A rage so strong it was impossible to contain sprang from my chest, made me form words, and pushed them out of my mouth, words that were like the waste that floated in the Esgueva's riverbank. My feelings for Diego, until last night as pure as holy water, had become fetid, and now all I wanted was to hurt him as badly as he had hurt me.

"Whatever you think you saw or heard, it's not true," he said, gazing at me in fear.

"I saw enough to understand the truth," I replied, more quietly now.

"Isabel, please! Listen to me!" Desperation lent his voice a fragile, almost feminine tone that confounded me; I was torn between wanting to protect him and spit at him. This was the person I had chosen as my husband, to whom I owed loyalty and fidelity until death did us part. Could I still think of him as a man?

"Isabel, you know me, you know I—"

"No, I don't know you. I don't know anything about you. Who are you?"

"I'm your husband and I love you. I never lied about that."

"But you can't love me, Diego, don't you see? You can't be what you are and love me."

"I can, Isabel," he protested, tears running down his cheeks, "if you give me the chance."

My incredulity must have shown on my face. "Give you the chance to do what? To invite sin into my bed?" I could hardly believe the words I was saying.

"Who are *you* to talk about sin?" he said, his tone suddenly defensive. "You acted so pure while I was courting you. Then the other night you were like an eagle hunting its prey!"

I was so upset when he said this that I slapped him. "The other night I was a normal wife, a wife who desired her husband—a wife who was unaware *she had married a sodomite!*"

At these words, Diego grabbed my shoulders. "Please, be quiet!" he pleaded, a look of terror in his eyes. He was right to be afraid; we were both in danger.

He sank onto the bed, crying. "I'll never do it again, I promise. Don't say anything, don't tell anyone! I'll do whatever you want. I never meant to harm you." I gazed down at him in anger and pity.

"You never meant to harm me? How is this false life"—I drew a circle with my hands to encompass everything around us—"how is this not harming me?"

"I gave you a place of your own, and your freedom. Wasn't that what you wanted?"

"Yes, but more than that: I wanted you to be my husband and act like a husband!"

"I'll try again. I'll do whatever you want." He pulled me towards him and kissed me. He kissed me as Simón never had. There was something sweet yet wicked in the way his tongue played around with mine, the way he bit my lips, and if I had allowed him to continue, I would have succumbed to temptation and allowed him to imbibe my heart and my soul, to consume my body. But everything had changed. As a Christian woman, it was my duty to reject the touch I had ached for as his wife. I pushed him away.

"You need to go," I said.

"Where?"

"Go back to your 'commission.' He'll welcome you back into his arms."

"The commission is real, Isabel! It's a fresco inside a rich man's house. I'm painting an image of the Holy Virgin. She will have your face." At this, another wave of rage surged up inside me.

"You expect me to believe that?" I demanded.

"I swear to God, it's true!"

"Sinner! You're swearing in vain!" I spat out, almost breathless with anger.

"I'll take you to see it! I've been working on it all week."

"No. I don't want to see anything," I said. The anger had suddenly evaporated, leaving only exhaustion. I had been rejected by my father and separated from my family to live with Diego as husband and wife. And now, here I was—more alone, more confused, more heartbroken than ever. "I don't want to see *you*. Just go."

My change of tone must have signalled to him that it was time to give up. He rose and headed to the door.

"I left something for you on the table," he said. I covered my face with my hands and fell back onto the mattress.

It was past noon when I ventured out into the hallway. My eyelids were swollen and my entire body was shaking. Diego was nowhere to be found.

On the table next to his key was a small leather pouch full of money—gold coins. Was that payment for the fresco or his body? Or both? I brought the pouch close to my chest. I would have given back all the coins if I could only unsee what I had seen, unhear what I had heard, unlive what I had just lived. I would have given back all the coins to hold Diego between my legs and grow his baby in my womb.

As I counted the coins, I thought of Ana and what I could provide for her with the money. I thought of Constanza and my aunts and me, working so hard to earn a fraction of this amount. I pondered my own future. I remembered Magdalena's words: "The money without the man is the best possible deal." Feeling a little like Eve when she bit the apple, like Mary Magdalene before Jesus, and like Judas himself, I decided to take the money, and I prayed for forgiveness.

XIV

June 1607
My dearest Miguel,

I know it was only a few weeks ago that I sent you a letter
expressing my concerns about Isabel, but those concerns
have only increased, and I need to alert you. Maria and I
were on our way to a customer's the other day when we
saw Isabel riding in a sedan chair. I almost did not recognize her (my eyes are not what they used to be, as you well
know) because she was dressed very elegantly, much more
so than her status allows. Could it be that Diego has found
a wealthy patron? I certainly hope so, but something tells
me this is not the case.

I am worried, Miguel, that going out alone, dressed above
her class, will bring Isabel trouble. I am also worried because
we saw Diego alone on *Santiago el Verde*, a day when they
should have been enjoying the festivities together. It took
me two days—and two nights of lost sleep—to gather the
courage to pay her a visit, but when I did, she was not home.
I happened to run into her neighbours, and they told me she
was very secretive about her comings and goings. They said
they have not seen Diego in several weeks. They noticed her
expensive clothing and clearly resent her.

I shiver when I remember Alicia de Ayala and the consequences of her evil tongue, for Isabel in particular. I do not want the story to repeat itself. Something is not right. Please come back to Madrid, I urge you. Your daughter needs you, even if she may not know it.

Looking forward to having you at home with us as soon as possible, I send you my love and my blessings for a safe journey.

Your sister,
Magdalena

XV

CATALINA

Sancte Michael Archangele,
defende nos in proelio,
contra nequitiam et insidias diaboli esto praesidium.
Imperet illi Deus, supplices deprecamur:
tuque, Princeps militiae caelestis, in virtute Dei,
in infernum detrude satanam aliosque spiritus malignos,
qui ad perditionem animarum pervagantur in mundo.
Amen.

SAN MIGUEL ARCÁNGEL, great captain of our souls, to You I pray for protection against all evil as Miguel returns to Madrid. I knew he would grow tired of the calm that inhabits the streets and homes of Esquivias and yearn for the excitement of the city. Because it took him so long to ask me to forgive him for his behaviour before and after Isabel's wedding, by the time he reverted to the warm, gentle man I fell in love with, something inside me had changed. I could forgive his errancy, his inconsistency, and his long absences, but not his coldness, his pushing me away when I tried to soothe his mind and body with my own. And now he is preparing to leave again. As I watch him pack yet one more time, I pray to You, Arcángel Miguel, to help him find the strength to continue writing his *Exemplary Novels*, which, as You well know, he has not touched since Isabel's wedding. I pray that his plays and interludes, which he reviewed and organized so carefully, will find producers who will stage them in Madrid's *corrales*, even though Lope de Vega is his foe. Help Miguel find solace in the fact that *Don Quixote* is doing better than anyone expected. I myself cannot believe that its third edition is already being sold in Madrid and that people continue to gather around fountains and squares to listen to it being read aloud. Even in foreign countries his work has caught readers' interest, and it is to be translated into many languages. And I know that we have to thank God, our Lord, and You, Arcángel Miguel, the strongest of Our Lord's warriors, for many of these blessings.

Miguel's return is set for December. Four long months away! What I request from You, great captain of our souls, is that You steer him safely back to me come Christmas. But more than anything, I beg You to guard his steps and protect him against the city's evil minds, evil hands, and evil tongues.

XVI

CONSTANZA

IT WAS LATE in the day when Miguel knocked on the door.

"We didn't think you would arrive so soon! You got here faster than usual," Magdalena said happily, taking his hat while Constanza took the leather bag that held his manuscripts. Thick and heavy, it contained pages and pages filled with his handwriting.

Constanza noticed the dark shadows under his eyes but didn't comment. Her uncle was home, and that was all that mattered. But Andrea placed her hand on her brother's cheek, and although she spoke playfully, her words didn't hide her concern.

"You're looking older than me, Miguel. What happened to you?"

"It is hard to compete against your beauty, *hermana*," he replied. "It would be different if you had a beard!" They laughed and headed to the kitchen, where they would soon ease back into the old family routine, eating and sharing the latest news. Judging by the amount of luggage her uncle had brought, he was planning for a longer stay than usual.

"How is Aunt Catalina?" Constanza inquired.

"She sends the three of you her warmest regards."

"Will she catch up with you here?"

"I don't think so, *hija*. Life in the city does not suit her well."

"And life in Esquivias," Magdalena asked, holding up Miguel's vest so she could brush it and hang it up to air, "Does it suit you?"

"Life without the theatre does not suit me," he replied. "I want to give my plays another chance."

"That is such great news, Uncle Miguel! I hope we can see them on stage soon," Constanza said as she poured her uncle a glass of wine. Magdalena stood close to the window. With the brush in one hand and the vest in the other, she asked,

"When will you pay Isabel a visit?"

Miguel choked. Constanza looked at her aunt with disapproval. It was so like Magdalena to never allow him a respite! Once he recovered his breath, he shook his head.

"I don't want to talk about that right now."

His sister protested. "I thought that was the entire reason for your trip."

"It's one of the reasons for my trip, yes, not the only one," he corrected her.

"Tell us about the other reasons, Uncle Miguel. I'm dying to know! Did you bring any of your writing with you besides the plays?" Constanza asked with excitement.

Smarting from her brother's reproach, Magdalena continued to brush the dirt from his suede vest. "I want to hear that, too, but I cannot stress enough how important it is that you see your daughter. Make sure she's doing well. I worry." Miguel frowned and Constanza rolled her eyes.

"You always worry, Magdalena," Andrea said. "I, on the other hand, have full faith in God Our Lord."

"You'll manage to kill this dead skin again if you continue

brushing it like that, *hermana*," Miguel teased, taking the vest from Magdalena's hands. "My first stop will be the *mentidero*. I need to catch up on the latest news."

"Are you going there now, looking like the mule just kicked you off its back?" Andrea scowled at him. There was something about the way she spoke and the things she said lately that startled Constanza. Her mother would never have spoken to Miguel that way before. He seemed to be taken by surprise, too. He exchanged a glance with Magdalena and Constanza.

"Of course not, dear sister!" he said with a smile that looked forced. "I will go tomorrow. Let me wash away some of this grime and then I'd like to eat. Is there anything tasty in this kitchen?"

CONSTANZA AND MAGDALENA were already at work when Miguel appeared early the next morning, dressed and ready to leave.

"Will you have breakfast with us?" Magdalena asked. "We have fresh bread."

Miguel shook his head. "No. But I promise I will be home for dinner tonight," he said. Constanza smiled. The house felt different when her uncle was living here. His voice, his presence, his soul filled every room and made her feel safe, protected.

"And when will you go to see Isabel?" Magdalena asked. Clearly she was not going to let up for a moment.

"Not today, I'm afraid."

Magdalena disapproved. "I wish you would take my concerns more seriously."

"I do take them seriously, but this is urgent," Miguel insisted.

He waved goodbye, and Constanza knew that every hour until his return would feel like a day. She couldn't wait to hear his stories! It was early evening when Miguel knocked on the door. Constanza dropped her sewing and ran to let him in. When she opened the door, she was surprised to see that her uncle was accompanied by a neatly dressed young man.

"I hope you don't mind, but I brought a guest!" Miguel announced cheerfully. Constanza immediately regretted not paying attention to her appearance that morning, knowing she would not be venturing outside. Her hair was carelessly knotted in a bun, and she wore a loose skirt and a shirt that were not meant to be seen in public or by visitors. She decided to say a quick hello, then head to her room to change and fix her hair.

Miguel introduced his guest. "Constanza, *hermanas*, this is Luis de Molina," The young man smiled and gave a little bow.

"Delighted to make your acquaintance, Señoras," he addressed Andrea and Magdalena, then turned to Constanza and said, "*Mucho gusto*, Señorita."

Constanza swallowed hard as they made eye contact. He was tall and slim, with dark hair and eyes and a neatly trimmed beard.

"*Igualmente*. And now, if you'll excuse me … " Constanza said. She curtsied and was about to head to her room when her uncle stopped her.

"Don't leave, Constanza," he said, indicating that they should all go to the kitchen. "Let's share some wine and cheese. It's not every day that you meet someone like Luis. He was a prisoner in Algiers, like I was."

"A prisoner in Algiers?" Magdalena exclaimed. "You look too young to have been there at the same time as Miguel. When was this?"

"About fifteen years after your brother was set free."

"In exchange for a ransom, you mean," Miguel said. "If not for my sisters and my mother, I would be a slave in Barbary now. That is, if I was still alive, of course."

"You?" Luis laughed. "You are a legend. I have heard so many stories about you!"

There was a sparkle in Luis's eyes that Constanza found very charming.

"Well, you're practically family, then! Welcome home, Luis," said Magdalena. Andrea assented, smiling.

"I'll just quickly change and—"

"You look fine, Constanza, please stay with us," Miguel insisted as they took seats around the table. "Maria, please prepare a platter of *chorizo*, grapes, and cheese, and bring some wine."

Luis sat next to Constanza. His skin was tanned and he looked strong.

"Your uncle has told me you're a very talented seamstress," he offered. Constanza blushed, looking at his lips, admiring his almost perfect teeth.

"The *most* talented seamstress in town!" Miguel corrected, raising his glass. "Here's to freedom, the most precious gift God gave to men."

Luis raised his glass and touched it against Constanza's, looking into her eyes as he repeated, "Here's to freedom!"

XVII

ISABEL

DIEGO HAD BEEN away for almost two months, and it was time for me to decide what to do next. Riding a sedan chair through the city helped clear my mind and kept my new dresses clean of Madrid's endless dust, but this was not a lifestyle I would be able to maintain forever. I had to consider ways in which I could earn an income—at least until the time finally arrived when I could claim the tavern. Two years seemed like a long time, but what choice did I have if Diego didn't return? And the prospects worsened if he did. What would I do, take him back? Sometimes I thought it could be possible for us to live under the same roof if we slept in different rooms. That would keep me free from sin. But would I be able to stand seeing him every day, risking my soul more than I already had?

I attended mass every day, praying for God to steer me in the right direction, and so it was that one August afternoon while leaving church our eyes met for the first time. I was lifting my mantilla to dry the perspiration from my face when a very elegant carriage slowed down and stopped across the street from where I stood. It carried a single occupant, a gentleman whose clothes gave away his rank: he wore *ropa negra*, a velvet so rich in colour that it had clearly been imported from the New World. His tight jerkin with golden buttons was of a quality not even Constanza at her best could aspire to create. He was bald, but there was something about him I found attractive.

I should have pulled down my mantilla, bowed my head, and continued towards the sedan chair that was waiting for me to take me back home, but instead I stood still, my head held high, barely breathing. The scene repeated itself the following day, and the day after that. Fearing that the man knew Diego or was associated with him, I hesitated to give in to my curiosity, but when I noticed that the carriage was heading towards the Alcázar, I crossed myself and instructed my sedan chair carriers to follow it.

The carriage had stopped not far from the gates in a spot with very few passersby, and as we approached, the gentleman got out and came towards me. Suddenly I felt as if I had just woken up. What did I think I was doing, following a gentleman's carriage? As if I wasn't already disgraced! I was about to instruct the carriers to turn back when the man called out to me.

"Don't leave, please!"

I froze. I had never spoken to someone of that position before. Remembering Magdalena's teachings, I exited the sedan chair to show my respect for his rank, but also straightened my back and lifted my chin.

"Forgive me for bothering you. I just had to tell you that you are, without a doubt, the most beautiful lady I have ever laid eyes on," the gentleman declared.

No man would ever again trick me with that kind of talk. "Shame on you, gentleman, for mocking a woman who is suffering," I replied.

"My apologies, Señorita. I spoke the truth. I have travelled through many countries and never seen a beauty as breathtaking as yours," he insisted. I couldn't help it; my face was on fire.

"And it pains me to hear that you suffer. If there is anything I can do to make you smile again, pray tell me so now." He stood still, looking very serious. I hadn't expected such an answer and was at a loss for words.

"Thank you, Sir," was all I could think to say.

"Juan de Urbina, at your feet," he said, giving me a gracious bow. His smile was genuine and gentle.

Juan de Urbina was a well-known man. He was secretary of the House of Savoy. A man at the direct service of the Duke of Savoy, a direct relative of His Majesty King Philip III. I curtsied with trembling knees.

"Now may I please know your name—if you don't mind?" he asked.

I had been through this before. Had I learned my lesson? "My name is Isabel," I said. Apparently not.

"Isabel! What a lovely name. Fit for a queen."

How original, I thought, remembering Simón. At least Diego had never said those words.

"Thank you. And now if you'll excuse me ..." I started to move back to my sedan chair.

"No, please! Wait!" he cried. "May I invite you to take a ride with me in my carriage? Perhaps you can tell me what is ailing you. I might be able to help."

A ride in that carriage, which looked like it was made of gold and ivory? It was tempting. He might, indeed, be able to help me, or better yet, become my protector. But I had to be careful.

"I would love to join you, Señor de Urbina, but I'm afraid I must decline."

He looked crestfallen. "May I ask why? It's just a carriage ride on a lovely summer afternoon."

"I'm a married woman," I confessed, looking him straight in the eye. I was a good Christian, I had to say the truth.

He took my hand in his and kissed it. "It's only a carriage ride." His lips and hands were soft. I had forgotten how good it felt to be touched. "As I said, I am at your feet."

I took a deep breath. I would accept a carriage ride—but not too quickly.

"I need to think about it," I said. "Perhaps tomorrow?"

"It would be my honour," he said with a smile, "if you allow me to meet you here tomorrow and *perhaps*," he emphasized the word, "enjoy the pleasure of your company." His lips hovered over my hand again and I caught the scent of verbena and bergamot. For some reason, the fragrance gave me a renewed sense of hope.

ACT FIVE

MADRID
OCTOBER 1607–APRIL 1616

In 1609, King Philip III intensified the expulsion of the Morisco or Moorish population, giving them only a month to leave the Spanish territory, a territory in which the vast majority had been born, and forbade them from taking any gold or silver with them.

The unfairness of this measure was reflected in the second part of the novel Don Quixote, *which was published in 1615, a year after the Moriscos were allowed to return to Spanish soil, but only if they married a Christian or joined a Catholic religious order.*

Everyday life became more difficult for Spaniards. The social and ethnic landscape of the nation changed in ways that affected the Cervantes family directly. Miguel's hopes were crushed when all the theatres were closed from 1611 to 1613 due to the death of the king's wife, Margaret of Austria.

As the king's incapacity to govern wisely became increasingly evident, Spain's control in Italy weakened. By 1616, irreconcilable differences plagued the Spanish Court. The beginning of the end of the Spanish Empire, whose extent was once so vast that Charles I declared it "the empire on which the sun never sets," was dawning.

I

ISABEL
November 1607

MEETING JUAN DE URBINA became my habit and my joy. To avoid being recognized when I went to see him, I always covered my face with a dark mantilla, and his carriage driver had strict orders to drop me off a block from home and wait until I was safely inside.

One chilly, leaden-sky afternoon, I lit the brazier, wrapped myself in a woolen blanket, and lay down on the bed. I was almost dozing off when I heard a knock at my door. Startled, I sat up, listening intently. No one ever visited me. Now that Juan was my benefactor and protector—although he preferred the term "admirer"—I kept mostly to myself and tried not to attract notice.

When the knocking was repeated, I rose to my feet. My heart racing, I stepped quietly towards the foyer, holding my breath. The knocking brought back memories—of the day Magdalena came to take me away; the night Mencía tried to escape her violent husband; and that fatal night in Valladolid.

I decided not to answer now that I was responsible not only for myself but for the life growing inside me. I had spent the first few weeks of pregnancy feeling sick, vomiting every morning. Sometimes I was sleepy and couldn't think clearly, but at times like this I felt sharp. I could see, hear, smell, and taste everything, as if a dormant beast with a hundred eyes, ears, noses, and tongues had awakened inside me.

"Isabel? Are you there, *hija*?" My eyes filled with tears. Father! How many times had I wanted to talk to him and ask for his forgiveness? How many letters had I wanted to write, telling him that I was sorry, that I needed his help, his advice, his protection?

"Is somebody with you?" I asked cautiously.

"I came alone," he said.

"Give me a minute, please!" I cried out. I was frozen to the spot, unsure what to do. Try to fix my hair? Change my clothes? How would he take the news of my pregnancy, especially once I told him that Diego had been gone for months? I tried to redo my braid, but my fingers were clumsy. In the end I received him with my hair loose, my voice shaking.

"Close your eyes!" I ordered, suddenly realizing the way I wanted to welcome him. "You have to promise that when I open the door, your eyes will be closed."

"I promise," he agreed, and after fighting with the locks, I opened the door and there he was in front of me. He smelled clean, and when I removed his hat, I noticed that he had combed his hair.

"Don't open your eyes just yet!" I said as I took off his cape and laid it, together with his hat, on the chair where I kept my mantilla and cape.

"Don't move! Just a second!" I was almost whispering, as if afraid that raising my voice would break some kind of spell. I studied his face. There were shadows under his eyes. His beard had grown whiter.

"Ready? Let me guide you." I took Father's right arm in mine and led him inside, closing the door gently behind us. Then I stood across front of him, took his hand, and placed it on my round belly. "Open your eyes," I said.

He stared at my face, then at my stomach, then back at my face. He did this a few times before erupting into a mixture of laughter and tears.

"Father, I'm sorry I—"

"No, *hija*, no. Let's not talk about the past. It's all about the future now." He held me against his chest and rubbed my back, rocking me gently. I allowed myself to be comforted by the soothing rhythm. If it had been possible, I would have prolonged that moment, that feeling, forever.

When he finally broke our embrace, he took out his handkerchief and offered it to me, though it was really he who needed it most. I smiled. I had missed him!

"Can I offer you some wine, Father? Something to eat?" Juan de Urbina kept me supplied with excellent wine and food. If I went out to the market it was mostly to get fresh air. When we met, he often surprised me not only with gifts—silk, velvet, fine jewellery—but with a basket of fresh oil, bread, cheese, olives, fruit, and meat that his servants prepared for me.

Father shook his head. I let him keep his hand on my belly until he felt the baby kick.

"Such a miracle!" He smiled. "Does the baby kick you all the time?"

"No, your grandchild does not kick me all the time," I replied.

"Your mother told me that *you* kicked her all the time!" he said. This was followed by a silent pause. I could tell he hadn't meant to blurt that out.

"Did she?" I said, aching to hear more.

"It just came back to me like it was yesterday," he said, caressing my cheek. "I'm sorry I couldn't be the father you deserved. But I would love to have the opportunity to be the grandfather this baby deserves, if you allow me to."

I nodded, and we embraced again. "Some wine, then?"

We headed to the kitchen. I lit the stove and brought out cheese, bread, and wine for us to share.

"This is a nice place," he said, looking around the room with curiosity. "That rug you have is very valuable. And the porcelains!" I agreed. Everything here was certainly much better than the apartment in Valladolid, or the house where my aunts were living. And it was a better neighbourhood, too. "I am happy that I was mistaken about your husband. I can see that he gives you a good life. Where is he?" he asked.

This was the question I had been dreading. I drank my wine in a couple of gulps and poured myself some more. Father frowned at this.

"I should have listened to you," I said. There was no use keeping it a secret any longer. "He left me."

"Left you?" Father's eyes opened wide. "How could he? You are with child!"

Realizing I had chosen the wrong words, I corrected myself.

"He still sends me money, but we don't live under the same roof anymore." I hoped that sounded better.

"Why? Where does he live?"

"He accepted a commission on the other side of town, and he stays there so he can work without interruptions."

"Who is his patron?"

The question took me by surprise, and I tried to think of something fast.

"He wasn't at liberty to say. It's a private project. But he mentioned it was a large fresco," I explained. I didn't enjoy creating a web of falsehoods. I felt ashamed, but I didn't know what else to say.

"And you don't have a servant?"

I shook my head. "Only a laundress."

Father looked baffled, but then he composed himself. "You will need help when the child comes."

"That is still a couple of months away," I said. I lamented not being able to reassure him. Juan and I had discussed the matter, and he had promised to provide me with support in the next few weeks. One of his maids, Francisca, a very discreet, middle-aged woman, would move in here. He had also promised me a wet nurse.

"Well, your aunts and your cousin will be elated when they hear the news. They will be only too happy to sew a new wardrobe for you and for the little one, I am sure!"

"Thank you, Father." We smiled and clicked glasses. "But enough about me. Tell me about you! What are you writing now?"

He bit into a piece of cheese and washed it down with wine. I watched him in awe, still in disbelief that he was here, sitting at my table. That we were together, just he and I.

"I am trying to find a producer for my plays. But I have not had any luck yet."

"Why not?"

"What do I know? They always find an excuse."

"But at least *Don Quixote* is doing well, right?"

"Who cares? My plays are my best work." His mood had darkened. I could tell he was hurt.

"Don't say that, Father. Nothing anyone has written is

as widely read as *Don Quixote*," I reassured him. Even Juan admired his book. He was the one who told me that it had been published in other countries already.

"They must all be envious of you. Especially Lope de Vega." I knew I was pushing it a little, but I wanted to show him that I cared.

"No, *hija*. There's a reason I call Lope the Monster of Nature: his talent is extraordinary. No one can write poetry like he does, but—" he suddenly paused.

"But?"

"Nothing."

"Tell me. I want to understand," I insisted. I was being honest. I wanted to know what was happening in his world. Perhaps if I talked to Juan, he could have some influence. Father sighed, helped himself to more wine, and tried to explain.

"The great Lope has convinced everyone that plays should have only three acts instead of five, and mine are too long, and too complex, to fit into that simple structure. Besides, he is promoting mixing comedy and tragedy, which results in bland, uninteresting plots that, to everyone's shame, our uncultured masses cannot get enough of. Sometimes I wonder if I am too old to understand the ways the world around me is changing."

"I'm sorry to hear you feel that way, Father," I said, putting my hand on his. I was especially sorry because there was nothing Juan could do to fix that kind of problem. Feeling sad for him, and hoping I could lighten his mood, I asked after the people in Esquivias. How were Catalina, her friend Juana Gaytán, and the others who had been our neighbours in Valladolid? He shrugged.

"I promised Catalina that I would be back in December, but I do not want to go anywhere now. I want to stay in Madrid, close to you."

I shook my head. "She will be angry at me again, Father. Go ahead with your plans. You don't need to worry about me."

"No, Isabel. How could she be angry when you are about to give me the greatest gift I have ever received? I will write to her tonight to let her know."

"Give her my regards, please." It felt as if the warmth of the stove had transferred itself to my chest, melting away all resentment. Now that Father had returned, in my new world—and in my baby's life—there would be room for every single member of my family. I couldn't wait to see my aunts again. Even Constanza. It had been far too long. Father caressed my hand as if confirming I had just made the right decision. Would my sister, Ana, be as welcoming, I wondered? Now that I had recovered Father's support, everything seemed possible.

II

CONSTANZA
November 1607

ISABEL HAD A GLOW about her that reminded Constanza of paintings of the Virgin Mary. Pregnancy agreed with her so much that even when she smiled at her, it seemed genuine.

"You did this for me?" It had been Andrea's idea to sew and embroider a christening gown for the baby as a surprise present, and Constanza had been forced to help, but now that she saw Isabel's eyes welling up, she was glad she had taken part.

"It is too small for you, I am afraid," Magdalena replied, making them all laugh, "but your aunt and Constanza worked really hard on it."

"I can tell. This is exquisite, thank you!"

Constanza had examined herself in the mirror before Isabel arrived to make sure that she looked her best, and even though she knew pride was a sin, she did not believe she was ugly. The way Luis had looked at her during the past few weeks made her feel desirable. But she was not Isabel. Her cousin had only become more bewitching, whereas age was already showing around Constanza's eyes, each line symbolizing a path not taken. Was this the destiny God had intended for her? It must be, because every time she had tried to escape, she had been drawn back, like a wild bird caught and placed in a cage, its wings clipped. Constanza was that bird, and seeing Isabel so full of life, and creating life, reminded her that she had even forgotten how to sing.

Today, Uncle Miguel had invited Luis de Molina to join them. He wanted to introduce his dear friend to his only daughter, he said. Constanza had thought about confiding in her uncle that she was fond of Luis de Molina. More than fond. She found him clever and interesting and attractive. She dreamed about his dark voice, his rich mane, his pointy nose. But now it was too late, because even though Isabel was married and with child, it was clear that Luis was smitten. He could not take his eyes off her. During his short visit, he had ears for her voice alone.

After the meal, they had all walked Isabel back to the sedan chair except for Constanza, who was finishing a shirt. As the others returned, their voices carried into the sewing room.

"Doesn't Isabel look glorious, Andrea?" Magdalena asked when they were back inside.

"She does indeed. And she loved the gown we made!" Andrea answered. Constanza could not remember the last time they had sounded this happy.

"It is the least we can do for her now!"

"I am praying for Diego to finish his fresco soon so they can be together again. Is it not peculiar that he would accept such a lengthy commission when she is expecting their child?"

"Yes, but these are tough times for everyone, *hermana*. Besides, it might be better this way. The money without the man, remember?" Magdalena said as she closed the front door behind them, and they both laughed.

"Did you see the way Luis looked at Isabel? It's too bad they met this late."

Would they ever be quiet? Constanza could barely stand listening to their conversation.

"Yes, if only she had married Luis!" Magdalena sighed. "But the Lord works in mysterious ways."

"You two talk too much," said Miguel. It was hard to tell if he was joking or telling the truth. He peeked inside the sewing room. "I think that you, Constanza, were lovely today. I am very happy to see you and Isabel getting along. You are my girls, after all."

Constanza acknowledged her uncle's compliment with a nod of her head, then turned towards the window and sighed. *His girls.* More like the spinster and the mother-to-be. The one who had nothing, and the one who had it all.

III

ISABEL
December 1607

I HOPED THAT the fact I was expecting a child would soften my Ana's heart. And I made sure to dress very simply when I visited her. This time I was fortunate enough to run into her on the street as she carried a bucket of water from the fountain. It was a relief to see that she was alone—or was she? I wasn't in the mood for Luisa's bitterness and resentment or her haunting toothless grimace. I felt vulnerable enough as I was venturing again down those familiar, godless streets on my own. Juan would be upset if he found out. I had to be cautious.

"Isabel?" At first, Ana raised an eyebrow when she saw me—a look that reminded me of her father, which gave me pause—but when she noticed the roundness of my belly, she smiled.

"You're with child?" she asked, putting the bucket on the ground and approaching me timidly, with curiosity.

I nodded. "Yes, Ana. Are you alone?"

"Did you marry? Do you have a husband?"

I nodded again. "Where's Aunt Luisa?"

"When did you get married? Why didn't you tell me?"

I looked around to see if Luisa was anywhere nearby. I wanted to have Ana to myself, even if only for a few minutes.

"I didn't tell anyone about my wedding," I said quietly.

Ana bit her lip just like she used to when she was a girl. I suppressed the urge to tap my finger on her mouth to make her stop, like I had done so many times before.

"You didn't tell anyone? Not even your father, the war hero and famous writer?"

These were the exact words Magdalena had used when she appeared at our door to take me away. Ana remembered them. Was that day engraved in her memory the way it was engraved in mine?

"I didn't tell anyone, *especially* my father," I replied.

"And where's your husband?" she asked.

The question took me by surprise. How could I explain things to her? I said the first thing that came into my head. "He's working."

"Working? You married a man who needs to work? Wait until Aunt Luisa hears that!" she exclaimed.

"Everyone needs to work to survive, Ana," I protested.

"Rich people don't. Aunt Luisa always said you'd marry a rich man."

"Aunt Luisa is not always right, you know. My husband is a painter," I explained.

"A painter?" she asked, looking skeptical. I nodded. "And how is that useful?"

I laughed. "People like art. They like paintings."

She shrugged. "Rich people, you mean. Not us."

"Yes, you, too! Don't you like the ones at church?" I challenged her.

Ana shrugged, and I felt sorry for her. It was not her fault she had grown up deprived of so much and surrounded by all that ignorance.

"Can I touch it?" Before I could realize what she was talking about, and without waiting for an answer, she placed her hands on my waist, then slowly slid them towards my belly button. I could see traces of dirt under her fingernails. Her dress was almost threadbare. How long had she been wearing that rag and why? I had left enough money for her to afford at least a couple of new dresses, what had Luisa done with it instead? Had she been wearing those same clothes the last time I had seen her? I couldn't remember.

"You're so fat!" she laughed.

"I'm not fat, silly!" I laughed, too. Who cared what she was wearing? This was still my sister. I had missed the sound of her laughter. "I have a baby growing inside me. When the baby comes out, my body will go back to the way it was."

She frowned and shook her head. "Nothing ever goes back to the way it was." Her eyes were fixed on my middle, her hands still on it, waiting to feel movement coming from inside.

"What will you call him?" she asked.

"Him? And what if the baby is a girl?"

Ana shook her head once more. "Aunt Luisa says girls are a curse. I hope you're not having a girl."

I wrapped my arms around my sister and pressed her against me, feeling her body, tense at first, melt little by little into my embrace. The baby inside me would bring us together again, I could feel it. What a blessing this pregnancy was. I closed my eyes and focused on Ana's breathing. It was peaceful and deep, like mine.

IV

CATALINA
December 1607

Anima Christi, sanctifica me. Corpus Christi, salve me.
Sanguis Christi, inebria me. Aqua lateris Christi, lava me.
Passio Christi, conforta me. O bone Iesu, exaudi me.

SOUL OF CHRIST, sanctify me. Body of Christ, save me.
Blood of Christ, heal my pain. Isabel will make Miguel a
grandfather and he says he has never felt so happy in his
entire life. *In his entire life.* Soul of Christ, how am I supposed
to take those words? You know how much I yearned to give
him a child. How much I prayed, begging for that miracle.
Must I understand that my barren womb has weakened our
bond now? Has our time together meant so little to him,
My Lord?

Miguel wants to remain in Madrid and is requesting
that I join him. Why uproot me again and force me to leave
behind everything I know and love to live in the filth and
vice of the city again? Did Valladolid not teach us enough
of a lesson?

God Almighty, please grant me strength and wisdom.
His absence this time is the bitterest of them all. I could
cope before, knowing it was his work that kept him away.

But now it is his own will. He promised he would return to me come December. And if I cannot depend on his word, I do not have anything. If I cannot depend on his word, My Lord, I lose it all.

V

A GUSH OF liquid slid down my legs and left a puddle on the floor. At first, I thought it was urine and felt ashamed. But the soreness creeping up my back made me realize it was time.

"Fetch the midwife and alert my aunts! Hurry!" Francisca, the maid that Juan had sent to look after me, wrapped herself in her shawl and ran outside.

I rubbed myself. *Please, baby, be gentle, don't hurt your mother too much.* Then a pain worse than anything I had felt before took over my entire abdomen. My skin tensed up, then relaxed, and a few minutes later tensed up and relaxed again. I was breathing fast, walking around my bedroom, unable to sit or lie down, sweating, praying, when Francisca returned with the midwife. My two aunts, Constanza, and Maria followed. Father came in last. The midwife took command right away.

"Quick, draw all the curtains and turn on the fire. All the braziers need to be on. We need a chair in the birthing room. And water, boil water!"

Maria headed for the kitchen.

"I brought silk thread in case sutures are required," Magdalena announced.

My belly tensed up again and I let out a cry. "Sutures?"

"Miguel, you are not needed here right now. Come back in a few hours," Magdalena said, holding the door open for him. The look of concern and affection he gave me before leaving filled me with hope.

"The apartment needs to be hot; no outside air is to be let in," the midwife ordered. "We need to protect the humours of Isabel's body, which will be hotter if the baby is a boy."

After she locked the door, Magdalena came and took my hand. "My poor girl. Your beauty makes you fragile. Your childbirth will be harder than most, just like Andrea's was. God has willed it that way: beauty is to be paid for with pain, especially at times like this."

"If we anoint your privates with oil or grease, you will have a swift labour and, perhaps, suffer a bit less," the midwife explained. "But first, you need to walk. Walk as much as you can, even if only around the room."

So I leaned against Constanza, who had offered me her arm, and took small steps around the bed. The midwife came over and said, "I also brought Rose of Jericho to assist with the birth." She held out a bowl that contained a dry plant with curled-up branches, resembling a ball, and asked me to touch it. "We shall put it in water, and as it opens up, so will your body. It is a very powerful herb, brought to me by Franciscan friars from the Holy Land."

I stared at the plant, and at the midwife, in disbelief. "This thing is dead."

She shook her head. "No. It's a miraculous plant. As it revives, it helps us tell whether you and the child will be all right. We must watch it closely over the next few hours." She placed the bowl on the floor by my bed, crossed herself, and asked for God's assistance. Then she turned back to me. "Your aunt is correct. Beautiful women like you go through the most painful childbirths."

At that moment, a lightning bolt of pain pierced my body. What curse was this? If a witch or a wizard had offered to turn me into a beast so my pain would subside, I would have accepted.

"Quick, we must undo our shoelaces and let down our hair!" Andrea said, unpinning her bun. "I remember it helped me when Constanza was being born—everything in the room must reflect openness and freedom of movement."

Magdalena, Constanza, and the midwife let down their hair, then undid mine. I was sweating—my head, my face, my entire body was burning. After what seemed like hours, they sat me down on the edge of a chair and told me to open my legs. I felt so exposed, so ashamed to be showing my body this way in front of my aunts and my cousin. And as time went by, the pain became worse. I cried. I yelled.

"Let's pray together, Isabel." Andrea sat on the bed. Constanza held me under my right arm, while Magdalena held me under my left, and the midwife fixed her eyes between my legs as she massaged my abdomen. Maria made sure there were clean linens at the midwife's disposal. I had never felt so taken care of, and so miserable, in my entire life. How could women go through this nightmare more than once?

¡Virgen del parto! Mirad
Que la noche de Belén
no hallávades vos también
casa, huésped ni piedad,
¡Señora, doleos de mí!

"*Holy Virgin of Childbirth, You who that night in Bethlehem could not find lodging or mercy, be merciful to me,*" Constanza prayed out loud and asked me to join her. But I couldn't even talk. I screamed again. I was panting, my hair was dishevelled, covered in sweat, sticking to my back and my forehead.

"Try to stay as calm as you can, Isabel," the midwife ordered, "the baby will push itself out. All you need to do is wait." She touched me down below and assured me that the baby was coming down headfirst. I screamed and breathed as if I had run a hundred miles, and my aunts and my cousin continued to pray, asking God for a good delivery, and for health for me and my child. There was blood, so much blood! Was I going to die? Where was Juan? If he had been here, I would have cursed him, why had he done this to me? It was as if my entire body was being torn in two. I lost my voice, and the wooden floor was soaked in blood. My aunts and the midwife looked exhausted, too. Then I heard crying. A baby's crying.

"It's a girl, Isabel!" Magdalena was weeping with joy.

They cleaned her with warm water, wrapped her in a clean bedsheet, and handed her to me. I brought her close to my face, and as I smelled her scent, something inside me stirred awake. Something with a life of its own that I had never experienced. I looked at my baby, red as she was, swollen, covered in a whitish ointment, and my eyes overflowed with tears. I would never be alone again.

"We should find Diego, he must come!" Magdalena said, drying my forehead with a clean cloth.

"No!" I cried, pushing her hand away. I immediately regretted my reaction. "This commission is too important, he is not to be disturbed. Our livelihood depends on it. I will send

330 • MARTHA BÁTIZ

him word of our daughter's birth the next time he sends me money." How long could I sustain my lies? I wondered. I forced myself to smile to relieve my aunt's worry.

"But—"

"What will you name her?" Andrea asked, and I was grateful to her for excusing me from further explanations. Constanza stood by her side, drying her eyes. When I saw her happy tears, I realized how powerful this tiny, helpless creature was. She alone had brought our entire family together.

"Her name is Isabel. She will be my Isabelita." Flesh of my flesh, blood of my blood. Kissing her forehead, I made a silent promise to her that we would never be apart.

"The Rose of Jericho is reviving in only one day!" the midwife exclaimed. She picked the bowl up from the floor, careful not to spill the water, and showed me the faint but definite signs of life in its branches. Relieved, I turned back to my baby. I wanted to celebrate her arrival—behold her, smell her, kiss her, count her fingers and toes and marvel at her tiny nails, her tiny mouth, her perfection. I could hardly wait for Juan to meet her, to see my daughter in her father's arms.

VI

CONSTANZA
January 1608

ISABELITA STIRRED SOMETHING inside Constanza she had never felt before. The moment she held her in her arms she was overcome by a desire to protect her, to take care of her, to ensure that she would always be happy and safe.

In the days following Isabelita's birth, Constanza and Maria took turns staying at Isabel's side to help her tend to the baby. There were so many diapers to change, so many linens that needed to be washed, that Francisca could barely keep up with the household chores. Isabel's breasts were swollen and bleeding, and applying cold cabbage leaves and poultice on her nipples was not enough. Constanza had already tried to find out when the wet nurse that Diego had promised would arrive, but Isabel said she had already sent him notice and they needed to wait. Constanza disapproved. That man! Had he bothered to come meet his daughter, he would know there was no time to waste. Isabelita needed to eat, and Isabel required rest. She had shadows under her eyes and her cheeks had lost their usual rosiness.

On her way to Isabel's that morning, Constanza was considering if she herself could hire a woman to help her cousin should Diego not send money or return soon. Constanza would need to take on additional sewing, but if someone else was available to help at Isabel's, she was confident she could do it. But when Maria, mantilla in hand, ready to return to her duties at the Cervantes household, let her in, she informed her that a wet nurse was in Isabel's room.

"Did Diego come back?" Constanza took off her mantilla.

Maria shook her head. "That wo—" She paused, correcting herself. "She arrived alone."

Puzzled, Constanza took off her outdoor clothing and entered Isabel's room. She was yearning to hold Isabelita in her arms, whisper sweet songs into her ears, rock her to sleep.

Isabel was in bed and a woman with skin as dark as night sat on a chair, holding Isabelita against her chest. Taken by surprise at the woman's appearance, Constanza was unable to contain her discomfort.

"Isabel!" She cried out.

"Shh!" Isabel put her finger to her lips. "Isabelita's finally feeding!"

Constanza stood by the door, her mind whirling with everything she wanted to say. Eventually the nurse placed the baby in Isabel's arms, satiated and asleep.

"Could you excuse us, please?" Constanza asked the nurse politely. She closed the door after her and approached the bed. Unsure how to begin a conversation she never imagined would be necessary, she vacillated for a second before speaking.

"Where is Diego working that he sent you a slave, cousin?"

"A slave? Gracia is a wet nurse. What are you talking about?" They were keeping their voices low, careful not to disturb the baby or be heard outside the room.

"That woman is not a Moor, like Prudencia. She's from Barbary! She must be a slave. Wait until your father finds out."

"She just arrived last night. I've barely spoken a few words with her! But I'm sure that—" Isabel stopped, seemingly uncomfortable, yet Constanza pressed on.

"Your father and our uncle Rodrigo, may he rest in peace, were prisoners for years in Algiers. Miguel was handcuffed and about to be sold as a slave himself when he was rescued. He doesn't like to talk about this, but I remember it, and believe me, we nearly killed ourselves working to pay the ransom to free him. You can't keep a slave, it's wrong. It's one thing to employ a servant, quite a different thing to own a slave."

"Don't you think I know that?" Isabel replied testily.

"You must talk to Diego!"

"Diego has nothing to do with this. It was Juan!" Isabel blurted out.

"Who is Juan?" Constanza asked, at a loss. She could see that her cousin was nervous and distressed, and she had to find out what was going on.

Isabel hesitated. "My uncle Juan! My mother's brother. The priest."

"Where does a priest find the money for a wet nurse? And how can a man of God be so heartless?"

"Isabelita needs her milk to survive."

Constanza shook her head in frustration, but then she turned her eyes on the baby and felt remarkably calmer. "Can I hold her?" she asked.

VII

CATALINA
February 1608

Requiem æternam dona ei, Domine.
Et lux perpetua luceat ei: Requiescat in pace.

LORD, GRANT ETERNAL rest unto him. May Diego Sanz del Avila's soul be swathed in Your gentle embrace. Although I only saw him on the day of his wedding, I cannot help but feel enormous pity for him, as he was young, far too young to die. And I pity Isabel, who is now left a widow alone with her newborn baby, not even knowing how, or why, her husband died. Miguel mentioned that Diego had sustained a head injury while he was a soldier, and that he complained of frequent, debilitating headaches. Whatever the reason, I am certain he is in a better place, Lord. The place where we sinners can only aspire to be one day. Please help Isabel find prompt resignation.

Please forgive me for not heeding Miguel's request to join him. I should have been at my husband's side at this difficult time. But it is never too late to mend one's ways and atone for one's sins. It has been Your sacred will that I should not carry his child, but I will now welcome his granddaughter into my life. Forgive my selfishness, dear Lord, and shed Your divine light upon me as I fight my inner fears and prepare to depart for Madrid.

VIII

"YOU ARE MOVING back in with us, and that is final."

Father was firm, but his voice was gentle. He and I were alone in my bedroom, sitting on the bed. I held Isabelita in my arms while he gently touched her cheek.

Avoiding his gaze, I took my time to answer. I had to find the right words. While Diego was away I had an excuse to be on my own, and I was able to keep my relationship with Juan de Urbina a secret from my family. But now that Diego was gone—his death had been sudden, yet, given his sinful lifestyle, not unexpected—it was impossible to hide the truth any longer.

Francisca had been a loyal messenger between Juan and me. Thanks to her, I learned how much Juan was longing to see me, and that he had promised to take care of us now that Diego was gone. We had agreed to see each other again once the novena for Diego's soul was completed.

The "arrangement" that we had would be impossible if I moved back to Father's house. And that house would afford me none of the comforts I had grown accustomed to, and which Isabelita, as Juan de Urbina's daughter, was entitled to.

"Isabel? Did you hear me?" Father repeated. "Give your wet nurse her freedom, and we will help you care for Isabelita."

I looked at him sadly. "I can't do that, Father. Isabelita needs Gracia's milk. I no longer have any."

"Set her free. Hire her as your servant. We will pay her."

I shook my head. If only it were that easy! I had sent Juan a message telling him that Gracia's status—the fact that I was using a slave as my wet nurse—had created trouble between me and my family. He replied, explaining that, while she was at my service, Gracia officially "belonged" to him and I had no power over her fate.

"Father, Isabelita and I cannot move back in with you. And it is not up to me to give Gracia her freedom."

"Why? Where will you live if you don't come with us? You cannot afford to rent this place any longer."

The time had come to confess the truth, but I felt ashamed. I knew he would be disappointed in me. There was no way out, however. I had a child whose future I was obliged to protect.

"We will move into a house of our own."

Father looked confused. "A house of your own?" he said. What do you mean?"

"I mean that we have a house. Isabelita and I will move into a house of our own," I said, my cheeks burning as I finally revealed the secret I had concealed for so long. "Isabelita's real father is taking care of us."

My words must have fallen like a blow, but Father persevered in his questioning.

"Her real father? Wasn't Diego her real father?" He was speaking louder now, and I shook my head, indicating Isabelita.

"Keep your voice down, you'll wake her!"

Lowering his voice to a whisper, which sounded more

ominous to me that the loudest scream, he asked the inevi-
table question.

"Who is your child's father?"

I swallowed hard. "Juan de Urbina."

For a few seconds, Father remained still, absorbing my
words.

"Urbina? The man who works with the Duke of Savoy?" he
said in disbelief. I nodded. "Isabel, what have you done? Don't
you know what life in court does to people?"

"Feed them well? Give them comforts?" I challenged.

He shook his head. "I am sorry you fell into that trap."

"You're sorry? Or you're envious?"

"Envious? Why?" he said in shock.

"Because I have a connection to the palace. Because I don't
have to worry about money or debts from now on," I replied
defensively.

"No, Isabel. I am not a palace dog," he said quietly.

I was speechless. I had not insulted him. Why was he
insulting me? I stood up.

"I think you should leave now, Father," I finally said.

"I will not leave until I have instilled some reason into you."

This was more than I could bear. "*You* will instill reason
into *me*?" I exclaimed.

"Why on earth would you accept to be the mistress of a
married man?"

How could I ever explain the horror I went through with
Diego? Or my wonderful relationship with Juan? He would
never understand. I decided not to lie; I would tell a half-truth.

"I fell in love," I said simply.

"And you thought it was fine to go ahead and have his
child?"

I nodded. "Yes, the same as you did, Father—except that you chose a taverner."

"Isabel!" he cried out, moving away from me on the bed. But I was not afraid of him anymore.

"Juan bought me a house on 33, Calle de la Montera, steps away from where he lives. His servant brought me the deed to sign this morning. It's all set."

"And you will live there as what, exactly?" he demanded.

"As the mother of Juan de Urbina's daughter, just like my mother *could* have done if you hadn't run away to Esquivias and a barren wife!" I couldn't contain myself. I had been harnessing my feelings for years. Father remained silent. Then he bit his lip, rose to his feet, and left the apartment. Isabelita began to cry.

"Don't cry, my girl," I whispered to her. "Everything will be fine. Your mother is here. I will give my life to protect you."

IX

CONSTANZA
March 1608

CONSTANZA SAT BY the window, feeling the warmth of the sun against her back. Spring was coming. She pretended not to care when she heard that Francisco Leal had returned to Madrid. She tried not to think about him. But her mother and her aunt insisted on going to see him to demand reparation on her behalf.

"Eleven hundred reales. That is all," Magdalena repeated.

"He should have paid much more for what he put you through, but this is all he had, so we took it," Andrea said. Constanza agreed. She knew her lost dreams were worth much more, but she considered that the money might come in handy now that her mother could not sew as much, or as quickly, as before.

The three of them were alone in the sewing room and her aunt had just started ironing a shirt when the front door opened and Miguel came in. After quickly removing his outerwear, he joined them in the sewing room and began pacing like a beast, his jaw tense.

"Isabel *cannot* live in that house alone as Urbina's lover. I don't care how powerful he is. My good name must count for something!" he declared. The news of Isabel's relationship with Juan de Urbina had made Constanza more resentful of her spinsterhood, their hardship, and the unfairness with which she herself had been treated by her own mother and aunt when she was younger. This time, while both had initially condemned Isabel's licentiousness, their anger had softened far too soon. Only her uncle had been restless. Restless, and so preoccupied he had not written a single word.

"I agree with you, *hermano*," Magdalena said. "But I don't see what we can do."

"She needs a husband, of course," Miguel said.

"But she just lost a husband!" Magdalena protested.

"Which is why she needs another man. Someone who can officially protect her and Isabelita. Someone I can trust."

"Juan de Urbina is so powerful, Uncle Miguel," Constanza said, her eyes following him as he paced. "I wouldn't worry about their protection."

"They need protection *from* Juan de Urbina, that is what I mean. People in the court are treacherous and deceitful. The day de Urbina decides Isabel no longer pleases him, the moment he is bored with her, she will be defenceless. This is what I want to prevent."

Constanza felt sorry for her uncle. Always trying his best to do well by his daughter, regardless of how many times she let him down. But in her opinion, the one they should be concerned about was Isabelita. She was pure and innocent, and her future had to be secured.

"You're right, Miguel," Andrea said.

"And who do you have in mind as Isabel's next husband?" Constanza inquired. Her heart was heavy in anticipation of his response. "And I wish you luck getting her to follow your advice."

"This is beyond advice. I will leave her no choice!" Miguel said emphatically.

"And the husband?" Magdalena echoed Constanza's question as she rolled the yarn that Andrea had finished spinning.

"Luis de Molina has agreed to marry her, and I cannot think of a finer man."

Constanza's heart was racing and her eyes began to water despite her best efforts to control herself. "He has? When did you talk to him?"

"Just now, in the *mentidero*." Constanza couldn't believe her ears. The *mentidero* was a place where men shared news and discussed political matters, not where they arranged marriages.

"I'm not surprised," Magdalena said. "That man was smitten by Isabel from the moment he saw her. They'll be good for each other."

"I have also requested a meeting with Juan de Urbina. I will offer to pay half of Isabel's dowry if he covers the other half. It is in his best interests to protect his own daughter as I protect mine. Luis de Molina has asked for two thousand ducats."

"Two thousand ducats?" Constanza nearly choked. That was nearly double what they paid to get Miguel out of Algiers! Where would he get such an outrageous amount of money? Her uncle had gone mad. She was the only one able to work at full speed, and he still hadn't sold any of his plays or finished his *Exemplary Novels*. Even half that sum was beyond their reach.

"Luis is a good man," Miguel declared. "He has agreed to receive the money in installments." If he were a good man, Constanza thought, drying her eyes, he would not ask for such a large sum of money from an old man like her uncle to marry a woman he clearly adored. Perhaps Magdalena had been right about men all along. Could they ever be trusted?

"Even if that were the case, Miguel ..." Magdalena began. Constanza hoped she would ask the question that she didn't dare to. "... how will you cover those installments? We have not been—"

"No need for you to worry, Magdalena," he said as he walked out of the room. "I will ask Catalina for a loan. She wrote telling me she would come to Madrid as soon as she finished dealing with some business affairs. Perhaps I can reach her before she leaves Esquivias."

"A loan?" Magdalena cried, but Miguel did not hear her. "Andrea, did you hear that?"

Constanza couldn't stand it any longer. Once again, Isabel was turning her life upside down. A loan that large would weigh heavily on her uncle, her mother, and her aunt—and consequently on her.

"I have a headache, I need to lie down," she said, excusing herself and fleeing the sewing room.

X

ISABEL
April 1608

"WHAT YOUR FATHER is proposing makes sense."

Juan and I were lying in his bed. My postpartum seclusion over, we had returned to our previous routine, except that now I lived on Calle de la Montera and it was easier for us to meet.

"No, it doesn't! He has no business talking to you, and he has no power over me." I protested. I was still hurt by the harsh words Father had used at our last conversation.

"But he does. You are not twenty-five yet."

"I'm a widow and a mother. He should not be able to control me."

"He's not trying to control you," Juan argued, kissing my neck close to my ear. "He's trying to protect his daughter and helping me to protect mine, like the sensible man that he is."

I couldn't believe what I was hearing. I pushed him away. But he continued.

"He doesn't want his daughter living by herself and being judged by people, don't you see? Because even an honourable widow is not supposed to live alone. And it would put Isabelita at a social disadvantage, even if she's officially Diego Sanz's daughter."

I hated to admit it, but he was right. "What your father proposes is that you marry his friend for appearances only. We will give this man a dowry, and you will have a more honourable marriage."

"A *more honourable* marriage? What do you mean?" I said. A chill ran down my spine. "I don't understand."

"You said Diego never touched you. Was that a lie?" I shook my head. "There you are. The world is a better place without that—" He stopped himself, but I felt nauseous. Was Diego's death related to Juan having discovered his secret? "You have nothing to worry about, Isabel. Luis de Molina is a man of integrity, a soldier and a former prisoner in Algiers. I received good reports about him. The house will be in Isabelita's name, but everything inside it will be yours. The marriage will give our daughter the honourability she will need to find a good suitor when she grows up. I will make sure of that. And in the meantime, you and I will still meet here, as always."

I would own the house and furniture, and have a husband in name only. In exchange, all I was required to do was preserve appearances. The deal sounded almost too good to be true, yet, at the same time, it was not nearly enough. He kissed me, but I did not return his kiss. I could not allow myself, and my daughter's future, to become prey to anyone's impositions.

"Are you all right?" he asked, with a look of concern.

It took me a moment to compose myself after the discovery I had just made. My view had undergone an enormous shift in the briefest amount of time. I saw who Juan really was: a predator. And no matter what I did or how much I fought back, as a woman I was condemned to be prey.

I was careful not to show how I felt after this revelation. "What about Gracia?" I asked.

"She is yours. Isabelita needs her," he replied.

"With an ownership title?" I added. He frowned, so I changed my tone, making it sweeter. "If you give us the owner-ship title, Isabelita will thank you. Gracia could become her lifelong maid."

He sighed deeply, then nodded. "Yes. With an ownership title."

"I need an ownership title for each piece of furniture that you give me and that I buy for us, all in my name." I was learn-ing quickly how to play this game!

"Fine."

"And two thousand ducats for Isabelita's dowry. That's in addition to the money to cover our monthly needs." I would no longer settle for whatever I was given.

"That is a bit too much. I still have to pay for half of your dowry," he protested.

"That dowry will not pay for your child's everyday expenses, or mine."

It had taken a while, but I was finally aware of how things worked. This was the time to fight for every *maravedí*. I couldn't count on the money from Mother's inheritance, and in any case, I would need to share that with Ana. I had to secure Isabelita's future.

"Can I pay in installments, perhaps?" Juan was asking. "I have a wife and three other children, remember."

I tried to hide my anger, but my words gave it away. "Can Isabelita eat and be clothed in installments?" Juan opened his mouth wide and was about to respond, but I didn't give him a chance. "There's your answer. The dowry is separate from our monthly expenses, and you will pay it as such. If Luis de Molina accepts installments, good. But your daughter and I definitely cannot."

"You're tough, did you know that?" he said with surprise.

"I'm only asking for what is fair. She's your favourite child after all, isn't she?"

My expression made it clear that only one answer was possible. Isabelita had to be his favourite child. She was our treasure. And treasures were not cheap.

"One more thing, Juan," I said, nibbling on his neck. "I would very much like to have those portraits hanging on the wall." I pointed at them. "Would you give them to me as a present?" I said, drawing my finger across his lips.

"My gilded portraits of saints? Why?"

"For Isabelita's protection."

"But they're mine. The Pope blessed them before giving them to me."

"Then you should be happy to share your blessings with your daughter," I said with a smile.

"Anything else?" he asked. He didn't seem to be enjoying this game much anymore, so I placed my hand between his legs. I couldn't stop now.

"Yes, a tapestry," I whispered.

"You can buy one yourself with all the money I'll be giving you!"

"No. I want a tapestry that could hang here, in this room, in this palatial house, because this is where Isabelita would grow up if she were recognized as your legitimate child."

"Now you're asking for too much," he protested. But his flesh surrendered to my touch. I had to go as far as I could.

"Doesn't your daughter deserve it all?"

"Yes, but …"

"And don't I deserve it, too?"

He sighed. "Fine, you win." He pulled me towards him, but I resisted. Spoken words meant nothing. Signatures did. I gently pushed him away.

"When all those belongings and their titles are in my possession, I will be all yours," I said with a coy smile. It was a gamble, but if it paid off, my child and I would be set for life. "It's late now, and I must return to our baby. I'm not used to being away from her this long."

"Isabel, please!" He looked desperate. I put my hand back between his legs and asked God to forgive me for my sins. It was only a few months until the wedding, and I had to ensure that Isabelita and I would be safe. Who was prey now?

XI

CATALINA
March 1609

Considerans autem dolum illorum dixit ad eos quid me temptatis
Ostendite mihi denarium cuius habet imaginem
et inscriptionem respondentes dixerunt Caesaris
Et ait illis reddite ergo quae Caesaris sunt Caesari et quae Dei sunt Deo.

YOU SAID UNTO them, my Lord Jesus Christ, render unto Caesar the things which be Caesar's and unto God the things which be God's. Why did Miguel wait until now to tell me the truth? Why didn't he share with me that Diego Sanz del Aguila was not Isabelita's father? He lied to me. Her real father is Juan de Urbina, Secretary to the Duke of Savoy, and Miguel brokered his daughter's marriage to Luis de Molina to safeguard her honour and his. And to think I was so happy to lend him the money for the dowry and attend the wedding! To think I felt grateful to be welcomed back into his home in Madrid! How foolish was I, how blind!

The fact that I was tricked into this arrangement and that I afforded legitimacy to Isabel, that adulteress, through my presence and support makes me tremble with anger now. The fact that Miguel asked me to be part of that charade and I agreed makes me feel ashamed. As if it wasn't bad enough that he recognized Isabel as his legitimate daughter! Yet I understood, My Lord. You are my witness. For Isabelita and her alone, I agreed to Luis de Molina's request that Miguel give Isabel his name. She walked into that marriage as Isabel de Cervantes, a legitimate daughter and a wealthy woman—the mother of Juan de Urbina's child, daughter of lust and sin. And I? I was the fool who was made to play along.

I pray to You, my Lord, for fortitude and guidance. I want to do what is right and I am following your example. Miguel needs to render unto me the things that are mine, and unto You the things that are Yours. The one thousand ducats I lent him to cover his share of Isabel's dowry must be repaid without delay. I refuse to believe that my mother was right about him. He has found generous patrons before. Guide his hand, dear Lord, so he can write more, and be paid what his work is worth. Guide his hand so he can pay this debt back to me and restore what little of my trust in him remains. I need strength, my Lord, to prevent all the love that I once felt from turning into bitterness. Listen to this, Your most humble of servants. I need courage, my Lord, to carry on.

XII

ISABEL
April 1609

NOW THAT WE were husband and wife, Luis de Molina and I ate our main meal together, and it became his little habit to tell me stories about his time as a soldier. I was particularly interested in his captivity in Algiers, and convinced him to tell me what he had heard about Father during his time there. Every day he volunteered more details, and I looked forward to our conversations.

As far as Luis knew, Father had attempted to escape Algiers four times. The first time, he and other prisoners were led through the desert to Orán during the winter. No matter how many times Luis described the desert and the ocean, I could not picture them. Endless untamed sand. Endless wild waters. Father and the others were abandoned by their guide and forced to return to their captors. They were very fortunate to have their lives spared. Had Father been killed, I would have never been born! The thought was unsettling. It meant Isabelita wouldn't exist either, and I was unable to conceive of a world without her smile.

During Father's second attempt to escape, he hid in a cave with fourteen other prisoners and waited there for his brother

Rodrigo, who had already been freed, to return for him. But someone betrayed the captives, and they rounded them up and imprisoned them again. As a punishment for that attempt, one of Father's companions was strung up to a tree by one foot and died choking on his own blood. How many people had died in front of Father's eyes during his lifetime? I didn't dare ask him, nor did I ever ask Luis. Soldiers were not keen to share their battle experiences, that much I had learned.

That warm spring evening, I put on a fresh dress and joined Luis in the dining room. The table could seat eight, but we sat close together, him at the head of the table, me on his right.

"You look beautiful, Isabel," he said, standing behind my chair, waiting to pull it out for me.

I bowed my head. Luis was a good-looking man. Well built and muscular, he had a gentle smile. I had learned that Aunt Magdalena was right. A woman should aim for the money without the man. Juan had given me everything I asked for, and we met only when he visited Isabelita. Father had requested that I end my relationship with him now that I was a married woman, and Juan could not argue that I was being disloyal.

"You were going to tell me about the third escape?" I prompted, once we had been served and began to eat.

"Yes!" Luis poured us some wine. "The third escape started when your father sent a message to the general in charge of the Spanish forces in Orán, pleading to be rescued. Unfortunately, the message was intercepted, and the man who carried it, a Moor, was impaled."

Impaled? I grimaced, wondering how Father felt about that. He never spoke ill of Moors, although, wise as he was, he was careful not to say anything that could be held against him by the Crown, especially now that King Philip III had ordered the Moors to be expelled from Spain. The memory of Prudencia still cast a shadow over my heart.

"For that attempt to escape," Luis continued, "the punishment should have been two thousand lashes, which would have meant certain death, but Miguel was spared because he was considered a valuable captive whose ransom Hasan Pasha, ruler of Algiers back then, was keen to collect. He knew your father was a man of integrity, someone held in high esteem by the majority of the other captives. "

Father had been fortunate in the most unexpected ways. "I toast to integrity and respect. *Salud*!" I said, lifting my glass.

"*Salud*!" We drank. "For his fourth attempt, Miguel plotted to escape on a frigate with sixty others. But a fellow Spaniard, a former monk, betrayed them."

"A monk?" I said in surprise.

"The Dominican order he belonged to had expelled him so he was, in effect, *defrocked*," Luis emphasized with contempt. "His name was Juan Blanco de Paz, a man shunned by everyone and so jealous of Miguel that he tried to tarnish the excellent reputation he had built for himself in Italy, first, and then in Algiers. Your father never mentioned this man to you?"

I shook my head. At my aunts' house I had heard bits and pieces about Father's time in captivity. I knew that thousands of Christians were imprisoned by Turks and Berbers, and had heard plenty about the huge sacrifices the entire family had been forced to make to pay for his ransom. However, this story was new to me.

"Blanco de Paz behaved like Judas Iscariot, but your father defended himself well against him. Before returning to Spain, Miguel even made sure to carry a legal statement of his time in captivity, signed by twelve witnesses, to attest to his honourable conduct while in Algiers. Unfortunately, slander by a sinner such as Blanco de Paz can be enough to destroy even the greatest of reputations."

With Valladolid and Alicia de Ayala in my mind, I nodded, sad to realize that Father had gone through such an acrimonious experience more than once.

"Don't look so gloomy, my beautiful Isabel!" Luis smiled. "Against all odds, this story has a happy ending. Miguel was about to be shipped to Constantinople to be sold as a slave. He was already in shackles on the ship when Juan Gil, the Trinitarian monk in charge of his rescue, found him."

"Already shackled?" I put my hand on my chest, barely able to tolerate the cruel image my imagination displayed in my mind. "But he was rescued. How did that come to be?"

"It was not easy, you see, because the ransom, five hundred escudos, was to be paid in gold, but Juan Gil had Spanish coins, so he had to return to land to exchange the money for gold, then return to the ship. The ship was about to sail, so he had only minutes to convince Hasan Pasha to free Miguel. They both jumped ship just in time."

"What a miracle!"

"A miracle thanks to which I am now your fortunate husband, Señora de Cervantes," he said, taking my hand. I should have been glad to bear Father's name at last, but I couldn't forget that he had agreed to give it to me only because Luis had insisted on it so that he would not be marrying a bastard.

"Or may I say, Señora de Molina?" Luis kissed my hand. "The Lord blesses those who wait," he said, and I could not help but smile at him sweetly.

XIII

‹›✣‹›✣‹›✣‹›

CONSTANZA
April 1609

CONSTANZA KNEW SOMETHING was wrong the moment Miguel entered the sewing room and took a seat between her and Magdalena. His shoulders were hunched, he looked worn out. Andrea was resting in her bedroom; she had been feeling weak lately and the heat made it harder for her to move around.

"What's wrong, Uncle Miguel?"

"Catalina is demanding that I pay her the thousand ducats she lent me for Isabel's dowry."

"Why? What happened?" Constanza was alarmed.

"How should I know? She simply wants her money back," he said, pulling his hair back from his forehead. No wonder he was upset, Constanza thought. It was a large sum to repay.

"And how are you going to pay Catalina back, *hermano*?" Magdalena asked, her voice brittle and tired.

"I don't know, Magdalena. But I don't think we can afford to continue living in this house."

"What?" Constanza cried out. "Where are we supposed to go? Renting in Madrid is so expensive now!" They should have never left the old family home! She knew that sooner or later this would happen. Her eyes teared up.

"I'm sorry to let you down, *hija mía*," Miguel said sadly. Constanza had never seen her uncle look this defeated. She wanted to hug him, but she was also angry. Hadn't he written the most successful book in all of Spain? So how could this possibly be happening?

"Can't you request any advances for your writing? Or any money on account of the new editions of *Don Quixote*?" she asked desperately.

Miguel shook his head. "No new advances are possible until I hand in a finished book, and my *Exemplary Novels* are far from finished. And you know the conditions under which I sold *Don Quixote*. I am not entitled to receive any money after its initial printing."

Resentment and sorrow fought each other in Constanza's chest. She wanted to say something but was at a loss for words. Magdalena broke the silence that hung heavy in the air around them.

"Miguel, you never mentioned that before. Why did you sign such a disadvantageous contract?"

"We needed the money."

It was true, Constanza thought. They needed money then, and they needed money now. Coming to think of it, they had always seemed to be in need of money. Now, she knew why.

"It took us years to be able to pay your ransom, Miguel," Magdalena said, her voice sad and weak. "How are we going to pay this new amount?"

Constanza shared her aunt's anguish. Magdalena could no longer embroider, and she herself could not work any harder. She had taken on so much work that she barely had time to visit Isabelita. At fifteen months, she was already starting to walk and say her first words, and Constanza didn't want to miss any of her childhood stages. She stared at her uncle, his head hanging down in shame and silence. Constanza's brain was racing. Did they have anything to sell? What did they have that was of value? The *bargueño* desk, perhaps. Some of the tapestries they hung on the walls during the winter, but that meant even less protection against the cold. Her grandmother Leonor's *talavera*? Constanza would be sorry to see it go. But they didn't have much more.

"For a few months now, I have been considering …" She realized that Magdalena was speaking, her gaze on the horizon, without looking at either of them. "I have been considering joining the Trinitarian Society as a novice. If I join the convent, you will no longer have to worry about my keep."

"Magdalena!" Miguel exclaimed. "What are you thinking? You are not a burden, on the contrary! Your keep is the least of my worries," he protested, placing his hand on his sister's arm.

Constanza's chin trembled, and she began to openly weep. "Uncle Miguel is right. We need to stay together."

Magdalena shook her head. "No, Constanza. You must take care of your mother. Our dear Andrea needs you now the way you needed her when you were little. But I will join the convent; that will allow the three of you to move into a smaller house or apartment. I will not need any of my belongings anymore, so you can sell them all. When I was born, my mother didn't even have a chair to sit on! I can't complain, as I have more than enough now. And as long as you visit me once in a while, I will be happier in the service of Our Lord, far away from the worries of the world and its wickedness."

XIV

ISABEL
July 1609

AT FIRST, I thought Isabelita's crying was taking place in my dreams. But when I opened my eyes, I remembered that she was with Gracia and that she knew how to calm her down. As the crying persisted, I got up as quietly as I could. Luis was still asleep by my side. I lit a candle and stared at him for a moment before putting on my chemise—there were scars on his arms and legs, probably from battles he had yet to describe to me, and his chest rose and fell with a peacefulness I envied. How could he not hear Isabelita's cries? I hurried to her room.

Gracia was holding her in one arm and pressing a compress on her forehead with the other. Isabelita wouldn't stop crying.

"Isabelita, my love, what's wrong?" I asked in alarm.

"She has a fever," Gracia said, "a very high fever. Nothing brings it down."

I touched my daughter, and her skin was burning. I took her from Gracia and kissed her, trying to calm her down, but the crying continued unabated. I tried singing to her, rocking her in my arms. Nothing worked.

"Perhaps it's an earache," Gracia said. "I've seen earaches in babies before. It makes them cry for hours."

"And how do you cure an earache?" I asked.

She placed Isabelita on the bed, asked me to hold down her arms, and took out her breast. Then she brought it close to the baby's head and, turning it gently, let a couple of drops of milk fall into her ear. Isabelita wailed.

"Are you sure this is the right thing to do, Gracia?" I was beginning to feel desperate. I hated myself, hated my body, for not being able to produce the medicine my daughter needed.

"*Sí*, Señora Isabel, I have seen this done before. I have done this before."

I nodded, and we repeated the procedure with the other ear. Then we waited. Isabelita continued to cry. We waited a little longer. Then I noticed that she had started to develop a rash on her face, and I sent Gracia to fetch a doctor—not a barber surgeon but a doctor. The noise must have woken Luis. He came into the room and was so upset by the state of Isabelita that he sent Francisca to call my family. I know I should have sent for Juan. He was her father. But I didn't want him. I needed my family. I needed a doctor, someone who knew how to help my child. I wanted her to be well, to be her usual happy self. Why was she crying like this? What was the rash on her skin?

The doctor and my family arrived at almost the same time, and by then I was crying almost as much as Isabelita. I was holding her close, kissing her, begging her to calm down, to stop wailing. The doctor asked me to place her on her bed so he could examine her. We were all standing around her, watching her turn redder by the minute. It seemed that now she was having trouble breathing. What was wrong with her? She was fine earlier that day, wasn't she?

No, Gracia reminded me. She had not eaten well. She had been tired and inattentive.

But I did not know that, because I had spent the afternoon with Luis.

When did the fever start? Surely she was fine in the morning. Perhaps a little irritable, but I thought it was due to the heat. I was ashamed of myself. Ashamed of leaving my child in her wet nurse's care to fall into my new husband's embrace. I looked at Father.

"Isabelita will survive this illness, won't she?" I asked, my eyes swollen. "Won't she?"

Father hugged me with his good arm and said, "Yes, of course. She will survive, she's strong like you, and like me. She's a Cervantes."

The doctor prescribed wax-based ointments for the rash and compresses to bring the fever down. I sent Francisca to the apothecary to fetch everything we needed, even though it was the middle of the night. If there was one thing I knew it was that money opens every door, no matter how late or how early.

We followed all the doctor's instructions, but when by dawn Isabelita was no better, I sent a message to Juan. Our baby was no longer crying; she had lost her voice and had no more tears. She was still burning hot. She was lethargic, limp.

When Juan arrived, he started screaming at me: Why hadn't I called him earlier? He would have brought the royal surgeon. But when he came, the royal surgeon was unable to help Isabelita either. He said this was common with small children, that they were weak, that they got sick easily. But Isabelita was not weak, she was strong. She alone had the power to erase resentments and repair wounded hearts. She alone had the power to instill the desire to forgive. She was a source of love, of understanding. An endless source of smiles. But now she was not smiling, she was not even crying anymore, she was breathing. Only breathing. Barely breathing.

When Father said we should call a priest, I refused. He said we had to be prepared. I refused again. I hit him, I screamed, I took my little angel in my arms and demanded to be left alone with her. I would breathe life into her mouth. I would tear my heart out of my body to make hers strong again. I would bring God himself down from Heaven to instill vigour in my baby again.

The priest came in and I spat at him. If my child dies there is no God. The priest prayed and gave my daughter his blessing. I threw one of Juan's gilded portraits at him. If my child dies there are no saints. The priest pronounced the last rites so my baby's soul could go to Heaven, and I yelled, No, there is no Heaven, there is no Heaven if it wrenches babies out of their mothers' arms. And if there really were a Virgin Mary, she would have made sure that no other mother suffered as much as she did, that no other mother lost her child the way she did. There was no God, there were no saints, there was no Virgin, there was no air, no heartbeat, and soon the fever turned into cold. The coldness of Hell. My baby became so cold that I wrapped her in blankets and curled myself around her body and blew warm air on her face. Be warm, my baby. Be warm.

Aunt Magdalena said Isabelita was with God, and I should be grateful that her suffering was over. Aunt Andrea said I had to submit myself to the Lord's will. Constanza said the Lord would comfort us in all our affliction. But no matter how hard they tried, no matter what they said, I did not let them have my baby girl. I did not let them take Isabelita away. She would wake up, she would wake up or I would never believe in God again. Father was scared, he said I shouldn't be blasphemous, that I could be punished.

"Punished?" I yelled at him with the last of my voice. "What punishment could be worse than this?"

XV

❧❧❧❧❧❧❧❧❧❧

CONSTANZA
August 1609

CONSTANZA AND MIGUEL found a less expensive house nearby, on Calle de las Huertas, for them and Andrea to live. When Constanza heard a knock on the door, she expected to find their new landlord, who had agreed to come by in person to settle their lease agreement. Instead, it was Juan de Urbina, dressed in *ropa negra* and a hat so fine she was certain it was fresh from Italy. She stared at it in silence, unable to utter a single word.

"May I please speak to Don Miguel de Cervantes?" he asked quietly. Outside, the neighbours were gathering around a carriage parked at the end of their narrow street, where it was still wide enough for its majestic girth. Constanza assumed the coachman had stayed behind with the horses, and that the man keeping watch in the middle of the road was a servant tasked with security. Miguel was in his studio but as soon as he heard Juan's voice, he came to the door and invited him to come in. Constanza returned to the sewing room but left the door ajar so she could hear their conversation.

Since Isabelita's death, her uncle looked older than ever. She was worried about his health. Now that it was just the three of them living together, she felt she had a right to know everything that was going on in their lives. *Her* life.

"Don Miguel, I have come here because I need to address an important issue related to your daughter. As you know, I bought the house where Isabel currently lives with Luis de Molina so that my daughter"—here his voice shook ever so slightly—"would have a suitable home in which to grow up. But now that Isabelita is no longer with us, my obligation, as you will surely understand, has come to an end."

Constanza brought her hand to her chest.

"I understand that the situation is certainly different now," Miguel said warily.

Urbina continued. "I need to sell the house in order to pay some private debts, among them the payments still pending for Isabel's dowry—which, at this point I must confess, I may not be in a position to make in their entirety."

Constanza gasped. Would her uncle be liable for Juan de Urbina's debt? They had signed the legal document together. There was an uncomfortable silence, then her uncle's angry voice.

"Sir, you have a legal duty, an obligation—"

"An obligation I will be in a position to meet as soon as I sell the house that Isabel is living in."

"And where do you imagine Isabel will go if she cannot be in her house anymore?"

"The house was Isabelita's. I bought it for her."

"My daughter told me the deed is in Isabelita's name but the usufruct is in hers. If you take the house back she will have nowhere to go."

"She is a married woman. I can offer her husband a good position. They will be able to live comfortably on his salary, you have my word. I care for Isabel and would never leave her destitute. They can stay in the house until they find a suitable place to move. With my daughter gone, there is no reason for them to continue living there."

XVI

ISABEL
September 1609

EXHAUSTED FROM WANDERING through the rooms of my house looking for remnants of Isabelita's life—traces of her scent, proof that she had lived—I decided to try to conceive another child with Juan. He was the only one who understood the emptiness that made my arms ache, the weight of Isabelita's absence. I wanted another baby who looked like him. Another baby with Isabelita's face.

I melted into Juan's embrace the moment I entered his bedroom. This was the father of my only child, and the only children I ever wanted.

"Isabel," he said, panting after we finished, "I have no words to thank you for the pleasure you have given me today."

"We can do this tomorrow, and the day after tomorrow, and every day after that."

"But you are a married woman now."

I frowned. Had I not been with Luis the day Isabelita became ill, I might have been able to call for the doctor sooner, hold her in my arms a bit longer. The mere thought of sharing Luis's bed, of having my skin brush his, sickened me.

"You know that marriage has never meant anything to me, Juan."

He looked into my eyes, then kissed my forehead. "I need to talk to you about something important." I sat up in the bed. "I didn't want to tell you while you were mourning."

"I am still mourning. Aren't you?"

"Of course, I am. But things have come up that have forced me to make a decision that will have an impact on you."

He paused and looked uncomfortable. I crossed my arms and waited. When he continued he wasn't looking at me.

"I have debts I need to pay besides your dowry to your husband, and I now find myself forced to sell the house you live in. You'll need to find another place to live."

There were a few moments of silence while what he said sank in. I had to push my words out through my clenched jaw. My entire body had tensed up.

"The house is mine; you cannot sell it."

"I can, because I am the one who paid for it. I have already spoken to your father. He agrees that the best way to proceed would be for Luis de Molina to leave the property first and find proper accommodations for you both. I am in a position to offer him a job, a job that will afford you comforts."

"You spoke to my father about this? When?"

"A few weeks ago."

"He hasn't said a word to me about it!"

"He probably will very soon. But I thought you might as well hear it from me."

"That is my house. It's the only place my daughter ever knew, where she lived and where her memories are. I'm not going anywhere."

"If I don't sell the house, I won't have money to pay my

debts. I won't be in a position to pay for your dowry. Your father will have to cover the full cost."

I was speechless. I looked around—at the silk bedsheets that covered our bodies, the silver cups and crystal glasses resting on the table, the fine carpets and tapestries and paintings. Then I looked into Juan's eyes and saw him again for what he was: the predator. I had given myself willingly to this snake who was now ready to regurgitate me out of his life and leave me without anything to indicate what we once had together. When I spoke, my voice was like ice.

"If you don't make my dowry payments in a timely fashion, I can have Luis sue you."

"Then he will have to sue your father, who will be legally responsible for the whole amount the moment I declare myself incapable of paying," he said. He got out of bed and started getting dressed.

"He will sue you, and my father, and whoever else needs to be sued," I said, my voice trembling, my hands shaking with anger. "You will not kick me out of my daughter's house. You'll regret it if you try."

He smiled. "Be careful, Isabel. Your father is old and can barely sustain himself. Did you know he is deeply in debt?"

"Yes, his ransom from Algiers and my dowry—"

He let out a guffaw. "No, Isabel. No. Your father is a gambler. He gambled away the money that your aunts and your cousin earned. And his luck has been notoriously bad for years now."

"You're lying!" I screamed.

"I am not lying. Perhaps you can't tell the difference because you've been surrounded by liars all your life."

"Be quiet!" I cried, covering my ears. This could not be happening. I felt like I was falling, falling into a pit.

"I think it's time I share some of the information I've gleaned since I met you."

"Information? What information?" I whispered, panic welling up inside me.

"Is the name Fernando de Lodeña familiar to you?"

I remembered the name. It had come up during the trial in Valladolid. Did Juan know about the trial? Did he know about Simón, too?

"Your aunt Magdalena was engaged to Fernando de Lodeña. He broke their engagement to marry another woman. De Lodeña was supposed to give your aunt three hundred ducats as reparation for her lost honour—and you know what I mean by that. But he disappeared. Then they found each other again in Valladolid."

No, I realized. He wasn't lying. De Lodeña must have been the man Prudencia said she saw with Magdalena!

"But there's more to your aunt's and your father's behaviour than you imagine!" he said, smiling, clearly enjoying the effect his information was having on me. "You know how they never let you visit your sister, Ana?"

I gasped. I had never mentioned Ana's name to Juan before. I sank into the bed, paralyzed with fear. He was a poisonous creature with eyes everywhere. Again, I covered my ears with my hands, praying to God that he would stop talking. But he went on and on, and his words seeped through my fingers and poured into my ears like molten wax.

XVII

CONSTANZA
September 1609

THERE WAS A loud banging on the front door. Constanza opened it to find Isabel. Two chairmen stood off to the side with a sedan.

"Is my father home?" she asked, with no preamble.

"Come in, cousin," Constanza said, making room for her in the small foyer. She was dressed in *ropa negra*, even though she was not in the ranks of the wealthy and powerful. Constanza wondered if she had chosen the dress simply to impress them.

Isabel's contempt for the modest new dwelling was evident. Constanza suddenly recalled the day Isabel arrived to live with them at age fifteen. That day, Constanza had been the one who stared at her cousin with derision. God had certainly had divergent plans for their futures.

Miguel was in his studio, writing. He was trying to complete his *Exemplary Novels*, but he had experienced so many interruptions that he hadn't finished adding new novellas to the volume. He was also working on some interludios. Now that Andrea had joined Magdalena in the convent, it was only Miguel and Constanza living in the home, and not a day went by that Constanza didn't miss her mother and her aunt. But she was aware that at the convent they were receiving the care and attention she and Miguel were unable to give them. There were so many debts to pay that all they did was work, work, work all day long. Even Maria had to find another job, but she still came by once a week to help with the laundry. Constanza was so tired, and she felt so alone. She didn't need Isabel disrupting the only thing she had left: her silence, her peace.

"Isabel, *hija*, come in. Are you all right?" Her uncle's voice made Constanza's heart shrink. He had aged so much in such a short period of time. They all had.

"No, I'm not," she said tartly. Without so much as another glance at her cousin, Isabel entered Miguel's studio and closed the door behind her. "I need to ask you some questions."

These walls were not as thin as those in Valladolid, but Constanza put her head against the door, hoping to hear whatever transpired in the study.

"Won't you sit down?" Miguel offered.

"No, thank you. I don't need to sit down. I just need you to listen." Constanza had never heard Isabel so angry. She stayed where she was, afraid of what might come.

"I had a very—how shall I call it—disturbing conversation with Juan the other day. He shared with me some stories I had never heard before. I came here to ask if they're true."

"What stories?" Miguel stammered. Constanza bit her lip. She could tell he was nervous.

"He said that you and Aunt Magdalena kept me apart from Ana so that I could adapt better to life with you. Is that true?"

"We thought it would be best for you at the time."

"You thought it would be best for me to lose my sister?"

"I'm sorry, Isabel. In my defence," he pleaded, "I made sure you married well and I am paying your dowry."

"Yes, and you're an ally to the man who wants to evict me from my own house."

Miguel sighed. "Juan de Urbina is the owner of that house. He purchased it."

"He purchased it for me!"

"He purchased it for Isabelita."

"And I am Isabelita's mother and always will be. And I live there. The fact that you are colluding with him on this matter makes my blood boil!" She was crying with anger and frustration. "How could you betray me like this?"

"I told you that I disapproved of that relationship to begin with, *hija*," he declared.

"I didn't ask you for permission then. But I am asking you for support now," she said more softly.

"I'm supporting Juan because there is such a thing as integrity. And as a man of integrity, I agree that the house belongs to him."

"Are you saying I don't have integrity?" she demanded.

"Isabel, you are too upset to think straight. Isabelita's loss is too recent."

"Don't you dare use my daughter's death against me!" she cried.

Constanza was shaking. There was a moment of silence, then Isabel continued.

"I am suing Juan de Urbina, Father. He hasn't complied with the agreement we signed, and he owes me money. He says he has debts? Wait until he's forced to pay what he owes me!"

"Isabel, have a little consideration for the man. He gave you everything you wanted and more," Miguel said reasonably.

"No, Father. *I* gave him everything *he* wanted and more. I gave him a child. And now he owes me money and wants to take my house away!"

"This is a battle you will never win, Isabel," Miguel warned her.

"I am willing to try," she said.

"If he doesn't get the house back, he will be in a very difficult situation."

"If Isabelita were alive, he would still be obliged to pay the same amount of money. And the house would still be mine. What's different now?"

"Circumstances have changed, *hija mía*," he said sadly.

"How understanding you are about Juan and his debts! Are you sorry for him because he's a gambler, like you?"

Constanza had to make an effort to contain a gasp.

"Do my aunts and my cousin know that all those years they worked for hours on end, spinning and sewing and embroidering, you were gambling their earnings away?"

Constanza threw open the door to the studio. She didn't want to believe what she heard, but it made sense. Why else had they been forced to live in such a small apartment in Valladolid? Why else was her uncle always short of money even after receiving generous advances for his books?

Considering the circumstances, Miguel and Isabel seemed only slightly surprised when Constanza burst in. Her uncle sat behind his desk while her cousin stood in front of him.

"Uncle Miguel, is it true?" she asked.

"Constanza, we can talk about this later," Miguel said wearily.

Isabel dried her tears. "But that's not all. Guess what else Juan told me, cousin?"

Constanza shook her head. She couldn't guess what else, but she had heard enough. She didn't think she could stand to learn any more.

"Isabel, enough." Miguel's voice was low, but firm.

"No! This is the most important part of it all, especially for Constanza."

"I don't want to hear anything you have to say." Constanza turned to leave the room, but Isabel grabbed her arm.

"There's something about your past that you need to know," she hissed.

"Isabel, I said stop!" Miguel insisted.

"No, Father. I will not stop, because according to Juan, I am not the only illegitimate child in this family."

Constanza looked at Miguel pleadingly. "Uncle, tell me. What is she talking about?"

"Isabel, you must leave now!" Miguel cried, rising to his feet. Anger blazed from her eyes and Isabel remained where she was. Ignoring Miguel, she spoke as if only Constanza were in the room.

"You see, cousin, you were lucky. Your father gave you his name even though he didn't marry your mother. You were born out of wedlock. It seems to run in the family."

Constanza was desperate for reassurance. Surely Isabel was lying! She expected to hear her uncle say so, to come to her defence, but it took him a long time to respond.

"What does that matter now?" he finally said, holding out his arm to Constanza, who had begun to cry in silence.

Isabel whirled around to face him once more. "Ah! Suddenly it doesn't matter anymore, does it? But it mattered when I was brought here against my will, forced to dress and pretend to be your maid and feel humiliated in front of everyone. You didn't object to that, did you? Where was your integrity then, Father?"

"Out with you, Isabel! Leave this house now!" he yelled, slamming his palm on the desk.

"Yes, I will leave! I don't want to see any of you again. I will not let you take my house away, and I won't give you a single *real* even if you come begging. Remember when Catalina said she wouldn't give me any money for my dowry? I will pay you back in kind."

"But Aunt Catalina did give you money!" Constanza protested. Her cousin's insolence made her cry out. "Uncle Miguel is in debt because of your stupid dowry!"

Isabel laughed with bitterness and shook her head. "No. He is in debt because he likes to gamble. And because he imposed a husband on me who demanded a dowry!"

"You are an ingrate! You never deserved any of the things we did for you!" Constanza shouted. When Isabel lifted her arm, Constanza thought she was about to slap her. But her cousin must have reconsidered; she did not touch her. She moved to the doorway and addressed them both from there.

"Don't look for me, don't write to me. Consider me dead because that's what you are to me now."

XVIII

CATALINA
December 1609

Deus meus, ex toto corde poenitet
me omnium meorum peccatorum, eaque detestor,
quia peccando, non solum poenas a Te iuste statutas promeritus sum,
sed praesertim quia offendi Te,
summum bonum, ac dignum qui super omnia diligaris.

O MY GOD, I repent for my sins and beg your forgiveness for having offended You. As I prepare to join the Trinitarian Society as a novice, together with my sister-in-law, soon to be my sister-in-God, Magdalena, I take this moment to reflect upon my past and what lies before me.

I was madly in love with my husband, and as You well know, I enjoyed his flesh, his mind, and his spirit the way only the most blessed of wives do. But it is time now to protect my soul and secure my place in Heaven. The sudden and unjust deaths of Isabelita and Andrea—may their souls be in Your presence—have made me question my existence. Miguel and I enjoyed a good life together, even though he left me on my own for years at a time. Now he owes me money—money for a dowry to which I swore not to contribute a single *vellón*, money for a daughter who is not mine and does not deserve any of the blessings she enjoys. Constanza wrote to me to share the news that Magdalena had written Isabel out of her will. Only You know her reasons, my Lord, but I hope You will forgive me when I say that I commend her for that.

After searching in my heart, I have decided to write my will as well, and name my brother Francisco my executor. For the great love and companionship we shared, I will give Miguel use of my estate for as long as he lives. Should You call me to Your side before him, I have indicated he is to inherit my bed and the linens and furnishings of my house, which we lovingly enjoyed during the best moments of our marriage, as well as two small plots of land outside Esquivias. I know I am being overly generous, God Almighty, and am satisfied with my decisions. I have destroyed all his letters, his words of love, all traces of the profound bond that we shared. What happened between us must remain between us, especially as I prepare to join the convent. No one shall read about our nights together, our mornings together, the way we learned to know and love each other. I will remain his loyal friend, and trust that his writing and the patrons he has found will help him provide for himself.

Please, God Almighty, protect Miguel as he takes on the battles that are still to come, and give strength to Constanza, who remains faithfully at his side. In the end, he is like his knight errant, and will live in the company of his niece for the rest of his days. That is his choice, and this is mine. There are no regrets on my part, just the firm resolve, with the help of Your Grace, never to sin again.

XIX

ISABEL
June 1615

I KNELT IN the confessional and made the sign of the cross.

"Bless me, Father, for I have sinned."

I breathed in the smell of wood and incense surrounding me. I enjoyed the darkness and intimacy of the space. On the other side of the screen I could hear Juan's soothing voice. All the years we were apart seemed to vanish when I ended contact with my Cervantes family and focused instead on Ana and Juan, Mother's brother. I often visited him in search of spiritual advice. I felt safe here.

"Tell me your sins, my child."

"Father, I have not been able to stop rejoicing since Juan de Urbina was arrested for bankruptcy. He will be in jail for almost a year, and I cannot be happier. Is that wrong?"

"Isabel, you know that in confession you can tell me your sins, but you can't ask my opinion."

"Yes. Forgive me, Father. As it turned out, de Urbina had bigger enemies than me."

"Isabel ... Your sins, please."

"I'm happy, Father, at another Christian's misfortune." But in truth, I was not happy. After years of court fights and proceedings, I felt like a soldier who returns home after a war.

"Isabel, if you simply want to have a conversation with me, we don't need to be here."

"Father, forgive me, for I have sinned. Just give me a moment to remember my list of trespasses."

I could hear Juan laughing quietly.

"You're incorrigible, you know that?"

I knew it, of course. Otherwise, I wouldn't have been able to make Miguel Hernández and Pedro de Herrera give us back the tavern on Tudescos Street and the house on Toledo Street. Magdalena had kept all the records so well organized, despite our move to Valladolid and back to Madrid, that when I finally faced the judge to claim what was ours, it could not be denied. Ana would have a dowry. I had fulfilled my promise to Mother, yet was now faced with other concerns.

"I have been asked to help my cousins, Jerónima and Marita, and I am finding it hard to say yes," I finally admitted. This was not the only thing oppressing me, but it was where my real confession began. "Ana asked me to help them."

"They are orphans now, and your family." Juan's voice became serious. Luisa had recently died. But Jerónima and Marita had never been good to me, and neither had their mother. Not since I was taken to live with my aunts. I was finding it difficult to forget that.

"Taking them in is a huge responsibility, Father. And I would need my husband to agree. The law will not allow me to intercede in their favour otherwise."

"Luis is your husband. You will know how to convince him," he said. I rolled my eyes, knowing Juan could not see me. Luis spent his days at the *mentideros* and pursuing businesses that never bore any fruit. Had it not been for me, for the properties I kept and acquired, we might have ended in the same position as my father. The mere thought made me shiver.

"It's hard to forgive and forget the past when it hurts so much, Father."

Something else weighed heavily on my chest, but I wasn't sure I could talk about it with Juan. I had just secretly finished reading the second part of *Don Quixote* and found in it all sorts of characters that reminded me of people we knew or had met. Some of them were in Valladolid, like Prudencia. Others were in Madrid, in the tavern where I grew up. But there was no mention of a daughter in it at all. Father had written a continuation of his most successful book and, in the end, the only character that remained with the deranged knight until the end of his days was his niece. I felt hurt, so hurt that when I finished reading the book I asked Gracia to dispose of it.

"I will say this again. You must try to forgive, my child. For your own sake. And because God wants it so."

"I will do my best, Father."

"Is that all you have to say, my child?"

"Yes." I would try to forgive Marita and Jerónima because they were my mother's nieces, and they had no one else in the world who could help them. But I could not forgive Father's betrayal. And I would certainly never forgive Juan de Urbina.

"God, the Father of mercies, through the death and resurrection of his Son, has reconciled the world to Himself and sent the Holy Spirit among us for the forgiveness of sins; through the ministry of the Church may God give you pardon and peace, and I absolve you from your sins in the name of the Father, the Son, and the Holy Spirit."

"Amen. What about my penitence, Uncle Juan—" I corrected myself, "I mean, Father?"

"Your penitence will be to make sure you truly forgive, my child. To be forgiven, you, too, must forgive."

XX

CONSTANZA
April 21, 1616

SO THIS IS how his life ends, Constanza thought. In this small rented house on Calle de León, at the corner of Francos, in poverty, but in the company of her and Catalina, the women who loved him the most.

"Father Martinez will be back soon, and our neighbours and friends have been coming to ask about his health." She was afraid of breaking into tears, so her voice was only a whisper. Catalina had been there day and night. It was easy to see that she still cared deeply for him, that despite everything that had happened between them there existed an unbreakable bond.

"His skin is so greyish! Even the palms of his hands, his lips, and his tongue are pale. But I managed to change him into a clean, dry chemise, and he is resting now. He is much calmer now that he has received the last rites," she said. Constanza was grateful to have her by her side.

"Is he still thirsty?"

"Yes, and he says his lips are tingling. It is as if his body cannot retain the water that he drinks," Catalina said, shaking her head. Despite wearing the Franciscan habit, she looked beautiful, Constanza thought. She had gotten used to seeing her uncle dressed in his coarse brown habit since he joined the tertiary orders of the Franciscans, but with Catalina it was different. Constanza remembered the beautiful dresses she wore in Valladolid and during her brief visits to Madrid, and it was still rather a shock to see her now in these humble garments.

"But his mind is as sound as ever," Catalina said.

"I know. The letter and prologue he dictated to you left me breathless. To think he can still *write* like that, even when he is so weak. So sick."

"He insisted on thanking the Count of Lemos for his patronage." Catalina sighed. "So much like Miguel. Besides, he considers this new book his masterpiece."

"I know. He told me so. The second volume of *Don Quixote* has been such a huge success, yet he still looks down on those books," Constanza said with a sigh. She wanted to stay strong, but the idea of losing her uncle and being completely alone in the world filled her with despair.

"I promised I would make sure *Persiles y Sigismunda* is published as soon as possible. And I will keep my word."

"I know you will, Aunt Catalina."

"Did you hear back from Isabel?"

Constanza lowered her eyes. "The messenger came back alone and empty-handed."

"Empty-handed?" her aunt said in disbelief. It hurt Constanza to give Catalina this additional sorrow.

"Does she understand that you are not asking for money for yourself, but for her own father's tombstone?" she asked.

Constanza nodded. "I said so in my letter."

"May God forgive her."

Yes, may God forgive her, because I cannot, Constanza said to herself. But to Catalina she said, "Why don't you rest a little? I will sit with him for a while."

Catalina went to lie down, and Constanza entered Miguel's room. The air smelled of urine and sweat. It was a sunny day, and birds could be heard chirping. *The world should go dark and quiet when our loved ones die*, Constanza thought. She tried not to make any noise as she sat by her uncle's side, listening to him breathe. He had lost a lot of much weight. His arms and legs, once so strong, resembled sticks. His cheeks were sunken. If he could only see how much he resembled his Knight of the Sorrowful Countenance! Catalina had combed his hair and washed his face.

Miguel opened his eyes and smiled when he saw her.

"Constanza, *hija*," he said, pushing each word out with great effort. "When is Isabel coming?"

"She should be here any minute," Constanza said, her eyes welling up. "Don't worry, Uncle Miguel. Try to rest." She caressed his head, his grey hair. Although the room was warm, his skin was cold. As cold as Isabel's heart.

AUTHOR'S NOTE

The desire to write this book arose many years ago when I was still a doctoral student at the University of Toronto, minoring in Spanish Early Modern theatre, and discovered that, while there are endless volumes of scholarly and creative work on Miguel de Cervantes, critics and scholars have mostly ignored the women he shared his life with. When they did refer to them—especially Isabel, his daughter—they oscillated between contempt and indifference. For far too long, Isabel has been judged an ingrate and a bitter, angry, unpleasant woman. Some have even dubbed her "the little bastard" ("*la bastardilla*"), minimizing her strength and her importance to her father.

The more I read, the more intrigued I was by this troubled father-daughter relationship and the Cervantes family as a whole. The bits and pieces of information I found were so compelling that I simply had to weave them together and try to bring these brave women's stories to life. There is much to learn from the social challenges and restrictions they faced in Early Modern Spain.

This novel is based, for the most part, on true events. I read a long list of peer-reviewed articles and scholarly books on Spain's Golden Age and Miguel de Cervantes, both in English and in Spanish. The ones I relied upon the most, besides Donald McCrory's *No Ordinary Man: The Life and*

Times of Miguel de Cervantes, were Emilio Maganto Pavón's *Ana de Villafranca, Amante de Miguel de Cervantes*, Antonio Pasies Monfort's *La vida canalla en el Madrid del Siglo de Oro*, and to orient myself around the Madrid of the time, Pedro López Carcelén's *Atlas Ilustrado de la Historia de Madrid*. The complete list of the resources I used, as well as my suggested readings, is too long to include here, but I will be happy to share it with whoever requests it (I may be contacted via House of Anansi or my website). The excerpts of *Don Quixote* included in Act Two belong to an English translation by Charles Jarvis (fourth edition, Volume the First) published in London, England, in 1766.

The use of everyday language to narrate this novel is deliberate. *Don Quixote* was written in the language of its time, so I decided to write this book in the language of ours and kept it simple—although, hopefully, still evocative and entertaining—so it would be understood by any and all readers.

And while I tried to remain true to the most relevant historical facts, it is important to remember that this is a work of fiction, so I took certain liberties for dramatic purposes. (SPOILER ALERT: For those readers who are only now familiarizing themselves with the Cervantes family, the following paragraphs contain information that might ruin the suspense built in the novel. Therefore, I recommend reading this note after finishing the book.) For example, I made Constanza younger in this story to bring her closer to Isabel. And because there are no records of the origin of Isabel's first husband, Diego Sanz del Aguila, what he did for a living, or the circumstances of his unexpected and early death, every detail surrounding this character in the novel is the product of my imagination. Likewise, Isabel's speech at the trial in

Valladolid, as well as the edicts, were fuelled by my imagination. I changed the name of Isabel de Ayala, whose accusation brought dishonour to the Cervantes women in Valladolid, to Alicia de Ayala in this book, to prevent any potential confusions between her and my protagonist. And while the reasons for the duel between Miguel de Cervantes and Antonio di Sigura remain a mystery, it is believed that their dispute was related to the Italian's dishonouring of Cervantes's sisters. I chose to support my plot on this hypothesis, weaving it together with "The Power of Blood," one of Cervantes's *Exemplary Novels*, whose protagonist suffers a fate similar to Magdalena's in this book. The lives of Isabel de Saavedra, Magdalena and Andrea de Cervantes, and Constanza de Ovando are so sparsely documented that there was plenty of room to use my creativity to fill in the gaps, but I tried to do so as respectfully and realistically as possible.

Miguel de Cervantes died on April 22, 1616, in Madrid, Spain, in the house he shared with his niece, Constanza de Ovando. *Don Quixote de la Mancha*, one of the most translated books in literary history and Cervantes's magnum opus, is considered by many the first modern novel in the Western world and the best book ever written in the Spanish language.

A few years before his death, Cervantes joined the Society of the Holy Sacrament, where he was in close contact with the most important intellectuals of his time. According to Donald P. McCrory in *No Ordinary Man*, the Society "was more of a club for writers, poets and artists and, significantly for a pauper like Cervantes, attracted wealthy patrons" (221).

He released the second part of his famous novel, *The Ingenious Hidalgo Don Quixote de la Mancha*, in 1615. He did this partly to reclaim his authorship and characters after an apocryphal version, published under the pseudonym Alonso Fernández de Avellaneda, appeared in 1614. His final literary work, *Trabajos de Persiles y Sigismunda*, was published posthumously in 1617 thanks to the efforts of his wife, Catalina de Salazar y Palacios. She died in 1626, and her remains were buried in the primitive church of the Trinitarias convent, presumably next to her husband's.

The nuns changed residence in 1639, and the church was rebuilt in 1694, by which time Cervantes had already been forgotten (the interest in Miguel de Cervantes's work, in particular his most famous novel, was rekindled in the eighteenth century). These events, and the lack of a headstone, are the reason the exact location of his burial site or his remains is still unknown.

Andrea de Cervantes died in October 1609, "four months after receiving the habit of the Tertiary Orders of St. Francis" (McCrory, p. 222). She died suddenly and without a will. Cervantes paid for her burial, something he was unable to do for his beloved sister Magdalena, who died in January 1611. "Her funeral was paid for by the nuns, [which] suggests that Cervantes once again found himself in financial difficulties" (McCrory, 228).

Constanza de Ovando passed away in Madrid in 1622. She lived alone with very scarce means and continued working as a seamstress until her death.

Miguel de Cervantes's life was full of adventures and misfortunes, and his daughter lived very intensely, too. Even in a *telenovela* it would be hard to find a character whose existence is so full of twists and turns (for example, in December 1606 she married Diego Sanz del Aguila against her father's will, and before 1608 came to an end she had already become a widow, given birth to her daughter, and married Luis de Molina, all while in a relationship with the powerful Juan de Urbina). She was clever and went on to amass a small fortune over which she kept control. Isabel lived off the income she received from renting her properties and died at age sixty-eight, the same age as her father, in 1652. She "had joined the Tertiary Orders of the Franciscans and laid claims to the arrears owed to her 'uncle' Rodrigo, which mostly remained unpaid." (McCrory, 213) During the course of her life as an adult, and while she was married to Luis de Molina, she gave financial help to her sister, her cousins, and her niece, and granted Gracia (whose real name was García) full freedom in her will. Her second husband, Luis de Molina, died on January 23, 1632. Isabel continued to fight Juan de Urbina's family over the house on Calle de la Montera, and the matter continued even after her death. Juan de Urbina's grandchildren ceased to fight, and Isabel's beloved niece, Ángela Benita, purchased the house in 1666.

Isabel's half-sister, Ana Rodríguez y Villafranca, married a man named Alejandro Gasi de Castro. It is not known what he did for a living, but they had two children—a boy, Fernando, who died young, and a girl, the above-mentioned Ángela Benita, of whom Isabel was very fond. The sisters recovered their mother's inheritance, but it is unclear whether Ana or Isabel ever took charge of the tavern again. Ana died sometime between 1640 and 1650.

Between 1580 and 1680, Spain experienced a flourishing of incomparable artistic production and achievements. This period came to be known as *El Siglo de Oro*, the Golden Age. Among its many talented and prolific writers, it is Miguel de Cervantes whose name became synonymous with his language; Spanish is known as *la lengua cervantina*.

Many centuries have come and gone, but women still find themselves bound by patriarchal rules in more countries around the world than we care to acknowledge. There is still much to be done to ensure equal opportunities and freedom for women. The so-called *Cervantas* were maligned because they lived as well, and as freely, as they could at the time. With this book, I humbly hope I have delivered them some justice, especially to Isabel.

A Daughter's Place is a tribute to all the daughters, mothers, sisters, aunts, nieces, and wives whose lives have been erased in order to highlight the important men in their families. Now, more than ever, it is time to hear these women's voices—our voices—in all of their vigour and power.

ACKNOWLEDGEMENTS

Writing may be a solitary activity, but it is by no means a lonely journey. I have so many wonderful people to thank for their support for this book that I wish their names and roles could appear the way closing credits do at the end of a movie.

First of all, a big thank you to my agent in Mexico, Verónica Flores, and my editor at the wonderful House of Anansi Press, Douglas Richmond, who believed in this project since its very beginning. Thank you, Doug, for your insightful comments, for your patience, and for your trust in my work. I'm also very grateful to everyone at House of Anansi for their support in making this book possible. *Muchas gracias* to Karen Brochu, Jessey Glibbery, Joshua Greenspon, Ricky Lima, Mariana Linares, Jenny McWha, and Alysia Shewchuk. Michelle MacAleese, thanks for your help putting the final version of the draft together and making sure that everything was perfect before the book went to typesetting. And since a book never goes far without the magic of the people in marketing, thank you to Emma Rhodes, Emma Davis, and Melissa Shirley. Also, all my gratitude to Alysia Shewchuk for the cover design, and to the incredibly talented, generous, and patient Allegra Robinson (the best copyeditor in the world), and Rachel Spence. It has been a huge honour to work with each and every one of you, and your guidance, support, care, and kindness mean everything to me.

Writing this novel would have been impossible without the Canada Council for the Arts' Explore and Create Grant, which allowed me to travel to Spain in August 2021, where José Fernando Corrochano Figueira took me around on a very enlightening tour of Madrid's El Barrio de las Letras, where Cervantes and Lope de Vega used to live. I want to thank Mr. Fernando Luis Fontes Blanco, Director of the Museo de Santa Cruz, for the luxurious catalogue of Spanish Golden Age clothing that he gave me as a present, and which was so useful to me as I navigated the garments that seamstresses back then could have been working on and what people wore. In Esquivias, Susana García Moya of the Casa Museo de Cervantes was very kind and answered all my questions, and in El Toboso, Dulcinea's picturesque town, I was welcomed and helped by Isabel Fernández Morales at the gorgeous Casa de La Torre, Brigitte at the Tourism Office (who guided me at the Museo Cervantino), and María Llanos at the Casa de Dulcinea. I was very fortunate not to take that trip alone. My dear friend from childhood, Julia Edler, travelled from Germany to spend a week with me in Madrid, and for her company and support, back then and always, I'm very grateful.

I would like to thank Dr. Stephen Rupp, who directed my doctoral dissertation and is a Cervantes specialist, for his book recommendations to inform this novel, particularly the biography I mention in my Author's Note. I also would like to mention Dr. Margaret Rich Greer, who was my dissertation's external advisor, and kindly agreed to read an imperfect early draft of this novel and gave me generous feedback. And I must mention David Fernández, Head of the Department of Rare Books and Special Collections at the University of Toronto's stunning Fisher Library, who allowed me to peruse a facsimiled edition of *Don Quixote* and helped me translate a few terms I had a bit of trouble with.

After all the research, of course, came the writing. The earliest attempts at putting this story together were read and guided by Marina Endicott at a summer course in Historical Fiction at the University of Toronto's School of Continuing Studies, where I received my very first feedback. Shortly after, I was mentored by Amy Stuart, in a private workshop I shared with Vicky Bell, and their comments were very helpful as I struggled to find ways to approach this complex project and develop its first chapters. Thank you so very much, Marina and Amy!

I joined the Muskoka Novel Marathon twice in an attempt to push out more pages and polish my very imperfect beginnings. I need to thank my generous sponsors, some of whom donated to the Muskoka Literacy Council two years in a row: Drs. Gillian and Ken Bartlett, Dr. Néstor Rodríguez and his son Mario, Dr. Arturo Victoriano, Miriam López Villegas, Frank Portelli, Pilar Miralles, Christina Kilbourne, José Antonio Villalobos, Carlos Chalico, and my husband, Dr. Edgar Tovilla.

I produced the first full draft of this book under the protection of an extraordinary woman I am blessed to call my Fairy Godmother, Dr. Gillian Bartlett. She and her husband, Dr. Ken Bartlett, who are family to me, welcomed me in their gorgeous home for a very intense week of writing during which they fed me and gave me wine, and encouraged me to keep going. It all started and ended with Gillian, truly, because not only did she host this book's full birth, but she gave me its lovely title, and I would have been lost without her careful editing of the final phase of this project. I have no words to thank you enough, dear FG, for your time, your input, and your love!

And what can I say to my wonderful friend Deb Bennett, who read and commented on every single draft I sent her way, from the first to the last? I lost count of how many there were, but I know it was a LOT to comb through! Thank you for your patience and kindness at every single round! I hope you are proud of this, your "godchild." *Gracias*, my dearest Deb!

My dear friends Miriam López Villegas and Flavia Hevia also read early drafts and provided me with valuable feedback that I am very thankful for as well.

A big thanks, too, to all my friends, near and far, who knew I was working on this project and encouraged me in one way or another. You know who you are, and I'm forever grateful to have you in my life.

What could I ever say to the five incredibly generous, talented, and successful writers whose blurbs grace this book? I'm such a huge fan of your work that I feel like the luckiest person alive for counting on your endorsements. Words are not enough, in any language, to convey my gratitude. Please forgive my shortcomings as I address each one of you all in alphabetical order. I hope that the next few sentences come close, even if only a little bit, to what I feel and what I'd like to say.

Danila Botha, you bring so much positive energy to everything you do, that I feel incredibly fortunate to have met you at this precise moment, and to be walking down this path in your company. Gracias for being such an example of grace and resilience, both through your actions and your writing. Thanks for your friendship!

Kim Echlin, one of my very first mentors in Canada, and my dear friend: your books have changed me and taught me things about humanity I would have never otherwise learned.

Your support means so very much to me! I aspire—hopelessly, of course—to one day have an ounce of your poise and gentleness in life as well as in literature. Te agradezco de todo corazón.

Marina Endicott, this novel would have taken even longer for me to write had I not enrolled in your Historical Fiction course. I had no idea how to start telling this story, how to go about untangling this web and tackling the obstacles I faced as I trudged along. For everything I've learned from you—in the classroom, and through your writing—I'm deeply grateful. Gracias for making me feel, in the most perfect of ways, like I closed a full circle, because you were here both at the beginning and at the end of this book. I hope you know how much that means to me.

Nita Prose, what a joy and privilege has it been for me to reconnect with you and share so many fun, magical moments together. You shine such a bright light on all of us who are lucky to know you, and you do it with such humbleness that every time I am with you, I am reminded of what it is to be not only a literary superstar, but a true mensch. ¡Te quiero tanto! Gracias por ser mi amiga. You (and Theo!) rock.

Roberta Rich, even though I have not had yet the chance to meet you in person, I feel like I know you because of your books and the complex, unforgettable characters that inhabit them. I am deeply, deeply grateful for the generosity with which you replied to my first email—a complete stranger's email—and accepted to read my book. I am forever honoured, and humbled, by your support.

At home, I would like to thank our dear family friend Norma Vázquez Lazcano, SuperNorma, for coming to my rescue so I could juggle life and the writing of this project.

And of course, nothing at all would have been possible for me without the generosity and support of my beloved husband, Edgar Tovilla, who also read early drafts of this work and not only tolerated my insecurities and stress but put up with my endless hours in front of the computer screen, typing away, writing and rewriting. Thank you for your love, Cielo. *Te amo*.

And to my three children, Ivana, Natalia, and Marco, sorry this project took your mom away from you for so long. The three of you are the biggest loves of my life, and I hope you will always remember that.

MARTHA BÁTIZ is an award-winning writer, translator, and professor of creative writing and Spanish language and literature. She is the author of five books, including the short story collections *No Stars in the Sky* and *Plaza Requiem* (winner of an International Latino Book Award), as well as the novella *Boca de lobo / Damiana's Reprieve* (winner of the Casa de Teatro Prize). Born and raised in Mexico City, she now lives in Toronto. *A Daughter's Place* is her first novel.